DARING TO LOVE

Colin reeled in his line and waded to the bank. Tossing the rod on the grass, he sat beside Mercedes. She looked deliciously relaxed. He bent his head and kissed her.

Her lips were damp, her mouth warm. She responded sweetly, without haste or pressure. It was a slow, languorous exploration, an appreciation of the tastes and textures that made them the same and different. Her tongue swept along the edge of his upper lip. She kissed the corner of his mouth.

His mouth touched her just below the ear. She lifted her chin and exposed the long line of her throat. He kissed her jaw, then the pulse in her neck.

The fragrance of the thick, damp grass mingled with the fragrance of her hair. Her elbows no longer supported her as she stretched languidly beneath him. Her arms circled his neck and the shadow cast by his head cooled her face.

"This is what I thought you had in mind last night," he whispered against her mouth.

Her smile was serene. "I know." Silent laughter brightened her eyes. "But you enjoyed star gazing—you know you did. It was lovely."

"*You* were lovely."

Mercedes felt heat rush to her face and welcomed the mouth he laid across hers. They kissed for a long time, unhurried, but not without hunger . . .

Books by Jo Goodman

PASSION'S BRIDE

CRYSTAL PASSION

SEASWEPT ABANDON

VELVET NIGHT

VIOLET FIRE

SCARLET LIES

TEMPTING TORMENT

MIDNIGHT PRINCESS

PASSION'S SWEET REVENGE

SWEET FIRE

WILD SWEET ECSTASY

ROGUE'S MISTRESS

FOREVER IN MY HEART

ALWAYS IN MY DREAMS

ONLY IN MY ARMS

MY STEADFAST HEART

A GIFT OF JOY
(with Fern Michaels, Virginia Henley and Brenda Joyce)

Published by Zebra Books

MY STEADFAST HEART

Jo Goodman

Zebra Books
Kensington Publishing Corp.

http://www.zebrabooks.com

ZEBRA BOOKS are published by

Kensington Publishing Corp.
850 Third Avenue
New York, NY 10022

First Printing: March, 1997
10 9 8 7 6 5 4 3 2 1

Printed in the United States of America

Prologue

London, October 1820

They came for the baby first. Colin remembered because he was eight—old enough to grasp the loss, too young to prevent it. He had expected it would happen but expectation alone did not prepare him. He had not been able to prepare his brothers.

Not that Greydon could have understood. He was the baby they came for. With his round face and engaging smile it was natural that he would be chosen. Grey had no real knowledge of his circumstances or surroundings, Colin thought. At five months he did not know he already had a family, albeit a smaller one than he had had three months earlier. Young Greydon was all gurgling laughter and chubby, flailing limbs. He charmed without effort and without conscience, as naturally as breathing and eating and crying.

So when Grey sighed contentedly as he was lifted into the woman's arms, Colin tried to remember that it didn't make his baby brother a traitor.

Beside the doorway, just inside the headmaster's office, Colin stood holding his younger brother's hand. Decker was only four but he was willing to stand at Colin's side, his small body at attention while the couple from America made their decision about the baby.

The next minutes were an agony as the headmaster indicated the two boys and asked the question of the couple with careless indifference: "Will you have one or both of the others?"

The man turned away from his wife and seemed to notice the boys for the first time. The woman did not glance in their direction.

"They're brothers," the headmaster said. "Colin. Decker. Come here and stand. You will make the acquaintance of Greydon's new parents."

Colin's last hope that the couple would not choose Grey vanished at the headmaster's words. Dutifully he stepped forward, Decker in tow. "How do you do, sir," he said gravely, extending his free hand to the man.

There was a surprised pause, then a low, appreciative chuckle from the man as he returned the handshake and greeting. Colin's narrow hand was swallowed in the man's larger one. In later years, try as he might, Colin could not put features to the man's face. It was the dry, firm handshake he remembered, the deep, lilting chuckle, and the momentary surge of hope he felt.

The man looked at his wife who was coaxing another smile from the baby in her arms. It was easy to see she was already in love with the child. There would be no difficulty passing the baby off as their own. No one among their family or friends would have to know it was an adoption.

"I'm afraid not," he said, letting go of Colin's hand. "My wife and I only wanted a baby." Because he was uncomfortable with two pairs of eyes looking up at him he added to the headmaster, "You shouldn't have brought them here. I told you from the first we were only interested in an infant."

The headmaster did not flinch under the rebuke. Instead he deflected it, turning his head sharply toward the boys and ordering them out of the room. His stiff, accusing tone made it seem that their presence in the office had never been his idea at all, but theirs.

Colin released Decker's hand. "It's all right," he said quietly. "You go."

Decker's wide blue eyes darted uncertainly between Colin and the headmaster. It was at Colin's urging, rather than the headmaster's stony glare, that Decker hurried from the room.

"I would like to say farewell to my brother," Colin said. He had a youthful voice, but the dark eyes were old well beyond his years and he stood his ground as though planted there.

The headmaster was prepared to come around his desk and bodily remove Colin. He looked to his guests for some indication of their wishes in the matter.

The man raised his hand briefly in a motion that kept the headmaster at bay. "Of course," he said. "Dear? This child would like to say good-bye to his brother."

With obvious reluctance the woman pulled her attention away from the baby. Her generous smile faded as she looked down at Colin. The dreamy, captivated expression in her blue eyes slipped away. "Oh, no," she said flatly. There was a hint of gray at the outer edge of her eyes, like the beginnings of ice on a lake. "I don't want that boy touching my baby. Look at him. Anyone can see he's sickly. He may harm the child."

It was as if he had been struck. The impact of the words caused Colin's thin body to vibrate. He could feel heat creeping into his cheeks as he flushed deeply with equal parts anger and shame. In that moment he knew he was standing there because he couldn't move, not because he didn't want to.

"Is the boy ill?" the man asked the headmaster. "My wife's right. He's very thin."

"He doesn't eat," the headmaster said. The glance he leveled at Colin darkened considerably and the warning was clear. "He's really had little appetite since he arrived. My wife believes the . . . um, incident . . . affected him more than the others. It's understandable, of course, being the oldest."

As if there were no other conversation in the room, Colin said again, "I'd like to hold my brother." This time he held up his arms.

The man prompted his wife gently. "Dear? Where can be the harm?"

She did not accede immediately, but considered her options for several long seconds. Colin watched her eyes shift briefly toward the door as though she were toying with the idea of fleeing

the room. In the end she gave him the baby accompanied by a
stiff, icy admonishment not to drop him.

Colin held his infant brother to his small chest, cradling the
boy as he had on so many other occasions these past three
months. Turning away from the adults, ignoring the woman's
sharp intake of breath, Colin adjusted the baby's blankets and
smoothed his muslin gown. "I'll find you," he said, his lips barely
moving around the words. "I promise, I'll find you."

Greydon cooed obligingly and beat his small fist against
Colin's shoulder.

"I think that's long enough," the man said as his wife took a
step forward to hover over the brothers.

The headmaster addressed Colin. "Give Greydon back now."

Colin did not so much return his brother as his brother was
taken from him. He did not wait to be dismissed a second time.
He could not leave the headmaster's darkly paneled office
quickly enough. His gait was stiff and his spine rigid. Only his
lower lip trembled uncontrollably as he crossed the floor. He
barely heard the woman's words and at the time didn't fully comprehend the impact they would have.

Tickling the baby's chin, she said softly, "I don't think I care
for the name Greydon at all."

It was only three weeks later that Decker left Cunnington's
Workhouse for Foundlings and Orphans. Colin had thought he
would have a longer time with Decker. It was not so usual for
four-year-old orphans to be placed with a family. The ones who
could understand their fate at so young an age were reconciled
to the prospect of servitude or apprenticeship. It seemed an infinitely more desirable alternative than remaining at Cunnington's until twelve years of age, then being put on London's
unforgiving streets. A boy who didn't know how to fend for himself might be taught thievery if he was judged to be quick-witted
and light-fingered by one of the London bands. If he caught a

pimp's eye, however, he was more likely to learn the skin trade and ply his wares until his looks faded or disease wasted him.

Colin wanted none of those things for Decker so he was resigned to the fact that Decker's departure from Cunnington's was necessary, if not welcome. He wanted to be happier for his brother, thought he *should* be happier, but in his heart of hearts he knew he was also jealous. And afraid. And now alone.

The couple who chose Decker among the score of other children were a more satisfactory pair in Colin's eyes than the couple who had taken Grey. The wife was handsome, not pretty, but she had a serene smile and a quiet way about her that smoothed the anxious lines between Decker's brows and eased Colin's mind. Her husband was reserved but polite, a bit uncertain what to make of Decker's constant questioning until his wife said indulgently, "Why, answer him, *cher.* Just as you do me." That was when the man spoke. His voice was a deep, rich baritone, the edges of his words crisp and defined. It was a voice that inspired confidence and Colin guiltily wished that he might be chosen in place of his brother or at least that he might be permitted to accompany him.

The headmaster tried again. "Perhaps you will consider Decker's brother also?"

The woman's kind eyes alighted on Colin. Sadness and pain warred in her expression and then Colin flushed deeply, recognizing pity when it was turned in his direction. "We'd take them all if we could," she said to the headmaster. *"Ce n'est pas possible."*

Her husband nodded. "She means it all," he said. "We would if we could. And the child must be healthy. There's the voyage to think of. We have a long trip ahead."

Colin slipped out of the headmaster's office quietly. In the dimly lighted hallway he sucked in a ragged breath and swallowed the hard, aching lump in his throat. If he closed his eyes he knew he would see the woman's piteous look. He didn't want her pity. In truth, he wanted her gratitude. Did she think her new son's sturdy little body was a happy accident of nature?

In anticipation of the evening meal, Colin's stomach actually growled. It had been a long time since he had heard that sound. In the months since coming to Cunnington's he had accustomed himself to eating less in order that his brothers might have more.

He had done what he could for them. Now he had to think of himself.

Malnourished and frail, his dark, opaque eyes like bits of hard coal in a gaunt face, Colin did not respond immediately or well to larger portions of dinner. Older boys who thought twice about tangling with him when he was championing his brothers, now found him an easy target. Soon he had little more to eat than when he was feeding Decker or Grey, and sometimes less.

Ten days after Decker was gone Colin developed a cough. At night in the chilly barracks, with one cot separated from another by mere inches, Colin kept the others awake with his deep, raspy hacking. He jammed a fist in his mouth to quell the sound but it wasn't enough. By the third night Jamie Ferguson and John Turley had worked out a plan of their own. When Colin started coughing they rose quietly from their beds, placed a blanket over his head, and took turns beating him with their fists. The following night there was no need to use physical force. They simply laid a pillow over his face and held it there until he went limp.

It was Mrs. Cunnington who first suggested that Colin's size might lend itself to a particular occupation. He was tall, it was true, but that was of little consequence. It was the width of his shoulders and narrowness of his frame that mattered. The headmaster, keen to be rid of Colin, was easily persuaded.

So it came to pass that he was apprenticed as a sweep. Although he displayed a remarkable aptitude for shinnying up and down chimney flues, he was too easily exhausted. His bright yellow hair, once so lovingly tousled by his mother's fingertips, disappeared beneath a film of greasy soot. Colin's unnaturally flushed complexion was hidden by ash and grime and the bruises he received from regular beatings were indistinguishable from streaks of coal dust.

He was returned to Cunnington's in a few weeks without fulfilling the terms of his apprenticeship. Mr. Cunnington cuffed him on the ears while his wife soundly scolded him. Colin's head rang without respite for twenty-four hours.

"I can't say that I like the idea of him living *here* until he's twelve," Mrs. Cunnington said. She set down her embroidery work, folded her hands on her lap, and looked at her husband expectantly. "He has the *most* accusing eyes. Had *you* noticed that?"

Indeed he had. The headmaster continued to clean his pipe.

"As if it were *our* fault that his wretched parents died. We *have* done our part. Everyone *knows* we have." Mrs. Cunnington could not speak without giving emphasis to at least one word. She believed it lent weight to her opinions. "I should say, they *could* have provided for their children. It was *obvious* they had the means to do so."

Mr. Cunnington laid his pipe cleaner aside and began to pack the pipe with tobacco. He felt the same disappointment his wife did. They had both pinned some hopes on finding relatives of Colin, Decker, and Grey. Using their own money they had placed ads in the London papers which described the three brothers and the circumstances of their parents' demise. No one had ever come forward to lay claim to the boys or suggest they might know the whereabouts of relatives.

It was the boys' clothes and Colin's polite and articulate manner that led the Cunningtons to believe there might be deep pockets in the family's coat of arms. No one at the Burnside Inn on the post road north of London knew anything about the family who had stopped only briefly for dinner. Thirty minutes after leaving the inn their carriage had been met by highwaymen. Murder was not the usual end to these encounters but there were always exceptions. The highwaymen made just such an exception for the boys' mother and father and their driver. Not knowing what else to do with three newly orphaned children, the local authorities sent the brothers to Cunnington's Workhouse.

The Cunningtons questioned Colin for facts about his family and upbringing but they found the stories somewhat fanciful and gradually came to believe an eight-year-old could not be counted on to know or tell the truth. The special attention given the brothers in the early days gradually waned and soon they were treated no better or worse than any other of the workhouse's charges.

When the headmaster finished packing his pipe he lighted it and puffed several times to begin the draw. Satisfied at last, his exhalation was more like a sigh. "You're right, of course," he said. He had learned it was always better to tell his wife she was right, even when he had every intention of disagreeing with her. Tonight, however, it was not his intention. "He can't stay here. He can't work, and I fear the consumption may infect the others."

Mrs. Cunnington's eyes widened. "Consumption?" They would have to get rid of Colin if that was the case. They couldn't wait for the boy to die. Too many other children might take ill. Why, they themselves were vulnerable. The workhouse would close and they would lose everything. "Do you *really* think it could be?"

He shrugged and drew on his pipe again.

To Mrs. Cunnington's way of thinking her husband was too indifferent. It could only mean that he had given the situation some thought and had decided on a course of action: *"Tell* me your plan."

Jack Quincy arrived at Cunnington's Workhouse for Foundlings and Orphans the following day. Everything about him was large. His voice rumbled and reverberated as though the barrel chest and throat from which it emerged were hollow. He had thick arms and legs as solid as tree trunks. His handshake was strong and warm, his manner a shade aggressive. Jack's eyes were widely spaced as if to suggest his peripheral vision was as good as his dead-on look. His nose had been broken on more than one occasion and mended badly each time. It was rumored that Jack Quincy was still looking for the fight that would set it right again.

When he swept into the headmaster's office he brought the smell of fresh air and salt water with him. And something else. Colin found himself leaning forward just to take in the scent of adventure.

Jack Quincy didn't wait to be offered the headmaster's hand. He took it in his, pumped it twice, and said without preamble, "Where's the boy you were telling me about?"

"Behind you," Mr. Cunnington said, looking past Quincy's shoulder to where Colin stood. "Won't you sit down and we'll discuss terms?"

Quincy gave Colin a cursory glance. "There's not much to him," he said in flat tones.

"He doesn't eat," the headmaster said. "At least not a lot. You won't find him terribly expensive to keep."

"And not terribly difficult to heave over the side." His eyes narrowed on Mr. Cunnington and he jabbed a thick finger in the headmaster's direction. "More to the point, I figure the fish won't take him as bait. They're likely to throw him back. Now, what kind of bill of goods are you trying to sell me, Cunnington?" He placed particular emphasis on the first two syllables of the headmaster's name. "My ship sails in two hours and you told me you had someone I could use. What do you think I can do with this boy?"

Mr. Cunnington bristled. He disliked the Yankee's boorish manner. "He's just as I promised."

"He's sick. You didn't tell me he was sick." As if on cue Colin began to cough. Quincy glanced backward again, assessed the boy's sunken features, the shadows beneath his eyes, the hollow cheeks and pale lips, and asked bluntly, "Is he consumptive?"

"It's a cold."

Quincy walked over to Colin, raised the boy's chin, then demanded, "Is that true?"

Colin thought he would be lifted off the floor by the finger under his chin but the large man's touch was surprisingly gentle. His lungs seemed to swell with the effort not to cough. "It's true, sir," he said. "No doctor's ever said as much."

Quincy was quick to understand Colin's game. There was no lie in his words—the truth was that no doctor had ever examined him. "Do you want to come with me, boy?" Quincy asked. He kept his finger on Colin's pointed chin and took measure of the grit and willfulness he saw in the boy's eyes. "Well?"

"It's Colin, sir," he said gravely. "My name's Colin Thorne, and yes, I want to go with you."

"Knowin' full well that I'll pitch you over the rail of the *Sea Dancer* as soon as look after you?"

In an effort to show strength where little existed, Colin held his thin body rigidly. "I'd like to take that risk, sir."

Jack Quincy released Colin's chin. "How much for him?" he asked the headmaster.

"Three pounds."

"That's a fortune," Quincy growled.

Colin grew suddenly afraid. What if Cunnington wouldn't negotiate and Quincy wouldn't pay? "If you wouldn't mind, sir," he said, interrupting, "I'd be honor-bound to give you recompense. With interest if you'd like."

Quincy blinked. "My God, he talks like a bleedin' banker," he said, more to himself than either to Colin or Cunnington. "How old are you, boy?"

"Ten," Colin said, crossing his fingers behind his back.

"Twelve," Cunnington said at the same time.

Jack Quincy grunted, believing neither. "Hell, it doesn't matter. I need the boy this trip." He opened his wool coat, reached for an inside pocket, and drew out three silver pieces. He manipulated one of the silver coins in and out between his fingers before he set them all on the headmaster's desk. "This is what I have. Suit yourself."

Mr. Cunnington picked up the silver quickly. "Get your things, Colin, then wait for Mr. Quincy at the front gate."

Colin hesitated, looking to Quincy for direction and approval, half afraid he might be set outside the gate with his bag and no one to take him away.

Jack Quincy rubbed his mouth to hide his brief smile. Damned if there wasn't something about the cheeky little boy that he liked. "Go on with you, lad. I'm not leavin' without you."

Colin looked for the truth in Jack Quincy's eyes, then he turned and walked out of the room, wearing his dignity like armor.

Quincy watched him go. When he was certain Colin was out of earshot he turned to the headmaster. "So help me, Cunnington, if that boy dies before the *Sea Dancer* makes Boston, I'll come back and take you and this workhouse apart."

"He'll arrive in Boston. After that . . ." His voice trailed off and he shrugged.

"It doesn't matter after that."

The *Sea Dancer* left London three hours behind schedule. Half expecting that one or the other of the Cunningtons would change their mind, or that Jack Quincy himself might think better of the bargain he had made, Colin had an agonizing wait.

The knot in his stomach didn't begin to untangle until England's coastline disappeared from view.

He was half an ocean away when Mr. Elliot Willoughby arrived in London from Rosefield and began inquiring about the direction of Cunnington's Workhouse for Foundlings and Orphans. The solicitor, it seemed, was particularly interested in the information on three children whose surname was reputed to be Thorne.

· *One*

It was the sound of thunder that roused him out of bed. Colin hadn't been asleep, or at least not deeply so, but he hadn't been particularly anxious to crawl out from between the sheets or remove the length of shapely calf and thigh that had been lying across his legs.

He padded softly to the window and drew back the yellowed curtains. Lightning flashed across the sky and for a moment his naked body was bathed in brilliant white light. He pressed the flat of his hand against the glass. When thunder rolled a few seconds later he felt the vibration all the way up his arm.

His trousers were lying over the arm of the room's only chair. He reached for them and pulled them on. Another ragged bolt of lightning illuminated the room as Colin glanced toward the bed. He had no difficulty discerning that his companion was still sleeping soundly. That was good, he thought as he unlatched the window and threw it open. It meant he had time to remember her name.

Warm, moist air swirled into the room and Colin put himself directly in its path. Drawing one leg up, he sat on the sill and rested his palms on his bent knee. The first fat droplets of rain touched his left shoulder on their way to the ground. He didn't move. The path of the water outlined his arm and elbow. One drop swelled strands of hair near the nape of his neck, darkening it to gold.

Colin leaned his head back against the window frame. This time when the thunder came it seemed to rumble through his entire body. He felt it in the soles of his feet, along his thigh, and across his chest. He breathed deeply and imagined the scent of the sea. He had only been ashore eight days and he'd been ready to return to his ship for six of them.

Rain began to fall faster and the shape of the drops changed from fat, spattering batter to thin water lances. The sting was mild compared to what Colin endured at the helm of the *Remington Mystic*. There the spray could be needle sharp and the pounding waves were known to scale the clipper's rails and carry an unprepared or unsuspecting sailor away.

The room Colin was shown at the Passing Fancy Inn faced the road to London. At this hour the throughway was quiet. Colin had been on the last coach from London and that had arrived at the inn before nightfall. He and Aubrey Jones were the only two to disembark. Aubrey had immediately caught the eye of the wench who served them dinner and they retired to his room shortly thereafter. Colin had expected to sleep alone but the serving wench produced a sister. Sibling rivalry, it seemed, had provided any number of travelers a playful romp in the upstairs rooms at the Passing Fancy.

"Here now," the voice from the bed whined sleepily. "Come away from the window. Ye'll catch yer death and toss it to me besides." When Colin didn't move or even glance in her direction she raised herself up on one elbow and patted the space beside her. "Come to Molly, why don't ye, luv."

Molly. So that was her name. "Go back to sleep," he said. His words were not delivered kindly or as a suggestion. Colin Thorne was used to giving orders.

"No need to bark at me," Molly said, quite able to hold her own. "Didn't get quite enough of the ol' slap n' tickle, is that what's keepin' ye up? I don't mind a bit more play." She yawned hugely. "If it's all the same to you."

It was so much better when she didn't talk, Colin thought. His gaze moved away from the quiet road and into the room. It did not alight on Molly, but on the bath that had been drawn for him hours ago. He'd never had the opportunity to use it; now he felt the need. "If it's all the same to you," he said, "I'd like my bath water warmed."

That brought Molly upright and she made no attempt to bring the sheet with her. Her heavy breasts heaved as she managed quite a show of her indignation. "Yer throwin' Molly out of yer bed?"

Apparently this was a first for Molly. "You should have gone back to sleep when I told you to," he said indifferently, turning away. Out of the corner of his eye he saw movement just below him. It had disappeared by the time he looked down. Someone just arriving at the inn? he wondered. But there had been no stage or horses. The sound of the inn's large door being slammed suggested to Colin that he'd been right about a new arrival. Probably a lone traveler surprised by the storm. Colin could have told him there was no need for panic. The rain was already letting up as thunder and lightning moved to points south and east of the inn.

Molly was of a mind to push Colin out the open window, but she remembered he hadn't paid her.

"On the nightstand," Colin said.

"So yer a bloody mind reader, too." Molly took the coins he'd put out for her and scrambled off the bed. Clutching them in her palm, she began to dress. "Me sister told me why you and yer friend are here," she said. "And here I was, feelin' like I should comfort a man about to look death in the eye. Well, I can tell ye it doesn't matter a whit to me now if his lordship puts a lead ball through yer head or yer heart."

"As long as he hits something," Colin said dryly.

"Yer too bleedin' right."

Colin came to his feet lightly. He could feel Molly's eyes on him as he walked to the door. He suspected she was glaring at him but when he turned he glimpsed something else there, something like regret perhaps, or longing. His dark eyes narrowed on Molly's pleasant, heart-shaped face. Had she imagined herself in love with him?

"Don't flatter yerself," she said sharply.

An edge of a smile touched Colin's mouth. "Now who's the bleedin' mind reader?"

Molly's reply caught in her throat. He had no right to look at her just the way he was looking now and stop her thoughts before they were formed. It was that hint of a smile that did it. That, or the flicker of interest that was darkening eyes already as dark as polished onyx. It was just as well he was throwing her out. Given the rest of the night with him she'd be a fool for love by morning.

"Arrogant bastard," she said under her breath. She finished fastening her skirt and shimmied into her blouse. The laces dangled and Molly made no attempt to tie them. He deserved to get an eyeful of what she was never giving him again, at least not unless he said please.

Colin was preparing to open the door for her when the knock came. It was a tentative intrusion, not a firm one. Colin knew it couldn't be Aubrey. His second in command had fists like hammers. Doors rattled under his pressure.

When Colin didn't respond to the first gentle rapping, the light staccato was tapped out again. He looked at Molly in question. When she shrugged, surprised as he, he placed a finger to his lips. She nodded her understanding.

Reaching for his boots by the door, Colin removed a knife from a leather sheath in the right one. He held it lightly in his palm, hefting it once to familiarize himself with the feel and weight of the weapon. He opened the door a crack.

The figure on the other side of the door was rain-soaked. The hooded cape dripped water onto the wooden floor. The person inside the woolen garment was shivering uncontrollably.

"What do you want?" Colin asked tersely. It was too dark in the hallway to make out the features of the stranded traveler.

"The innkeeper said I would find Captain Thorne here." The voice was husky and interspersed with the click of chattering teeth, but the timbre was unmistakably feminine.

Colin opened the door wider and let his visitor see the dagger in his hand. When she visibly started, he was satisfied that she was not a threat. He let her cross the threshold. To Molly he said, "Perhaps you'd better see to that warm water now."

"So I'm dismissed, am I?" she snapped. "And ye already with a replacement in me bed. Heat yer own bleedin' water."

The stranger interjected, "I don't require anything."

Colin managed to grab the door before Molly slammed it on her way out. "I wasn't asking for you," he said. "I've been trying to get a hot bath since I arrived." He saw his visitor shift her head toward the bed and imagined she was able to draw all the correct conclusions. "Yes, well, you're not my first interruption this evening."

Colin thought there might be a reply, better still, the beginnings of an explanation. It seemed his visitor was mesmerized by the tangle of sheets and blankets on his unmade bed. Colin placed the flat of his knife under her chin, let her feel the cool metal, and slowly drew her attention back to him. "That's better," he said.

The tip of his weapon vibrated slightly as she continued to shake with cold. His dark eyes narrowed. Her sodden hood fell too far forward for him to make out her features. "Take off your cape."

The command shook her out of her stupor. "I'll leave it on, thank you."

"It wasn't a suggestion."

She raised her hands as far as the fastener at her throat but there they froze again.

Colin neatly sliced the satin closure. The hood fell back and the cape opened. "Do what I say when I say it," he said, giving no quarter, "and you and your clothes will leave in one piece."

She nodded once and averted her gaze, uncomfortable with the way he was examining her. She didn't blush. Even if she could, it wasn't that kind of stare. His interest was more remote, almost clinical. She might well have been inanimate, a preserved specimen prepared for scientific study.

Colin lowered his knife. With a quick snap of his wrist he sent it spinning end over end until it stuck in the headboard. The sudden movement made her flinch but she didn't cower. That in itself was intriguing. "Take off the cape."

She responded this time, slipping it off her shoulders. It was heavy now that she had to hold it, but the weight was preferable to giving it up. She clutched it in front of her.

Colin walked over to the chair and pulled his shirt off the back. He shrugged into it and tucked the tails in his trousers. He noticed her eyes were still averted.

"I take it you're not one of Molly's sisters," he said.

"Who?" Then she understood. "No. Oh no. I've never seen her before."

Colin pitched the remainder of clothing on the chair toward the bed. He sat down and stretched his legs in front of him. As though uncertain if she were coming or going, the stranger hadn't turned yet in his direction. He studied her slender silhouette while she made up her mind. Beneath the cape which covered her forearms and hands he could make out the spasmodic clenching and unclenching of her fists. There was tension in the line of her shoulders and a lift to her chin that suggested she was not yet resigned to whatever fate or purpose had brought her this far.

Her teeth stopped chattering and her profile became still and smooth. He couldn't be sure, but he thought she might be worrying her lower lip. The full line of it was drawn in slightly.

He gave her time. He wasn't tired. In the best circumstances sleep often eluded him and at this moment he would wager that even if Aubrey Jones was now enjoying the pleasures of Molly's sister *and* Molly, this little diversion was bound to be more entertaining.

Colin watched his uninvited guest take a breath and let it out slowly. She hung her cape on the peg by the door and smoothed it out, squeezing water from the hem. Apparently she was staying.

"I'll heat that water for you," she said softly.

He was going to tell her the water could wait but she was already bending to the task, scooping water from the tub into the kettle on the hearth. She knelt on the brick apron of the fireplace and laid down kindling. After a few clumsy failures with the flint and striker she was able to start the fire.

He followed her movements with interest. She was small and rather delicate, with slender arms and shoulders and a high, narrow waist. Her hair was the color of bittersweet chocolate. Until he saw it in the firelight he thought it was merely black. Now he could see shades of sienna and russet and coffee gave it its deep, rich shading. She wore it pulled away from her face in a loose plait that hung down the middle of her back. The style was more for service than fashion. Colin knew women who plaited their hair at night, in preparation for bed and after giving it the requisite hundred strokes. He liked the ritual, liked lying in bed waiting for the women who did it, counting the strokes and watching the hair dance and swirl as the brush was pulled through.

Her hair shone in the firelight. Strands of dark umber whispered across her smooth cheek. Had she brushed her hair this evening? Had she done it while someone waited in bed for her?

She rose to her feet slowly, brushing her hands on her gown, and looked uncertainly at Colin. He was still watching her with that distant, narrowed glance of his. She cleared her throat.

"I imagine you're wondering who I am," she said.

"No," he said casually. "I think I've figured that out, Miss Leyden." Her widening eyes were confirmation. Were they blue or gray? In the light it was difficult to tell. "I suppose I even know why you're here. What I don't know is what you're prepared to offer in exchange for his miserable life."

Resigned now, Mercedes Leyden let her hands fall to her sides. "How did you know?"

"Weybourne Park isn't far from here. I know because that's where I'm going in the morning. One could manage the distance on foot; even at night it wouldn't be difficult. And you arrived on foot. I glimpsed your entrance into the inn. I'm aware the earl has two daughters and two sons. I make it a point to find out something about a man who's called me out. Since you're most definitely not one of the sons and your clothes are too fine to belong to one of his servants, it occurs to me that you must be one of the daughters."

"Actually I'm his niece."

Colin considered that. "Aaah," he said slowly. "I remember now. The poor relation."

She winced at the description but she didn't deny it or object to it. Mercedes had heard it before, though never so boldly pointed out. "The polite way to introduce it into conversation is to wait until my back is turned. In that manner you can console yourself with the pretense that I haven't really heard the remark. Although I understand that with Americans proper form counts for little."

One of Colin's brows raised in appreciation and approval. The corner of his mouth edged upward ever so slightly. "At least with this American," he said. "And you should be relieved. If I were an Englishman, proper form would forbid me from entertaining you in my room. Then where would you be?"

"In the hallway?" she rejoined. Mercedes noticed that her comment did not broaden the glimmer of a smile on his lips. He was not a man given to easy laughter or sudden, careless grins. She imagined the lines at the corners of his eyes were beaten into his face by sun and salt spray. His youth was captured in the sun-drenched color of his hair. It covered his head like a helmet of light and shimmered at his nape. In startling and unsettling contrast were his eyes, so deep brown they could have been black, so polished and penetrating they reflected an image while shuttering private thoughts.

Colin stood. "Why don't you sit here, Miss Leyden? I'll see to my own water. Unless you're comfortable by the fire."

She would not feel comfortable until she was out of his room, and perhaps not even then. She shivered when he brushed past her.

"Take a blanket from the bed and wrap it around you."

Mercedes recognized it as an order. She glanced at the dagger in the headboard. It wouldn't take much effort on his part to use it on her again. She picked up a blanket and did as she was told.

Colin poked at the fire. Although the rain had stopped, there was still a breeze eddying about the room. Flames flickered and danced. Shadows leaped on the bare walls. Colin dropped the poker against the fireplace and shut and latched the window. The curtains lay still again. Crossing his arms in front of him, he leaned back against the glass. "Did Weybourne send you here?" he asked.

She had to turn slightly in the chair to see him. It was natural for her to draw her feet up under her. Her leather shoes and socks were damp and the heat of her own body felt good against them.

"Oh, for God's sake," Colin muttered. He pushed away from the window and dropped to his knees in front of her. "Give me your feet." When surprise made her too slow to respond, Colin reached under her gown and pulled on her ankles. He removed both shoes, then the stockings, then rubbed her bare feet briskly between his hands. "Did Weybourne send you here?" he asked again.

Mortification. It was the word that came to Mercedes's mind. But she was asking herself why she wasn't experiencing it. In all of her twenty-four years no one had ever touched her so intimately, man or woman, and yet she wasn't at all embarrassed by it. Quite the opposite. The sensations filled her with exquisite relief. It was only when he paused that Mercedes realized he was waiting for an answer to his question.

Drawing her feet away and pushing her gown back to modestly cover her legs, Mercedes found time to recover her voice. "My uncle doesn't know I'm here."

Colin wondered if he could believe her. The Earl of Weybourne was a nasty piece of work. "Really?" he asked skeptically. "Then I confess I'm curious as to what prompted your trek to the inn and why you sought me out."

Mercedes watched him rise easily to his feet and walk to the fireplace again. There was an unmistakable edge to this man, whether it was his smile or the aggressive line of his nose. He did not merely stand; he took a position. The eyes were guarded, the stare fixed. He had a well-defined, clean-shaven jaw and he held his head at an angle that suggested he was not merely listening, but alert, even wary.

"I know you plan to meet my uncle tomorrow morning."

Without consulting his pocket watch, Colin knew she was wrong about the time. "It's after midnight," he said. "I think you mean this morning."

Her hands folded in her lap. Her fingers ached with the effort it took to keep them still. "Yes, you're right, of course. This morning. Near the pond at Weybourne Park. I believe you chose pistols."

"That was . . ." He paused, searching for the phrase. ". . . *proper form,* I believe. It was your uncle who called me out."

"He was in his cups."

"I'm sorry," Colin said, his tone indicating sarcasm, not regret. "But I don't recall seeing you in London at the club Tuesday a week past."

"You know I wasn't there. They don't allow women."

"Well, yes, I do seem to recall that. I wondered if you did." He dipped his fingers in the kettle. The water was only tepid. "What makes you think he was drunk?"

"He told me."

"And you believed him," Colin said flatly. "Why, I wonder?"

Why wouldn't she, Mercedes thought. He drank a great deal. Wallace Leyden, the sixth Earl of Weybourne, was frequently three sheets to the wind before he left his bedchamber. It was inconceivable to her that he would spend an evening at his club without a decanter of brandy at his side. "I have my reasons," she said.

"Oh, I don't doubt he's a sot most days of the week and most hours of the day, but last Tuesday he was sober. Do you require proof?"

"No." Mercedes shook her head. She believed him. It was natural that she would take the word of a stranger, even an American stranger, over her uncle. The point was simply that she knew the Earl of Weybourne, knew him as well as his own children, perhaps better. She would count lying as one of his smaller sins. "He may have been sober," she said. "But he wasn't thinking clearly."

"I'll concede that point. I believe a number of people, including several who call themselves his friends, tried to dissuade him from the action he took. He was set on the matter."

"He had everything to lose," she implored.

"He had material things to lose," Colin said. "Until he called me out, his life wasn't one of those things."

Mercedes's face paled. The strain of this past week showed in her clear gray eyes. The cobalt ring at the edge of her irises darkened and she drew in her lower lip again, worrying it. After a moment she said softly, wearily, "So it's true, then. You intend to kill him." She watched him carefully, wondering if he would deny it, and if he did, if she could believe him this time. She needn't have bothered. There was no denial.

"If he doesn't kill me first."

She closed her eyes briefly. She tried to imagine her life away from Weybourne Manor. Where would she go? What would she do? Chloe, at least, was already engaged, and Sylvia might still make a reasonably good marriage even without a dowry, but the twins would be her responsibility and they would have no inheritance. How was she supposed to keep food in their stomachs and a roof over their heads?

Mercedes could feel her stomach lurch and roil as her thoughts began to tumble out of control. It was not like her to get ahead of herself. She was the unfailingly practical one, the responsible Leyden, heiress to virtues like honor and honesty, loyalty and trust. And where had it gotten her? She would do well, she thought, to embrace a bit more in the way of larceny and deceit. This evening's escapade was a good start. On the heels of that thought Mercedes found she could still smile.

Watching her, seeing the glimmer of a sweet, satisfied curve on her lips, Colin said, "You find the idea of your uncle killing me amusing?"

For a moment she had difficulty following him. Then she recalled his previous comment. "Oh, no," she said quickly. "I wasn't thinking about that. . . . I was . . ."

"Yes?"

She shook her head. "Nothing." How could she explain that she was not quite like the person he was talking to tonight, that in other circumstances she wouldn't have left Weybourne Park after nightfall, at least not alone and never on foot. She wouldn't cross the threshold of an inn like the Passing Fancy and she'd never even entertained the notion of joining a man in his room.

Colin tested the water in the kettle. It was finally hot. He yanked a sheet off the bed and used one corner to keep from burning his palm on the iron handle. In one easy, sweeping motion he poured the scalding water in the wooden tub. That made the temperature warm enough. After setting the kettle on the floor he began to pull out his shirttails.

"You're going to bathe now?" she asked.

"I'm not waiting until the water gets cold again."

"But I'm still here."

"Are you planning on leaving any time soon?"

"Not without discussing—"

"That's what I thought." He finished pulling off his shirt and hooked his thumbs in the waistband of his trousers.

That's when Mercedes did a surprising thing. She didn't turn in her chair or avert her head. Mercedes didn't even blink. What she did was stare.

Colin pushed at his trousers. She still didn't look away. He lowered them a fraction. The flat of his muscled belly was fully exposed and she hadn't twitched. He swore softly and kicked the tub with his bare foot in frustration. Water sloshed on the floor and pain shot through his foot. "Very well," he said gracelessly. "I'll wait, but state your business then get out of here."

Taking little comfort in her victory, Mercedes said stiffly, "If you insist on showing up at Weybourne Park, then you must find some way for honor to be served without killing the earl."

Colin sat on the edge of the bed and nursed his stubbed toe. "Must I? I suppose you're going to tell me why."

She leaned forward in her chair, her expression earnest. "We'll lose everything. You can't appreciate what that means else you wouldn't insist on this manner of addressing a fault."

He understood better than she could know about losing everything. He didn't explain because it made no difference; it was something *she* would not understand. What he said was, "You call it a fault? Is that your word or the earl's?"

"His word," she admitted apologetically.

Colin stopped rubbing his toe. "The Earl of Weybourne made a wager. A wager he hadn't the means to honor at the outset. I wouldn't have accepted the terms if I had known, but it would have been less than proper form if I had made an overt inquiry about his finances. I was prepared to cover the wager if I lost. The earl was not."

Mercedes felt a tightness in her chest. It was every bit as bad as she thought it could be.

"Do you want a drink?" asked Colin. She looked as if she might need one. Indeed, she looked as if she might faint. The only positive thing that might come of it, as far as Colin was concerned, was that he would finally have his bath. "Never mind," he said before she could answer. He could see she was preparing to reject his offer anyway. "I'll pour you one and you'll finish it. A second, if I say so."

She nodded weakly. There was no point in arguing. She had learned living with the earl that one must choose one's battles and over the years she had become something of a good strategist.

The bottle of whisky on the nightstand had been thoughtful Molly's contribution. Colin poured two fingers of alcohol into his own unused tumbler and passed it to Mercedes. "All of it," he said.

Mercedes wrapped her slender fingers around the glass and raised it to her lips. Over the rim she caught Colin's intent stare. He looked as if he'd hold her nose and pour the stuff down her throat if she didn't drink it on her own. She tipped her head back and let it slide.

"Good girl." He took the tumbler from her and put it aside. "Let's see how you get on with that."

Her insides were on fire, that's how she was getting on. Gamely, she nodded. She hardly recognized her own voice when she was able to get a few words out. "Tell me about the wager."

Colin stuffed a pillow behind his back and leaned against the headboard. Thinking back, he raked his fingers through his hair. "You're familiar with Lloyd's?" he asked.

"The insurance house."

"That's right. They've been insuring ships and cargo for over a hundred years and they have a good system for communicating departures and arrivals. News always seems to reach them first if a ship's foundered somewhere on the coast, or if the cargo's been spoiled, or if there's been hands lost to storms or pirates. There's an opportunity for fortunes to vanish or be made depending on the fate of ships. Lloyd's policies are really shares sold to investors, and if their ship comes in they're rewarded handsomely. If it doesn't . . ." Colin shrugged. "Well, you can imagine."

Indeed, Mercedes was having no difficulty imagining. In her mind's eye she was seeing men who had risked everything going quietly into a back room of the coffee house and putting a pistol to their head. Her knuckles whitened around the empty tumbler.

"Recently Lloyd's has been the site of more reckless wagering. Men are not only betting on a ship coming in, but putting down extra money if she comes in on time. There's always more to be made if a ship carrying certain valuable goods is the first of its kind to make port. Tea, for instance, from Hong Kong. Or wool from Melbourne. If a clipper captain can be the first to reach Liverpool or London with cargoes like those, he can do well for himself, his crew, and his company."

"That's what you are?" she asked. "A clipper captain?"

"Master of the *Remington Mystic*."

Some men would have said it as a boast, or at least with a trace of pride. Mercedes detected nothing like that in Colin

Thorne's tone. He said it merely as a statement of fact. She held out her tumbler. "I think I'd like more, please."

Colin considered her request. There was a bit of color in her cheeks that hadn't been there during any part of their brief acquaintance. Her eyes—gray, he could see now, with the smallest ring of cobalt blue—were clear and steady. Mercedes Leyden appeared to be holding her own. "All right," he said, leaning forward with the bottle. He gave her half as much as he had before. "Don't knock it back like a sailor this time. Sip it."

She did as she was told. The sensation was quite pleasant. "Was it a wager like that that my uncle made?" she asked. "Was he betting that you'd come in on time?"

Colin set the bottle down. He drew his knees up and rested one arm across the caps. "No. That sort of wager wouldn't have had the return the earl was looking for. He challenged the *Mystic* to come in *ahead* of schedule."

"Break a record, you mean?" Ignoring Colin's earlier admonishment, Mercedes finished her drink in one gulp. "My God," she said lowly. "What was he thinking?"

"Probably that he couldn't lose," Colin said practically.

"And what prompted you to take him up on it? Was it the same for you? Did you think you couldn't lose?"

"On the contrary. I didn't think my chances of winning were very great. Your uncle only had to record his wager and wait. I had to make it happen."

Again Mercedes could detect no boast in the statement. He said it simply, accepting his role as part of the risk. "How much was the wager?"

"A quarter of a million pounds."

She blanched. It was more than everything. "The run?"

"Liverpool to Boston to London."

"And the record?"

"Twenty-six days, thirteen hours."

It was becoming easier to understand why her uncle thought he had made a winning wager. She might have been tempted herself. Mercedes leaned forward and set her tumbler on the floor. When she straightened she was a little light-headed. At the moment it seemed like a very good thing.

"Twenty-six days, four hours," Colin said, answering the question she had yet to ask. "The *Remington Mystic* logged in nine hours under the record."

Mercedes stared at him. "Nine hours," she said hollowly. "My family is going to lose Weybourne Park because of nine hours."

Colin pushed off the bed and stood. "You talk as though it hasn't happened yet. Your family's already lost Weybourne Park and not because my crew had an outstanding run, but because his lordship didn't think for a moment that it was even possible."

Mercedes pressed her spine rigidly against the back of the overstuffed chair as Colin towered over her.

"Lloyd's documented the run," he told her. "It's a matter of record now. By the time I walked into their offices, people already knew your uncle had lost his wager. I found him at his club that same evening. I, too, thought he'd be drunk but apparently his friends feared what he might do and they managed to cut his drinks with water." Colin suddenly realized he was leaning over Mercedes, and that she had pushed herself as much into the corner of the chair as was possible. She was looking up at him, her eyes watchful and wary as though expecting a blow and preparing herself to take it on the chin. Disgusted, Colin straightened and removed his hands from the arms of the chair.

"I'm not going to hit you," he said tightly. When he noticed her position didn't change a whit he took a step backward and finally moved to the window. She had to turn in her chair to see him. It made her seem less like a cornered fawn. "In front of half a dozen witnesses the earl called into question the legitimacy of the *Mystic*'s run. He went so far as to suggest that the *Mystic* had a twin ship in the Remington line and that I had never taken the clipper the entire way back to Boston."

Mercedes's eyes widened a fraction. Her uncle had to have had some understanding of his situation to act so recklessly. Impugning a man's honor was no peccadillo, but a breech with serious consequences.

"I showed him the dated newspaper I picked up the day I arrived in Boston harbor. He claimed it was all arranged and all of it a fraud." Colin now saw on his guest's face an understanding of where this was leading. She nodded once, slowly, bidding him to continue. "Your uncle said a number of other things. I would have been well within my rights to call him out for any one of them."

"Why didn't you?"

"Because there was no point. I was already aware that he couldn't pay the debt without borrowing against the value of Weybourne Park. If he wasn't willing to do that then the estate would be mine by default. It's all quite legal, I assure you."

Mercedes didn't doubt it. She had come to understand that Colin Thorne took calculated risks, not blind ones. What she could not comprehend was that he had a quarter of a million pounds to wager. How was it possible for a clipper captain to amass a fortune? "So when you didn't take the bait?" she prompted.

"He called me out. To his way of thinking he had no other choice. If he kills me tomorrow he won't have to make good on his wager. If I kill him . . ." Colin shrugged. "Then he has no more worries, does he?"

The Earl of Weybourne worried very little. That was left to Mercedes. She was the one who took on the burden of managing Weybourne Park. It had been her home first.

Unfolding her legs, Mercedes moved to the edge of the cushion. She sat there a moment, perched like a skittish bird, her head darting first one direction then the other. She picked up her stockings, rolled them on, then slipped into her damp shoes. When she stood she felt water squishing out from between the stitching. She wriggled her toes uncomfortably.

In spite of the warmth supplied by the fire, her cloak was still damp. She swung it around her shoulders and drew the hood up over her head. Mercedes glanced once at Colin. He was merely watching her with the same detached curiosity she had noticed earlier. She rested her palm on the door handle, searching for something to say. In the end she left as quietly as she had come.

There were no words.

There was a light on in the library when she arrived home. It meant her uncle was waiting up for her. No one met her at the door to take her cloak or inquire if she wanted tea. The manor had been understaffed for years and the servants Mercedes was able to retain were taking a well-deserved rest in their own quarters.

Her uncle appeared in the dimly lit hallway before she could put away her cloak. "I'd like to heat water for tea," she said, opening the closet beneath the stairs. Mercedes placed her damp garment inside. When she stepped back to shut the door the Earl of Weybourne was directly behind her. Her entire body went rigid as she bumped into him. Before she could pull away he had caught her plait in his hand and was wrapping it around his fist.

"Tea can wait," he said lowly.

His mouth was near her ear but Mercedes could smell his breath. He'd been drinking since she left. Knowing how futile it was to fight, Mercedes willed herself to remain quiet.

"Let's go into the library, shall we?"

It was anything but an invitation. Mercedes nodded once and felt the tug on her scalp for her effort.

Wallace Leyden, the Right Honorable Earl of Weybourne, drew his niece into the library by the scruff of her neck. When he let her go to close the large oak pocket doors behind him, she stepped quickly out of his reach. Her movement did not go unnoticed. He was smiling narrowly when he turned away from the doors.

Lord Leyden was not a particularly tall man, but Mercedes had to look up to him. In her eyes he had remained remarkably unchanged over the last score of years. His brown hair had begun to gray at the temples soon after his forty-eighth birthday and the lines at the corners of his eyes and mouth had deepened, but that was all she had ever noticed. Years of drinking had not appreciably thickened his waistline or reddened his nose. Even when he'd been without a drink for days, his hands never shook. His tolerance for liquor was something of a legend among the peerage, and snippets of this dubious accolade had become known to Mercedes over time.

The earl was a popular escort among the widows and neglected wives of his set. With his trim, athletic figure and rather elegant, austere features, he was considered handsome by many women and at various times kept a mistress in London. The extent of his debt was known to his family and his creditors but not widely suspected among his peers. Few friends were ever invited to Weybourne Park and when a party did arrive it was left to Mercedes to make certain that appearances were kept.

In some ways the manor bore a resemblance to the earl. It had not changed overmuch on the outside. The grounds were maintained. The lawn and gardens were regularly trimmed. The face of the stone house was kept in good repair. It was only when one looked more deeply that the signs of trouble were apparent: the water stains on the ceilings on the third floor and in the servants' quarters; the thin carpets in the north wing bedrooms; the dwindling artwork in the gallery; the clogged chimneys; and the sagging floor in the upstairs parlor.

And so it was with the earl. Decay and deterioration were there upon closer inspection. The wit for which he was known could politely be called acerbic. At home, when it was turned on his family, it was cruel. Drinking or not, his moods were unpredictable, and when accompanied by violence, they were frightening. He had the judgment of a spoiled and willful child. He was impatient and demanding, ignorant or merely heedless of consequences.

When she was younger Mercedes didn't understand why he had so many friends. He was always being called away from the country estate to visit this person or that. She had once asked her Aunt Georgia that very question, but her aunt knew better than to answer it. In time Mercedes was able to draw her own conclusions as she learned that his lordship saved his cruelty and vicious temper for his family at Weybourne Park. They were an outlet for him. The longer he was away the more they could expect to pay some terrible price upon his return. And when her aunt died giving birth to the twins, Mercedes discovered how often Georgia Leyden had shielded her children and niece from the earl's blackest side.

Wallace Leyden's hooded glance was leveled on his niece. His hands rested behind his back, clasped. "Well?" he asked. "You don't look the worse for your encounter. He didn't throw you out, I take it."

Mercedes inched toward the fireplace. The flames were meager but they radiated warmth. There was also a poker nearby. Mercedes never walked into a room with her uncle without assessing what could be used as a weapon, though the one she most often had to fear was his hand. "No, he didn't throw me out. He was quite accommodating, actually. Given the circumstances, I don't know that I would have been as gracious." It was pushing the truth a bit, Mercedes realized, but something his lordship deserved to hear. "You lied to me."

The flecks of gold in Weybourne's brown eyes splintered. A muscle worked in his cheek but he managed to say with credible calm, "How so?"

A strand of damp hair lay against Mercedes's temple. She pushed it back impatiently. "You told me you were drinking that night, that Mr. Thorne took advantage of you in your cups. You said he provoked your response."

"There's no falsehood there."

"Liar!" In her mind she screamed the word. In reality it was given little more sound than a harsh whisper.

He crossed the space that separated them in three strides and raised his right hand. "You dare," he said with soft menace.

Mercedes was suddenly transported back to the Passing Fancy. She could picture herself sitting in the chair while Colin Thorne prepared for his bath. She had stared him down then. Hadn't turned away. Hadn't blinked. He was the one who thought better of his actions.

The same tactic did not work with his lordship. In fact, it seemed to inflame him. Mercedes took the blow on her cheek. The sound of it hurt her ears and the sting sent her rocking back on her heels. She wavered a moment, tried to steady herself by grasping the edge of the cherry desk, then went down on her knees, catching her hip on the sharp corner.

His hand was raised for a second blow but he was satisfied when she cried out. He lowered it slowly and let it rest at his side, his fist still clenched. "What else did he say?" he asked evenly.

Tears touched the corners of her eyes and lined the lower lids. By lifting her head she kept them from falling. "That you accused him of cheating to win the wager."

"He *did* cheat."

"What proof do you have?"

"Where's the proof that he didn't?"

"He said there was a newspaper. One dated the day he put in at Boston Harbor."

Weybourne dismissed that as evidence. "Carried to him at sea by another ship. What he says he did couldn't have been done."

Mercedes placed one hand on the desk and pulled herself up. Because her uncle did not back away, she skirted the corner to put distance and an obstacle between them. "Why do you say that? He broke the record by nine hours. He only needed to break it by one minute. Why shouldn't he have been able to do it?"

The Earl of Weybourne's tight jaw clamped shut. He stared hard at his niece and remained silent.

"Oh, dear God," she said on a thread of sound. "You made some arrangement, didn't you? With whom? A crew member? Someone on the dock? What did you do?"

Lord Leyden was stoic in the face of the accusations. All he said was, "He couldn't have accomplished what he did."

"You've shamed us all."

For a moment it looked as though he might hit her again.

"Captain Thorne cheated," he said quietly, reining in his anger, "and I'll find some way to prove it."

"If he doesn't kill you first."

"That's why I require your services."

"I can't talk him out of meeting you."

The earl leaned forward on the desk and faced her squarely. "How hard did you try, Mercedes?"

"I tried." Even to her own ears her effort sounded feeble.

"That's what I thought." He straightened and pulled on the sleeves of his tailored jacket, smoothing the material as he pretended to consider what to do next. With practiced deliberation he opened his jacket and removed his pocket watch. Glancing at it, he then held it in his palm for Mercedes to see. "It appears there is still time."

Mercedes felt herself pale. "Oh, I couldn't, my lord," she said quickly. "I couldn't go back there."

Wallace Leyden shrugged. He returned the watch to its pocket and left the desk for the sideboard. The decanter of brandy was still open. He poured himself a drink. When he turned in Mercedes's direction again he raised the glass in a mocking salute. "That's your decision, Mercedes. But I feel I must remind you of the consequences. Do you really think he'll let any of you stay here? He probably has plans for the manor that don't include the brats or their governess. He'll marry Chloe and Sylvia off. It will be the easiest way to deal with them and cause the least scandal, but you and the twins will find yourselves on the streets." His tone became intimate, silky. "Have you thought of what you might do on the streets?"

Over the rim of his glass he let his eyes graze Mercedes from head to toe. Her thick, dark hair and clear gray eyes, easily reminded him of her mother. Mercedes took her looks from Elizabeth Allen, not the Leyden side of the family. She had the same stature, the same delicate turn of her wrists and ankles. What she did not have was Elizabeth's stubborn willfulness. He had seen that disappear in the early years and had never missed it. She could be bent to his will in a way her mother never could. Lord Leyden knew how to make it happen. "You really are a striking young woman, Mercedes," he said in a low voice. "I've regretted a number of times in recent years that your father was my brother. I could easily entertain thoughts of setting you up as my mistress. A few friends have suggested to me that I'm too fastidious. They would not be so restrained if you lived under their roof."

Mercedes flinched but it only showed in her eyes.

"I make mention of it," he went on, "because it seems to me that Captain Thorne, with a bit of effort on your part, could be made to desire you."

"No," she said quietly. "You're wrong. I'm sure you're wrong. He didn't show the slightest interest."

The earl ignored that. He cocked his head toward the library doors. "I think I hear the twins."

Mercedes's head snapped up. "What?" There was a thread of panic in her voice. "No, you couldn't have. I'm sure—"

He held up his hand. "I'm sure I did. Perhaps I should pay a visit to their rooms. Who do you think it is this time? Britton? Brendan? Perhaps both of them. You know I don't like them moving about at night. They could get hurt. It's a simple thing to fall on the back stairs."

"Oh, please." She came around the desk and approached him. "Leave them be. This doesn't have anything to do with them."

His dark brows came together. "I'm afraid it does. You've seen that it does." Ignoring her approach he started for the door.

"Wait!"

The doors opened silently and the Earl of Weybourne passed through them.

Mercedes followed, grabbing his sleeve at the foot of the stairs. "No," she said, despair edging her voice. "Give me another chance. I'll go back."

One of his brows cocked and he looked pointedly at the small hand on his jacket. "Really?"

Her hand slipped away. Mercedes rubbed her damp palm against the skirt of her gown. "I'll do it this time. I swear it."

Two

Colin hauled himself out of the tub when he heard the commotion belowstairs. The banging on the inn's front door rattled the shutters. Colin had no doubt the intrusion was somehow related to his business at Weybourne Park. Most likely the earl himself this time, he thought as he dried himself off. "Come here to tell me I've spoiled his virgin niece and now I have to marry her," he said under his breath. "Does he think that will stop me from killing him?" Colin caught his dark, ironic smile reflected in the window pane. To his way of thinking it was all the more reason to do the deed. The Earl of Weybourne would make a poor sort of in-law.

Tossing his thin towel over the back of the chair, Colin stepped into his trousers. He was pulling on his shirt when the outside noises finally reached the other side of his door. The knock that came this time was not tentative. Swearing softly, Colin started to cross the room. Out of the corner of his eye he saw his knife embedded in the headboard, a reminder of his earlier encounter. If this visitor was the earl, he was likely to be served well by it again. He drew it out and carried it half concealed in his palm.

Colin didn't open the door. Rather he called through it. "Who's there?"

It was the innkeeper's raspy, guttural voice that responded. He made no attempt to hide his impatience. "The wench is back to see you, guvnor. Told her if she was thrown out once ye weren't interested in a—" He stopped as the door was opened.

"Molly?" asked Colin before he got a clear look.

The innkeeper's large hand was placed firmly around the neck of the intruder. The hood of her cloak was all that kept her from being bruised by his grip. As before, her face was shadowed and her figure shrouded by the dark and damp cape. "Not Molly, guv," the innkeeper said, though it was clear to him now that Colin recognized the troublesome visitor.

"You can let her go," Colin said.

The innkeeper dropped his hand. The directive that he do so was delivered almost carelessly, as if it were a matter of indifference. It was what the innkeeper glimpsed in Colin Thorne's black eyes that prompted his quick response. "Now see here," the innkeeper blustered momentarily. "She can't come an' go as she pleases all night. There's other guests to think of."

"I'll settle with you in the morning," he said. The way he said it closed the subject. Reaching out with his left hand, Colin drew Mercedes into the room and closed the door on the innkeeper. Mercedes began to speak but Colin backed her against the door and placed his hand over her mouth. He felt her panic in the stiff, unyielding length of her body, and saw it in her widened eyes, but he made no explanation and no move to release her until the innkeeper's footsteps had receded in the hallway.

Colin placed his knife on the scarred dresser top before he let his other hand fall away. He didn't step back. "The innkeeper doesn't know who you are, does he?"

Mercedes was crowded by his presence. It was difficult to draw an even breath. "No," she said. "I've never been here before."

"That's not quite true."

"You know what I mean. Except for tonight I've never—"

"I knew what you meant."

"Then you shouldn't pretend to be obtuse."

A single eyebrow lifted archly. "Are you taking me to task?"

Mercedes could detect no humor in his tone yet there was the faintest suggestion of a smile lifting one corner of his mouth. "I . . . I suppose I—"

Continuing to watch her closely, Colin finally moved away.

"What are you doing back here? Is your uncle waiting some-where nearby, hoping to catch us out?"

She didn't answer, but leaned weakly against the door and drew in a slow, deep breath. As if she had been deprived of air for hours, it shuddered through her.

His eyes narrowed. "What's wrong with you?" he asked.

There was no concern in his voice, only that detached curiosity that maddened her. "Nothing," she said.

Plainly it was a lie and Colin had no patience for them, at least when they were being told to him. He closed the space that sepa-rated them and yanked on her hood. Strands of dark, damp hair were matted to her cheeks and temples. The weave of her thick plait was loose now and it hung over her shoulder, her hair barely contained in the braid. Her pale skin had taken on a grayish cast and there were the first faint markings of a bruise along her jaw.

Colin raised his hand. With his forefinger he traced the line of the discolored area without really touching it. Still, her head jerked back against the door as if he had slapped her. "What happened?" he asked.

When Mercedes didn't answer Colin opened her cloak and drew it off. Belatedly she made a grab for it. It was out of her reach and on the floor behind Colin before her arm was fully extended. Her arm fell uselessly to her side and she averted her head as he assessed the damage.

Other than to note the expensive cut and color of her gown, Colin had not given much attention to what she was wearing when he first met her. Now the finest details were observed be-cause of what had happened to them.

The rich emerald silk was mottled by dirt and water. One of the tight-fitting sleeves was ripped at the seam, exposing the skin of her shoulder. The neckline was also torn and two smudged fingerprints were visible at the base of her throat. There was a small, right angle tear near her hip. The material was rent at her waist and at the hem a tattered flounce from one of several pet-ticoats peeped out like a white flag of surrender.

Without asking her permission, Colin raised the hem of her

gown enough to see that her black kid slippers and stockings were wetter and muddier than on his first encounter with them.

He let the gown fall back in place and straightened. He said nothing, merely looked at her and waited for an explanation.

Mercedes's heart hammered against her breast. Whalebone stays were the only thing holding her in and holding her up. She didn't dare look at him. "I never made it back to Weybourne Park," she said lowly. "I can't go back like this . . . my uncle . . . he'll . . ." She bit her lower lip briefly, then said in a rush, "I didn't know where else to go. I thought you might—"

He swore softly. Colin hooked his forefinger under her chin and forced her to look at him now. "You thought I might what? Sweet Jesus, woman! What am *I* supposed to do with you? Like as not I'll be the one strung up for accosting you!"

"No! I wouldn't let anyone say that!"

Colin didn't give any indication if he believed her one way or the other. He gave her another hard look as he weighed his options. Finally he stepped aside. "Go sit down on the bed. I'll heat more water. It won't be fresh since I've already had my bath, but it'll do."

"Oh, no," she said quickly. "I don't want—"

He didn't say anything this time to interrupt her. It was his narrowed black glance, the vaguely menacing way his body shifted, that made her reconsider reckless words.

She dropped to the edge of the bed.

Colin rapped out orders in short bursts. "Shoes. Stockings. The gown, too." He tossed her a brush. "Do something about your hair." He didn't give her any more overt attention while he heated water. Without seeming to, he watched her stiff, almost dazed compliance to his commands. Her movements were mechanical and detached, as if she were undressing someone other than herself. After she had removed her shoes and stockings and pulled the brush through her tangled hair a few times, Mercedes stood with her back to Colin and began to unfasten her gown. She stopped when she was only half done. Her arms fell and her hands clenched at her sides.

"I can't," she whispered. Then even more softly, "I won't."

Colin was of no mind to debate the issue. He came up behind her and made short work of it. He felt her resistance when he began to pull the material over her shoulders and down her arms. "If you fight me, you'll tear it beyond my ability to make it right. Now, step out of it."

She had little choice. The emerald bodice and sleeves were already hanging at the level of her waist. An odd thought occurred to her: he was considerably talented at getting a woman out of her clothes. She placed a hand over her mouth to quell her nervous laughter.

"Are you going to be sick?"

Mercedes noted that the question was asked with genuine curiosity this time. Perhaps he was human after all. "No," she said. "At least not—"

"Sit back down then," he said, the last vestige of feeling gone from his voice. Colin snatched up the torn and muddied gown, the shoes and stockings, and began rooting through his valise at the foot of the bed. He came up with a small cedar box. "I'll repair these things downstairs while you bathe," he told her.

Her eyes widened.

Colin ignored the look. Her surprise was hardly flattering. "Finish undressing and get in the tub. When you're ready to go I'll see what Molly or her sister might have to cover that bruise." It was only at the point of leaving that he paused again. "Were you raped?"

Mercedes blanched under the hard, penetrating look he gave her. "No," she said. "It didn't come to that." If anything, Colin's expression seemed to search her more deeply.

"I wonder why."

He was gone before she could tell him her invented story, that she had fought off her attackers. Perhaps, given his cynicism and scrutiny, she'd better amend her attackers to the singular. He might believe she had fended off one drunk, but never two.

Mercedes realized she hadn't given enough consideration to her tale or Colin's reaction. On the way back to the inn from

Weybourne Park, her mind had mostly been numb. Her promise to deal with Colin Thorne hadn't been enough to stop her uncle from going to Brendan's room. There was no better way for the earl to ensure her cooperation. It was not surprising that Britton had been there too, sleeping soundly beside his twin in the large four-poster. It may have been the door flying open or Mercedes's own cry of alarm that alerted the boys, but they were roused to attention immediately, darting to opposite sides of the bed in a strategy of flanking the enemy that they had perfected as small children.

But for the fact that Britton tripped on the long tails of his nightshirt, they might both have escaped. As it happened, the young boy's stumble sent him directly into his lordship's hands. Britton took a fist so solidly in his gut that it drove the air from his lungs. He went down on his knees and curled fetally, the protective posture part instinctual and part practiced. The boot that kicked out at him only glanced off his shoulder.

Mercedes put herself between Brendan and the earl as that boy tried to save his brother. Her interference gave Lord Leyden an excuse to touch her. He seized the neckline of her gown, tearing it as he removed her from the fight. She stumbled back but still managed to catch and hold Brendan. Mercedes knew better than to let him join the fray. It would be the same beating for both of them. Now she only had to concern herself with nursing one.

Chloe and Sylvia heard the muffled screams and came rushing from their rooms to Britton's. They stood on the threshold and watched the last blows of Britton's beating. When it was over, when their fear subsided, they looked to Mercedes for direction. They stepped aside until their father strode out of the room, then ran in to care for their fallen brother.

Mercedes forced the scene from her mind as she lifted the kettle. Water splashed the hot hearth bricks and sizzled. Embers hissed. She poured the warm water into the bath, replaced the kettle, then knelt beside the tub. She washed quickly, never removing her undergarments. Bits of dirt and humus that she had so carefully placed on her person were now wiped away. She scrubbed her face and arms and let water sluice her throat and run between her breasts. The edge of her bodice became wet.

Looking down at herself, Mercedes could see the hilt of the dagger riding above the edge of her corset. She got up and walked to the window where she was reflected in the dark glass. This view assured her that the dagger was hidden by her camisole. She dipped three fingers below the laced edge of the camisole and between her breasts. The hilt was easy to grasp. She raised the dagger a few inches, accustoming herself to the movement, then slid it back in place.

Behind her she caught sight of the headboard. Mercedes turned and saw clearly that Colin had removed his knife. Was he carrying it on him? She glanced around the room and spied it on the dresser. Her first thought was to hide it from him. Her second thought was to think better of her first. If he saw it was gone then he would naturally assume she took it. Mercedes didn't doubt he would search her and that would reveal her own dagger. Her ill-conceived plan would be aborted then and there.

She let his weapon lie.

Her gaze turned from the dresser to the nightstand. The bottle of whisky was still there and beside it, the glass tumbler. It didn't look as if it had been touched. Perhaps Colin Thorne didn't drink, or at least not to excess. The novelty of it intrigued Mercedes. Her knowledge of her uncle's habits and her acquaintance with those he considered friends prepared her to believe that sobriety was the exception, not the rule. It was another way in which Captain Thorne stood well outside her experience.

The valise at the foot of the bed became another point of interest. Mercedes wondered if she dared. Then she wondered how she dared not.

Setting the case on the bed, Mercedes opened it. Her first observation was that he was meticulous about his packing. Nothing was simply thrown in. She sifted carefully through the shirts and stockings. Pressing down a pair of trousers was a book. She lifted it and read, *The Hunchback of Notre Dame.* His tastes in literature raised more questions than answers. She wouldn't have anticipated he would be drawn to something widely acknowledged to be so romantic. Perhaps he was only using it to press his trousers after all.

Mercedes set the book aside and delved deeper. At the bottom of the valise she found a black lacquered box, large enough to take up the entire base of the bag. The enameled wood was smooth to the touch and when she had completely removed it, her reflection was somewhat hazily visible on the surface. She sat down, placed it on her lap, and opened the lid slowly.

Because of the weight of the box she had suspected what the contents would be. She was only left to be surprised by the beauty of the weapons.

Like exquisite stones, the pistols lay in a bed of dark red velvet. Mercedes had no doubt the setting was deliberate. It was the proper background to display weapons that ended life in a pool of blood.

She knew something about pistols. Her father had had a large collection of them. At one time the present earl had added to their number and then, when fortune reversed itself, had begun selling them off one by one.

These weapons were American flintlock pistols. The handles were maple, oiled and shined so they had the warm red and brown tones of a polished chestnut. The fittings on the butt and trigger guard were brass; the barrel was steel. These were pistols made for dueling, for responding to questions of honor and slights against one's reputation—real or imagined.

How often had they been used? she wondered. And by whom?

Feeling sick to her stomach, Mercedes closed the case and set it back in the valise. She carefully replaced the trousers and book, the shirts and stockings, then returned the valise to its place on the floor. Because she was sitting so still she could feel the fine tremor in her hands without seeing it.

It was some thirty minutes later that Colin returned to his room. He didn't knock or ask permission to enter. He figured his footfalls in the corridor were fair warning.

Except to lift her head slightly, Mercedes didn't move when he entered. She was much in the same position as when he left her and at first he thought she hadn't made any use of the tub and water at all. On closer inspection he saw that she was no longer looking quite so gritty as when she had arrived. Her complexion was essentially colorless but the gray cast had disappeared along with the streaks and smudges of dirt. The bruise along her jaw was a shade more evident and to accompany the faint discoloration was the beginning of a swollen line.

Colin pulled out the top drawer of the dresser a fraction of an inch and hung Mercedes's cleaned and mended stockings over the edge. Her shoes, which had also been scrubbed, he placed on the floor. He held up her gown just long enough for her to see that he had done his best to remove the stains, then he thrust it at her for her closer inspection.

His stitches were neater than her own. The shoulder seam was flawlessly repaired. The neckline, a more difficult thing to make right since the material itself had been rent, was mended with all but invisible stitching. The small tear on the skirt had disappeared and at the waist another seam had been restored.

For reasons she couldn't fathom, she felt the unfamiliar ache of tears in her eyes and throat. The pressure subsided almost as quickly as it had come and she remained curiously dry-eyed. The lump in her throat was merely swallowed.

Still sitting, she held the dress in front of her. "Thank you."

He didn't acknowledge her gratitude. Instead he indicated the cedar box in his left hand by raising it and pointing to her petticoat with the torn flounce. "Take that off and I'll fix it as well."

"Oh, no. You don't have—"

"Take it off."

"Must you always interrupt?" she asked, regaining some spirit. "At least allow me to finish my protest."

"Miss Leyden," he said, drawing out her name with exaggerated patience. "When a fly alights on my nose I don't wait for him to finish his business. I brush him off as soon as I can."

"Are you comparing me to—"

"I don't believe I could be any clearer." He watched her lower jaw sag a notch. "You're gaping, Miss Leyden. It's not very flattering."

"I have no intention of flattering you, you great ignor—"

"I meant the expression didn't flatter you," he said. Her jaw clamped shut and the full line of her lips compressed. "There, I see I've made my point. Now take that petticoat off or I swear I'll strip it off myself."

This time she didn't argue. Standing, holding her dress up modestly, Mercedes wriggled out of the petticoat and threw it at him.

"Have a care, Miss Leyden," he said. "Or I might think your thanks was all form and no substance."

"Go to—"

He did not interrupt her with words, but with a single arched eyebrow. "Yes?" he asked when she didn't finish.

Mercedes's gray eyes flashed. "Hell," she said forcefully. "Go to hell!" She dropped back on the bed hard, stunned by her outburst.

"Good for you, Miss Leyden," Colin said. He crossed the room to the chair behind her, moving out of her vision so she couldn't see the narrow, satisfied smile that raised the corners of his mouth. When she was angry her eyes were like a lightning storm. It was a sight worth seeing again. "Perhaps the fly is really a wasp," he mused aloud. "I swear that was a little sting I felt."

His observation gave her a start. The dagger between her breasts suddenly felt as big and as obtrusive as a jousting lance. Did he know it was there? Was his comment a veiled reference to it? How could—

"No riposte?" he asked casually.

"Must you even interrupt my thoughts, Captain Thorne?"

That narrow smile became a little wider. Colin bent his head and opened his sewing box. When his silence drove Mercedes to near distraction and she finally turned around, he was blithely threading a needle.

Anything she had planned to say was gone from her mind. "Why do you carry a sewing kit?" she asked.

"Every seaman does, leastways if he wants to look presentable on shore."

"Are they all so good with their handiwork as you?"

Colin tacked the flounce with large, even stitches to hold it in place. "Some are better, some worse," he said matter-of-factly.

"How did you learn?"

"The usual way a sailor learns. Mending sail." He threaded the needle again, this time with finer thread, and began repairing the hem with tiny stitches. Mercedes moved to the other side of the bed to watch him more closely. "Aren't you going to put that on?" he asked.

"What?" Then she realized he was speaking of her gown. She was still holding it in front of her, although with less concern for her modesty now. "Oh, yes . . . yes, of course."

Colin's head cocked to one side but he didn't raise his eyes in her direction. "It was only a question," he said. "Not a command."

A small shiver slipped along Mercedes's skin. What was he saying? That he approved of her state of *dishabille?* This was the trickiest part of her plan. Mercedes had no clear idea how to go about seducing any man, let alone one as seemingly indifferent as Colin Thorne. Perhaps she had made a good start after all. "Then I'll wait until you've finished with my petticoat," she said softly. His shrug was not all that she could have hoped for. She allowed the gown to fall a fraction. Her camisole strap slid over one shoulder and she let it remain.

He glanced up, his eyes alighting on her bruised jaw. "How did that happen?" he asked.

Mercedes almost grimaced in frustration. It was knowing the unattractiveness of that expression that kept it in check. He hadn't noticed the smoothness of her bare shoulder or the curve of her breasts. No, his dark eyes had narrowed on the blemish. Mercedes lifted her hand to it self-consciously. "He hit me."

"Who?"

The question confused her. He asked it quickly, as if he suspected some lie and could surprise the truth out of her. "I'm sure I don't know."

"How did you get away?"

She was tempted to say she fought her fictional attacker off. Instead she stuck with a more plausible answer. "There was a noise in the brush—an animal probably—but he didn't know that. It frightened him and his grip loosened."

"And that's when you were able to get away?"

"That's right."

"Then you came here."

She shook her head and her eyes wandered off, away from his penetrating stare. "Not at first," she said quietly as if retrieving a painful memory. "At first I hid . . . and I stayed hidden for a long time. He searched for me, then I think he tired of it. He just seemed to disappear. Even then I was afraid to come out. Once I did, I didn't know where to go except here. You don't know how the earl would have reacted to my appearance."

Colin said, "Tell me."

His soft command made her flinch. This would be more difficult because it wasn't exactly a lie. There had been any number of occasions in recent years when her uncle had made unpleasant accusations. "He already thinks I'm free with my favors," she said. "He would reproach me for . . . for whoring. He'd say I'd gotten no more than I deserved."

"And this is the man you *don't* want me to kill?" Colin asked.

Her head snapped around. "Is that supposed to be amusing? Do you think I'd want him dead because of that?"

"Let's say I wouldn't blame you."

"You don't understand," she said sharply. "It doesn't matter what he says or does. It only matters who he is."

"He's your uncle."

"He's the Earl of Weybourne!" Her raised voice drew no reaction from him, but she did not like herself for it. Mercedes drew in a calming breath. "You can't appreciate how powerful he is."

Colin finished the last stitches, bit off the thread, and returned the needle to the cedar box. "I understand that he's mismanaged a fortune, brought creditors to bear, abused his authority, and browbeaten his niece into believing he has a life worth saving."

It was all true but it wasn't all of the truth. Her clear gray eyes implored him. "There will be consequences you can't imagine."

"Consequences?" he asked. "For me?"

She shook her head and said quietly, "For me."

Intrigued, his brows raised slightly. "How's that?"

Mercedes came up off the bed. Agitated by his relentless questioning, she was unaware she was no longer dragging the gown with her. Moments earlier such an action would have been deliberately flirtatious. Now it was without design or guile. "If he's gone they'll come after me," Mercedes said softly.

He watched her skirt around the edge of the bed, out of his reach. Her underpetticoats swayed against her legs. There was the first faint rise of color just at the level of her breasts. Her throat was taut as she lifted her chin at a defiant, challenging angle. In contrast, Mercedes's slender arms were crossed in front of her, the posture shielding and defensive. He supposed she meant to look inviolate. What he saw was her vulnerability.

Colin dropped the sewing box on the floor and let the repaired petticoat lay over the arm of the chair. He stood. Even done slowly his movement caused her to take a step backward. He saw her bump her hip against the bedside table and wince. It was evident to him that she was not reacting to immediate pain but a previous one.

Forgetting his other questions, he asked, "Where else were you hurt?"

She held out an arm to ward him off as he approached. "It's nothing."

He started to push her arm aside, thought better of it, and let his fingers close around her wrist instead. She tried to pull away but she simply hadn't the strength. He waited for her to understand she was outmatched and surrender to the inevitable. "Let me see," he said.

In response Mercedes's mouth flattened in a mutinous line.

"So that's the way it's going to be." With no more warning than that, Colin flicked his wrist and yanked her into his arms. In one swift motion she was lifted off her feet and cradled against him, one of his arms under her back, the other under her knees.

Mercedes was all outraged dignity and clenched teeth. She refused to say the obvious. He would put her down when he was ready and not one moment before. Entreaties on her part at this point were laughable.

Colin laid Mercedes on the bed. Her clumsy attempt to sit up was swiftly dealt with. His large hands clamped over her wrists and held them down at the level of her shoulders. His hip nudged hers. As Colin leaned forward, his head bending over hers, a lock of sunshine yellow hair fell across his forehead.

Seized by the unreasonable desire to brush it back for him, Mercedes stopped struggling.

"That's better," he said.

Nothing was better, she thought miserably. She was supposed to want to kill, not caress him.

"Now, let me see what's been done to you."

For a moment she'd forgotten what all his strong-arm tactics had been in aid of. "It's a bruise," she said. "I looked at it myself when I bathed. I assure you I'm going to live."

He let her finish then proceeded as if she hadn't spoken, raising her petticoats almost to her waist then lowering the left side of her cotton drawers. Where her skin was uninjured it was pale and creamy. The lividity of the bruise made it seem even more so. The bruise itself was about the size of a sovereign, so dark at its center it was almost black. It blossomed outward in vivid purple hues.

Colin whistled softly. "It's about a quarter of the size it's going to be tomorrow."

"Have you had your fill?" she asked with some asperity. "I told you it was only a bruise."

He didn't right her clothes just yet. He had seen enough injuries to be able to guess at the origin of this one. "Your skin was nearly punctured. Did he have a weapon?"

Mercedes's low growl at the back of her throat spoke eloquently to her frustration.

Colin watched her, fascinated. Belatedly he realized what the growling was in aid of and he straightened her drawers and petticoats. He still didn't release her wrists. "Better?"

She didn't deign to answer that question. "He didn't have a weapon," Mercedes told him. "At least not that he used on me. I ran into something as I was making my escape." She thought it was sufficiently vague to satisfy him. She couldn't very well tell him that the corner of a desk had been the culprit.

Colin stared at her a long moment, considering. "Probably a fallen branch," he said. "You were fortunate it didn't pierce you."

"Yes, well, I'll be certain to remember that in my prayers tonight."

Her acerbic tone caught his fancy. It seemed so much at odds with her mannered airs and delicate features. "Your wit doesn't appear to be overly addled by tonight's events."

"I wasn't accosted for my wit," she said. Mercedes fell silent as Colin's eyes darkened above her. He was studying her face and she felt the graze of his interest touch her hair, her forehead, then slip along the arch of her brows. His head tilted slightly to one side as he took in the shape of her nose, her ears, and the curve of her cheek. He didn't pause on her bruised jaw but rather on her mouth. Mercedes felt her lips part slightly of their own accord as the breath she had been holding escaped.

His eyes lifted to hers and that's when she noticed his regard was not so remote this time, that there was an element of warmth in the way he was watching her now.

"Why did you really come back here?" he asked.

There was a husky timbre to his voice that startled Mercedes more than his question. "I told you," she said.

His head bent a fraction closer. "I know what you told me."

Mercedes caught her lower lip. He made it sound as if she hadn't been telling the truth—which, of course, she hadn't—but not in the way he seemed to be thinking. "Then you should listen to me."

Colin shook his head. "Not bloody likely."

She did not duck the kiss. Mercedes wasn't certain it was going to happen until his mouth was on hers. Even at the very last moment she thought she was merely calling his bluff. It was only in retrospect that she understood Colin Thorne didn't bluff.

It was not her first kiss. Others had been stolen, a few given freely. She had even experienced one lying down. But this one was different and it was her ability to compare it to the others that made her sure of it. For once, Mercedes did not regret them.

Colin's lips were warm and dry. The first touch was tentative, as if he expected her to shy away. When she didn't, the pressure increased, the shape of his mouth on hers became firmer. The edge of his tongue parted her lips.

A slip of pure sensation shuddered through Mercedes. At her side, where Colin still held her wrists, her fingers slowly uncurled. She closed her eyes.

He traced a damp line along the underside of her lip. His teeth nipped her gently. Beneath him, Colin felt her body stir even as she relaxed. His hands loosened on her wrists so that it was the weight of his palms, more than his grip, that was securing her.

He pressed the kiss more deeply and she gave him entry. It was only a matter of time before this thing that was being done *to* her was being done *with* her.

Mercedes felt herself being drawn into the kiss. Her tongue swept his. She touched the slightly uneven ridge of his teeth. Somehow the pressure of her mouth pulled him closer. His hip that had rested beside hers now touched her more intimately. He hovered over her, separated by only a small space of air. When pleasure made her arch restlessly, her breasts grazed his chest.

He swallowed the puff of air that was her gasp. His mouth slanted across hers a second time, insistent now, driving. Colin was stretched out beside her. His bent knee pushed intimately between her legs. Her own knee rose and her calf rubbed his leg.

Her heels dug into the mattress to give her purchase as she raised herself against him.

Colin's mouth slipped from hers. He touched her cheek, her chin, the base of her throat. He sipped her skin, tugged with his teeth. His hands finally left her wrists and slid along the length of her arms. The skin at the underside of her elbows was as soft as a newborn's.

Freed, Mercedes's hands lifted. Her fingers dipped into the hair at his nape and sifted threads of butter yellow and gold. Her nails lightly scraped the back of his neck. At her fingertips she felt the shudder that ran under his skin and down his spine.

The pads of Colin's fingers were rough, his palms slightly calloused. His touch on her bare shoulder and arm was gently abrasive. He dragged his fingertips along the inside of her arm and past her breast. Mercedes sighed sweetly when his mouth closed over hers again.

She pushed at his shoulders once and Colin seemed to understand what she wanted, obligingly rolling on his side, then his back, taking her with him until she was lying fully on top of him. Mercedes trapped his wrists at the level of his shoulders. There was no force behind it. Colin was very much a willing captive and there was no resistance as she kissed him deeply.

She raised herself slowly, her gray eyes vaguely unfocused, and drew her hands along his arms until her palms were flat on his chest. Her petticoats fanned out below her waist like the sun's corona and beneath them she straddled his hips with her thighs.

His hands came up to cup her waist and practically enfolded her. He watched her raise her head. Her upper body stretched in a sensuous arc, exposing the length of her throat and thrusting her breasts forward. Her slim hands rose gracefully to her neck and she traced the defined line of her collarbones with her fingertips. A siren's smile held his full attention.

Her thick braid fell across her shoulder and behind her back. The tip of it brushed his fingers. He caught the tail of it in the same moment Mercedes tore her dagger free.

She stabbed futilely at the air as Colin wrapped her braid

around his fist and jerked her away. Mercedes fought back, pushing herself sideways to strike her target. The tip of the blade caught his shoulder and split his shirt. A thin streak of blood followed in its wake.

Colin yanked harder on her hair. His tug toppled her and she was slammed against the mattress, precariously close to the edge of the bed. She had a vision of herself falling off, Colin still tightly holding her hair while she screamed in agony at being scalped. The fleeting thought of that kind of pain was enough to make her quiet.

Having no reason to trust her sudden stillness, especially while she was armed, Colin brought down the side of his hand in a swift chopping motion. It fell across the narrow bones of her wrist like a cleaver. Mercedes's hand opened convulsively and the dagger slipped out. Colin grabbed it and flung it across the room. It clattered across the dresser top and came to rest very near his own.

There was a short silence, punctuated only by their harsh breathing. Then Colin released Mercedes's hair and shoved, sending her tumbling out of bed and onto the floor. She came down hard on her bruised hip. The jarring rush of pain brought tears to her eyes. She cried out, curling into a ball to protect herself from another blow. When it didn't come she remained there without moving and bit her lower lip to keep from whimpering out loud.

Colin rose from the bed on the opposite side and shrugged out of his torn shirt. He yanked the petticoat he had repaired off the chair and tore at the flounce. It came away easily in his hands. He dipped it into the tub, wrung it out, then used it to wipe away the blood on his chest. The scratch was mostly superficial. There was a deeper puncture at his shoulder where she had first made contact, and Colin let it bleed freely for a few minutes to reduce the chance of infection. Finally he wadded a piece of the wet bandage and placed it squarely against the wound until the bleeding stopped.

Colin came around the side of the bed. His upper lip curled

in disgust. Mercedes was still lying on her side. He kicked at her feet, not hard, just enough to rouse a response. There was none. Hunkering down, Colin placed his palm on her hip and gave her a nudge. She didn't stir.

Mercedes had fainted.

It didn't move him to gentleness. Colin plucked the tumbler off the nightstand, dipped it in the tub water, and tossed it in her face.

She sputtered, coughed. Mercedes opened her eyes and water ran between her lashes. Sitting up, momentarily panicked, she swiped at her face with her hands and gasped for breath.

"It's only water," he said. "You're not blinded."

Mercedes lifted a corner of one of her petticoats and wiped her eyes and cheeks. When her vision had cleared she didn't look at him, but stared down at her hands instead.

"I hope you're working on an explanation," he said. "I'm not interested in any lies."

"There's nothing to explain," she said dully. Her head ached. Just behind her temples there was a steady throb that made her ears roar. Colin's voice came to her as if distorted by water or wind.

"I beg to differ."

"I think I'm going to be sick."

Colin reacted swiftly, taking the empty chamber pot from below the nightstand and shoving it into her hands. Mercedes retched immediately. Spasms gripped her body and she clutched the pot to steady herself. Colin pushed her back against the bed frame so she could lean against it. The bed shuddered under the force of her retching. She held the pot until she had been made helpless by the experience. It began to slip out of her hands. Colin caught it and held it for her. His other hand went to the back of her neck where he kept her braid from falling forward.

In the end her feeble cough signaled she was done. Colin put the chamber pot outside the door. He filled up the tumbler again, this time with fresh water and a touch of whisky, and told her to rinse out her mouth.

"Rinse," he repeated when she swallowed the first mouthful. "The last thing you need right now is a fire in your belly."

She nodded weakly and did as she was told. She spit into a second tumbler then repeated the process twice more before he was satisfied. Mercedes rested her head against the mattress while Colin stepped into the hallway and emptied the tumblers into the pot. When he came back, her eyes were closed and she was breathing shallowly.

"Let's put you back in bed," he said.

That brought her head around and opened her eyes, but there was no protest. She allowed herself to be hauled to her feet and laid back on the bed. A pillow was stuffed under her head. She never mistook his attention for kindness. If he seemed to be solicitous now it was because he wanted something in exchange.

Mercedes closed her eyes as Colin washed her face with a damp cloth. When he tossed it aside, she knew her respite was over.

"Look at me," he said. His voice brooked no refusal.

She looked.

"I'm waiting."

"I think I should go now," she said feebly.

He raised one brow. The planes and angles of his face were taut and there was no humor in the edge of the dark smile that touched his mouth. "You're going to have to talk to me first."

"What do you want to know?"

"Did you have that dagger with you the first time you came here?" he asked.

She nodded again.

"But you didn't use it."

"See? You don't need me to answer questions. You can work it out all by yourself."

Colin got up from the bed and went to the dresser. He looked at both daggers, testing hers for its feel in his hand before choosing his own. Mercedes was sitting up by the time he returned to her side.

"What are you going to do with that?" she asked, eyeing him warily.

"This." Colin's knife cut through her corset like butter.

"What are you doing?"

"Waiting," he said. "For answers. Don't make me wait too long, Miss Leyden. You don't have that many ribbons on your camisole."

"You can't just—"

He flicked the tip of the dagger once and severed the uppermost ribbon.

Mercedes's hands flew up to hold the material together. "Ask me another question," she said.

"Good," he said approvingly. "You're getting the idea. Now, why didn't you use the knife the first time?"

"I thought I could talk you out of it." Mercedes wasn't watching Colin's face. Her eyes were centered on the point of his dagger. It appeared to be wavering slightly as he moved it closer. "You know," she said quickly. "Talk you out of killing the earl." The dagger stayed where it was. "It seemed possible at first, then you told me things I hadn't known and it confused me. I didn't know what to think."

"So you left."

"That's right."

"But you came back."

"I told you why."

Colin had no difficulty slicing another ribbon. He poked the point of the dagger in between Mercedes's splayed fingers and flicked. No other prompting on his part was necessary.

Mercedes pressed herself back against the headboard. "I was attacked," she said hurriedly. "On my way home."

"Get your hands out of the way."

"No."

"I'll cut you."

Afraid he meant it, Mercedes spread her fingers a fraction. The dagger darted in and did its work. She really had to grip the camisole now. The material was loosened by the cuts and Mercedes knew she was in danger of spilling out of it. She tried to draw her knees up but Colin forced her legs down.

Colin watched fear crystallize in her clear gray eyes. He did nothing to alleviate it. "The truth, Mercedes. There was no attack between here and Weybourne Park."

Her face paled. "Why won't you believe me?"

"Why are you so desperate to make me?"

Her hands were shaking now as was her voice. "Because it's the truth!"

Colin cut through her camisole.

Mercedes cried out when the camisole hung in shreds. She tried to hold the thin material together to preserve her modesty. Her mouth was dry, making it impossible to swallow or speak. She simply stared at him.

"I think you made it all the way back to Weybourne Park," he said. "There was a tear in the skirt of your gown but not anywhere in your cape. That suggests you weren't wearing the cloak. In fact much of the damage to your gown appears to have happened when you were out of the cape."

"You cut the fastener, remember?" she said. "The first time I came here." Her throat ached. Her voice didn't sound as if it belonged to her. "He had no difficulty getting it off me."

"I don't think so. You told me you fled and hid. I don't think you would have gone back for your cloak. Your attacker might have been waiting for you."

Mercedes was silent.

"The smudges on your neck would lead one to believe your attacker's hands were dirty, yet where the material of your gown was split there was no sign of dirt. That neat tear on the skirt of your gown wasn't made by running into a branch." He paused a beat. "Talk to me, Mercedes."

She found she couldn't. His hand was on her shoulder, plucking at the strap of her camisole. The point of the dagger was under her chin.

"Is your uncle involved in this?" Colin asked. Her stricken

look was answer enough. "Did he ask you to come here this evening?"

Her voice was only a pathetic whisper. "Please," she said. "Let me go."

"Did he force you?"

"No!" There were some truths that could not be told.

Colin's eyes narrowed darkly. "You said before that there would be consequences if the earl died . . . something about someone coming after you."

Mercedes felt the last vestiges of color drain from her face. She didn't want to think about it. Beneath her chin was the cool length of Colin's blade and she concentrated on that. Her clenched hands ached and her knuckles were white from holding the edges of her camisole together. It was suddenly borne home to her that his interest had never really been personal; everything he did was to bring her to heel.

"Tell me what you meant by that," he said.

Mercedes finally understood that she didn't have to tell him anything. It didn't matter if he saw her naked because his own arousal wasn't his purpose. Taking away her garments one ribbon at a time was only a tactic to keep her off balance. He couldn't shame her if she wasn't ashamed.

It occurred to her that her hands weren't tied or even restrained. He had accomplished the same outcome by keeping them busy. In order to use them she had only to give up her modesty. Staring down the length of Colin's dagger, it was an easy choice.

Mercedes let go of her camisole and slapped at Colin's wrist. The blade missed nicking her throat by a fraction of an inch but she was successful in pushing it sideways. She ducked and kicked out swiftly, shoving him away. He lost his balance on the edge of the bed and before he could recover, Mercedes scrambled to the opposite side.

Colin straightened. "So what are you going to do now?"

The bed was certainly between them but she was on the wrong side to reach the door. Her brow furrowed as she considered her predicament.

"Or hadn't you thought that far?" Colin deliberately allowed his eyes to wander to the level of her gaping camisole. "Take your time."

Mercedes fought the urge to close the material. She had better uses for her hands than to protect her modesty. Keeping her eyes on Colin and the dagger resting lightly in his palm, Mercedes sidled carefully toward the dresser.

"Don't pick up that knife," he warned her.

"I'm getting my stockings." Her tone made it seem a perfectly reasonable thing to do.

Colin couldn't fathom her intention. "Are you going to flail me with them?"

"No," she said sweetly, reaching the dresser. "I'm going to tie you up with them."

He didn't think that was possible. That's why he was still looking at her breasts when she flung the drawer at his head. One corner caught his temple and Colin Thorne went down as if he'd been felled. He was groaning, trying to raise his head and clear his vision, when Mercedes clobbered him with the whisky bottle.

His last thought was that since she had promised to tie him up, she probably wasn't going to kill him.

Three

Mercedes let herself in the tradesman's entrance at the rear of the manor. She was relieved to be able to do so. She had no wish to face her uncle immediately upon her arrival. Using the back stairs, Mercedes reached her room in the north wing without being accosted.

A great cheval glass with an elaborately scrolled walnut frame was one of the few amenities left in her room. Mercedes did not pause in front of it or even glance in its direction. She had no wish to see the wretched mess she had become. Standing in the middle of the threadbare rug, she stripped out of her clothes and tossed them in a corner. She could not afford to be so careless with her belongings, but the need to feel clean, the need to have this evening behind her, hammered at her practical nature until she surrendered, at least conditionally. There was still a small voice telling her to get rid of the clothes entirely, but Mercedes rebelled against that kind of wastefulness.

It wasn't as if she had his blood on them, she thought. Only she knew what she had done.

Mercedes pressed the heels of her hands against her temples and closed her eyes tightly. She didn't want to think about it anymore. She *wouldn't* think about it anymore. The dull, pounding ache in her head was relentless, and like the steady beat of kettle drums, would not be silenced. She swayed a little on her feet, moaning once, softly, with pain.

Mercedes let her arms drop mechanically to her sides and opened her eyes. It was the sheer force of her will that propelled her to the armoire in the adjoining dressing room. She removed her nightgown and slipped it over her head. Like a cloud descending, the voluminous cotton shift swallowed her whole. Mercedes fastened the satin ribbon at her throat and adjusted the sleeves at her wrists. The hem brushed her ankles as she reached for her robe. As secure as a babe in swaddling clothes, Mercedes derived a measure of comfort from putting on her dressing gown and tightening the sash about her waist.

The ladderback chair beside her bed held a washbasin and pitcher and a few toiletry items on its seat. At one time the bedroom had been appointed with a dresser, two bedside tables, a vanity and padded stool, and a writing desk. Two cream brocade wing chairs used to be arranged in a conversational setting near the fireplace. The dressing room had held a daybed and a commode in addition to the armoire. The missing, exquisitely crafted pieces by Chippendale and Windsor now filled an unoccupied room in the south wing for the earl's occasional guests.

Mercedes had become accustomed to the arrangement. She no longer missed what wasn't there.

At the basin Mercedes scrubbed her face hard, as though she could erase the bruise along her jaw. The ache that developed there was a diversion from the pounding in her head so she counted her effort as some kind of success. Sitting on the edge of the four-poster, Mercedes unwound her thick plait of hair and began to brush it out. She was careful to give it long, gentle strokes, starting at the ends and working her way up to her scalp. The braid had rippled her hair and when she was done it framed her face and shoulders in waves of dark chocolate.

From under her pillow Mercedes pulled out a small brown bottle of laudanum and measured out a spoonful. The bottle was her secret, her protection against pain inflicted on those occasions when the earl was in his foulest moods. She rarely had cause to use it, not because she was seldom the target of her uncle's aggressions, but because of her well-developed tolerance for pain.

Even as she swallowed the opiate, Mercedes acknowledged

that it was not merely physical pain that made her seek out the medicine's dubious comforts. She could have endured that. What she required was relief from her deepening sense of shame.

It was an effort for Mercedes to leave her bed. It beckoned her to stretch out beneath the covers and welcome drugged sleep. No one who knew her would have been surprised that other responsibilities weighed too heavily. Instead of lying down, Mercedes went to check on her young cousins.

"I told you she'd come," Britton said as soon as Mercedes let herself into his room. "Didn't I say it?" He was sitting up in bed, a pillow plumped behind his back and surrounded by a mound of blankets. He wasn't talking to his twin. That worthy fellow was sleeping soundly at the foot of the bed like an old guard dog. His gleeful whisper was directed at Martha Hennepin, who, along with her husband, had served at Weybourne Park in one capacity or another for the past forty years. Every so often Lord Leyden would take it in his head to get rid of one or both of them, but they had been blithely ignoring those directives for as long as the earl had been issuing them.

"You did indeed, Master Britton," Mrs. Hennepin said. She clapped her hands together lightly, just once, to applaud his observation and to punctuate her own relief. Getting to her feet, she smoothed the wrinkled folds of her apron where she had been twisting the material between her gnarled fingers. "And I was thinking the same, the truth be told." She waved one hand in a beckoning gesture, urging Mercedes to come in the room and shut the door. "Best to be quiet, dear. His lordship is sleeping in his own room but no one can ever say for how long or what incidental sound might wake him."

Mercedes nodded. She closed the door quietly. "Did you hear the commotion from your rooms or did Brendan get you after I left?"

"It was Sylvia that came for me as soon as you and the earl were gone downstairs. She was beside herself, poor girl. Didn't know half of what she was saying." Mrs. Hennepin crossed her arms in front of her, supporting her shelf-like bosom. "Mister wanted to come with me, of course, but I told him I would do better managing on my own." Her frown became even more substantial. "He worries so about the boys."

Britton piped in with more than a bit of bravado. "He needn't fret about me. I did fine. Sylvia loses her head about the least little thing."

Mercedes found it in herself to smile faintly. "I'd like it better if you'd let me look for myself," she said. She watched Britton wrestle with her request. He didn't like to be coddled, not in these circumstances anyway. It hurt her heart to look at him, with his wide blue eyes and brave face. Britton's sandy hair was tousled and a cowlick made several strands stand at attention. She fought an urge to sweep her hand over his head and smooth the wayward curls. He was only eight years old. He deserved to be fussed over for something besides being able to take a beating on the chin. "Well?" she asked, sitting beside him on the bed. "May I?"

"Oh, very well," he said with a long-suffering air. Pulling up his nightshirt, he missed the half-amused, half-heartbroken glances that Mercedes and the housekeeper exchanged. "See? Not even a cracked rib this time."

Mercedes placed the flat of her hand along Britton's small ribcage and pressed lightly in a number of places. He winced a little when her fingers touched the edges of a bruise but she noticed he wasn't experiencing any painful breaths.

"He only caught me in the gut," Britton said, his voice muffled under his nightshirt. "You saw how I curled in a ball. Just the way you taught me, Mercedes. You can see how well it worked."

She could see. There was no substantial damage this time. Mercedes wondered what other governesses taught their charges. It didn't seem likely that measures for self-defense were part of the standard curriculum for the schoolroom. She helped him lower his nightshirt and before he could duck away, she leaned forward and kissed him on the brow. "You were very quick this evening."

It was just as well that in a few more months Britton and Brendan would be going away to boarding school. Mercedes made certain there was money for that. The boys could hardly be expected to take their place in society without a proper education. It was low on the list of the earl's priorities so Mercedes put it at the top of her own.

Mrs. Hennepin moved closer to the bed. Her rounded figure blocked light from the bedside lamp and cast a shadow across the quilts and comforter. "He wouldn't let me wrap his ribs. Just to be safe, I told him, but he wouldn't have any part of it."

"It's all right," Mercedes said soothingly. "Britton knows better than anyone what it feels like when his ribs are cracked or broken." She leveled her gaze on the boy. "And you don't feel like that now, do you?"

He shook his head, his eyes solemn.

"We'll have to take his word for it," she said. "Thank you for staying with him."

Mrs. Hennepin pooh-poohed Mercedes's thanks. Her chin jutted toward the foot of the bed where Brendan slept. "And that one wouldn't leave at all. Even Chloe couldn't get him to go to his own room."

"I understand," Mercedes said. "I'll carry him back when I leave." Out of the corner of her eye she saw Britton flinch. It wasn't an actual movement, she realized, but only something he did with his eyes that suggested he had just bit back some pain or swallowed his fear. Something else they learned from me, she thought miserably, for she had seen the same reaction in Brendan a time or two and recognized it as a reflection of her own expression.

"He has to go to his room," Mercedes explained. "If your father comes back and finds him here it will only be worse for both of you."

Britton blurted out the thing that bothered him the most. "He's not my father."

"Don't say that," Mercedes said.

"Even Chloe says he's not," he said stubbornly. His bottom lip was thrust out.

Mrs. Hennepin clucked her tongue. "This is no kind of talk for a child your age."

"Well, I can't be a child *your* age," he rejoined.

Mercedes's slender smile widened a fraction. "I'd say he's feeling quite the thing."

"There's nothing wrong with his mouth," the housekeeper said. "Or his wit. Too smart by half, these twins. What one doesn't have the gumption to say, the other one does." Knowing it would get his goat, she laid one hand over Britton's head and ruffled his hair. "I'll check on you in the morning." She glanced in Mercedes's direction, her sharp eyes missing nothing in their assessment of the pale complexion and bruised and swollen jaw. "You, too. I don't know what havey-cavey goings on there's been tonight, but I hope this affair is settled at dawn."

Mercedes didn't reply. No one save her uncle and her victim needed to know what had been done this night.

Mrs. Hennepin sighed. "I doubt I'll sleep soundly myself," she said on her way out of the room. "You know where to find me."

When she was gone Mercedes glanced at the clock on the mantel. It was after three. In a few hours the earl would be rising and demanding to know if she had accomplished her task. When he discovered her answer he would go about preparing to meet his adversary, confident now of the outcome. She wished she dared lie to him. It would almost be worth it to witness his re-action, to see if he would still keep the dawn appointment believing that Colin Thorne would meet him there.

Britton studied Mercedes's profile. He could see the structure of her tension in the perfect stillness of her pose. It frightened him when she became so withdrawn, as if she were unaware that anyone else existed, and in some way ceased to exist herself. He slipped his small hand under hers. For a moment there was no reply and his heart raced as loneliness and fear closed in. Then he felt a gentle squeeze around his fingers, reassurance in the slight pressure, and she turned her face toward him and graced him with her smile.

"You're a good boy, Britton," she said quietly. "Mrs. Hennepin thinks so, too—most of the time."

Britton ducked his head, afraid he might be subjected to another kiss or some more hair ruffling. He slipped lower in the bed until he was lying on his side but he didn't remove his hand from under Mercedes's palm. "Did you kill him?" he asked. His voice was grave.

The slender smile that had crossed Mercedes's face vanished. "What are you talking about?"

His disappointment showed momentarily. Did she really think she could hide it from him and his brother? "It's no good pretending. Mrs. Hennepin likes it better that way but I don't. I think even Chloe and Sylvia know what's going on this time."

He was too old, she thought. So was Brendan. The twins were privy to things they shouldn't have seen or heard and they understood too much of it. They spoke with oddly mature intonation and solemn tones that belied their small statures and childish features. "What do you think you know?" she asked carefully.

"The earl asked you to do that American fellow in," Britton said. "You know"—he made a cutting motion across his neck with his index finger—"separate his head from his shoulders."

"Britton!"

"Perhaps that wasn't the precise phrase," he allowed.

"Nothing of the sort was said."

"*Something* of the sort was said. Brendan and I both heard it." Before Mercedes could stop him he kicked out with his right foot and nudged his brother awake.

Brendan's head bobbed up wearily. "Mmmm?" he said sleepily. He yawned hugely before his eyes alighted on Mercedes. It was as if his mind suddenly came to attention. "Oh, I say, you're back. Have you killed him then?"

Britton sniggered. "See? I told you."

Brendan sat up, pushed a lock of sandy hair back from his brow, and said, "Told me what?"

"Not you," Britton said. "Mercedes. I told Mercedes we knew what his lordship said."

"His lordship is your father," Mercedes said.

"Oh, no," Brendan said. "Even Chloe says he's not."

Mercedes sighed. Something else they had overheard listening at doors and hiding behind drapes. It wasn't a point worth arguing, not at this particular hour. "Brendan, come with me to your room now. It's time everyone, including me, was in bed."

Brendan crawled off the mattress as Mercedes came to her feet and obligingly put his hand in hers. His comment, however, was directed at his brother. "She did it," he said with assurance. "You know she'd say if she didn't and she hasn't, so she must have."

Britton nodded sagely. "I agree with you."

Mercedes shook her head helplessly. "I don't even know *what* you said." Brendan opened his mouth to explain but she placed one finger over his lips. "And I don't want to know." She pointed to the door. "Bed. Goodnight, Britton."

"G'night, Mercedes. 'Night, Brendan."

"Sorry I fell asleep," Brendan said. "You know I would have wakened if the earl had come back."

"I know," said Britton simply.

Mercedes marveled at the exchange between the boys, at the deep, abiding trust they had in one another. It was hard to say if it would have been the same if the earl hadn't been who he was. In other circumstances some healthy rivalry might have existed between the boys, but with them looking to themselves and each other for protection, there was no opportunity for it to flourish. Britton always found a great deal of satisfaction in Brendan's successes, and Brendan derived a certain comfort from his brother's accomplishments. Mercedes doubted the situation would change when they attended boarding school in the fall. She almost pitied the first student who thought one of them might be an easy target for ridicule or tormenting. The twins were quite capable of making that poor lad's life a miserable hell.

Mercedes escorted Brendan to his room and bed and tucked him in. "Don't let the bedbugs bite," she said.

He turned on his side, one arm under his pillow, in a position almost identical to his brother's in the other room. "You needn't worry that Brit or I will think badly of you," he said. "The earl was prepared to kill Britton if you hadn't promised to do as he said. We know you did it for us."

It wasn't quite the truth, she thought as she climbed into her own bed. She had done it as much for herself.

It was the certain knowledge that she was no longer alone in her room that woke Mercedes. The soft, steady breathing was not her own and the faint tapping sound she heard was not the movement of her shutters against the window.

Mercedes bolted upright as the Earl of Weybourne sat on the edge of her bed. She noticed he looked none the worse for his bout of drinking the night before. His eyes were clear, their focus sharp, and there was a thinly agreeable smile lifting the corners of his mouth. It was as pleasant an expression as he ever showed one of his own family.

Pushing a lock of hair behind her ear, Mercedes's eyes dropped to the source of the tapping sound. The earl was carrying a leather quirt with him. The tip of the braided leather lash hit the bed frame each time her uncle flicked his wrist. Mercedes knew he was carrying it less to signal his intention to ride out to the meadow, than as a subtle threat. She willed herself not to stare at it.

"I'm waiting," he said casually.

Mercedes's mouth was dry. It was an effort to keep her eyes from darting toward the quirt.

The Earl of Weybourne flicked the whip's short handle a bit more intentionally. "You should have awakened me upon your arrival. You knew I would want to hear the outcome of your visit to the inn."

She recovered her voice. "When have I ever failed to do as I was bidden?" asked Mercedes. Paper-thin layers of light slipped between the window shutters and slanted across the hardwood floor and area rug. It should have brightened the finish on the floor or the colors in the carpet but it did neither. It was too early for the sun to have burned off the morning fog and all of Weybourne Park was still shrouded in mist. And now it was seeping into her room. On any other morning she might have risen from her bed and closed the louvers more securely, barring any light from entering. Today, she didn't move. Mercedes didn't think she was being too darkly imaginative in believing it was a fitting accompaniment to her uncle's presence.

The Earl of Weybourne was satisfied with Mercedes's response. "I'm scheduled to meet Colin Thorne in just under one hour," he said. "Will he be there?"

The steady tattoo of the quirt against the bed was so loud in Mercedes's head that she could hardly hear the question. "No," she said after a moment. "He won't be there." She pressed herself back against the headboard, much as she had done in Colin Thorne's room when his dagger had been under her chin. This time it was the short handle of Lord Leyden's whip that nudged her. "No!" she said with more conviction.

"You did as I asked?" he said. He raised her chin a notch to better catch her eye. "You used the knife?"

"He won't be there." Mercedes turned her head aside. The quirt's leather handle jabbed at her bruised jaw. Pain made her breath hiss as she sucked in air between her teeth. "He won't be there," she said again, enunciating each word stiffly.

The quirt slid along her jaw to a spot just below her ear. The braided end was drawn softly across her neck and shoulder. Mercedes fought against brushing it away. She did not want to give the earl the satisfaction.

"That's quite a bruise," Lord Leyden said blandly. "I don't think I hit you that hard. I've always noticed you tend to mark easily. More so than the boys, I think. Or Chloe or Sylvia, though they've never given me as much cause to punish them as you."

Mercedes had heard this observation before. It was always delivered in the same tone, fascinated, oddly surprised, and with no hint of regret. It was never meant to elicit a comment so Mercedes offered none now. The quirt was slowly withdrawn.

The earl stood. "You know it will go badly for you if you're lying to me," he said. He watched her expression carefully, looking for any nuance of expression that would warn him he was walking into a trap. No aspect of her appearance was altered in the least. "I have no choice, do I?" he said. "I have to believe you."

"You could have done it yourself," she said, slanting him an accusing glance. "Or met the challenge you made fairly."

Lord Leyden had taken to slapping the quirt lightly against his leg. He stopped moving it now. The silence itself became threatening.

Mercedes could not sustain her look. Her eyes fell away under the earl's more sharply drawn glare. She cursed herself for being weak. Britton and Brendan showed more courage.

"I thought so," Wallace Leyden said softly, satisfied that she had nothing more to say. He took pleasure in quelling Mercedes's brief rebellions. He would not find her such a satisfactory opponent if she never returned fire. "Perhaps we'll talk later. In the meantime, think on this."

There was nowhere for her to go. Her eyes darted toward the opposite side of the bed but her body couldn't follow. Even her attempt to raise the covers was too slow and awkward to protect her. The braided leather whip snapped against her shoulder, raising an immediate welt beneath her nightshift. It was more than the searing pain that took her breath away. It was the viciousness of the act, the unprovoked, almost playful cruelty that she would never get used to.

She braced herself for another stroke but it didn't come.

The Earl of Weybourne merely smiled at his niece. He left her room as quietly as he had come.

Aubrey Jones had two fannies to pat as he hopped out of bed. Molly and her sister didn't stir. Aubrey accepted that as a compliment of sorts. He washed and dressed quickly, mindful of the fact that he had slept longer than was his wont. That said something about his bed partners. He'd spent a snug night comfortably nestled between the sisters—after he wore them out.

Feeling a bit full of himself, eager to relate the story to the crew of the *Mystic*, perhaps embellishing it a bit, but not much, Aubrey Jones was looking forward to ending the business that had taken him away from London in the first place. To that end he packed his valise and carried it down the hall to his captain's room.

His first knock brought no response. That was unusual because Aubrey was well aware he didn't have a light touch. With a broad face, bull neck, and fists like mallets, everything about Aubrey Jones was big. He hammered on the door again, laughing heartily this time, thinking to himself that perhaps Molly's brief appearance in Colin's room had worn his commander out. Or better, perhaps it was the captain's other late-night visitor, the one Molly described as a skinny wench of no consequence.

When Aubrey was met by the echo of his own laughter a second time, he decided he'd had enough. Although a large man, he was blessed with a surprisingly gentle and good-natured temperament. It did not give him any particular pleasure to push through the door with a swift kick and the thrust of his shoulder.

The door flew open, swinging crookedly on broken hinges. Aubrey stood just inside the threshold and surveyed the scene. His strong, square jaw dropped a fraction as he shook his head. He whistled softly and grinned as crookedly as the door. "I'll be damned."

Colin Thorne was lying on his side on the floor, trussed like a calf for the slaughter. His wrists had been pulled behind him, bound, then bound to his ankles. Even though his knees were bent to accommodate the position, the effect was to bend him awkwardly in the middle. He had obviously been wrestling with his bonds for some time. Above and below where the stockings secured him, his skin was burned from his struggles. It didn't look as if he'd made any headway.

Aubrey felt the full force of his captain's glare but it didn't make him move any more quickly. First he glanced around to make certain he wasn't going to become a victim of the same assailant that had laid Colin low. A brief survey of the room, including under the bed, assured him there was no one hiding.

Picking up Colin's knife, Aubrey used it to slice through the gag.

"It took you long enough," Colin said thickly. His mouth was dry, and getting the words out was like trying to cough up gravel. "Did you really think someone was hiding under the bed?"

"No, I did that just to irritate you." One could never be certain just how serious Aubrey was about some things, and he liked it that way. "Don't make me regret removing your gag first." He cut through the stocking that held Colin's ankles and wrists together, then the bonds that secured them separately. "Quite a job that was done on you," he said. "I never heard anything. How many were there?"

"One less than was keeping you occupied and deaf to my troubles," Colin said.

Aubrey sat back on his heels. "One man did this to you?"

Groaning softly, Colin slowly unfolded himself. His arms and legs began to tingle as circulation was restored. "Almost right," he said. "One woman."

The possibility had never occurred to Aubrey. "You mean the skinny wench of no consequence?" he asked. He caught Colin's sharp look and shrugged. "Molly's description, not mine. I didn't think her story was worth investigating."

"It wasn't," Colin said. "At least not the first time." Sitting up, he rubbed his wrists carefully, then his ankles. The return of feeling to his limbs was prickly and painful.

"What do you mean, not the first time?" Aubrey asked, studying the stockings. "Are these hers?"

"They're sure as hell not mine," Colin muttered. "What time is it?"

"Time for you to be up and moving if we're going to make it to Weybourne Park." He stood and pulled Colin to his feet. "What do you mean, not the first time?" he asked again.

Colin's fingertips were engaged in the ginger exploration of his left temple. "Later," he said, steadying himself against the end of the bed.

Aubrey held up three fingers directly in front of Colin's aquiline nose. "How many?"

Colin pushed them aside. "Not now. Get my clothes out while I wash. I don't believe the earl's expecting us any longer. All the more reason not to be late."

Bemusement sat comically on Aubrey's broad masculine features. His dark red brows were raised a notch, furrowing his forehead, and his green eyes widened but remained slightly vacant. In the end, rather than ask another question which would be summarily dismissed, Aubrey shrugged philosophically. He lifted Colin's valise to the bed and began to remove his captain's clothing. "You have a bit of blood on your face," he said.

Colin turned away from the basin. "What?"

Aubrey tapped his temple. "Here," he said. "Blood."

"Oh." Colin dampened a wash cloth and began to scrub. "Better?"

"Well, the blood's gone."

It was the best Colin thought he could hope for. He lifted the small hand mirror and examined the injury. The corner of the drawer had struck him hard. A stitch or two wouldn't come amiss. "Damn her," he said softly.

"What's that?" Aubrey asked.

"Nothing." Colin set the mirror aside and finished washing. He shaved with less care than he normally used, adding another drop of blood to his chin. Cursing, he stopped the bleeding with a bit of alum while Aubrey chuckled. "Check the weapons," Colin said.

"Any particular reason?" Aubrey asked as he removed the lacquered box.

"She might have tampered with them."

Aubrey examined the outside of the box first. "Does she have dainty hands?"

Colin was studying the wound on his shoulder where Mercedes had tried to plunge her knife. She might have done serious damage had she been able to drive it deeper. "I don't know that I'd call them dainty," he said, stripping out of his shirt. "Capable, perhaps. Certainly strong." He recalled those hands on his chest and shoulders and arms. She'd had a light touch. Gentle but insistent. Colin grabbed a clean shirt. "What sort of question is that anyway?"

"You're missing my point," said Aubrey. He held the box up to the light coming from the bedside lamp. As he turned it this way and that the lacquered surface could be seen to be smudged with prints from careless handling. "I polished this box before I packed your bags. There was nary a fingerprint on the lacquer when I was through. These prints are too small to be yours, so I'd say they belong to Molly or your other guest."

"They're not Molly's."

"Then Miss-Dainty-Hands was all over it."

Colin fastened his shirt, slipped on clean trousers, and sat on the bed to put on his socks. He glanced toward the foot of the bed where Aubrey was carefully going over the weapons. "Miss-Dainty-Hands has a name," he said.

Aubrey didn't pause in his inspection. "I'm sure she does," he said. "I wonder if you'll get around to telling me what it is." He took out the second flintlock pistol and gave it the same examination as the first, checking the barrel and trigger mechanism.

Colin reached for his boots, tugged them on, and began tossing articles into his opened valise. "Mercedes Leyden," he said. "Any part of that familiar to you?"

Aubrey closed the pistol case and tucked it under his arm. "Leyden," he said softly, thinking. His mouth screwed up to one side and his eyes widened as realization seemed to hammer him in the face. "Isn't that the earl's name?"

"Wallace Leyden," Colin said.

"His daughter?" asked Aubrey.

"She says she's his niece."

Aubrey considered that. "You believe her?"

Colin glanced around the room looking for anything he might

be leaving behind. He noticed that except for the stockings Mercedes had bound him with there was no hard evidence of her having been in the room. Her dagger was gone as were all her clothes—even the strips he had torn off her petticoat to stem the bleeding in his shoulder had disappeared. "Half of what she says is lies," he told Aubrey. "The other half is mostly fiction."

Aubrey laughed. It seemed to him that Colin Thorne had a talent for finding those wenches.

Colin shot him a quelling glance. "You have something to say, Mr. Jones?"

Aubrey made a show of clearing his throat. "Not a thing, sir."

"That's what I thought." He didn't need Aubrey Jones to remind him of the last woman to spin him a web of lies, or the woman before that. Colin had already decided he was much better off with women like Molly or her sister, who offered pleasure honestly, than those with a pedigree who invariably wanted something from him. "Let's go," Colin said. "You arranged for horses?"

"Last night. They should be waiting for us in the stable."

Everyone at Weybourne Park was up earlier than usual. On her way to the breakfast room Mercedes said good morning to Mr. Hennepin, Janie Madison, Emma Leeds, and Ben Fitch. It was not odd to see Mr. Hennepin up and about. Maintaining the grounds of Weybourne Park had been his position since he first arrived. In the beginning it meant caring for the expansive gardens and bordering hedgerows. Now, with the reduced staff, he made repairs to the exterior of the manor and all the outbuildings. On this morning he was headed for the north turret, ostensibly to patch the roof. Mercedes knew Mr. Hennepin had another motive. If the fog lifted, the north turret roof would give the best view of the duel.

The Earl of Weybourne's morning assignation was the reason most everyone was busy. Janie Madison had been rung by either Chloe or Sylvia to assist them in dressing. Emma was carrying freshly baked bread from the kitchen when Mercedes saw her, and Ben Fitch tipped his hat on his way to the stable.

No one mentioned the reason for all the early morning activity. It was the pretense of normalcy that was seeing them all through. Not one among them was willing to think on how their lives or their livelihood might be different if the Earl of Weybourne did not return from the meadow.

Mercedes was greeted in the breakfast room by the twins. They were sitting on opposite sides of the walnut table, swinging their legs energetically to see who could kick whom first. As soon as Mercedes walked in they made an effort to stop and she pretended not to see the fidgeting as one of them finally connected with the other.

"You're both up very early," she said as she drew back the heavy drapes. On a clear, cloudless morning the room would have been filled with sunshine. Mrs. Hennepin would have complained that Mercedes's penchant for sunlight was fading the carpets and closed the drapes as soon as the room was vacated. Mercedes doubted that it would be the housekeeper's concern today. She fastened the drapes open even though the only light filtering into the room was gray and misty. Turning back to the boys, she said, "I thought you'd both welcome a chance to sleep in. I haven't prepared any lessons for you. I suppose, since you're both up, I shall."

The twin looks of pleasure and secretive, knowing glances faded into something between consternation and horror. Under the table the playful battle stopped completely.

Mercedes was hard pressed not to laugh as the boys put forth their objections in unison. She held up her hand, stemming the flow. "We'll see," she said. "Let's wait to hear what plans Chloe and Sylvia might have."

Britton and Brendan settled back, appeased for the time being. With the hope that school lessons might be put aside, they regained their good humor. Brendan even scooted off his chair to hold Mercedes's out for her.

"How are you feeling, Britton?" Mercedes asked. She unfolded her napkin on her lap and began lifting the lids to the dishes Mrs. Leeds had already set on the table. She had little appetite for the sausages and tomatoes, but mindful of the boys' presence, Mercedes took a soft-cooked egg and the heel from the warm bread. "Are you quite certain you should be out of bed?"

"It depends," he said frankly. "If we're going to do lessons I suspect I'll be feeling quite poorly. If not, I believe a picnic later today would be just the thing."

"Well, I can't fault you for your honesty," said Mercedes. She placed a helping of everything on Britton's place, then did the same for Brendan. It was a treat to have the twins in the breakfast room. Normally, when the earl was in residence, they were strictly forbidden to take their meals anywhere but their own chambers or the schoolroom. Today they were willing to risk his censure. Mercedes didn't think it had occurred to the boys that their father may arrive home in just as foul a mood as always. He would have the pretense to maintain, that of being slighted by Colin Thorne a second time for not showing up for the duel.

Mercedes encouraged the boys to eat. The more she thought on it, the more she didn't want them around when the earl returned.

"This is the place," Aubrey said, pulling up his mount along the side of the road. "There's the grove of trees. The pond. And we're at the edge of the meadow." He looked around to see if there was another location with similar features. There was nothing like it on the other side of the lane. Aubrey shrugged and looked to Colin. "This is Weybourne Road. It appears everything's here except the earl."

The thickest layer of fog had finally lifted. Although the sky remained overcast there was no difficulty in taking in the lay of the land. Colin could even make out the yellow underbelly of a finch that had alighted on a pine bough some thirty yards away. Further in the distance was the gray slate roof of Weybourne

Manor itself. The turrets at either end of the massive stone house were still only partly visible through the lowest layer of mist. In another half-hour that shroud would be peeled back and the gray stone mansion would rise unencumbered, a formidable presence on the landscape.

Colin dismounted and began leading his horse through the meadow. Aubrey followed suit. They walked to the edge of the grove where Colin secured both horses while Aubrey collected the lacquered pistol case and consulted his pocket watch.

"We're not late," he said. It was six-thirty.

Colin checked his own watch. He had the same time. "How long should we give him before we consider it a forfeit?"

One of Aubrey's large hands came up to rub his temple as he considered the question. "The thing of it is," he said after a moment, "the damn Limeys probably have some rule about it."

A narrow smile edged Colin's mouth. "Proper form," he said dryly.

"How's that again?" asked Aubrey.

Colin dismissed it with a wave of his hand. "Just something I recalled. No importance."

"Well," Aubrey drawled. "I say we wait a half-hour. If we haven't seen the earl or his second by then, we'll go to the house and drag him out. I may shoot him myself."

Colin made himself comfortable leaning back against a pine. He crossed his arms in front of him. He wasn't entirely surprised by the earl's absence. "I didn't think he would be expecting us," he said. "Not after his niece's second visit last night. He's probably slept in."

"You really think he knows what she tried to do?"

Colin shrugged as if it were of no consequence. "We'll find out," he said softly. "Won't we?"

Aubrey wasn't certain he liked the tone. On the few occasions he'd heard it before it always boded trouble. He forgot about that as he caught some movement out of the corner of his eye. "Here, what's this?" he said, pointing to the road. Two men on horseback were approaching. "Is one of them the earl?"

Colin's eyes narrowed as he watched the progress of the riders. They paused along the road where he and Aubrey had also stopped. Rather than dismounting, they followed the beaten-down path on horseback. "The one on the roan is Lord Marcus Severn, Viscount Fielding. I believe he's a viscount. I met him at Weybourne's club. He's serving as the earl's second."

"So the other one's the earl?" asked Aubrey. The pair were closer now. Aubrey had not given much thought to the earl's appearance or age but he would not have guessed Lord Leyden was so old. "You won't need to shoot him," he said. "Blow on him and the geezer will keel over."

"That's not Weybourne," said Colin. "If I'm not mistaken, that would be the physician."

Lord Severn drew up on his horse but didn't dismount. He carried himself very straight in the saddle and had no difficulty keeping the roan quiet in spite of the other animals. He nodded once in Colin's direction, his narrow face almost devoid of expression. "Thorne," he said briskly in way of acknowledgment. "This is Dr. Barclay. He's agreed to serve in the event that either party requires medical attention."

Dr. Barclay tapped the medical bag that was attached to his saddle. He lowered his head and looked down at Colin and Aubrey over the rim of his spectacles. His pale blue eyes were rheumy and slightly unfocused. The doctor's complexion had the mottled color of someone who was familiar with the use of liquor as a personal anesthetic.

Aubrey stepped closer to his captain. "Don't worry," he said under his breath. "I won't let him touch you."

"I'm heartened."

Marcus Severn had no patience for these private asides. His flattened mouth and raised chin were evidence of his disdain. "Where is Weybourne?" he asked.

Colin pushed away from the tree. "Don't know," he said lightly. "We've been waiting."

It was not the viscount's way to make an explanation. The doctor, however, did not demonstrate the same reluctance. Some excuse could always be offered, even if it was a lie. "I was called out early this morning to the vicar's. A birthing, don't you know. It delayed us. Those things can't be hurried."

"That's quite enough, Barclay," Lord Severn said. "They can see we're here now."

"We can see that," Aubrey said agreeably. He was satisfied to see that his lordship's mouth tightened even further. Thin-lipped toady, he thought. "Do you want to examine the pistols?" he asked. He made no effort to hand them up.

Marcus Severn had no choice but to dismount. Although of medium build and quite able to hold his own in most gentlemanly sports, he was dwarfed by Aubrey's proportions. He took the case in his gloved hands, stepped back out of Aubrey's shadow, and opened it. Like Mercedes, Lord Severn had an appreciation for the quality of the flintlocks. He admired them together, then individually, removing each from its formed depression in the velvet and turning it over in his hands.

"I take it they're satisfactory," Aubrey said.

"They'll do," Severn said curtly. He returned the one he held to its place, trying not to reveal his reluctance to do so. He could envy Weybourne the opportunity to use so fine a weapon.

Aubrey closed the case and slid it under his arm again. "How long do we wait?" he asked. "Colin and I thought thirty minutes was fair."

Severn looked toward the manor. From their present location a slight rise in the meadow made it impossible to see if someone was approaching from that direction. "Weybourne is rarely late," he said. He was careful not to let his concern show in his voice. "I should think something has happened at the house to delay him. Perhaps I should ride to the—"

Aubrey was shaking his head. "I don't think so," he said amiably. "Surely the earl's got himself a timekeeper in that mansion of his. Probably has a room filled with nothing but clocks and another one with servants who do nothing but wind them." He glanced at Colin. The captain's narrow smile told him he was enjoying Severn's discomfort as well. Aubrey stepped closer to the viscount and said confidentially, "It's better if you stay right here with us. That way if the earl's missing this appointment on purpose, we'll *all* know it."

Mercedes paced the length of the parlor, from time to time going to the large windows facing the semi-circular drive to look out. Except for Ben Fitch who was clipping the hedgerow near the house, there was no one else about. She wished she might have taken her cue from Mr. Hennepin and found some reason to go to the north turret. It was probably where Britton and Brendan had run off to, though they were supposed to be in their rooms right now.

Sylvia and Chloe, after joining Mercedes and the boys at breakfast, had retired to the sewing room on the second floor. Mercedes wasn't fooled by Chloe's interest in repairing the hem of her lilac gown. The sewing room faced the meadow and they would be likely to see their father's approach soon after Mr. Hennepin caught sight of him. She didn't know if, like the twins, Chloe and Sylvia had a clear idea what the earl had asked her to do, but Mercedes suspected they knew something. Clearly they knew she had balked at his command, and Britton's beating had been the result. Mercedes remembered Chloe's fearful and faintly accusing glance as she stood in the doorway last evening. Chloe and her sister were helpless, too, she reminded herself. They looked to her to keep the peace, and last night she had failed them.

Lost in her thoughts, Mercedes didn't hear the parlor door sliding open. She actually jumped, her heart slamming in her chest, when she saw Mrs. Hennepin standing on the threshold.

Mercedes forced a calm expression that she was nowhere near to feeling. "What is it, Mrs. Hennepin?"

The housekeeper's distress showed clearly in her deepening frown. The parenthetical lines on either side of her mouth appeared to be engraved there. Between her silver-white brows was a vertical crease that disappeared into her mobcap. Her gnarled hands were not smoothing her apron, but twisting one corner of it. "We have visitors to see his lordship," she said. She looked over her shoulder to make certain they hadn't followed her. "I put them in the library."

Mercedes was surprised. "You explained the earl isn't here, didn't you?"

"Well, yes, I explained but they wouldn't be moved. I think one of them actually wants to search the house."

"That's quite out of the question," said Mercedes.

"That's just what I thought." Mrs. Hennepin's anxiety began to lessen in the face of Mercedes's serene confidence. "You'll speak to Lord Severn, then?" she asked. "Shall I show him in here?"

"Severn?" Mercedes felt a rush of panic. What was the viscount doing at Weybourne Park without her uncle? "But he was going to serve as his lordship's second."

"That's what I'd heard, too."

"And he's come looking for my uncle?"

Mrs. Hennepin nodded. She was worried again. "That's what he said. Do you want to speak to him in here?"

Mercedes supposed she had little choice. "Who else is with him?" she asked.

"Dr. Barclay."

Mercedes nodded. She had forgotten a physician would be in attendance. Severn must have arranged it. One of the duties of the second. "And someone else besides?"

The housekeeper held up two fingers. "They weren't introduced," she said. "And they didn't have a word to say, though it was the bigger of the two that looked as if he might want to turn over the furniture."

A shiver chased a chill all the way up Mercedes's spine. "I'll see Lord Severn now," she said. "In here. The others can wait."

Mrs. Hennepin turned to go. She stopped abruptly, brought up short by the appearance of one of the guests just beyond the parlor door. His smile was polite but cool as he stepped around the housekeeper. Leaning against the door jamb, an edgy watch-

fulness in his posture and his expression, Colin Thorne's dark
eyes leveled on Mercedes.

"I think you should see me first," he said. "You may not want
Severn to hear what I have to say."

Four

Mercedes simply stared. She was aware that just beyond Colin Thorne's shoulder, Mrs. Hennepin was looking to her for guidance. The housekeeper was both agitated and curious and the expressions warred for dominance on her careworn face. Mercedes could find no words to satisfy Mrs. Hennepin. Feeling Colin Thorne's presence as a real pressure against her chest, she left things that came to her mind unsaid.

In the end she was saved having to respond by the commotion on the stairs. Mercedes didn't have to be able to see what was happening to identify the source of the noise. She recognized the twins' youthful voices over the more mature tones of their sisters. The girls were hurrying down the steps in the direction of the parlor while the boys opted to use the banister to beat them to the bottom. There was some high-pitched laughter from the boys and breathless scolding from the girls. The party of four came to an abrupt stop in the open doorway.

Colin's head turned slowly in the direction of the intruders. He gave them all a cursory glance, his features expressionless, then turned back to Mercedes. "I suspect they've come to warn you," he said. "These are the same faces I spied pressed to various windows on our approach."

Chloe and Sylvia were eighteen months apart and it often seemed that it was the only thing separating them. They were invariably mistaken for twins, especially when they wore their pale blond hair similarly styled. Sylvia, the younger of the pair, was taller by a mere inch. They shared the same delicately winsome character, which upon first acquaintance sometimes all fluff and no substance. Nothing could have been further from the truth. Though possessed of the fine, beautifully realized features of a porcelain doll, Chloe and Sylvia were made of sterner stuff.

Knowing the picture they must have made at the windows, both blushed at Colin's comment. Neither stammered apologies or looked away guiltily, however. Mercedes wondered that Colin didn't feel them boring holes into the back of his head.

Britton and Brendan weren't satisfied with glaring at the visitor's back. They skirted around their sisters and darted into the parlor, placing themselves squarely between Colin and Mercedes.

Colin didn't spare another glance for the twins. He continued to look over their heads at Mercedes. "Your protectors?"

Mercedes was spared answering this time by the arrival of Severn. She did not look on his sudden appearance as either timely or particularly welcome. He gave Mrs. Hennepin no notice and walked past Chloe and Sylvia with only the slightest nod to acknowledge their presence. His brief glance at the twins was cold and clearly meant to dislodge them from the parlor. Mercedes knew that the effect was the opposite. Britton and Brendan would remain frozen in place rather than leave her with Marcus Severn.

Severn crossed the parlor to stand directly in front of Mercedes. Without asking permission he placed his gloved hands lightly on her elbows and bent his head, kissing her on the cheek. "I would speak to you alone," he said, straightening.

Stricken, Mercedes felt as though she couldn't draw a breath. No matter how she willed her feet to move she remained exactly where she was.

Severn's examination became more thorough. His eyes fixed on the bruised jaw that her light application of powder failed to cover. "What happened?" he asked.

Had Lord Severn not been holding Mercedes's arms, she would have raised one hand to her face. It wouldn't have been a gesture of self-conscious acknowledgment, but one of protection. Severn's question had the appropriate nuance of concern for everyone in the room to hear. Only Mercedes could see the edge of excitement that had darkened his eyes.

She drew back, forcing him to let her go unless a struggle was to be obvious. "It's nothing," she said.

"That's not what I asked."

In the doorway, Mercedes saw that Colin Thorne had abandoned the pretense of his relaxed posture. A thread of tension seemed to vibrate through him though he hadn't moved in the least. His very stillness, his predatory calm, was the threat now.

Britton left his post beside his brother and went to Mercedes's side. "I caught her on the chin with my noggin," he said, patting himself on his head. He even winced as he tapped the pretend injury. Blithely ignoring Severn's dark, impatient look, he carried on. "Brendan and I were having a bit of a spat, you see, and Mercedes took it on herself to separate us. That's when we collided. She knows I'm sorry. Don't you, Mercedes? You were ever the good sport about it."

Severn looked back to Mercedes, his mouth thinning impatiently. "What is this child doing here?" he asked tersely.

Britton looked as if he was going to take exception to being named a child and by association, Brendan appeared to be taking it as a slight as well. "Sylvia. Chloe. Take the twins back to their rooms and keep them there. I'll be up directly with an explanation as soon as I get one. Mrs. Hennepin, you may close the doors. I will see these gentlemen privately." Mercedes noticed that no one was happy with her. Sylvia and Chloe did not want to be relegated to the position of nursemaids. The boys disliked being dismissed out of hand. Mrs. Hennepin's curiosity remained unsatisfied, and Severn and Thorne had each wanted a private audience. "Now," she said sternly, eyeing the girls.

The parlor was cleared quickly. Lingering protests could be heard in the hallway but eventually there was quiet. Mercedes had enough time to collect her thoughts. She moved beyond Severn's easy reach and stood with her back to the fireplace.

"Mrs. Hennepin tells me you've come to see my uncle," she said without inflection.

Colin Thorne marveled at her recovered composure. Mercedes Leyden had the reserved, regal bearing of a queen holding court. There was no evidence that she had ever been caught off guard by the presence of either himself or Severn. His eyes darted briefly around the room, taking in dark paneled walls, elaborately framed landscapes, jade and ivory figurines on the massive mantelpiece, and finally the vases on every polished table filled with freshly cut flowers. When his gaze alighted on her again he saw her differently than before, recognizing how much of her poise was derived from her surroundings. This parlor, with its heavy draperies and polished floors, was a far cry from any room at the Passing Fancy Inn.

Just as a diamond might sparkle more brilliantly against black velvet, Mercedes Leyden was shown to her best advantage in this setting.

Colin knew the difference went deeper than her physical appearance. The change was more subtle than the obvious alterations in her clothing and hair. In truth, her plain gray day dress was less attractive and fashionable than the emerald gown she'd worn the previous evening. Her hair had known more freedom confined in the thick plait of last night than it did now swept back and coiled at her nape.

Still, there was a difference in her demeanor that was quite remarkable yet tantalizingly indefinable.

Aware that Colin Thorne was studying her again, Mercedes addressed Lord Severn. "I can't think why you've come to the house. My uncle left here more than an hour ago to meet you at the meadow."

Severn's mouth flattened. "I'd think it would be obvious that we haven't seen him."

Mercedes's brows raised a fraction. "Oh?" she said, affecting credible calm. "I don't see how that could happen. Are you certain you were at the correct location? Weybourne Park is quite large, as you well know. Perhaps you—"

"I'm very certain," Severn said, watching her closely. "Did he say anything to you before he left?"

Mercedes had no difficulty remembering exactly what the earl had said—and done—before leaving the manor. She also had no intention of relating any of it to Lord Severn. Beneath the high collar of her day dress the welt from the earl's quirt was a snake-like brand. She resisted placing a hand there and drawing attention to her discomfort. Instead she looked at Colin and said in mannered accents, "I'm sorry, but I don't believe that Mrs. Hennepin gave me your name."

Colin's narrow smile returned as if to remind her she was playing a dangerous game. He had only not to join in and she would be exposed. "I don't think I told her," he said.

Mercedes waited, pretending a patience she didn't feel. Her clear gray eyes darted to Viscount Fielding for an introduction.

Severn did not hide his displeasure. "He is not your concern, Mercedes," he said. He glanced over his shoulder. "Get out, Thorne, so I can talk to Weybourne's niece alone. You can see for yourself that she's not going to tell me anything in front of you."

Colin didn't move. Ignoring Severn, he spoke to Mercedes. "I believe you got half my name," he said. "Thorne being the last, Colin's the first."

Mercedes feigned surprise. "Then you're the one my uncle's supposed to meet," she said, as though realization was just dawning. "The accent . . . I should have known . . ."

Colin considered applauding her performance. He simply saluted her with a brief nod instead, then added, "And you're the poor relation."

"For God's sake, Thorne," Severn snapped.

"It's all right," Mercedes said, not sparing his lordship a glance. Her eyes were leveled on Colin. "I find it more to my liking to be insulted to my face than behind my back."

Severn frowned. "What does that mean?"

It was Colin who answered. "It means the lady is willing to

make allowances for ill-mannered Yankees." To Mercedes he said, "My apologies, Miss Leyden."

She nodded once, coolly, accepting it. With seeming indifference, Mercedes walked to one of the tall windows, parted the drapes, and looked out. "I don't know what I can tell you," she said. "I didn't see my uncle actually leave the house but I know that was his intention when we last spoke. I can only imagine that there has been some miscommunication regarding the site— or that there's been an accident." Mercedes let the drapes fall back, eliminating the sliver of light that had lain across her face. She turned to her guests. "Do you think we should organize a search?"

"Of the house?" Colin asked.

"I was thinking of the grounds," she said. "My uncle's not a coward. You won't find him here. He would never hide from you."

Severn nodded, satisfied with her defense of the earl. "That's what I've been telling him."

"Then you agree with a search of the grounds?" she asked.

"I do."

"Very well," Mercedes said. "If you'll excuse me, I'll speak to Mr. Hennepin about organizing it." She hesitated, affecting uncertainty as she looked back at Severn. "I'm not sure he'll know how to go about it. I wonder, my lord, if you'd be willing to speak to him."

"Of course." Severn reached the doors before Mercedes and opened them. He stepped back to allow Mercedes to precede him, only to realize she wasn't following. She was standing at Colin Thorne's side, a rather tight smile on her face.

"Go on," she said. "Mrs. Hennepin will direct you to her husband. I'll only be a moment."

Marcus Severn drew himself up as if preparing to issue a challenge. His austere features were set in cold disapproval. He looked from Mercedes to Colin and back again. "A moment," he said tersely.

Mercedes waited until Severn was out of earshot. "Let go of

my dress," she said stiffly, a brief angry pause between each word.

Instead Colin pulled her closer, gathering up handfuls of material in his fist until she was against him. He held her just that way, ignoring her attempts to free herself, until he shut the parlor doors. Once privacy was assured, he let her go.

Mercedes spun away from him. She ran her palms over the folds of her gown, trying to smooth it and erase the evidence of Colin's grasp. "Are you quite mad?" she demanded. "Severn might have called you out for touching me that way."

Colin was more interested than perturbed. "Really?" he asked, leaning back against the doors. "Then why didn't you tell him? I'd have thought you'd welcome the opportunity for someone to finish off what you started last night."

Mercedes refused to rise to the bait. "Let me pass," she said. "You're blocking my way."

"Quite intentionally, I assure you."

"Severn will come back."

"Are you threatening me with him?" asked Colin. "Perhaps you imagine you can provoke us both into a duel."

"You're ridiculous."

"Am I? I'd wager you'd be relieved if we killed each other. From what I've observed, you don't have much liking for the Right Honorable Viscount, and I already know what you think of me."

Mercedes threw up her hands. "I'm trying to prevent the very thing you seem bent on making happen. Now, let me pass and speak to Mr. Hennepin myself. He's not likely to take orders from Severn no matter how sternly they're issued."

Colin straightened but he did not move away from the doors. "So you're going to make a show of it?"

She was visibly bewildered. "A show of what?"

"The search."

"You're daft."

"It could be because of the blow I took to my head last night, but then you probably wouldn't know anything about that."

"Of course I know about it. I flung the drawer, didn't I?"

"So you admit it."

"I'm not likely to deny what we both know is true."

"At least when there are no witnesses."

Mercedes's smile was as sweet as it was insincere. "Exactly."
Her smile vanished. "Now let me pass."

Colin stepped out of her way. "You have a lot to answer for,
Miss Leyden."

"Excuse me," she said politely. "I'm interested in finding my
uncle, even if you're not."

Colin put out a hand as she would have passed him. "You're
a tad too confident for my tastes," he said lowly. "Just because
I didn't expose you to Severn, don't think I won't. I believe he'd
be very interested in hearing that you've already spent time in
my bed."

Mercedes didn't look at Colin. She couldn't. She had no wish
for him to see her fear. Drawing in a shallow breath, she waited
him out.

Colin studied her three-quarter profile and sensed her withdrawal. He let his hand drop away. "Go," he said. "But know
this isn't over."

Without a sideways glance, Mercedes hurried away. She was
on the point of reaching the stairs to the kitchen, when a scream
from above halted her steps. Running back down the hall, Mercedes raised her skirts and took the main stairs two at a time,
heedless of the fact that Colin Thorne was on her heels. Knowing
the source of that scream and the ones that followed, Mercedes
automatically turned toward the north wing when she reached
the first landing.

The door to Sylvia's room was already open. Mercedes was
brought up short on the threshold by the melee that confronted
her. At the center of the disturbance was a man she didn't recognize, but all the other participants were very well known to
her.

The red-headed giant at the eye of the storm easily stood six
and a half feet. That Brendan was clambering up the man's back

emphasized his height and the breadth of his shoulders. That he did not fling Brendan across the room when the boy began to clobber him about the head and ears spoke to his temperament. He actually dislodged Brendan as if he were no more irritating than a pesky puppy and tossed him on Sylvia's bed. That's when Britton head-butted him in the brisket. The giant took a step back with the blow, not because it staggered him, but because if he had held his ground Britton might have hurt himself. Throwing oneself head first against the man's hard middle was rather like diving into a shallow pond.

Chloe screamed this time as Britton was picked up by his waist, turned upside down, and pitched onto the bed beside his brother. Sylvia charged next, flinging herself at the giant's back much as Brendan had done. Her wrists were grabbed, stilling their blows, and as the man bent at the waist he actually flipped her over his head. Her shout was muffled by the flurry of skirts and petticoats. She landed on her feet directly in front of the giant, this time with him at her back. Sylvia's arms were crossed and locked, secured by his hold on her wrists. It was at that point that Chloe picked up the pitcher on the bedstand and flung it at his head. He ducked easily, making certain Sylvia cleared the missile as well, and let it fall harmlessly at Mercedes's feet.

"Are you just going to stand there?" he demanded.

At first Mercedes thought he was inviting her to join the fray, then she realized his question was directed to someone behind her. It was the first she knew that Colin had followed. She turned on him, her eyes flashing. "Do you know this man?" she asked angrily.

It was then that Colin understood that his approach had been all wrong. Mercedes Leyden was quite capable of dismissing him and his questions as long as she was the one being threatened. Now he remembered how quickly she had acted to remove Weybourne's children from the parlor when one of the boys had caught the edge of Severn's temper. It seemed she would take on anything to protect the others.

Colin Thorne studied Mercedes a moment. Anger was the

overriding emotion she turned on him but he didn't think he was wrong to believe that fear had provoked it. None of his own satisfaction at this discovery showed on his features. This was not the moment to reveal he had found her Achilles's heel.

Colin stepped past Mercedes and over the shards of the broken pitcher. "You look as if you have it—" He dodged another missile, this time as Chloe threw the washbasin. "Well, perhaps you don't have it under control after all." Chloe's screech actually hurt his ears as he took a step in her direction. She looked around frantically for something to throw. Britton and Brendan scrambled off the bed and ran headlong at Colin's legs, stopping him much more successfully than they had their other target.

"Everybody stop!" Mercedes hardly recognized her own voice but she noticed no one else seemed to have any difficulty. Not so far off she could hear Severn and several others nearing the top of the stairs. Whatever search had been organized was now on its way to the north wing. "Now they're all coming," she said sharply. "Chloe, put down that book. Brit and Brendan, let go of Captain Thorne right now. And you—" She pointed to Aubrey. "Put Sylvia down. She's not an acrobat and this, whatever you've been given cause to think, is not a circus ring."

Her directives were no sooner complied with than Lord Severn reached the door. "What is going on?" he asked "Thorne. What's your second doing in this part of the house?"

Colin shrugged. "Ask him yourself."

Aubrey brushed himself off, straightening the shirt that was twisted around his waist. When Sylvia stepped away he casually touched her wrist and brought her to stand in front of him. "The doctor wasn't good company. And I didn't think much of joining your search. Thought I'd have a look around and see if I couldn't scare up the earl myself."

Mercedes spoke before Severn could respond. "It's all right, my lord. No harm's been done."

Severn was not appeased. "Then what was all the screaming about?"

This time Sylvia spoke up. "Girlish silliness, my lord," she said. Her head was tilted at a coquettish angle. "I saw a mouse and started screaming. People have been coming to my rescue ever since. It's really rather overwhelming. I had no idea I had such a compelling cry."

God bless you, Mercedes thought. She addressed Severn. "You see, it was nothing. High spirits is all."

"High strung is more like it." He surveyed the room again and, seeing that everything was reasonably at peace, he motioned to Mrs. Hennepin, her husband, and the others who were going to be part of the search to back out of the doorway. "Are you coming?" he asked Mercedes.

"Yes," she said. "In a moment. I've decided to permit Captain Thorne and his second to look through the house. It's clear they're not going to be satisfied with less." Ignoring Severn's glowering look and Mrs. Hennepin's hand-wringing, she addressed the twins. "Boys, why don't you take them on a tour? Sylvia and Chloe, you may go along if you wish. Be particular to show them everything. Even the turret rooms."

"North and south?" they asked in unison.

"Of course." She turned back to Severn. "I'm ready," she said.

A thorough search of the grounds took until midday to complete. In the end there was only one conclusion that Mercedes could reach: The Earl of Weybourne had fled. Severn, she discovered, had come to another one.

She offered him a drink in the earl's library, too tired to wonder at her foolishness in being alone with him. "Are you quite serious?" she asked when he offered his explanation.

Marcus Severn nodded once and raised his glass. "Quite," he said, his voice clipped. "They killed him."

"But there's no evidence."

"That's only because we haven't found the body."

Mercedes began to think she may want a drink herself. She sat down slowly. Even in her confusion she had enough sense to take a chair rather than the narrow divan where Severn might be tempted to join her. "Don't you believe we would have seen something?" she asked. "Some sign of blood, torn clothing from a struggle?"

"We'll keep looking, of course," he said. "Tomorrow I'll bring help from my father's estate to comb Weybourne Park. I'll also alert the authorities. They'll want to speak to the Yanks at length, I'm sure." He sat behind the earl's desk and rolled the tumbler between his palms. "Where are they?" he asked.

"I believe that after they finished with the house they joined Ben Fitch's group at the pond."

"Not surprising. That isn't far from where they were supposed to meet your uncle in the first place. They may have even gone there to make sure their tracks were covered."

"You can't know that," Mercedes said.

"But I can find out." He set his tumbler down firmly and came to his feet in a single motion. Marcus Severn's ice-blue eyes rested thoughtfully on Mercedes. "You know, Mercedes, if Thorne murdered your uncle it raises all kinds of questions about the future of Weybourne Park. It isn't as if Thorne can collect on the wager under those circumstances."

That thought had also occurred to her. "This is all supposition," she said. *"Your* supposition." She was uncomfortably aware that Severn was studying her again, and that his look could not have been more different than the one she experienced from Colin Thorne. There was nothing remotely disinterested in Severn's expression. Mercedes even allowed that some women might have been flattered by his attention; she simply did not count herself among them.

He was not a strikingly handsome man but he wasn't unattractive. His features were refined, with high cheekbones and a narrow jaw. His dark hair was casually styled. He had an athletic build, and Mercedes knew he rode frequently for pleasure and boxed with friends from his club. It was his widely spaced eyes that set her skin crawling, or more precisely, the way he looked out of them. Mercedes could not escape the sense that he removed her clothes each time he met her. His speculative glances had more to do with what she looked like outside of her chemise and petticoats than any question he had about her character.

"I think it would be better if you left," Mercedes said.

Severn's smile did not reach his eyes. "Have a care, Sadie," he said. "I might believe you're eager to be rid of me."

Mercedes schooled her features and did not take issue with the use of his pet name for her. "I'm exhausted. Surely you can appreciate that. I've been up since dawn along with every other member of this household. The search has achieved nothing except to confirm that my uncle has disappeared. And now you've given me something else to consider. My plate is full, m'lord."

"Marcus," he said. "I've given you leave often enough to use my Christian name."

Mercedes regretted her slip because it extended their conversation that much longer. "Very well," she said. "Marcus." It was a measure of how much she wanted him gone that she deigned to use the familiar address with him. She came to her feet to avoid him coming around to her chair and towering over her.

"I should like to talk to Thorne and the other fellow before I leave," he said.

She sighed. Marcus Severn was well aware of the other fellow's name. It was typical of him not to use it when he considered the man of so little consequence. "Please. Tomorrow will be soon enough. It's not as if we're even certain where they are right now."

"All the more reason to find them and warn them not to leave until they've fully accounted for themselves."

"You're not suggesting they remain here, are you? I'd really rather have you and the sheriff speak to them away from Weybourne Park."

"Of course," he said. "One of the local inns will do as well. I believe Thorne's second mentioned the Passing Fancy." He rounded the desk and approached Mercedes. As was his habit, he reached for her, this time taking her wrists in a light clasp. "Don't worry, Sadie. This will be settled quickly. I'll see to the matter myself." He bent his head and kissed her on the cheek.

Mercedes did not think it was her revulsion that made his lips seem to linger longer than usual. She shut her eyes and prayed he would withdraw quickly, not understanding the invitation she appeared to be offering with her closed lids and patient expression. She almost cried out when his mouth touched hers.

Except for falling back in the chair, there was nowhere for her to go. His clasp on her wrists became noticeably tighter. Mercedes found she simply couldn't breathe.

When Severn raised his head it was to discover Mercedes staring at him. "That's an accusing expression," he said calmly, letting her wrists go. "One might think you found my touch not to your liking."

Mercedes drew in a shallow breath. "I did not give you leave," she said.

He smiled lightly as he picked up his gloves. "That's something else you'll have to consider about your future, won't you? If you want to keep Weybourne Park there will have to be some allowances made." Severn watched her flinch. It was accomplished with a mere blink but he understood it for what it was. He was satisfied Mercedes knew what he was saying. He could always change her mind about liking it. "Good day, Sadie."

"They took us in, didn't they?" Aubrey said.

"So you've noted." It was not the first time Thorne had heard the observation. By his recollection, since being locked in the north turret room, Aubrey Jones had pointed it out five times. Colin was considering engraving it in the plaster. For all the good it was doing them, he still had his knife. "Why don't you sit down, Aubrey? You must have already memorized the view from each of the windows."

The turret's six windows offered a panoramic view of Weybourne Park. From this vantage point Colin and Aubrey had been able to watch most of the search. It was their initial interest in the view that had made it so easy for the twins and their sisters to lock them in.

Aubrey leaned against the wall and inched his way down until he was sitting on the hardwood floor. "The southern turret was furnished," he said. "You'd think they'd have had the decency to make a prison out of that one."

Colin pointed to the waterstained ceiling and the stain on the bare floor. There was also what looked like a permanent shadow on the cream plaster caused by water damage. Colin had already spent a considerable amount of time looking for shapes and figures in the odd marking. "The room's in need of some repairs."

"Did they have to remove *all* the furniture?" Aubrey grumbled.

Colin gave Aubrey a critical glance. Even folded as he was, his legs crossed in front of him like a tailor, Aubrey took up a fair amount of space. "You'd have broken that delicate stuff by now anyway. From what we've been allowed to see, I'd say they couldn't afford to replace it."

"Is that why you wouldn't let me break one of these windows?"

"It may still come to that," Colin said. "I may throw you through one. Be glad I'm more interested in discovering what she has planned than in making an escape."

Aubrey snorted. "That's because you haven't been trying to ignore one of nature's calls. I had a quick drink with the doctor before I started my search. I have certain needs."

Colin grinned at that. "It shouldn't be much longer," he said. "You saw yourself that the search parties are coming back to the house. She'll be here directly."

"You're confident she doesn't intend to starve us, then," Aubrey said dryly. As if on cue his stomach growled. "I swear I may just gobble her up." He patted his stomach to settle. "Though, truth be known, I fancy one of the younger ones."

One of Colin's brows kicked up. "Really? Britton or Brendan?"

Aubrey shot his captain a sour look. It was too bad there was no furniture, he thought. He might have been moved to throw something. "Sylvia," he said, stretching out his long legs. "She was pleasing to my eyes."

"As I recall she doesn't look so different from her sister," Colin said. "Your interest in her wouldn't be because the other one told us several times that there are plans for her to marry a vicar?"

"She looks nothing like Chloe," Aubrey said. "Her eyes are more blue than green, for one thing. And she must be a full inch taller. There's only a suggestion of a dimple in her chin while Chloe's looks like a thumbprint. You must have noticed that—"

"That you could go on and on," Colin interrupted. "I take your point. I'm convinced you don't mean to have them both."

Aubrey scowled. "They're nothing like the wenches last night," he said. "You'd do well to remember that."

Both of Colin's brows lifted as he considered Aubrey's statement. "I thought you liked Molly and her sister."

"I did. I do. And I mean no offense to them by pulling you up short, but they'd be the first to tell you that there's a world of difference between them and the earl's daughters."

Colin was unconvinced. He shrugged. "Only in the breeding, Aubrey. Not in the bedding. They're more similar than different."

Aubrey decided he did not want to be drawn into an argument, certainly not an argument about women. He'd observed for himself over the years that he'd been with Colin Thorne, that his captain preferred to hold himself aloof from female entanglements. Neither did he have much to do with men beyond what was demanded by business. Aubrey counted himself as Colin's friend but he was never certain that Colin did. Colin Thorne preferred to keep his own counsel and Aubrey figured he'd gotten as close as he had by respecting Colin's right to do just that.

Aubrey leaned his head back against the wall and closed his eyes. "You think about women your way," he said. "And I'll think about them mine. But ask yourself how it is that I passed a pleasant night wedged comfortably between feminine bookends while you spent it battened down to the floor."

"You're with me now, aren't you?" Colin pointed out. "And

unless I've confused the two, it was your dear Sylvia who actually pushed the door shut on us."

Aubrey's smile was serene. "Yes, but she did it gently. I could see it troubled her."

"Oh, well that's all right, then," Colin said.

Aubrey chuckled at his captain's dry sarcasm. "She was following orders I'm sure. You must know that."

Colin nodded. "It occurred to me."

Another vision suddenly leaped to Aubrey's mind. "She's someone to be reckoned with."

"I assume we're talking about Mercedes now."

"Hmm-mm. It's hard to believe that bit of a thing was able to truss you like my Aunt Esmy's Christmas goose."

"You're really enjoying yourself, aren't you?"

Aubrey's broad shoulders heaved once in a massive shrug. "Trying to make the best of a bad situation." He opened his eyes just enough to dart a glance in Colin's direction. He didn't think he imagined the smile that was edging his captain's mouth. "Have you considered what you're going to say to her?"

"I'm considering it now."

So that sliver of a smile wasn't prompted by anything he'd said, Aubrey realized. Poor Mercedes. It didn't bode well for her. "Don't be too hard on her," he said. "She's probably only following orders herself."

"Aubrey," Colin said flatly. "She tried to kill me."

"Maim you, more likely."

"I was there, Aubrey. *Under* the knife. She tried to kill me."

"I'm only saying that she could have killed you after she knocked you out and she didn't. It makes me wonder what her intentions really were."

"You can ask her yourself. I think I hear her on the stairs now."

Aubrey didn't ask what made Colin so certain he could distinguish Mercedes's footfalls from any others he could have heard. That question was sure to be answered with a dark look. Aubrey figured he'd already risked as much of that as he dared for now.

Both men sat up a bit straighter as the bar across the door was lifted and set aside. The door itself resisted easy opening because of hinges that had begun to rust. The grating sound raised the hair at the back of Colin's neck but he didn't offer any assistance.

Mercedes only cracked the door wide enough for her to slip inside. It didn't open directly into the turret room. She was confronted first by the narrow and steep stairwell that wound up to the room. There was no handrail so she placed one palm on the wall to steady her climb and raised her gown a few inches to keep from tripping.

"My God," she said when she reached the top and saw both men seated casually on the floor. "You really *are* here."

Colin gave in to temptation. He put his hands together slowly and rhythmically, applauding what he was certain was a performance.

Mercedes's chin came up and she said coldly, "I don't know what that's in aid of, Captain Thorne, but I'm sure you mean to be insulting."

He stopped clapping. "I'll add perceptive to all your other traits."

She ignored him, turning her attention instead to Aubrey. "Mr. Jones, is it?" she asked. "My most heartfelt apologies. When you and Captain Thorne didn't return with Ben Fitch's search group, I asked the twins if they'd seen you leave. They seemed surprised by the question."

"I wonder why," Colin interjected dryly.

Mercedes went on as if she hadn't heard. "Sylvia and Chloe have admitted their part in it. I'm afraid between them and the boys they were quite convinced this was *my* wish. It simply isn't so. In fact, I purposely set out to look for you to warn you." She offered Aubrey her hand to help him to his feet.

Aubrey looked at her extended hand, then looked at her. She was hardly more substantial than either of her female cousins. "Miss Leyden," he said frankly. "If I was to take that hand I'd still be sitting here in the end—only you'd be in my lap. Now, I won't be insulted if you take it back."

Mercedes's smile momentarily transformed her face. The small vertical crease between her brows was erased and her gray eyes cleared. "I'm stronger than you might think."

Aubrey chuckled. "I'm not going to risk it."

"Good thinking, Aubrey. You haven't checked for weapons."

Aubrey saw that while Mercedes's smile remained, it was forced now, more a parody of what she thought a smile should be. Requiring no assistance, Aubrey came to his feet fluidly. "Beggin' your pardon, ma'am, but the captain doesn't take well to being confined. And this *is* the second time in as many days that it's been done to him. Not that I find it a pleasure either," he added. "But I suppose your cousins were getting a little of their own back after that business in the other Miss Leyden's room."

"You mean Sylvia's," said Mercedes.

"Is that her name?" he asked. Over Mercedes's shoulder he caught Colin rolling his eyes. He pretended he hadn't seen and went on politely. "Well, then I must mean her. One of them looks a lot like the other."

"I wouldn't mention it to them," she said confidentially. Her first impression aside, Mercedes found Aubrey Jones very easy to like. "Perhaps you can tell me what really happened. I've never known Sylvia to take much notice of a mouse before."

"Perhaps you should ask her," he said.

"Oh, I have. For some reason she's sticking to her story. When I first heard it I was certain she merely invented it for Severn's benefit."

Colin smirked. "Adept liars, all of them." He saw Mercedes's shoulders stiffen but she didn't turn. Aubrey looked a little pained. Colin found his response to Mercedes interesting. It seemed he wouldn't be able to count on Aubrey Jones to watch his back.

"Perhaps there was a mouse," Aubrey said, not willing to disclose that Sylvia was lying. "I know for a fact that I startled her when I entered her room. I heard a noise and that's what led me there. I thought it might be the earl. Instead I surprised Miss

Leyden. She'd been reading, I think. There was a book on the floor beside her chair. It may be I heard it drop."

Mercedes considered this explanation, her head tilted slightly to one side. "I was afraid you'd barged in on her while she was changing her clothes," she said. "I noticed when she somersaulted over your head that the back of her gown was undone."

Aubrey shifted his weight from one foot to the other. She was very observant. Even Colin hadn't noticed that. He was sure he'd have heard about it sometime during these last interminable hours. He managed not to stutter in replying. "I wouldn't know about that."

Colin was finally enjoying himself. "It seemed to me that when Severn and the others arrived you were careful to keep the young lady's back to yourself. Either you took note of her state and were playing the gentleman, or you were oblivious and merely being cruel."

Aubrey was saved from choosing either explanation for his behavior by Mercedes. She spun on her heel and fixed Colin with an icy glance. "I don't remember inviting you to join this conversation. Mr. Jones and I have come to our own understanding. He knows now that I'm not a fool and I know he's infinitely more gallant than his captain." Having put Colin firmly in his place, she added for Aubrey's benefit, "And it's no good smirking at him behind my back. It's hardly becoming."

"And disrespectful to boot," Colin said.

Aubrey's eyes widened. Dumbfounded, he swept his fingers through his thick red hair. "Damn me if she doesn't have eyes at the back of her head."

Mercedes turned around. "If you'd excuse us, Mr. Jones. I'd like to speak to Captain Thorne in private."

Colin got to his feet. "Not here. I'm not taking a chance on getting locked in again."

"You were hardly locked in," Mercedes said. "The door was barred, yes, but there is an access right here that leads to the roof." She pointed to a marked section of the ceiling. Virtually concealed by the water stain was the outline of a panel which could be lifted to exit to the roof. "Someone on the grounds would have heard you shout."

Aubrey sighed and spoke as if to himself. "And didn't I suggest we look for such a thing?"

Colin's dark look was quelling. "Didn't you also mention some business of a personal nature you wanted to be about?"

Mercedes saw Aubrey flush and took pity on him. "You may use any of the bedrooms in the south wing, except the earl's, to refresh yourself. Mrs. Hennepin will direct someone to get whatever you require. You're invited to join us for dinner, but after I speak to Captain Thorne you may decide quite properly that it isn't in your best interest to do so."

"Thank you, Miss Leyden. I'll keep that in mind." He started down the stairs, practically filling the passage with the breadth of his shoulders.

Mercedes watched Aubrey duck through the doorway before she spoke. "The same offer is open to you," she told Colin. "If you wish, I'll wait for you in the earl's library. Anyone can show you where it is."

Colin was not of a mind to let her out of his sight, but like Aubrey, he had certain needs even if he hadn't been vocal about them. He consulted his pocket watch. "Twenty minutes," he said.

She nodded. "I'll have Mrs. Hennepin prepare some tea and cakes."

Eighteen minutes later Colin joined Mercedes in the library. A silver salver held the promised tea and cakes. He politely but firmly refused her offer. He was not going to make this easy for her, and allowing her to play the role of the gracious hostess, when she was anything but, would have made her more comfortable. When she sat down in the large leather wing chair, he chose to remain standing, ostensibly to look around the room, but in fact, to keep her on edge.

The library, he observed, was one of the manor's better appointed rooms. He supposed that was because it was the earl's domain. His lordship apparently hadn't seen fit to deny himself what he denied members of his family. The furnishings were all

cherry wood, buffed to a high gloss without a random scratch
on any surface. The large desk had brass fittings and was situated
near the fireplace. In the winter and cold, damp springs it would
be the most comfortable place in the room. Shelving comprised
two walls complete from floor to ceiling. They were crowded
with leather-bound volumes, some shelves devoted to the complete works of writers like Shakespeare and Jonson.

The carpet beneath Colin's feet wasn't worn as so many others
in the manor were. He wondered at it until he noticed slightly
faded sections in the shape of furniture that wasn't of this room.
He correctly surmised it had been brought from another room
in the house to accommodate the earl's need to keep up appearances. He also imagined that it fell on Mercedes's shoulders to
make it so.

Colin hooked his hip on the edge of the earl's desk and
stretched one leg out to support himself. He saw Mercedes worry
her lower lip as he idly rearranged some of Weybourne's personal
items to make more room.

"Won't you have a seat?" she encouraged politely.

"No."

Mercedes sank back a little. So far, this meeting was not going
as planned. She looked forlornly at the tea and cakes and wondered if she dared offer him any a third time.

Catching her look, Colin said, "And no. I don't want any."

"But you haven't eaten since breakfast."

"Not even then." He was silent, his light brows slightly raised,
his expression expectant. When she had the grace to look away,
he said, "I see you *do* remember why that would be so."

"I take it Mr. Jones is the one who freed you."

"That's right. I don't suppose you considered that I would
have a second, else you might have killed me after all."

Mercedes didn't want to think about that possibility. What was
done, was done. Afraid of the answer, she was not going to ask
herself how she might have handled things differently. "I'm not
sorry that you're all of a piece," she said. That, at least, was
honest. It had never been her wish to see him dead.

"You'll understand if I don't believe you," Colin said. "Just as I don't believe that tale you handed Aubrey upstairs." Mercedes looked at him blankly so he laid it out for her. "You told him that your cousins planned our imprisonment on their own."

"That's quite true."

"I distinctly remember you telling them to show us the turret rooms. North and south."

"I believe I was responding to a question from one of the twins."

"It's convenient for you to recall it that way. I remember an undertone to the exchange."

Mercedes folded her hands in her lap and regarded Colin for a few moments without speaking. "You're a very suspicious man, aren't you?" she said when she was through with her appraisal.

He was not offended. "I've learned to be."

"Why didn't you tell Severn what I did last night?"

"I've also learned not to rush my fences."

She frowned. "What does that mean?"

"It means that I can wait."

"Wait for what?"

"Just wait," he said. "Everything happens in its own time. I'll know when it's time to give up our secret."

Mercedes felt her heartbeat quicken. He'd said *when*, not *if*. He made it sound as if he had every intention of telling. All the more reason to encourage him to leave Weybourne Park. "You haven't asked about my uncle," she said.

Colin picked up a letter opener and turned it over in his palm. The silver handle was inscribed: Winston, my love. Elizabeth. "Aubrey and I could see a lot of the activity from our crow's nest," he said. "We never saw anything that looked like Weybourne's return." He held up the opener. "I thought the earl's name was Wallace."

"It is. That was my father's."

"Elizabeth?"

"My mother. She was his countess." She saw Colin's skeptical look. "I wasn't always the poor relation, Captain Thorne. Before my father and mother died this was truly my home. I was born here. That turret where you say you were imprisoned was once my very special room. That's where I kept my dolls and books and childish treasures and I passed many more hours in a single day there than you did or are ever likely to."

Colin was taken aback by this information though his expression remained unchanged. He looked around the room but the vision in his mind was the rest of Weybourne manor, the bed-chambers that needed airing, the threadbare carpets, the water-stained walls and ceilings. When his dark eyes alighted on Mercedes again he simply asked, "Then how?"

She understood. "The how of it is rather simple," she said. "Do you know what it means when an estate is entailed?"

"The inheritance is passed from father to son."

"If there is a son. If not, it goes to the closest male relation. That's how my uncle became the earl. He was my father's brother and my father had no sons."

Colin put down the letter opener. He ran his fingers through his hair, thinking. Her desire to see that her uncle wasn't killed in the duel didn't make any sense to him. One of the twins would have inherited the title at least. As far as Colin was concerned, he was now the rightful owner of Weybourne Park. He said as much to her.

Mercedes shook her head. "You don't understand at all. Severn believes you murdered the earl before the duel was to take place. That means you wouldn't get the property."

"Then the older of the twins would inherit. That must be to your liking."

"My uncle has never recognized them as his sons. He's always believed Lady Georgia, my aunt, had an affair."

"Then who would claim Weybourne Park?"

"Haven't I made that clear?" she asked. "No, I suppose I haven't. It's Viscount Fielding, of course. Marcus Severn is our closest male relative."

Five

She thought she might get a reaction. When Colin continued to look thoughtful, Mercedes had good reason to wonder if she'd been heard. "Severn," she repeated more loudly. "Our closest male relative is Severn."

This time one of Colin's brows came up. "There's no need to play the parrot," he said. "I heard you the first time."

Embarrassed, she glared at him accusingly. "Then you might at least make some response."

"Miss Leyden," Colin said, sighing. "If I jumped each time you surprised me, I'd have exhausted myself by now."

"Then you *were* surprised? You didn't already know about Severn?"

"Perhaps *I* should speak up. I thought I just said that." Colin gave her full marks for not shrinking back in her chair at his withering tone. She blinked once, shuttering whatever hurt he had inflicted, then faced him squarely. "You may tell me how he's related," he said. "I don't know that either."

She had never felt such an overpowering urge to throttle someone. In her lap, Mercedes's hands folded primly. "It would be more correct to say it is Severn's father who stands to inherit. The Earl of Rosefield and my grandfather were cousins."

"So you and Severn are third cousins."

"Something like that."

"Kissing cousins."

Mercedes reacted with her entire body. Her head whipped up and her shoulders stiffened. The hair on the back of her neck stood erect and beneath her gown she could feel the prickle of gooseflesh. She was unable to help herself, and a shudder actually rolled through her. "That's a vulgar expression," she said tightly.

Fascinated, Colin's head was cocked to one side watching her. "You've never heard it before."

It pained her to admit it. "No."

"It merely means the blood relation is far enough removed that there's no incestuous impediment to marriage."

"I surmised its meaning," she said coldly. "I'm not without some intelligence. It's still a vulgar expression."

Colin's tone was one of complete indifference. "Perhaps you're confusing the expression with the act."

"I hardly think that—"

"Kissing cousins," Colin said under his breath, mulling the words over. "No, it doesn't have any vulgar connotation in my mind. I admit though, when I saw Severn lay his mouth against your cheek, not once, but twice, I wondered that you were able to stand your ground." He almost smiled as she came out of her chair as predictably as a jack-in-the-box.

Mercedes rounded on him. "My duties as hostess don't extend to allowing you to amuse yourself at my expense. I asked you here to warn you of the danger you're in. If you cannot be sensible to that, then I'll excuse myself." She waited several heartbeats, trying to read his inscrutable expression. His eyes were like polished obsidian, darkly reflective and damnably unrevealing. "Very well," she said when he gave no response. "Good day, Captain Thorne." Mercedes made a graceful turn, her full skirt sweeping the air in an arc. She was permitted one step in the direction of the door before she was brought up short.

Colin grabbed a handful of her skirt and drew her inexorably closer. Repositioning himself on the edge of the earl's desk, Colin drew Mercedes directly between his splayed legs. He did not mistake her lack of struggle with compliance. She was merely trying to save her gown from being torn. When she was close enough for him to control in other ways, he turned her around and laid his palms on either side of her waist.

Mercedes said nothing. She stared at him mutinously as though she could shame him into releasing her.

"That look's wasted on me," he told her. "You'd best find another."

Her clear gray eyes narrowed.

"Better," he said, unruffled by her anger.

"You're intolerable."

"So I've been told."

He was completely maddening. Mercedes looked over her shoulder toward the door.

In anticipation of her next move Colin said, "I locked the door when I came in. You shouldn't leave keys dangling in the keyholes if you don't mean for them to be used."

Mercedes noticed the key was no longer there.

"In my pocket," he said when Mercedes faced him again. "I suppose you were too preoccupied with tea and cakes to notice." His eyes fell to her mouth as her lips parted. Colin couldn't be sure if she was preparing to scream or simply gaping at him. He was not taking any chances. "If you attempt to shout for help, I'll kiss you." Her mouth clamped shut so quickly that Colin wondered if he shouldn't be insulted. A narrow smile played on his lips as he continued to study her. It was clear she was uncomfortable beneath his scrutiny but she seemed unwilling or unable to look away. Perhaps it was a bit of both, he thought. What was it she was expecting him to do?

Colin's hands dropped away from her waist but his thighs tightened fractionally. Even though his grasp on her was more intimate, he noticed she wasn't moved to blush. Her eyes remained steady on him but Colin sensed that she was now looking through him rather than at him. It was a subtle withdrawal on her part as was her very stillness. It was as though she were willing herself to be invisible, yet none of the effort of this wish showed on her face. In her own way, Mercedes Leyden could be inscrutable.

"Tell me about this danger I'm supposed to be in," Colin said.

He was close enough that Mercedes could feel the rush of his breath as he spoke. It was not unpleasant. Like an echo, his words came to her consciousness a second later. She blinked slowly. At her sides her arms hung uselessly, her hands trapped between herself and his thighs. She felt very exposed, horribly vulnerable. Mercedes only hoped that Colin could not guess at the depth of her distress. She didn't want to give him that much power over her.

"Lord Severn believes you and your friend have murdered my uncle," she said quietly.

"You've already mentioned something to that effect," Colin reminded her.

"He's going to have the authorities question you in the morning."

"Really?"

She thought he didn't sound disturbed by the news, only interested. "You or Mr. Jones must have made mention of the Passing Fancy. He plans to seek you out there."

Colin didn't comment on this. He was more curious about her motives. "Why are you telling me?"

"I thought that was obvious."

Little about Mercedes was obvious. He almost said as much, then thought better of it. She didn't deserve to know how successful she'd been at keeping him intrigued. "Tell me anyway," he said.

"It occurred to me you might appreciate the opportunity to get away."

"I do."

"I can't imagine that you want to answer questions."

"I don't."

"Well then?"

Colin shook his head. He was amused by her now, and the glimmer of a smile returned. "You might convince someone else that you have my best interests at heart, but I'm the man you tried to murder last evening. This noble gesture of yours strains the boundaries of logic."

"Your logic perhaps," she said tartly. "It makes perfect sense to me."

No surprise there, Colin thought. "It occurs to me that the turret room in the north wing may be a small family asylum," he said. "I'm moved to wonder if you aren't a lunatic." He felt her fingers twitch against his thighs. He had no difficulty guessing at the reason for the movement. She itched to slap him. "Did the earl let you out specifically to wreak havoc on my head or did you escape and make more a success of doing him in?"

Mercedes's jaw went slack. She gaped at him.

Colin bent his head and laid his mouth across hers. Her lips were warm, her breath sweet. Tea and cakes. He moved to deepen the kiss, drawing his tongue along the edge of her upper lip, pressing against her teeth.

Mercedes's head snapped back. She tore her hands free and pushed at his thighs. Colin was immovable and Mercedes remained trapped between the vise-like grip of his legs. She raised her hands to push at his chest but the look in his eyes made her think better of it. Her arms lowered slowly. Now there was nowhere for her hands to comfortably settle. They lay uneasily against his thighs. "Why did you do that?" she asked. Her voice was not as accusing as she would have wished. To her own ears it sounded rather soft and tremulous. Her heart sank as she considered what he might make of that.

"I told you if you tried to shout I'd kiss you."

"But I wasn't going to shout."

"Oh." Colin shrugged. "My mistake."

Mercedes's mouth flattened. He knew very well she hadn't been about to call for help. "You did that deliberately," she said.

"I thought that was obvious."

Although no laughter accompanied this statement, Mercedes knew she was being laughed at. To her horror she felt an ache in her eyes and throat that was the precursor to tears. She drew in a shallow breath and steadied herself. It was not her way to cry even when she was alone—she would be damned if she'd cry in front of Colin Thorne. "You should leave," she said after a moment. "If my uncle still hasn't appeared in the morning, you stand to be accused of murder by Severn. You and Mr. Jones will want to be on your clipper ship as soon as possible and away from England."

Colin heard what she said but it wasn't what he was answering. His words were for the hurt he had glimpsed in her eyes before she'd blinked it away. "I'm sorry," he said.

She thought he was apologizing for not hearing her. Mercedes began to repeat herself, more loudly this time.

Colin held up one hand, cutting her off. "I told you, my hearing's fine. I'm sorry about the other . . . about laughing at you."

Flustered by this apology as she was flustered by little else, Mercedes looked away. It was only fair that he was holding her upright, she thought, since he was also the one continually setting her off balance. She believed that some concession on her part was probably appropriate and called for. "I wasn't trying to kill you, you know. Not really. I know how it looked, but it wasn't like that."

Colin used his raised hand to turn her chin back in his direction. "Then how was it?" he asked.

His fingertips were cool on the underside of her jaw. They exerted no pressure and yet she found it impossible to speak until he removed them. "I thought only to injure you," she said. "It seemed to me it would be enough."

"Enough?"

"Enough to prevent you from killing my uncle."

"How do you know I didn't?" he asked. "Your cousin seems to think I managed the deed."

Mercedes disliked the reminder that Severn was her cousin but she didn't take issue with it. "Because in spite of what I said in front of Severn, my uncle *is* a coward. If he saw you arrive at the meadow, he would have fled rather than face you."

"Perhaps you know it for a fact."

"If you're suggesting that the earl's taken me into his confidence, you're off the mark. I only *know* my uncle." Mercedes watched him weigh her words. It pained her not to be believed but she was well aware of the reasons for it. "You should go," she told him again. "I have no intention of telling Severn or the authorities what I've told you."

"By all means," Colin said, his tone derisive. "Don't tarnish Weybourne's sterling reputation."

"My uncle is what he is," she said calmly. "It matters to hardly anyone that he drinks to excess, not when alcohol sharpens his wit. And few people know the extent of his gambling debts. No one would believe he fled a match with you when he sought the challenge in the first place."

"You believe it."

"I told you, I know my uncle. But I'm only the poor relation. I'm not likely to be listened to." Mercedes thought Colin would finally be through with her. She tried to step backward, out of his grip, but he was not giving her up. "Did you think I might make some flattering point about your character?" she asked. "Some nonsense about how I believe you're an honorable man and could not have done what Severn's accused you of?"

"Now that you mention it," Colin drawled.

"The truth is," she said, as if he hadn't spoken, "I don't know anything of the sort. Your behavior toward me has been nothing short of reprehensible."

He was amused again in spite of himself. "Don't you think that's a bit like the pot calling the kettle black?"

Mercedes graced Colin Thorne with her rare and radiant smile. "Go to hell, Captain."

Colin wondered if she knew how close she was coming to being kissed again. Probably not. She didn't seem to have any sense about that beautiful mouth of hers. He watched the shape of it change slowly from a sweetly generous curve to a more wary line. Well, perhaps she was learning to exercise some caution with it after all. His implacable gaze lifted to her gray eyes. "What time is dinner?" he asked.

She stared at him, stunned. "Haven't you heard anything I've said? Yes, of course you have. You've pointed out twice there's nothing wrong with your hearing." She frowned deliberately. "It must be another problem, then. Is it a difficulty with the language, perhaps? Do they speak no English in America?"

Colin offered his observation casually. "For someone I could snap in two without much effort, you demonstrate remarkable effrontery." Satisfied that she was momentarily silenced, he added, "Now, I seem to remember that you made an offer of dinner earlier. I can't see that anything you've told me changes that, so I'm asking what time you expect it to be served."

"Seven."

He looked at his pocket watch. "That gives us an hour," he said.

"Us?" she asked uneasily. "An hour for what?"

"I can't quite tell if you're hopeful or frightened." He thought she might take the bait he dangled, but she was learning not to snap at everything. Pity. "There's no reason to be either," he said. "I was only going to suggest a tour of the gardens."

All of Mercedes's reasons for not accompanying him were summarily dismissed. By the time she had offered the last of them she was already on the terraced flagstone path winding away from the manor. The delicate scent of lavender was lifted on the back of a breeze. Mercedes's skirt fluttered against her legs. Beside her, Colin was hatless. He didn't seem at all bothered by the wind ruffling his hair.

She suddenly had a sense of him at the helm of one of the great clippers, the air rushing past the bow of the ship, filling the sails until they strained the supporting masts and arms with their pressure. Colin would stand facing that wind, welcoming its lift and strength, greeting the power that was inherent in its nature. His shirt would be flattened against his chest, his trousers beaten tightly to his thighs. Strands of bright yellow hair would whip across his forehead.

Mercedes glanced sideways at him again. His stature hadn't changed. He was still leanly muscled, tall and straight. There was no tension in him, just the suggestion of potential strength in the line of his shoulders, the tapering waist, and the light, rolling walk. Still, quite without warning, it was as if his very presence had been altered, that he had somehow become as compelling a force as the wind he harnessed.

Colin wasn't looking in Mercedes's direction. He was appreciating the display of generously cupped roses along the retaining wall. What he was thinking about them had more to do with the woman on his arm. Their soft pink and peach petals were surely no smoother than Mercedes's skin, nor their hue more delicately tinted than her complexion. At the moment he thought he might be overwhelmed by this fanciful digression he reminded himself that their thorns were also no less sharp. "What are you thinking?" he asked.

Mercedes gave a little start as her own thoughts were interrupted. She was pulled off the swift and stately clipper in her mind's eye and brought back to the present. "I'm wondering what we're doing here," she said. It wasn't what had been at the forefront of her thoughts, but it wasn't a lie.

"Admiring Weybourne Park's gardens doesn't please you?"

"I wonder that it pleases you."

Colin pointed to the carpet of silver-tinted foliage bordering the flagstones. Each stem radiated a deep red flower and the delicious scent of cloves. *"Dianthus deltoides,"* he said. Next he indicated the lilies-of-the-valley growing in the shade of a stone fountain. *"Convallaria majalis."*

Remembering her earlier, sarcastic comment about the language barrier between them, Mercedes ducked her head. For all that he could be maddeningly, deliberately obtuse at times, he was clearly an educated man. "Point taken," she said quietly. "You've put me in my place."

"That wasn't my intent."

Finished with her brief penance, Mercedes slanted him a skeptical look.

"Well, perhaps I took a little satisfaction in it."

She looked away again, this time to hide her smile. It didn't seem quite fair that he could prompt one from her so easily.

"I have no liking for being indoors," he said.

Mercedes realized he was finally answering her question about why they had come to the garden.

Colin's steps slowed. "At least not for hours on end and not on such a day as this one." A skylark circled above them, marking off its aerial territory with melodious song. Colin's eyes lifted to watch the bird's acrobatic antics.

Mercedes's eyes lifted only as far as Colin's face. The mere absence of the taut and edgy smile was in itself evidence of his pleasure. She considered how he had spent most of his day in the small turret room and knew he must have chafed at his confinement. The windows would have been a mixed blessing, permitting him to see the sunshine but not feel it on his face. A little like viewing paintings in a museum, Colin would have seen the effects of the wind but not been able to touch it.

Mercedes was suddenly conscious of his arm supporting hers. She drew away, putting some distance between them.

Colin was immediately aware of her absence but he made no move to correct it. "Without a body there's no proof of foul play," he said. Colin put more feeling into an observation about the weather than he did into this statement. Weather mattered to him more.

To Mercedes the air seemed to take on a chill. It was true the sun was noticeably lower in the sky than when they had first stepped onto the flagstones, but there was actually a lull in the breeze. She turned a little toward the west to better feel the sun's rays slanting across her face. "I said much the same thing to Severn," she told him. "He plans to bring help from his father's country estate and make another search."

"He can bring on a hundred men." It wasn't said with bravado.

"He has that many at his disposal."

"It doesn't matter," Colin said. "I didn't kill Weybourne." He paused. "Tell me about your cousin. I believe you said it was his father who would inherit if your uncle dies."

"That's right. But the Earl of Rosefield will let Severn take over Weybourne Park. He's wanted it for a long time."

"Wanted it?" he asked pointedly. "Or wanted you?"

Mercedes didn't answer but her arms rose protectively and crossed in front of her. She strayed off the flagstones toward the arbor. The wooden archway was covered with the lush, dense foliage of purple clematis in full bloom.

Colin followed. When she would have ducked under the deep green and purple canopy, he stopped her, placing one hand on the curve of her neck and shoulder. Her reaction was out of all proportion to the gentle pressure he applied there. She actually gasped and twisted out of his reach.

"Don't touch me," she said sharply. "I've never given you leave to think I welcomed your touch."

Colin gave no attention to her words. His dark glance shifted from her pained expression to her shoulder. One of her hands had come up to shield it. "I didn't hurt you," he said. No amount of words to the contrary would convince him otherwise and he didn't give her an opportunity to try them. "Show me your shoulder."

Now Mercedes did back under the cover of the arbor, instinct warning her to move out of Colin's reach. "Get away from me," she said. He seemed to fill the space under the canopy. In an attempt to avoid him, she found herself pressed against the side lattice.

"I'm not going to assault you," he said.

"You *are* assaulting me."

Colin didn't wonder that she thought so, but he refused to give up any ground. She had proven too many times already that she was as difficult to hold as a bead of mercury. "Let me see your shoulder."

"It's nothing. A small bruise."

In the shade of the arbor her eyes were like quicksilver. It hardened his resolve to press through her lies. "You had no bruise there last evening," he said. "And I did nothing to give you one. Now, let me see or bear the consequences." He reached into his boot and pulled out his knife. "I always carry mine. Can you say the same?"

Mercedes couldn't easily reach the buttons at the back of her gown. That morning she had struggled for ten minutes and finally left two of them for Mrs. Hennepin to fasten.

Colin motioned to her to turn around. "I'll play the lady's maid."

It had been years since Mercedes had had a servant free for that duty. More often she was the one who assisted Chloe and Sylvia with their gowns and dressing their hair. She turned around slowly and bent her head. She held onto the lattice, weaving her fingers in the slats and among the foliage.

"No one from the house can see," he said.

His voice was very close to her now. The deep timbre moved a strand of hair at the nape of her neck. She heard the sound of steel on leather and knew he was putting his knife away. She could duck and run, she thought, and though her mind willed her to make a move, there was no follow through by any part of her.

Colin had to unfasten five of the small, cloth-covered buttons before there was sufficient give in the material to free Mercedes's shoulder. Shadows lent her skin a gray cast and darkened the weal to a color as livid as the purple petals above her. The stripe snaked around half her throat like a broken necklace. He didn't touch. Colin's index finger traced the air above it, measuring the full-length at six inches and the width slightly more than a quarter of an inch.

He laid the strap of Mercedes's chemise in place, then carefully closed the back of her gown. Her fingers, he noticed, tight on the wooden lattice, were steadier than his own. Colin stepped away but Mercedes didn't turn toward him. "It's over, Mercedes."

"Go away." A dry sob lifted her shoulders just once. A breeze returned to the garden and fluttered the carpet of green leaves around her. There was movement then silence. "Go away," she said again.

She turned and realized she was alone.

* * *

The evening meal was served in the family dining room. It had been years since the manor's cook prepared anything but plain fare. On the occasions when the earl had guests he brought in the cook he employed at his London townhouse.

In the earl's absence, Mercedes took the seat at the head of the table. Britton and Brendan sat on either side of her with Aubrey and Colin next to them. Sylvia, she noticed, took pains to have Aubrey's escort into the dining room and therefore, the chair beside him. Chloe sat opposite her sister, on Colin's right, and competed with Sylvia to see who could be the most charming. Even the twins came to the table politely subdued. Mercedes could only imagine that this rather remarkable display of good manners was to make up for their antics with the turret room. At any given moment she could glance up and catch one of her cousins looking a bit chagrined.

Mercedes wished she had given some thought to the menu. By the time it was clear to her that Colin and Aubrey were staying for dinner, it was too late. Not that there was anything wrong with beef and potatoes, but Cook's roasted fare was always on the well done side. Mercedes noticed, however, that everyone ate their fill. In the case of Mr. Jones, double that. The bread was fresh and warm and the carrots and onions still retained some of their natural flavor. The twins were delighted to discover there was custard for dessert.

Mercedes spoke little during dinner. There was enough conversation going on that she felt no need to contribute. When a comment or question was directed to her she responded, but it was an effort to stay with the topic at hand. Britton and Brendan were eager to know about the workings of the clipper ships, and in other circumstances she would have found Aubrey's colorful discourse as fascinating as everyone else, but this evening she could only think on what lay ahead for her and her cousins. Nothing about their future was settled. On the morrow she would have to deal with Severn and his demands while contending with the earl's disappearance.

The only bright spot Mercedes could see was that Colin

Thorne and his second would be gone from Weybourne Park. Upon her return from the gardens, Mrs. Hennepin informed her that Mr. Jones had arranged for his mount to be readied and his belongings secured. Mercedes doubted she could have made it through the meal if she hadn't been assured the Americans were leaving, not when she still burned with humiliation. She counted it as a success of sorts that she was even able to sit at the same table with Colin Thorne, though she expertly avoided making eye contact. She did not need to see herself reflected in his dark glance to recall every humbling moment of their last encounter.

At the end of the meal Mercedes politely offered her guests drinks while excusing herself and her cousins from their company. She waited until she had reached the far end of the hallway before she rounded on them. Her voice was quite deliberately a harsh whisper that would not carry back to the dining room. "It's all very well for you to be civil to our guests, but have all of you forgotten why they're here in the first place?"

The twins exchanged sheepish glances with Sylvia and Chloe. The cheeks of the young women flushed.

"All of you are acting as if there's nothing wrong," she said. Mercedes hadn't meant to share the burden she was carrying with them. There was nothing to be gained by distributing the weight of her worries to those who couldn't lift them anyway. She closed her eyes briefly and placed four fingers against her throbbing temple and rubbed. Her fingertips were a counterpressure to the ache building inside her head. "I'm sorry," she said after a moment. "It's not your fault. I'll think of something." Mercedes turned to go, placing her hand on the newel post at the base of the staircase. She had gone only one step when she was halted by Britton's earnest voice.

"We don't miss him," he said. "If that's why you think we should be sad, we can't."

Brendan chimed in as Mercedes turned to face the quartet. "We've already talked about it."

Mercedes looked to Chloe. "You've talked about it?"

"We've talked about little else," she said. "And we think—"

"It's better that he's run off," Sylvia finished for her.

It was Britton's turn again. "We don't mind losing Weybourne Park to Captain Thorne."

Mercedes's beautifully drawn brows arched at this comment. "You don't mind . . ." Her voice trailed off as she realized how little any one of them understood their predicament.

"He's won the wager," Brendan said simply. "This will be his home now though I don't think he should change the name. It's always been Weybourne Park."

Chloe patted her younger brother on the head, silencing him as he tried to wriggle out from under this attention. "We didn't realize at first that the captain meant for us to stay here. In my case, at least until I marry Mr. Fredrick."

"And the rest of us for as long as we like," Britton said.

Sylvia rested her hand on his shoulder, quieting him. "The twins will still go off to school. There's to be money for that." She flushed a little as she added, "And I shouldn't wonder that I'll find a suitable partner."

"I shouldn't wonder," Mercedes said slowly. She felt as though she were adrift on a turbulent sea. Each one of her cousins, from the safety of their own boat, was extending her some life-saving device and she was too stupid to comprehend its purpose or reach for it. In another moment she was going to drown.

"It will only be left to find someone for you," Chloe said. "But you needn't worry that the captain will make you seek other employment. We told him we couldn't possibly stay without you."

Mercedes surrendered to legs that were already wobbly and slowly lowered herself to sit on the stairs. Her hand drifted along the banister spindle until it, too, was beside her. To hear these words from Chloe who had looked to her for guidance the day before, was beyond any of Mercedes's expectations. To hear them in the context of all that had come before was the outside of enough. "You *told* him?" she asked, disbelieving. "You've had a discussion with Captain Thorne about my future?"

"About *our* future," Sylvia said, coming to her sister's rescue.

"The future of all of us. There's no getting around that we depend on one another and that mostly we've depended on you."

Chloe nodded. A tendril of pale hair fell over her forehead and she blew it away impatiently. "You didn't expect us to be comfortably settled by the captain's promises and not think of you?"

"The captain's promises . . ." she said on a thread of sound.

Britton giggled. "I say, Mercedes, you're just like that parrot Mr. Jones was telling us about at dinner."

"A parrot," she said dully, her face drained of every vestige of color. It was the second time today she'd been compared to that bird. "Yes, I suppose I am." Mercedes heard her own voice and realized how she must look to them. The bright expectancy in their faces was fading as they realized she was sharing none of their views. She took pains to force a smile. "I think it would be best if you'd retire to your rooms. I'll speak to the captain and hear these promises for myself." She noticed this statement did nothing to relieve their consternation.

Sylvia's pale brows had drawn together. "Oh, you're not going to ruin it for us, are you? Please say you won't."

"It's not as if it's charity," Britton said. "Well, not *exactly* charity."

"You mustn't be all stiff-necked about it," said Brendan.

Mercedes watched his glance stray to Chloe and she knew where he'd first heard the phrase. It was clear the four of them had spent a great deal of time discussing it. But when? she wondered. Had Colin Thorne already filled their heads with the way things might be before they locked him in the turret? That didn't seem likely. There only remained one other time when he might have spoken to them outside of her presence, and that was after he left her at the arbor.

Mercedes had been deliberately slow to return to the house, and when she finally arrived, she immediately went to her room to change for dinner. Now that she reflected on it, the north wing bedrooms had been suspiciously quiet and when dinner was announced, she was the first to arrive. The others, including Aubrey Jones and Colin Thorne, came *en masse* from the conservatory.

She had thought her cousins were showing Colin the indoor gardens, and perhaps he was sharing a bit of botanical knowledge with them. In retrospect, she doubted there had been any conversations about the hothouse orchids.

"I'll speak to the captain," she said again, trying not to sound too stiff-necked.

Perforce, they had to accept it. Chloe took Brendan's hand in hers and led him past Mercedes up the stairs. Sylvia followed with Britton in tow. The looks they cast in her direction were alternately pleading and concerned. None of them could catch her eye. To a person they all recognized her withdrawal.

Mercedes was still sitting on the staircase when the doors to the dining room parted and Colin and Aubrey exited. She rose to her feet as they approached the wide entrance hall.

"Miss Leyden," Aubrey greeted her. "We were just on our way to the drawing room to find you. I wanted to thank you for your hospitality."

Even standing on the first step, Mercedes was still not eye to eye with the red-headed giant, yet she was not at all uncomfortable looking up at him. "It's kind of you to say so, Mr. Jones. You're rather generous to offer thanks in the aftermath of your confinement in the north turret."

He shrugged that off. "The truth of it is, ma'am, that it gave me seven winks. I didn't pass a restful night at the inn."

Not knowing the reasons for his lack of sleep at the Passing Fancy, Mercedes was politely solicitous. She murmured all the proper things and wished him well on his journey back to London and then to Boston.

Unused to so much gracious attention, Aubrey shuffled a little uncomfortably. He couldn't know that she was immediately put in mind of the twins who would have also chafed at her concern. He made a brief nod, signaling his intention to go. "I'll only catch the coach at the inn if I leave now," he said.

"Yes, of course, I didn't mean to delay your departure." All she had meant to do was avoid speaking to Colin. In spite of what she told her cousins, Mercedes didn't think she could speak to the captain this evening. Or any other evening. It occurred to her as she sat alone on the stairs, that a letter would better suit her purpose. She could address her concerns with more thoughtfulness and not be distracted by anything he might say. "Good evening, then. To both of you."

It was only when she saw the look that passed from Aubrey to his captain that she knew she had mistaken the matter.

"Good evening," Aubrey said.

Colin's flat statement came simultaneously. "I'm not leaving."

Aubrey's widely spaced green eyes darted from his hostess to his master and he realized his presence was superfluous. In spite of his large size he managed to slip away unnoticed.

Mercedes was glad for the banister's support. Although she hadn't been able to face Aubrey squarely on this same step, she was almost eye to eye with Colin. "What do you mean you're not leaving? How can that be?" She immediately regretted the questions because she didn't care about the answers. Mercedes simply wanted him gone.

"Do you really want to stand here and discuss it?" Colin asked calmly. His eyes strayed with significant intent to the top of the stairs.

Mercedes followed his gaze behind her. She was quick enough to spy the tousled head of one of the twins though she couldn't say whether it was Britton or Brendan. It didn't really matter. Where one was, the other was lurking. Turning back to Colin, she said, "The library?" Again, she wondered at the question in her own voice, as if she were already deferring to him as lord of the manor.

"That will be fine."

Colin stepped aside to allow Mercedes to precede him. She had exchanged her plain gray gown for summery blue silk and the material, accented by the hallway's candlelight, shimmered as she moved. Like her day dress, this gown's neckline was cut high, showing off the slender length of her throat without revealing the livid weal arced around it.

Once inside the library, Mercedes lighted several candles on the narrow side table and the lamp on the earl's desk. She did not sit down, preferring to keep her disadvantages to a minimum. "So you can have no excuse for missing the London stage," she told him, "I'll keep my comments brief."

Colin realized that somewhere between the grand staircase and the library doors, Mercedes Leyden had found her voice. He nodded once, as if in agreement, and allowed her to have her say.

"I can only guess at what nonsense you filled my cousins with," she said. "They're of the singular opinion that you've won the wager for Weybourne Park and that you mean to accept it. They don't seem to view the earl's absence as a bad thing, though none of them are aware of Severn's alternate view of their father's disappearance. Further, they've got it in their heads that you mean to support them until such time they can fend for themselves. In the case of the twins that's a commitment of at least ten years, though I doubt they realize it."

Colin had eased himself into the chair behind the desk, picked up the letter opener, and leaned back. He turned it over absently in his palm as he listened to Mercedes. When she paused for a breath he looked up, his expression thoughtful. "Are you quite finished?" he asked after a moment.

"No."

His nod was meant to encourage her. "Go on, then."

"It's still to be seen whether you can collect on the wager in the earl's absence. And there's the matter of Severn's charges. Ceding Weybourne Park to you will only occur after a great deal of scrutiny. If indeed every turn of fate favors you, and Weybourne Park falls under your control, you've yet to show that you can manage the estate. It's all very well and good to make promises of financial generosity to my cousins, but do you have the means to support them? Weybourne Park takes a great deal of capital to run and if you think to turn a profit, as you Yanks are so fond of doing, think again. This estate will demand the last shilling from some very deep pockets before profit is possible—and that's if you hire a competent manager who knows how to treat the tenants and won't alter the books for his own benefit."

Colin continued to look at her consideringly. He wondered how long it would take before she exhausted herself. "Finished?"

"No," she said firmly. "Absentee landowners are a blight on this country. There are already too many men like my uncle who believe they can be supported with very little effort on their part. The tenants are neglected, the land overused. When crops fail, the weather, the pests, or the tenants are blamed. No one looks to the policies that are strangling trade and the will of the workers. What do you, an outsider, know about our politics? And how will you respond thousands of miles away plying your ship through the China Seas? Your roots aren't here. There can't be anything about Weybourne Park that you find satisfying beyond the means by which you think you earned it. What happens to the people who live here when you decide you've played overlong with this toy? Are all of them ever subject to the same whims that brought you here in the first place?"

Passion gave Mercedes's voice a husky resonance and her cheeks were touched with high color. She glanced at the clock on the mantel behind Colin. "You can still make the London stage, Captain Thorne. It would be better if you left. No one wants you here."

Colin said nothing for several long moments. Then, "Have you said your piece?"

Disheartened that he wasn't running for the door, Mercedes merely nodded.

"Then have a seat, Mercedes," he said. "I'm weary of looking up at you."

She knew the use of her given name was quite deliberate, meant to remind her of a familiarity she would rather not think about. There was no point in taking issue with him. He would simply do as he pleased. "I'm comfortable standing," she told him.

"It wasn't a suggestion."

As if the rug had been pulled out from under her, Mercedes

sat. Her small rebellion was not to do it comfortably. She perched on the edge of the wing chair, holding her back rigid, her shoulders stiff, and her hands clasped tightly in her lap. In minutes her muscles would begin to protest her uncompromising posture but Mercedes set her mind to withstand it rather than surrender.

Colin stopped toying with the letter opener and laid it down. In contrast to Mercedes, he was almost stretched out in his leather chair. His elbows rested casually on the arms and his fingers were folded over his flat abdomen. He tapped his thumbs together. Inclined as he was, with his head at an angle against the back of the chair, Colin's obsidian glance appeared to be more hooded than usual. He looked down the length of his aquiline nose at her, his firm mouth slightly parted. Even the cut of his chin was more defined by this angle.

"That was quite a speech," he said at last. Without warning he rocketed to his feet and shook off the cloak of patient deliberation as if it had been a hair shirt. Colin came around the desk and hooked his hip on the edge as he had done during his earlier meeting with Mercedes. In this way he teetered somewhere between relaxation and readiness, comfortable yet primed. It was Colin's most natural state. "As you might imagine there are some things with which I take issue."

Mercedes nodded regally as if bidding him continue when in truth she knew she couldn't have stopped him.

"Aubrey is on his way to London, not to board the *Mystic* as you assumed, but to seek out the solicitor I've hired. I agree that it may take some time for me to lay claim to Weybourne Park, but have no doubt that I will do so. To me, your uncle's disappearance is little more than an annoying complication. It's interesting that his own children don't see it so differently." Colin saw Mercedes open her mouth to interrupt and he held up his hand. "I gave you your piece," he said. "Now I want mine."

He watched her swallow whatever thoughts had made it to the edge of her tongue. Satisfied, he went on. "You have a great deal to say about me taking the helm at Weybourne Park, but can you honestly tell me things will be better with Severn in control?

When I put the question to Chloe she didn't think so. Sylvia actually shuddered, though perhaps she's given to dramatics. The twins made faces and I felt safe in taking that as a 'no.' "

As he spoke he saw Mercedes draw in her lower lip and worry it gently. She stared straight ahead, her gray eyes fastened on the wall of books opposite her. There was nothing there that interested her, he was sure. It was simply better than looking at him.

Her face was gravely set, but all the more lovely because of the simplicity of the attending features. Her brow was unlined and dark lashes shaded her eyes. The gravity of her expression was in the tilt of her chin and the thoughtful composition of her mouth. Except for the slight tug on her lower lip, the shape of her mouth was full and unmarked by a frown. She had not redressed her hair for dinner and the long day's activity had taken its toll on the severe style, softening it by loosening some of the pins and letting wisps of it free to frame her face with rich chocolate color.

His eyes dropped to her neck. As if she could feel his stare she broke her rigid posture long enough to lay one hand over it. It was the briefest touch, more soothing than protective. That gesture angered him almost as much as what lay beneath it. Mercedes Leyden shouldn't have had to comfort herself.

"As to my pockets," he said, "I can assure you they're deep. Not bottomless, but deep. I've mostly been rewarded for the risks I've taken and sometimes I've just been damn lucky." It was as much as she needed to know about the state of his finances. "I've looked around Weybourne Park and I'm quite aware of the money it will take to make her yare again."

He paused at her puzzled look. "It's a sailing term. It means make her ready."

For Mercedes it only bore home the obstacles facing him. Weybourne Park wasn't a ship. She'd never even considered the land having a gender, yet Colin referred to the estate as if it were a woman.

Colin went on, ticking off points on his fingers. "The main grounds are well kept but I doubt the same can be said for the land the tenants farm. There are repairs needed on the roof. Water damage to various rooms. The artwork's been decimated. Carpets need replacing and the wine collection's been savaged. And I haven't been privy to every room or the stables."

At the end of his recitation he saw Mercedes blink once. It was the only sign of her pain.

"As for employing a manager, I already have one in mind. I have confidence this person will be able to handle all the things you mentioned: the tenants, the land, the crops, the finances, the policies, and the politics. I have reason to believe my manager can gain respect of the locals and return Weybourne Park to the showplace it was meant to be."

Mercedes cringed. Weybourne Park wasn't a showplace. *It was her home.*

"As for being an absentee landlord," Colin said, "that's yet to be decided. I have no intention of being kept ignorant of what progress is being made here. If I leave, I'll visit often and stay as long as I'm able."

She wondered how he defined "often" and "long." Mercedes didn't ask. It shouldn't even matter to her, she thought. She wouldn't be at Weybourne Park to notice.

"As for roots," he told her, "they were torn out from under me when I was eight. In the twenty-one years since, I've taken pains to see that it can't happen again."

The sea was a perfect home for him, she realized. No one could uproot what wasn't planted. Then he surprised her.

"Weybourne Park is the closest I've come to taking back what might have been mine. I don't take this acquisition lightly, in spite of what you think. It wasn't a whim that put it in my hands. It was *my* effort and the effort of all those at *my* command that made it possible. I'm not the Earl of Weybourne and I don't aspire to his title. Let Severn have that dubious distinction if it's something one inherits.

"I don't look upon Weybourne Park as a trifling toy. I'm a man, not a child, and my interests are sustained, not fleeting. No one here needs to worry that I'll show the same disregard for this property as your uncle. If the tenants and the servants and those in my employ work with purpose and dedication they'll be provided for because they've earned it."

Colin let this last sink in before he made his final point. "And you're wrong to think there's nothing beyond the getting of this estate that satisfies me."

Mercedes had had enough. "Really?" she asked coolly, raising her face to him. "And, pray, what else is there you find satisfying?"

The edge of a smile shaped his mouth. He uttered a single word, "You."

Six

Mercedes had every reason to hope she would fall asleep easily that night. The events of the last thirty-six hours had exhausted her and she hadn't enjoyed much rest the evening before. As if that weren't enough, she drew her own bath water and lingered in the tub until the water went from steaming to tepid to cool. It was only as she was facing the prospect of actually climbing into the four-poster that she realized it would serve no purpose to do so. She would never sleep while the thoughts she had now were still tumbling through her head.

Colin Thorne's voice would not be silenced. His surprising announcement echoed without becoming any weaker. Repetition did not reduce its volume or power as it rolled through her mind. She could hear herself ask faintly: *And, pray, what else do you find satisfying?* And the answer, clear, distinct, and reverberating: *You. You. You.*

He had excused himself then. Mercedes only counted herself fortunate that he had not kissed her, for she had a picture of herself gaping at him and he had taken that as an invitation once before. If she could have found her voice, she might very well have screamed.

It was the idea of becoming hysterical that actually calmed her. It had never been her way to draw the notice of the others when she was upset, and she had no intention of allowing Colin Thorne to be the catalyst for change now.

Mercedes chose not to follow him and demand an explanation. It was her preference to pretend the exchange had never taken place, and she was successful for a time. The twins' bedtime rituals provided her with an agreeable diversion and if she went about the routine of turning down their beds and scrubbing behind their ears with more enthusiasm than usual, neither boy brought it to her attention. Both of them agreed, however, that her storytelling that night was unusually inspired.

After settling Britton and Brendan in their separate rooms, Mercedes prolonged the moment when she would be alone by checking on Chloe and Sylvia. The girls weren't artful enough to mask their surprise at seeing Mercedes, but their invitation to have her join them was genuinely felt. The topic of conversation was weddings, specifically Chloe's, and while Mercedes knew her cousin's lavish plans were only dreams prompted by Colin Thorne's promises, she wouldn't let herself think about that and entered into the spirit of the conversation.

Now, as she slipped her nightdress over her head, Mercedes wondered that she had done it. On the heels of that thought guilt arrived as her emotional companion. Mercedes sat down heavily on the edge of her bed and stared blankly at the opposite wall. It had been irresponsible to let Chloe go on making plans as if they could happen, but to join in and make extravagant contributions of her own was reckless.

Turning back the bedside lamp, Mercedes curled on her side on top of the coverlet. It was a fleeting thought to place blame squarely on Colin Thorne's shoulders, but the problem wasn't his promises, only that everyone wanted so badly to believe in them.

Everyone.

Including her.

Weybourne Park restored. It was a gloriously heady thought, the power of it almost seductive. Even the fact that she would have to accede to the demands and directions of an estate manager seemed secondary in importance to having the park's affairs in order again. She might have to give up some say, but she would not have to give up her home.

Suddenly chilled, Mercedes sat up. *You. You. You.* She could hear Colin's voice again and came to realize it had never been completely silenced. At what price, she wondered, would she be allowed to remain at Weybourne Park? And in the same vein, what was she willing to do?

The second question frightened her more than the first.

Mercedes went to her armoire and removed her robe and kid slippers. When putting them on did not arrest the chill, she was forced to recognize that her present state had nothing to do with the temperature of her room.

Mercedes set a lighted candle stub in a pewter holder and carried it with her to the library. Her attempt to find something to read was half-hearted at best. In the end she had to admit that there was nothing in the library that would capture her interest this evening.

In the hallway she paused again, torn between returning to her room and wrestling sleep into submission unaided, or arming herself for the bout with a cup of warm milk. The decision did not take long to make. She turned in the direction of the kitchen.

Mercedes thought later that perhaps it was because she had no real liking for milk, warm or cold, that made her pass by the stairs to the kitchen. She could think of no other reason that she was drawn further down the hallway. The manor was almost eerily quiet, so there was no sound that attracted her attention, and except for the passing of her own shadow on the wall, there was no movement. It didn't make sense to her that she would be compelled to seek out the sanctuary of the gardens, yet a compulsion was exactly what she felt. She tried to justify it as a purging of sorts, an opportunity to be done with the humiliation of her experience under the arbor.

The last person she expected to see when she stepped out onto the portico was Colin Thorne.

He was sitting on the wide granite balustrade, one knee drawn toward his chest, the other stretched out along the length of the gray stone. His right arm rested casually on his knee cap, the left was crooked behind his head, supporting it as he studied the night sky.

His hair, touched by starshine, was a pale beacon. The strong lines of his profile were clearly defined against the darker sky. Mercedes was struck by his quiet pose, the almost unnatural stillness of his posture, and was reluctant to intrude. It occurred to her that Colin Thorne was not a man who found peace easily, yet by design or accident, it had come upon him now.

Mercedes meant to step back into the house but she found herself lingering instead, her eyes drawn to the heavens as his were. Softly blowing out her candle, she allowed her vision to adjust. Pinpoints of light sharpened in the blue-black curve of the sky and the dusting of stars in the Milky Way became visible. On the horizon she could make out Sagittarius and overhead, the brighter lights of Cassiopeia.

"Do you know the stars?"

His voice came to her as if from a distance, but still calm and clear like the passage of sound over water. She lowered her eyes to look at him and realized he hadn't moved, had never turned in her direction. It had been her candle, she thought, that had given her away. The brief flash of light when she stepped onto the portico would have disturbed his night vision. She didn't know if she would have been so charitable with a breech of her privacy.

"I'm sorry," she said quietly. "I didn't mean—"

He didn't let her finish. "I asked if you knew the stars."

"A few."

Still looking up, he nodded. "Polaris," he said. "The north star. That's one worth knowing."

"I can rarely find it."

He made a casual beckoning motion with his right hand. "Come here. I'll show you."

Mercedes looked down at herself. The voluminous cotton nightshift she wore, as well as her robe, covered her modestly from neck to ankle, yet she could not deny that she was bothered by the impropriety of being in his company dressed as she was. It did not seem incongruous in the least that the previous evening she had been less troubled at finding herself half-naked in his bed. That, at least, had had some purpose attached to it. She knew that it was all in aid of carrying out her uncle's orders, and while it was not much comfort, it did help distance her from her actions.

There was nothing to protect her now except her own sense of what was right and proper. More troubling to Mercedes was that in the presence of Colin Thorne she seemed willing to redefine those notions.

Her wavering stance had physical expression as she swayed slightly on her feet, but it was only when he turned and his dark eyes rested on her face, that she finally stepped forward.

Mercedes cinched the belt of her robe tighter as she came to stand beside him. The protective, almost panicked gesture was not lost on Colin but he raised his face just in time to hide his smile. Pointing out the Big Dipper, he showed her how to use the two stars in the ladle to locate Polaris. "It's the tip of the handle of the Little Dipper," he told her.

"I suppose I always expect it to be brighter," she said, sighing. "The way I hear it talked about, it seems it should outshine every other star in the sky."

"It's not valuable for its magnitude," Colin said, "but for its steadiness. That's why it's critical for navigation."

Mercedes thought it was an apt description of herself. At Weybourne Park she was hardly a shining star, but everyone depended on her to provide guidance. Sometimes, as now, she felt the burden keenly. "I wonder where it finds its center?"

Colin looked at her, his eyes narrowing slightly as he studied her profile. Her eyes were still raised skyward and he doubted she even knew she had spoken aloud. The troubled journey of her thoughts was only hinted at by the slight downward turn of her mouth. As he watched, a small shiver ran through her. He did not mistake its source as outside her. He knew something about the demons that arrested one's sleep and chilled one's bones; it wasn't difficult to recognize when they were visiting someone else.

"That's Draco," he said, drawing her attention to his hand as he lowered it a fraction. "The Dragon. Its tail lies between the Dippers."

She nodded. "I see it." It was quite natural to move closer to him to take in the same vision as he, as though she might view the sky more clearly if she could see through his eyes.

Colin took the candle from her and set it aside. "Over there's Gemini. The brightest stars are Castor and Pollux."

"The twin sons of Zeus."

"That's right."

"Which is the brighter one?"

"Pollux."

She made a soft sound, something between awe and contentment. "My father used to watch the sky," she said after a moment. "He'd come out here on nights like this with his telescope and stay for hours. Sometimes I'd sit with him but usually I was shooed off to bed. Later, from my window, I could see that my mother had joined him. I think I was a little jealous of her for that." The admission surprised Mercedes. She ducked her head and stared at her feet a moment, wishing she might laugh the comment away. "I haven't thought of that for years," she said softly.

It was exactly the sort of night, Colin reflected, for thinking on things that were normally pushed to the back of one's mind. Something about the vastness of the blue-black sky and the singular clarity of the stars prompted the mind to wander as the eyes drifted from point to point.

"You must have been young when your parents died," he said.

The comment helped Mercedes focus. "Four."

It was as Colin suspected. Mercedes and Decker were of an age. He often found it difficult to think of his brother in any way other than as the child he'd been when he was led away from the workhouse. Looking at Mercedes now, it helped him imagine that Decker had grown up, too. "Are your memories of them very clear?"

"What do you mean?"

"Do you remember the way they looked? How they acted? Things you might have done together?"

The questions were not the ones she had come to expect, but then their deaths were rarely mentioned any longer. If it came up in conversation, it was usually behind her back in the guise of explaining how she had come to be the poor relation. "It's hard to say if I remember how they look," she told him. "I've always had the portraits in the gallery to remind me when my own vision became less distinct." She had been adamant that her uncle not sell them off. Mercedes always believed he gave in because it would have been too embarrassing to haggle over family portraits with outsiders, not because he couldn't get a great deal of money for them. "Next year I'll be as old as my mother was when she died, and I don't think I've ever appreciated how young that was."

"What about your father?"

"Twenty-nine."

"My own age," he said quietly. "It does shift one's perspective, doesn't it."

She nodded. "I don't know that I can tell you more. I've already mentioned about the star gazing and I hadn't even remembered that before tonight . . . or that I wished my father hadn't sent me away." She paused, trying to draw on other thoughts. "I know my parents were a popular couple among their set. Aunt Georgia told me that. But I also know they spent more time here at Weybourne Park than in London, even during the Season."

"And you? Did they take you to London?"

"No, I don't think so. At least not that I recall. My only memories of them are here. My father put me on a pony on my third birthday. I can see my mother standing by the paddock, her hands over her eyes, watching us through splayed fingers." Mercedes chuckled softly. "Poor Mama. It must have been torture for her, wondering if I'd be dropped on my head. Papa was adamant that I should learn to ride."

"Did you?"

"I must have. I can't imagine that I would have disappointed my father. But I don't ride any longer."

"Why not?"

"I'm terrified of horses," she said simply. "Oh, don't think my father was some ogre who insisted I get on a pony regardless of my fear. I'm quite certain I wasn't afraid back then."

"What happened?"

She glanced at him sideways and shrugged. "I'm sure I don't know. There are times I even imagine I miss it. I screw up my courage and get as far as the entrance to the stable, then I bid good day to the groom and pretend I only meant to go walking. My riding skirt gives away my real intentions, but Ben is polite enough not to mention it."

For all that she made her explanation lightly, Colin suspected the reality was more troubling for her. The fact that she made the admission at all impressed him. In his brief acquaintance with Mercedes Leyden the one thing he knew with certainty was that she was not given to vapors. If she could say she was terrified of horses, then her fear must have approached near paralysis.

"How did your parents die?" he asked.

Mercedes had been anticipating the question. There were any number of ways she could answer it, and each answer evoked a slightly different response. She chose the one that elicited the greatest reaction and left people stammering apologies. "They were murdered."

Colin merely tilted his head to one side and studied her gravely. After a moment he said, "Was their murderer found?"

She might have known he wouldn't think anything of pursuing the topic. Far from having put a period to his line of inquiry, she seemed to have piqued his interest. "There were two men charged and hanged," she said.

"Were they guilty?"

"What sort of question is that?"

"A reasonable one, I think. Or have I mistaken where Severn's accusations might lead? Doesn't he hope there's a noose waiting for me at Tyburn tree?"

Mercedes was caught off guard by this reasoning, but she understood where it was heading. "My parents' murderers were two highwaymen who were found wenching and drinking in a tavern not five miles from where they committed their crime. Besides my parents, the driver was also killed. They had items of jewelry that belonged to my mother in their possession. It was enough to convict them."

"They didn't confess?"

"My parents were the last in a string of robberies and murders along the same stretch of road. Only six months earlier another couple met the same fate. They had the misfortune to have had their three children with them."

"What happened to the children?"

Mercedes frowned slightly, thinking. "I don't know if I was ever told," she said finally. "I haven't thought of it for a long time. As for the murderers, Mrs. Hennepin says highwaymen don't confess to their crimes."

"That's probably true," Colin said. He leaned his head back against the marble post behind him and studied the sky again.

Mercedes turned a little so she could see him better. His silence was telling. "You don't believe it," she accused.

"I didn't say that."

"You didn't have to. You have a way of not saying anything that says everything anyway."

He slanted her a look. "How's that again?"

Mercedes's mouth twisted in a wry smile. "I don't think I can repeat it," she said. "But you knew what I meant."

"Yes, I did."

When this admission didn't lead to further explanation, only more silence, Mercedes didn't press. She had noted before that he had a suspicious nature and this was simply further confirmation. "What about your family?" she asked.

He had known, given the direction of his own questions, that a similar interest would be turned on him. It didn't mean he welcomed it. "What about them?"

"Do you have one?"

"No."

"No one?" It seemed incredible to her. Even she had cousins. "How can there be no one?"

"Because there's not." He relented a bit when he saw her thoughtful frown. She was sincerely troubled by this piece of news. "Not family, not the way you mean."

Mercedes realized she would have to be satisfied with that. For now. It hardly made any sense to her. A wide, childish yawn took her off guard. It was the first inkling she had that she was finally tiring. She picked up her candle and had to stifle another yawn. "Good night, Captain Thorne."

He let her get halfway across the portico before he said, "Lock your door, Mercedes."

In her dream it was the steady pounding of waves against the rocks that made her cover her ears. It was only when there was no abatement in the incessant, intrusive rhythms that Mercedes woke up. Groaning softly, she turned on her side and opened bleary eyes. She saw the door shudder in its frame and finally recognized the source of the noise.

The fact that there was knocking at all was a novelty. The twins seldom bothered to be so polite, no matter how often she admonished them to the contrary. It was unusual for Sylvia or Chloe to come to her room and Mrs. Hennepin and the maids announced their intention to enter with more of a scratching sound. The tempo of the pounding changed suddenly and became a staccato rat-a-tat-tat. The quickness of the beat led her to believe there was more than one pair of hands at work.

"Come in, Britton!" she called. "You too, Brendan. But softly, please." She lay back and waited for the onslaught. The door rattled but didn't open. From the firmness of the vibration Mercedes suspected this had been tried before. It wasn't until Brendan complained that it was still locked that she remembered Colin's parting warning and her decision to take him at his word. "Just a moment."

Mercedes slid out of bed. Her robe was lying over the arm of the chair and she picked it up, shrugging into it just before she let the boys in.

"Why did you lock it?" Britton wanted to know.

Mercedes noticed he was looking around guardedly as if he expected to find someone hiding.

Brendan boldly asked what his brother was only thinking. "Is it the earl? Has he come back to make trouble for us?"

That gave Mercedes pause. "The earl?" she asked sleepily. "Don't you mean Captain Thorne?"

Britton's suspicious expression vanished. "Oh," he said happily. "Is the captain in here, then? Severn's looking for both of you."

"Severn's here already?" Mercedes put a hand to her temple as the boys barreled into the room. They jumped on the bed in unison as if they hoped to dislodge Colin Thorne from beneath it. "There's no one under there," Mercedes said, glancing at the mantel clock. It was gone ten. She leaned against the door and continued to rub her temple. It was as though the boys' pounding had been transferred to her head. Their bouncing on the bed didn't help. She held up her hand and they stopped immediately, forgoing even one last rebellious rebound. They collapsed so dramatically the bed frame shook.

"Have you had breakfast?" she asked.

"Hours ago," said Brendan.

"Hours and hours ago," his brother echoed.

"Sylvia? Chloe?"

"They ate with us," Britton said.

Brendan nodded. "Now they're entertaining Severn in the drawing room. He said we should get you but we were going to do that anyway."

"That was very good of you," she told them. "Tell him I'm on my way and stay with your sisters until I get there."

Brendan pulled a face and his brother mirrored his distaste. "He doesn't like us underfoot," said Brendan.

Mercedes merely smiled. "When has that ever stopped you

two?" Indeed, annoying Severn was one of their most enjoyable pastimes. "Now go." She stepped aside to open the door and usher them out.

They jumped off the bed and gave her cheeky, dimpled grins as they scampered past.

She had no time to feel sorry for Severn even if she were so inclined. Mercedes washed quickly and purposely chose a floral print dress to wear. Severn could not possibly mistake it for mourning attire. She brushed out her hair and plaited it quickly in a French braid, then tied it off with a spring-green ribbon that matched the tiny leaves in her gown. She pinched her cheeks to lend them the color they'd lost when she realized Severn was in the house. For extra measure she pressed her teeth against her lips until they reddened satisfactorily. At the entrance to the drawing room she secured her mouth in its most gracious smile.

"My lord," she said, as she walked into the room. "My apologies for keeping you waiting. Chloe? Did you offer his lordship tea?"

Chloe nodded. Perched on the edge of the divan as she was, she made no secret of the fact that she wished herself elsewhere. Sylvia was beside her, similarly postured. Their eyes strayed in unison toward the heavy drapes.

The gesture was so lacking in subtlety that Mercedes marveled that Severn missed it. She supposed it was her own entry into the room that pulled his attention away from the girls and for that she was thankful. Chloe and Sylvia would not have forgiven themselves, or been forgiven, for spoiling the twins' fun. The two pairs of shoes peeking out from under the drapes were warning enough of how they planned to bedevil Severn this time.

A breeze eddied through the open window, shifting the drapes enough to reveal their ankles, and they decided it was time to strike. Jumping out from their hiding places, they screamed like banshees before they bolted for the door. Even prepared as she was, Mercedes gave a start. Chloe and Sylvia were moved to high-pitched giggles as much from relief as from surprise, while Severn actually came out of his chair with a cry. When he realized that he had been the target of the rear attack, his face flushed and his mouth thinned.

Mercedes motioned to the girls to leave quickly then she shut the door so he couldn't follow the boys easily. She rushed to placate him. "I shall punish them myself, Severn. I asked them to tell you that I was on my way, so you see, it's me they were disobeying. I never know what tricks they'll get up to."

"They're brats," Severn said tightly, his eyes still focused on the door.

"They're high spirited."

"They need a good caning."

Mercedes almost flinched at the suggestion. When her uncle wanted to mete out disciplined punishment, caning was the method he used. The boys already had stripes on their buttocks. Mercedes was only glad that the earl didn't often have the patience to manage it and could be goaded into using the flat of his hand or his fists before he found the cane. "I'll take care of the boys," she said again.

"You'll coddle them. Weybourne says you always do."

Mercedes took the opening Severn gave her. "You're speaking in the present tense," she said. "You've seen my uncle then?"

"A slip of the tongue, nothing more." Severn motioned to Mercedes to sit. Before he lowered himself into his chair he made a point of closing the window. He'd be damned before giving the twins another opportunity to make him the fool. "I have forty men with me this morning covering Weybourne Park."

"You're not joining the search?"

"My time is better spent here, with you. I hope you can be made to see reason."

Mercedes impressed herself by remaining calm. Statements to the effect that she was the one being unreasonable almost always got a rise from her. "Is that right?" she asked.

Severn was on his feet again, this time pacing the floor with slow deliberation. He paused only when he addressed her. "I suppose you imagine that you'll be permitted to remain here at

Weybourne Park," he said. "Have you asked yourself in what capacity you may serve?"

She simply stared at him, her clear gray eyes widening only marginally.

"You would be better off agreeing to come with me," Severn went on. "I'll see that the twins are placed in school and the girls have a proper dowry. I'll set you up in London, Mercedes, or the lodge at Rosefield if you prefer. You may choose the location and furnish the house to your liking. I'll see that you have a full complement of servants to manage it. You will finally be able to spend your days without worrying about finances and crops and tenants and . . . and whatever else it is that occupies your time at Weybourne Park."

Mercedes smiled politely. "You make it sound liberating, Severn."

"I'm certain you would find it so."

She went on as if he hadn't spoken. "But I'm unclear as to what would occupy my time if I had none of my usual concerns."

Severn paused again, this time taking full measure of Mercedes, gauging her sincerity. Color suffused his defined cheeks as he realized she was having him on. His mouth thinned and his narrow jaw tightened. The stare he leveled at her was cold. "I see you wish me to state it plainly," he said. "Very well, Mercedes. You will have enough to occupy you in my bed."

"Your bed? But I thought the house was mine. Surely that would make it *my* bed and give me the right to decide who I would entertain there. That is what you're suggesting, isn't it, my lord? That in exchange for the boys' schooling and the girls' dowries, I'll open my legs for you?"

Severn's eyes narrowed. "Weybourne didn't beat you often enough."

Mercedes heard the thinly disguised threat in his tight voice. Clearly it was a circumstance he meant to rectify. She could not help the shudder that went through her.

One of Severn's dark brows arched approvingly. "I see you understand," he said coolly.

Mercedes didn't respond. She watched him walk to the fire-place and stand on the green-veined marble apron. He raised one arm and let his elbow rest casually on the mantel. Mercedes recognized it as a practiced pose, one that he knew showed off his trim figure to its best advantage and made him seem more careless than he was.

Severn regarded her closely. "Are you really so eager to crawl into the Yankee captain's bed?"

"I haven't been asked," she said calmly. There was a tightening in her abdomen as she saw Severn's fist clench. With almost de-tached curiosity, as if she might not be his intended victim, she wondered how much damage he could inflict with that fist. Mer-cedes knew he boxed at his club. Did that make him more skillful with his blows than the earl, or was he just as viciously ham-handed? "Is this your idea of making me see reason?" she asked. "That I should believe your offer is somehow more sensible than the one Captain Thorne has yet to make? Don't bother answering. I can see for myself that it is. I'm only confused as to why you think I'd accept."

"What else will you do?" he demanded. "Take up employ-ment as a governess? What about the twins? You may find a position for yourself but no one will allow you to have the boys around. It *is* reasonable that I take up the responsibility of your care and welfare. After all, we're cousins, distantly related, to be sure, but blood nonetheless. Thorne may have rights to this prop-erty but he won't get the title. That will be mine someday."

A small vertical crease appeared between Mercedes's brow. "It sounds as though you've talked to the captain already."

"Of course I've talked to him," Severn said impatiently. "Not above an hour ago at the Passing Fancy."

"At the Passing Fancy," Mercedes repeated softly. She should have known. She wondered if he had spent any part of the night at Weybourne Park or if he ever had planned to. His parting comment that she should lock her door had been intended only to get a rise out of her. Now, knowing that he'd meant to nettle her, Mercedes wished she hadn't followed his advice. "Yes," she said. "I'd forgotten. You questioned him, then?"

"I had the sheriff with me. Mr. Patterson asked the majority of the questions."

"And?"

"And Thorne had a solicitor there to assist him with the answers." There was something faintly accusatory in Severn's tone. "You must have told him more than was good. He was very prepared for the meeting. He'd sent his second to London to fetch his man of affairs."

"I had to tell him something," she said. "You didn't want him to leave the area."

Severn dismissed her defense with a wave of his hand. "It seems that Thorne can make a decent account of himself on the night before the duel. The innkeeper supports his story that he had a woman in his room. The whore herself came forward to admit it." Had Severn not been distracted by a movement outside the window, he would have seen that Mercedes had blanched. "Damn," he swore softly. "He's coming now."

Mercedes twisted in her seat and followed the direction of Severn's glance. "Captain Thorne? He's here?"

Severn's mouth twisted. "You needn't sound quite so eager, Mercedes."

She came to her feet. "I'm not eager," she said. "You were so certain that he'd be charged with a crime, I confess I'm relieved that it hasn't happened. If I truly believed my uncle had been murdered, I'd feel differently, but it appears even the sheriff is not accepting your theory without the proof of a body."

Severn held his response. Beyond the drawing room they could hear Mrs. Hennepin greeting Colin and directing him to where he would find Mercedes and the viscount. Only seconds passed before the doors parted.

"Miss Leyden," Colin said politely, nodding in Mercedes's direction. His acknowledgement of her guest was considerably less warm. "Severn. Somehow I'm not surprised that you're here in spite of what you heard this morning. Though I expected you'd be dredging the pond for the earl, not making small talk with his niece."

Mercedes spoke so that Severn couldn't. She did not care for the way he was looking at Colin, as if the captain were an insect he'd enjoy torturing before he squashed it. "His lordship was explaining that you had your man of affairs present at the inn, while he brought the sheriff, but I have yet to learn what has been resolved by their presence."

"Then I'm in time," Colin said. "It's better that she learn it from me, don't you think, Severn? If you have any doubts that I'll be less than honest, you're welcome to stay and hear it again."

Severn stepped away from the fireplace, the expression on his sculpted face stony. "I'll excuse myself," he said stiffly. "Mercedes, you know you may count on me if what you hear is not to your liking. I am ever at your service." He made a short bow and left the room, deliberately brushing close to Colin as he passed.

Colin went to the window. He stayed there, saying nothing until he saw Severn leave. "He's a disagreeable sort, don't you think?" he said. "Did he offer for you?"

Mercedes wished she had had Mrs. Hennepin bring some tea to the drawing room. It wasn't because she was thirsty or hungry. Indeed, her appetite had fled and her mouth was so dry it was difficult to swallow at all. A teacup would have occupied her hands. Now they twisted in the folds of her gown and she could only hope they did not draw Colin's attention. She didn't want to know what he would make of her nervousness. "Yes," she said. "Severn made an offer."

One of Colin's brows lifted. "And?"

"And that would be between Severn and me."

He smiled narrowly. "Then you haven't given him an answer." Confident that was the case, Colin went on. "That means you're willing to listen to what I have to suggest."

"It only means that what I had to say to Severn is none of your business." Rather than being angered by her directness, Mercedes noticed that Colin's expression seemed appreciative, as if he might applaud her if it were appropriate to do so. It softened her a little. "But as it happens, I'm also willing to listen. I take it your presence here means you haven't been charged."

He nodded. "Much to your cousin's dismay, the sheriff was clear on that account. There can be no formal charges without proof that the earl is dead. Though the sheriff advised against it, that's why Severn brought his men to Weybourne Park. He thinks he can uncover what wasn't found yesterday. Mr. Patterson was sympathetic to Severn's concerns and is not dismissing the earl's disappearance as of no account, but he was clear that he wants to conduct his own investigation. He seems competent to the task. He's not accepting Severn's explanation without proof, but he's not dismissing it out of hand, either. Enough suspicion's been leveled at my head." He touched his throat. "The rope's on my shoulders waiting to be tightened around my neck."

Mercedes blanched a little at that picture. She sat down slowly and folded her hands in her lap. "But with no charges," she said, "aren't you free to go?"

"Not quite. Mr. Abernathy, my solicitor, says I could engage a counselor-at-law to fight it, but that's moot. I've already agreed to abide by Mr. Patterson's directive."

She frowned slightly. "Then you're not free to leave?"

"Let's say that for the next six weeks I've promised to be a relatively compliant prisoner of your fair country."

"Six weeks," she whispered hollowly. "How will you ever stand it? What about your ship . . . your crew?"

There was a hint of derision in his smile. He left the window and sat in the chair that had been last occupied by Severn. "Your concern for me is duly noted," he said. "But don't overplay your hand. It will make it more difficult for you to be gracious when you hear the rest of what I have to say."

Mercedes's chin came up as he questioned her sincerity. "I take it back now," she said, "before you go on. I hope you rot."

"That's better," he said approvingly. "As for rotting, you'll be certain to know. After all, Weybourne Park is to be my prison."

Air whistled as Mercedes sucked in her breath. "Here? You

mean they're making you stay here? At Weybourne Park?" For a moment she was actually dizzied by the implications. "I can't believe that Severn would permit it. Are you quite certain you heard Mr. Patterson correctly?"

"Should I ring for tea?" Colin asked with grave politeness. "No? Then something stronger? Perhaps not. You look as if you'd throw it in my face."

That he had correctly read her mind bothered Mercedes. She made an attempt to school her features and react with less abandon. "How did this come about?"

Colin leaned back in his chair. "You were quite right to suppose that Severn didn't approve," he said. "As it happens, he had no say in the matter. Mr. Abernathy had all the papers in order, showing the wager as agreed to by Weybourne and me. There was supporting documentation from witnesses as well as evidence from creditors that clearly showed the earl couldn't make good on his wager without forfeiting this estate."

"Quite a lot to come by on such short notice," she said coolly.

"My man's been working on it since Weybourne issued this last challenge. I like to be prepared for any eventuality."

"Still, it's rather suspicious, isn't it? One might be led to believe you put your house in order in anticipation of this very thing happening, perhaps even that you are the architect of the plan."

Colin gave her an arch look. *"Et tu?"* he asked. "Severn said that very thing." He knew she had no liking for being painted with the same brush as Severn. Though he didn't show it, her struggle not to pull a face amused him. "Once Abernathy showed Mr. Patterson that everything was in order, the sheriff really had no choice but to agree that I could take temporary possession of Weybourne Park. It's a clumsy compromise at best, but for six weeks it's a tolerable inconvenience."

Tolerable for whom, Mercedes wanted to know. She stopped worrying her lower lip and actually bit her tongue to keep from asking the question.

"I'll remain in England, available to the magistrate and

authorities for questioning, while the search for your uncle continues. At the same time, I'll be afforded the opportunity to make Weybourne Park mine by legal means. At the end of six weeks, if the whereabouts of your uncle are still unknown, my petition for the Park will be ready for review in court."

"Then you don't actually own the estate now," she said.

"No. But neither do you." He saw her shoulders sag a little at this reminder. "And you have no means to get it."

"You not only stab," she said quietly, "you also twist the knife."

"I get no pleasure in it."

That, at least, was true. His expression was stoic, not gloating. "And what of Severn's claim to Weybourne Park?"

"As you noted yesterday, it's really his father's claim if he chooses to pursue it. I get the impression the Earl of Rosefield may not be as eager as his son to take on this estate. Nothing was said to that effect; it was merely something in Severn's manner that made me suppose it."

"I told you this estate would draw heavily on one's financial resources. The earl is of a more temperate nature than his son, and considerably more cautious."

"Perhaps Severn's father doesn't know *all* of Weybourne Park's assets."

In spite of her best intentions, Mercedes bristled. "What do you mean by that?"

"I think you know. You said Severn made an offer. That's a pretty clear indication that he wants you."

"Oh, Severn was quite clear," she said.

"I also have an offer."

Mercedes steeled herself. It crossed her mind to wonder if she'd slap him, but then the thought was gone. She knew she wouldn't. Whether for herself or someone else, she abhorred hitting out as means of expression. "Well, Captain Thorne?"

Colin studied her with his darkly reflective eyes. He liked her hair. The way she'd braided it close to her scalp altered the shape of her eyes, lending them a faintly provocative slant. Her features were clear and composed, though he suspected that composure was a struggle to maintain. Her complexion was smooth, but pale. The unnatural flush that he had noted when she'd been speaking to Severn had long since faded. Her long, dark lashes were lowered to half mast, shading her expressive gray eyes. Somehow she was managing not to tug on her lower lip, a mannerism that invariably signaled she was worried or deep in thought.

Colin appreciated the way she faced him, with her head held up and her slender throat exposed. It was rather a fearless pose and his eyes skimmed the line of her neck before they lifted to meet her gaze squarely.

"As you know," he said, "I spoke to Sylvia and Chloe and the twins yesterday before dinner. I think they must have told you some of it. It's the only explanation for your tirade after Aubrey left for London."

Mercedes smiled wanly. "Please," she said. "Get on with it."

Colin nodded. "I will see that Britton and Brendan are educated in the public school of your choice and I will support Chloe and Sylvia with dowries, provided you approve of the matches."

Had he talked to Severn? she wondered. Though Colin made some noises about consulting her, thus far the offers were remarkably similar. Mercedes felt confident in finishing for him. "And in return, Captain Thorne? Is it a house for me in London complete with new furnishings and a full staff to do my bidding? Or did you think to keep me here at Weybourne Park and frequent my bed at your will? That would be less expensive for you and tolerably convenient for both of us." She placed an index finger on her chin as though musing about her future. "Perhaps you will see fit to give me an allowance for new clothes and jewelry. That would make you more agreeable than Severn. He never got around to mentioning an allowance at all. We argued for a while about whose bed it would be, mine or his, but I think you can see my point that if it's my London house, it must be my bed." She feigned puzzlement. "There might be some confusion here, though, what with your bed and my bed both being so readily available." She brightened, her face clearing. "I know. I'll come to your room on the even days and you may come to mine on the odd ones. That's fair, don't you think?"

Colin had been following Mercedes's line of reasoning carefully so he didn't have to think long about it. "Very reasonable," he said pleasantly, watching her closely. "I assumed that if you accepted my offer to manage Weybourne Park, I'd have to pay you a wage, but if you're willing to barter your skills for my services in bed, I find I'm agreeable."

Mercedes blinked.

Her reaction was so priceless, like a baby owl seeing the world for the first time, that Colin actually laughed aloud. It was a deep sound, low and rumbling and hearty. For all that he did it so rarely there was nothing tentative about it. A lock of his bright blond hair fell forward and he raked it back, tempering his laughter at the same time.

Lowering her head, Mercedes stared at her folded hands. She waited for silence. "You didn't have to let me go on," she said quietly. "You've never hesitated to interrupt me before."

She probably didn't want to hear that she'd never been so entertaining. "I apologize," Colin said. "You're right. I could have stopped you."

Mercedes didn't ask him why he didn't. It wasn't hard to imagine that he had found her speech something of a wonder. In his place she might well have been struck dumb. Right now her tongue was cleaved to the roof of her mouth.

Colin's gaze rested on her bowed head. "I take it Severn's offer was not a marriage proposal."

The gentleness of his voice washed over her. She shook her head.

"I didn't know that," he said. "I wondered about it before, but today . . . well, today I thought he meant to marry you. I was less certain what your answer would be."

"I told him no." She lifted her head slowly but her eyes did not meet Colin's. She looked at a point past his shoulder. "It was easy to do."

"And if it had been an offer of marriage?"

"My answer would still have been no. Severn and I wouldn't suit."

"I see."

"I doubt it," she said. "Severn may be closer to your age than the earl's, but he was always my uncle's friend. That doesn't endear him to me or my cousins. The twins can't abide him and the girls merely tolerate his presence. He's never been a frequent guest at the Park, but then no one has. The earl was particular about that. As for Severn liking any of us, I can't imagine that it's true. He took pains to mention that he would send the boys to school and provide for the girls, but that's because he doesn't want to think about them or have them underfoot."

"And they would be outside of your protection," Colin said.

Mercedes gave him full marks. "You *do* understand." She twisted a tendril of hair and tucked it behind her ear. "Severn's only interested in controlling me. With the boys at school, out of my reach and sponsored by him, he supposes I'll be amenable."

"Amenable?"

"To whatever he wants." She saw Colin's frown and supposed that plain speaking was in order. "I know what's expected of a mistress," she said, "but I've heard that Severn's tastes aren't—"

Colin held up his hand. "I've heard the same thing."

"You have?"

He nodded but didn't explain. Molly and her sister had been his sources. Prior to the meeting with Severn and the sheriff he had talked to both women. When they realized it was the viscount who was making the accusations, they had a few of their own. It seemed that slap and tickle with Marcus Severn was more slap than tickle. "That leaves my offer," he said after a moment.

"You would hire me to manage Weybourne Park?"

"That's what I meant when I said Severn's father didn't know *all* of the estate's assets."

Mercedes pressed her lips together remembering how she had reacted to that statement.

"You'd be in charge of the daily operations," he said. "I would have final approval on the larger expenditures, of course, but in most things I imagine I'll defer to your judgment. During the six weeks that I'm here, I'll expect you to teach me about the estate. Your main task will be to make certain I understand what crops are raised, how the tenants are dealt with, what taxes I must pay, and all the rest. Together we'll establish a list of items due attention and decide which will receive priority."

Mercedes thought surely he could hear her heart slam. The roar in her ears made it difficult to hear. He was not forcing her out of Weybourne Park and he was not demanding her in his bed for the privilege of staying. He was offering the very thing she wanted.

"Well, Mercedes?"

She knew he was waiting for a reply. She could see the expectant look in his dark eyes even though the edges of her vision were blurred now. She saw his mouth moving but his voice was muffled by the rush of blood to her head. To give him her most heartfelt reply Mercedes came to her feet.

And dropped like a stone.

Colin looked over at her slender body slumped across the divan. She had narrowly missed falling on the floor. He shook his head as he moved to lift her. "I hope I can take this as a yes."

Seven

Mercedes came to consciousness while she was still in Colin's arms. There was little time to protest the arrangement or even to wonder if she enjoyed it. Moments after waking she was being lowered to her bed.

A veritable crowd hovered in the hallway. Mr. and Mrs. Hennepin were there. The twins. Two of the upstairs maids and the cook's helper. Chloe and Sylvia. She realized they must have trailed after Colin while he was carrying her. Colin, she noticed, was ignoring the on-lookers or oblivious to them. He didn't turn in their direction until Mercedes struggled to rise to a half-sitting position, supporting herself on her elbows.

Colin placed one hand on her shoulder and pushed her back. The gentle pressure he exerted was met with no resistance. He interpreted her small sigh as gratitude for not leaving the explanation to the gathering to her.

"Rest," he said. There was more command in the single word than tender admonition. Colin had been in charge of others too long for it to be otherwise. But he had also spent enough time with Mercedes to know she rarely responded as one of his crew. It was a true measure of her exhaustion, he thought, that she didn't argue with him.

The group in the hallway parted as he approached. Colin shut the door behind him as he stepped outside. "Miss Leyden will spend the day in her room," he said. "Mrs. Hennepin, if you would be so good as to see she has a light breakfast. Otherwise, all of you, let her be."

As an explanation it was lacking in content and there was an exchange of apprehensive glances. None of them moved.

Mutiny, even as tentatively staged as this one, was a new experience for Colin. He studied their faces, wondering at their motives. When it came to him, his dark eyes became even more coldly remote. "I didn't beat her," he said. Colin didn't wait to see if he was believed. He simply walked away.

Mercedes was horrified when the story was related to her, first by the twins, then by Mrs. Hennepin, and still later by Chloe with Sylvia offering breathless asides. Now that they knew she was truly all of a piece, they were embarrassed by the question they had never put to the captain. To a person they described Colin Thorne's anger as more terrible to look upon than anything they had ever experienced from the Earl of Weybourne.

Mercedes found she could not broach the subject with her new employer. It would have raised other questions that she was equally reluctant to answer. It was humiliating enough that he had seen the welt raised by her uncle's quirt. To discuss the extent of the abuse she had suffered at the earl's hands would have been difficult, but even more troubling for Mercedes was the fact that she had been unable to protect others from the same punishments. If that came to light, how could Colin Thorne judge her in any way less harshly than she judged herself? If he suspected she could be so weak-willed, ineffective, and powerless, would he still want her to manage Weybourne Park? To Mercedes's way of thinking there could be only one answer.

Mercedes's confinement to her bed accounted for only a fraction of her renewed energy over the next ten days. The real source of her vigor lay in her sense of purpose, and in smaller measure, her panic. She set herself the task of proving to Colin Thorne that she was firm and capable and strong and that his decision to set so much responsibility on her slender shoulders was not a misguided one.

Weybourne Park was eight hundred acres of prime agricultural land. At a distance the open fields appeared to be a patchwork quilt of organic productivity. It was upon closer inspection that the true state was revealed. Although the soil was rich for corn and wheat, sections had been allowed to go unseeded and bore no crop save for weeds. With too few tenants to manage the fields, the perimeters had been ravaged by birds and deer. Some of the stone cottages had been abandoned and others looked as if they should have been. As with the manor, there were roofs in need of repair and rotting timbers in the floor. While each family seemed to have enough vegetables, compliments of the carefully tended gardens at the rear of the cottages, Colin saw their stores of meat were low or nonexistent.

This observation puzzled him because there was much of Weybourne Park that was not given over to raising corn or wheat or sheep or cattle. In addition to the acres of farmland and pasture, there were deeply wooded areas where game was abundant. So abundant in fact, that it was destroying the crops.

The answer, he discovered, was that the earl had strictly forbidden hunting on his land. He did not deny himself or his friends that right, only his tenants. With pained honesty Mercedes told him that her uncle had made criminals of them all, forcing them to poach on the very land they tended, and placing her in the difficult position of covering for them.

Although Colin was certain Mercedes did not intend it, each day brought him some new revelation about the Earl of Weybourne. His crass disregard for his family's welfare and his selfish dedication to his own pleasures were at the root of the park's steady deterioration. That the decline had neither been swift nor complete was not the earl's fault. The single-minded pursuit of his personal satisfactions should have destroyed Weybourne Park years ago. It was the presence of Mercedes Leyden that had drawn out the denouement for more than a decade.

Colin had evidence of it again and again. Whether they were touring the fields or the pasture or the wood, he was given reason to be impressed by Mercedes's knowledge. She understood the demands of the land and what it required to make it productive.

The remaining tenants stood fast in their loyalty to her. The ones who had been forced to abandon their cottages had done so reluctantly and often because they had been threatened with eviction by the earl.

It was a similar story in the manor. Soon after Wallace Leyden had inherited the title and the estate, the servants came to the realization they could not expect the same treatment from this earl as they had received from his older brother. For those who had known both men as children it was more anticipated than not. There were some immediate defections. Those who had not worked at the manor long looked for positions elsewhere, sometimes even leaving their employment without a character to recommend them at another post. There were those who remained out of fear of not being able to find positions elsewhere, but most who stayed did so because they held a sense of duty to the late earl, his countess, and their daughter.

Mercedes may have come to this loyalty by default but it remained hers because she earned it. When her aunt died at the birth of the twins, Mercedes was sixteen. Responsibilities she had previously shared with Georgia were now hers to manage alone.

It wasn't from Mercedes that Colin learned these things, but from Mrs. Hennepin and others. While they toured the house and the grounds and made their lists of priorities and expenditures, Mercedes spoke little on any subject save Weybourne Park. She opened doors to him throughout the manor and was free with information about the use of the rooms, but allowed no entry into her own thoughts.

Colin learned there was a specific location for almost every imaginable task occupying the servants: lamp trimming, boot blacking, laundering, ironing, mending, polishing, and cooking. Like rabbits in a warren, the servants moved freely out of sight of the family as they went about their assignments in the nether regions of the house.

The family's movements were in the open but with no fewer choices. One could spend an afternoon in the gallery or the conservatory. There were two dining rooms, neither of which should be confused with the banquet hall, a library, a music room, and three distinct drawing rooms where one might entertain guests of different stations. On the upper floors, areas for dressing adjoined the bedchambers and reading rooms were available if one didn't want to go to the library. There was a school room for the twins and a nursery that had never been given over to any other use. Then there were the turrets, one sparely furnished and one not furnished at all.

Colin's polite refusal to spend much time there prompted Mercedes's beautiful smile. He was struck by what a rare thing it had become these last ten days. He had not been ignorant of the fact that she wanted to prove herself competent. He only wondered that she considered it necessary.

"Would you like to ride this afternoon?" she asked as they wended their way down from the turrets.

He was aware of her small considerations. Mercedes never kept him indoors all day long. She structured his education of Weybourne Park so there were activities that took them outside. An inventory of a half-dozen rooms would be followed by a walk to one of the streams that cut the southern portion of the property. Careless of staining her dress, Mercedes would sit on the grassy bank beside him while he fished. She felt no need to fill the silence with the sound of her own voice but Colin often found himself asking questions just to listen to her. She had a pleasant, almost husky timbre that was as soothing as it was engaging. As a fishing companion she was most agreeable. It was also in her favor that she didn't mind baiting the hooks, a task that had never been to Colin's liking.

Fishing was not the only outdoor activity she made available to him. Explaining that he could learn about the state of the Park's financial problems just as simply on the portico, she had Mrs. Hennepin serve them tea there and they studied the ledgers in the bright sunshine while sharing cakes and pots of spiced orange tea.

Sometimes they were joined by others. The twins liked to ride and they flew hell bent for leather over the rolling pastures in pursuit of Colin. Mercedes stayed back, arranging a picnic lunch on a shady knoll, and watched with dread and longing as the trio scattered clusters of sheep across the hillside. When they returned, Britton and Brendan would have healthy color in their cheeks and flash happy grins that Mercedes found deeply satisfying. That Colin found their company enjoyable filled her with unexpected pleasure.

Chloe and Sylvia could be counted on to escort Colin to the village. They could be as energetic in chasing down a new hair ribbon as their brothers were at dispersing sheep. Mercedes did not attend Colin on these shopping ventures, and though she was quite specific with the girls about not pressing him for favors, they invariably returned with some astonishingly fashionable adornment for their bonnets. Mercedes wished she could be more suspicious of his charity and less accepting of it.

She thought of that now as she walked along the narrow lane to the Thayers' cottage. Under her arm she carried a basket of fresh linens, ointments, and infant gowns for Mrs. Thayer's newborn. There was also a flask of brandy for Mr. Thayer. All of it was made available through Colin's generosity. The Thayers had been in immediate anticipation of the arrival of their fifth child when Mercedes had introduced them to the captain. On that occasion she had been struck by the ease with which he lowered Mrs. Thayer's guard by inquiring as to her health and showing an interest in her four other children. Mr. Thayer, laconic by nature, was almost verbose as Colin consulted him about the management of the dairy. Mercedes knew Colin could not have prompted those responses had his interest been anything less than sincere. Mr. Thayer had had plenty of dealings with the earl and was not one to be taken in easily.

On a second visit, one day following the birth, Colin was accepted with almost as much warmth as Mercedes. The initial misgivings, as brief as they had been, were gone now. If there was any doubt, Mr. Thayer proudly announced they had named their new daughter Colleen. Mercedes hid her smile behind her hand as the curtain was lifted on Colin's normally unreadable expression, and he demonstrated without words that he was capable of great feeling.

Caught up in this memory, wondering at warmth that came to her face as she thought of it, Mercedes didn't notice that her shadow had been joined by another until it was too late to react. A gloved hand closed over her mouth from behind and she was dragged into the abandoned tenant's cottage she had just passed. What had been dusk outside became as dark as pitch once she was thrust inside and the door was pulled closed. She expected release but it wasn't given. The leather glove smelled of horses and sweat. It pressed against her mouth with such force that her teeth were ground into her lips. She tasted blood and could do naught but swallow.

"You would do well not to scream," the voice at her ear said. "It can't go but badly for you after that."

The sibilantly whispered threat could have been expected to strike a chord of terror in any other victim. It was too familiar to Mercedes to have that effect. She was not so much a fool that she wasn't afraid. This was her uncle, after all, and she knew fear would keep her sharp, while terror would have paralyzed her. Forcing herself to remain quiet, giving him no reason to tighten his brutal grip, Mercedes managed a small nod.

His lordship felt the movement that signaled cooperation. He had expected nothing less from her. He eased the punishing pressure of his hand but did not lift it away entirely. "Hear me out," he said lowly.

She nodded again and this time the hand was removed. Mercedes spun away from him and stumbled on the uneven floor. In some distant part of her mind she found it odd that her uncle could so naturally step forward to assist her, as if he had no part in causing her distress in the first place. This ability of his to act in ways that were so incongruent was the part of his character that alarmed her the most. Mercedes was careful not to spurn the hand he held out to her. More pain had always followed that incautious gesture. Using his hand to steady her, Mercedes drew herself up.

Her eyes were gradually becoming accustomed to the darkness. It was not as impenetrable as it first appeared. There were shades of blue and black that defined her uncle's shape against the background of the door. The narrow breadth of his shoulders was evident but the rest of his body was made indistinct by the cloak he was wearing. The gold splinters in his brown eyes glittered even more brightly in a face that was so deeply shadowed. She realized that her uncle hadn't shaved in all the days since his disappearance. In a man as fastidious as the earl, this omission could only have been deliberate.

"You're so pathetically predictable," he said. He pointed to the basket she still clutched under one arm. "A basket of goodwill for Weybourne Park's newest addition. Food?"

Mercedes thought he said this last rather hopefully. She wondered if he was hungry. She had never given a moment's thought as to how he might have fended for himself. If she had, she would have supposed that some friend could have been pressed into offering assistance while remaining silent about it. It occurred to her now that perhaps the earl had no acquaintances who could provide help *and* confidence.

Lord Leyden took the basket from Mercedes when she was too slow to answer. Rooting through it carelessly and spilling the clean linens on the floor, he came across the flask of brandy. He tossed Mercedes the basket and while she stooped to gather the discarded items, he opened his prize and drank deeply. "Better than food," he said after a moment. "Tell me. Was the brat a boy or a girl this time?"

"The Thayers have a baby girl," Mercedes said carefully. She didn't mention the child's name. Her uncle might make the connection and it would only sour him.

The earl's grunt could have meant anything. "As soon as I heard the brat squealing I knew you'd be coming around. I just didn't know if you'd come alone this time." He heard the small gasp she was too slow to stifle. "Yes, I've been watching you. I don't know why that would surprise you. No one is observing mourning so I surmise that all of you believe I'm alive."

"Severn did his best to convince us otherwise."

He ignored that. "You must have known I wouldn't go far from Weybourne Park, not at least until I have all I need."

"You've been here all this time?" It didn't seem possible. The entire estate had been searched. Then she realized that following Severn's lead, the search parties had been looking for a body, not tracking a man on the move. An experienced, exceptional hunter himself, the earl had probably found it almost laughably simple to elude them. "Why haven't you shown yourself?"

Lord Leyden took another swallow of brandy. He was of no mind to answer her questions. "There are several things I require of you," he said. "All well within your power to accomplish, so you needn't think I've set forth the labors of Hercules. I will need several changes of clothes. You will go to my room and neatly pack two valises. Do not stuff them so full that they become a burden to carry."

He was speaking of the burden to himself, she thought, not of the trouble she might experience in bringing them to him. Mercedes held the basket up in front of her, as if it might shield her from subsequent requests.

"You will also pack each valise with foodstuffs. Bread and fruit will be adequate." Almost as an afterthought he added, "Another flask of this brandy would not come amiss."

There would be more, Mercedes knew. It could not be so easy.

"Pack my pistols," he said. "The ones in the mahogany case." There was a slight pause, then, "I will need money, of course."

Mercedes was visited with a gnawing sensation in the pit of her stomach. His request for his dueling pistols was of little concern next to his demand for money. "Money? But there's nothing. My jewelry—"

"Bother that," he said dismissively. "I'm not going to call attention to myself by pawning jewelry, especially that which is of so little value."

The cruelty of this last remark almost made her cry out. Her most precious pieces, her inheritance from her mother, had been sold off long ago, years before she had had any understanding of their worth in terms of wealth. For Mercedes it was the sentiment attached to the ear clips and necklaces. They had glittered around her mother's neck and adorned her ears. There had been diamond-studded hair combs and delicate gold lockets, bracelets that sparkled with rubies and a choker of emeralds that was like a circle of green ice around her slender throat.

Some items had been especially valued by Mercedes: ivory combs, a string of pearls, a sapphire ring in a platinum setting. These were the pieces her mother had been wearing the night she was murdered. They were the same pieces recovered from the highwaymen. Four years later they were irretrievably lost to her, on this occasion because the earl made an unconscionable wager involving his pair of matched grays and the speed in which they could make Land's End from London. Her Aunt Georgia had waited until bedtime to tell her of the earl's folly and its consequences. At eight years of age, Mercedes had been inconsolable.

Some of her profoundly felt anger returned and threatened to overwhelm her ability to reason or think. She swayed on her feet and was glad for the cover of darkness that hid this weakness from the earl. "If you don't want jewelry," she said, "then I don't understand. There's nothing left." There was the money she had set aside for the boys' education, and the earl, if he knew about the fund, also knew she couldn't touch it. She had made that arrangement deliberately, knowing there could come a time when pressure might be applied. "I don't know what you think I can do for you."

She felt his eyes boring steadily into her and then she knew. "Oh, no." Mercedes actually backed away. There was a chair behind her and it caught the back of her knees. Still clutching the basket, she dropped into it. "You can't expect me to—"

The earl cut her off. "What I expect is that you'll get it from Captain Thorne."

"Steal it, you mean."

"Acquire it," he corrected. "In whatever manner suits you. Don't forget, I've seen you with the captain . . . walking through the gardens . . . picnicking in the fields . . . you may only have to ask him for it. He seems to be in your thrall."

"Then you mistake your eyes. Captain Thorne is in no one's thrall, least of all mine."

"And you underestimate your allure. You always have."

A shiver snaked along Mercedes's spine. It was no compliment the earl paid her, not when it was said in those insidiously intimate accents. "I can't ask him for money," she said. "Every expenditure is made with some purpose. He would know if I didn't use the money as planned."

"So? By then I'd be gone." It was not his concern.

"He manages the finances with drafts," she told him. "They're drawn on his bank in London. There's no coin to be had."

Far from being dissuaded, the earl found this news to his liking. "Better yet," he said. "You'll make a draft to me in the name of . . . Ashbrook and Deakins"

"Your tailors?"

His mouth tightened at her needling. "Merchants. You may decide the specifics. From the activity surrounding Thorne's ill-advised acquisition, it seems that you must be conducting business with any number of tradesmen. You'll think of something that will allay his suspicions."

Mercedes doubted it. "He has to sign the draft himself."

"Not if you practice his signature."

"I can't do that!"

"That's not a choice, Mercedes." He paused, letting her take that in. "You're probably wondering what I can do if you deny me. You'd be better to think on what I *can't* accomplish. It would occupy less of your time. I see the boys come and go from the manor as they please. Separately or together, they make easy targets. For capture or killing. How long do you think they would willingly stay inside?"

What he was suggesting took her breath away. Mercedes could only stare at him.

"Do you imagine you'll go to the good captain with this story?" he asked. "What will protect any of you then? Not Thorne. He ha obligations to his ship and his men. Even your estimable captai cannot be everywhere at once. You will always have to look ove your shoulder, Mercedes. Can you imagine living what's left o your life like that?" He let the silence that followed speak fo itself. "You *do* understand," he said at last.

"How much?" she asked hollowly.

"Two thousand pounds."

Mercedes did not have the presence of mind to be shocked by the sum. She was numb. "And what does this purchase?" she asked.

"Your freedom," he said, shrugging. "My freedom. I suppose it depends on your point of view." He chuckled lowly, pleased by his ability to wax philosophical at such a time. "I intend to leave England. You can be assured my fortune awaits on another shore."

Hope soared in her. "You mean it?"

"Your eagerness is less than complimentary," he said dryly "but I suppose you have your reasons. Yes, I mean it. My destination, however, is to be my own secret. Once I'm gone you may be inclined to tell the captain where I'm going. I have no desire to look over *my* shoulder."

Being free of the Earl of Weybourne would be worth keeping the secret, she thought, but she didn't tell him that. Two thousand pounds suddenly seemed a paltry sum. She would have been willing to forge Colin Thorne's name to a draft for twice that amount and take any punishment he delivered for her crime. "Have you spoken to Severn?" she asked. "Does he know of your plan?"

The earl waved her questions aside. "By morning," he said. "I'll require everything before first light. And don't think to trap me here. I'll know if you have an escort."

Trapping him was the last thing on her mind. Gone. She wanted him gone. And one more thing. Mercedes believed she was finally in a position to press it. "Accept Britton and Brendan," she said.

Leyden blinked. The flask rested lightly against his lip and he didn't drink. He lowered it slowly. "What?"

"Acknowledge the twins as your rightful heirs," she said. "What difference can it make to you? You're leaving. The estate will be in Captain Thorne's hands. Why should you care if Britton has the title? More to the point, why should Severn get it? You've always known the twins are yours. It's been spite that makes you hard-hearted against them. Aunt Georgia was never unfaithful to you. You only despised her for not being my mother."

Mercedes had pressed her point too hard. The cover of darkness had given her foolish courage. The silver-plated flask came whirling in her direction and glanced off her temple. She froze with pain, teetered on the edge of her chair, then slumped over and onto the floor.

When she woke it was dark even beyond the cottage walls and she was alone.

Mrs. Hennepin took Mercedes's bonnet and shawl. "How did you manage to flatten this ribbon?" she asked, giving the bonnet a critical eye. "And your shawl looks to have been dragged on the road. Did you take a tumble?"

Mercedes brushed dust from the back of her gown. "Head over bucket," she said. It was an effort to keep her voice light and pleasant when agitation was running high. "I was a sight."

The housekeeper shook her head, clicking her tongue. "You should be more careful, child."

Mercedes accepted the admonishment, bowing her head slightly for good measure. "What time is it?"

"Long past when you were expected, I can tell you. Gone ten. The boys went to bed an hour ago. Chloe's been asking for you. She and Sylvia want to show you what they bought in town."

"That will have to wait until tomorrow. I want to soak these bruised limbs of mine. Will you see that a bath's prepared for me?"

"Of course. Go on with you."

"Has the captain already retired?"

"No. I don't think that man ever sleeps. I've never known the like. I can stumble on him in the library before dawn and I'd swear he's never even been to bed."

Mercedes tried to be patient. She, too, had noticed Colin seemed to be able to manage with very little sleep, but she didn't want to talk about it now. "Then he's in the library?"

Mrs. Hennepin's head bobbed once. "I just carried some hot chocolate in to him. He was asking after you. I think if you hadn't returned soon he was going to make a search of it."

That information was helpful to Mercedes. It meant she could probably count on him remaining in the library for several more hours as long as she let him know she was home. She found his routine of keeping late hours away from his bedchamber suddenly very comforting. "I'll speak to him," she told the housekeeper.

"Very good."

Mercedes waited until Mrs. Hennepin was well on her way before she approached the library. A few moments alone was what she needed to calm herself and strengthen her resolve. She slid open the doors but remained there, framed on the threshold. "May I come in?"

Colin had already lowered his book. Now he closed it and set it on the table beside him. He made a small beckoning gesture. "Of course."

She closed the doors behind her but only took a few steps forward. Surely he would understand that it was an indication she did not intend to stay. "Mrs. Hennepin said you might be moved to search for me. I wanted you to know that I've returned."

"That's good of you. More considerate than it was to be gone so long to begin with."

So he had no intention of making this easy for her. In a way it hardened her to her task. "I'm sorry."

"Where have you been?"

She did not have to feign surprise. "You remember, we discussed my going to the Thayers earlier today. The basket . . . for the baby. I thought you realized I was going when you escorted the girls to the village. Wasn't that clear?" Mercedes knew it had been and that he had obviously forgotten. She almost smiled. She had needed this reminder of his fallibility.

"All this time?"

"It didn't seem so long when I was with the Thayers." That was true. She had given them the basket with her best wishes and refused all their invitations to join them for tea. The lateness of the hour was her excuse and they accepted it. "Mrs. Thayer was delighted by the gifts. She exclaimed excitedly over each one of the gowns. She hopes you'll honor them by attending Colleen's christening." This was also true.

"And Mr. Thayer? Did he appreciate the brandy?"

Of its own volition, Mercedes's left hand came up to rub her temple where she'd been struck by the flask. The earl hadn't left his silver-plated weapon behind. Mercedes had made a quick search for it but with no success. She wondered that she had even wasted her time. "Most definitely," she said. "I think he means to save it for a special occasion." Mercedes wished she did not have a need to embellish her lies. Colin might well expect to see the flask brought out at Colleen's christening. Now she would either have to dissuade him from going or draw Mr. Thayer into covering her story in some way. The floor under her feet began to feel as thick and as murky as bog water.

"Indeed," Colin said pleasantly.

Mercedes had heard it said that a guilty conscience needs no accuser. There was nothing in Colin's tone or his expression that pointed to distrust of her story, yet she felt it keenly. In her mind's eye she saw his one brow arching skeptically and his narrow smile curling faintly at the corner. The single word had been drawled, giving it the nuance of cynicism.

She blinked. He was still watching her, his manner patient,

even indulgent. Could he see her distress? Mercedes wished he
would throw her a lifeline.

"Would you like some hot chocolate?" he asked. "I'm afraid
Mrs. Hennepin's taken it in her head that I enjoy the stuff."

Mercedes felt her breath come more normally. The bog waters
receded a little and she believed she could leave the library now,
her soul only slightly soiled by her lies. "I'll take it to my room,"
she said. "Mrs. Hennepin's having a bath drawn for me." This
time his brows *did* rise. There was no mistaking the keen interest
in his dark eyes. Mercedes knew that if she were given to blushing, her cheeks would be beacons of color.

Colin raised the cup of cocoa and held it out for her. "Here,"
he said. "Enjoy. That bath won't come amiss either. You look as
if you've taken a tumble."

Once in her room, Mercedes studied her reflection in the
cheval glass. She didn't have time for a long inspection, but then
one wasn't necessary. It was easy to see why Mrs. Hennepin and
Colin had both remarked on her appearance. Not only was her
gown stained with dust from her spill in the cottage, her injured
temple was printed with her own fingertips where she had tried
to massage the pain away. Wisps of hair rose at odd angles
around her head. The dark strands, the color of bittersweet chocolate, would not be flattened easily. An unkind voice that resisted
all efforts at silencing told her she looked like Medusa.

She remembered how she had reacted to Colin's final look at
her. What she had mistaken for keen interest could have only
been his sharp amusement. Just below the surface of her skin,
heat rose again. This time she burned with embarrassment.

Turning away from the glass, Mercedes quickly undressed.
She was in her robe by the time the hot water for her bath arrived.
She watched the progress of the maids with ill-disguised impatience and dismissed them before the tub was even half filled.
When they were gone she ignored the bath altogether and washed
at the basin by her bed. She brushed out her hair until every
tendril was tamed, then secured it loosely with a red ribbon. The
nightgown she chose from her wardrobe was a sleeveless shift

of white cotton. There was no ruffle at the hem or bric-a-brac along the scooped neckline. She had picked it purposely because of its lack of adornment, and when she glanced at herself in the glass again, she recognized the choice as a good one. The shift's simplicity was flattering and the scarlet ribbon in her hair was exactly the right foil.

Mercedes hoped she wouldn't be seen, but she was dressed in the event the opposite occurred. The robe remained discarded at the foot of her bed and she deliberately left her slippers behind.

The north wing was quiet. All the doors were closed. This made Mercedes's passage in the hallway much easier. Small alcoves along the wide corridor held lamps that lighted her way. The glow seeped into the warm, walnut wainscoting and distorted her shadow as she passed. She counted the doors as though they were milestones marking her way from Weybourne Park to London. The distance from the north to the south wing of the manor seemed almost as long.

Mercedes hesitated only when she reached the landing on the grand staircase which connected the wings. She listened, waiting to hear some noise that would confirm Colin's presence in the library. All she was privy to was the thumping of her own heart.

Turning back was not an option. Mercedes had been committed to this end since the earl had dangled his bait. Just as her uncle had suspected, freedom could motivate her powerfully. She hurried past the landing into the darker recesses of the south wing.

Mercedes and Colin had never discussed that he would take a room anywhere but in this section of the manor. It was a comfortable outcome for all of them. Mercedes did not have to worry that he would be bothered overmuch by the twins, or find the affairs of the girls tedious. She also didn't have to concern herself with tripping over him at every turn. The north wing had always been a sanctuary for her, the turret its bell tower. Colin's presence there would have been intrusive and cause her to reevaluate her own desire to stay at Weybourne Park.

Likewise, she imagined he found his accommodations similarly advantageous. He must welcome the opportunity it afforded him to be outside the range of Britton's and Brendan's antics, Chloe's pre-wedding insecurities, and Sylvia's chatter. He must also appreciate time spent away from her, Mercedes thought. He was used to the company of men and no doubt sometimes chafed at the mere sound of her voice.

The door to Colin's suite of rooms was closed. She stood outside, her ear pressed flat to the wood, listening. She forced her own calm so she could hear. When she was certain the chamber was clear, she entered. The door clicked softly into place behind her.

An oil lamp burned on the bedside table. The wick had been turned back so it provided only a fingernail of flame. Even this small light was sufficient for Mercedes's needs.

She knew where he kept his bank drafts. More than once she had been the one who retrieved the account book from his room and carried it to the library for him. It would be revealed eventually, probably sooner than later, that his trust in her had been misplaced. Mercedes had regrets but she didn't allow herself to dwell on that aspect of what she was doing. It was far simpler to reason that he would view this discovery not as some great revelation, but as confirmation of all that he'd believed about her from the beginning.

Besides the four-poster and chest of drawers, Colin's bedchamber was furnished with a writing desk and a large fan-backed chair. An upholstered footstool usually was slipped under the desk for the writer's comfort. She noticed that since Colin had occupied the room, the footstool was always at the side so he could stretch his long legs under the desk and lean back in his chair. He had written a few letters since his cooperative incarceration had begun. Mercedes knew because posting them had become her responsibility. One had been to Mr. Abernathy, Colin's solicitor in London. Another, to his bank. More interesting were the ones addressed to a Miss Jonna Remington in Boston. The name teased her memory until she recalled the great clipper that Colin Thorne commanded was the *Remington Mys-*

tic. It seemed likely she was the daughter of his employers. He obviously had some intimate message for her that he could not trust to Aubrey Jones.

Mercedes's mouth flattened in disapproval but she didn't reflect too deeply on the source of her censure. She pushed any thought of those letters to the back of her mind and raised the polished lid of Colin's secretary.

Cream writing paper lay in a neat stack in one corner. Several crumpled pieces were scattered around, attesting to Colin's frustration at putting words to paper. The rest of the storage space was occupied by the book of drafts. She opened it and glanced through the tally of his accounts. He could easily settle two thousand pounds on her uncle. Carefully removing one of the specially watermarked pages from the middle of the book, Mercedes held it by a corner while she lifted one of his discarded letters to provide a sample of Colin's penmanship.

Her palms were damp as she lowered the lid on the desk. It slipped from beneath her fingers. The sound of it slamming back into place was like a gunshot in the quiet room. Mercedes actually jumped away from the desk. She dropped both pieces of paper. The blank draft fluttered gently to the floor, drifting back and forth on an invisible current of air, eluding her efforts to snatch it up. Her last attempt to grab it disturbed the flight enough to send it flying under Colin's bed. The crumpled letter rolled there as well.

Mercedes sighed.

She was on the point of dropping to her knees when a movement in the doorway caught her attention. It was the first she noticed the door was open and Colin Thorne was standing in the entrance.

Mercedes jerked to attention. Had he seen? What had he seen? She was no longer standing beside the desk. Had he heard the crack when the lid fell? Did he recognize the sound for what it was or could he be persuaded it had no bearing on her presence in the room. Question after question tumbled through Mercedes's head, and none were accompanied by ready answers.

Colin took a step into the room. He used the heel of his boot to close the door. "This is unexpected," he said quietly.

Mercedes strove for calm and managed it. "Is it?"

He smiled narrowly. "Perhaps not. All these nights when you've locked your door, mine has always been open."

How did he know? Had he actually come to her room? Her expressive eyes gave away the nature of her questions as clearly as if she had spoken aloud.

"No," said Colin. "I've never visited your room. I gave you an order and expected that you had sense enough to follow it."

For once Mercedes did not bristle at the notion she had been ordered. She stood very still, her hands at her sides, and took pains not to look anywhere but at him. The last thing she wanted was for his attention to drift to the underside of his bed where the evidence of her deceit lay.

"This changes things," he said. When she didn't reply, but merely continued to stare at him, Colin added, "Doesn't it?"

Mercedes nodded. The small movement was an effort. Her head felt very heavy on the slender stem of her neck, like a peony in full flower drooping on the end of its slim stalk. She opened her mouth to speak and nothing came out. Colin did not make it easy for her. The words, she realized, would have to come from her. She had known this could happen. She had even dressed for this eventuality. It was only the words she hadn't considered. Mercedes had no idea what she might say when she opened her mouth a second time. "I think about you."

"Oh?"

One of his brows was arched. Mercedes couldn't tell if he was genuinely curious or laughing at her. "Often," she said. There was a pause, then she amended, "Constantly." It was difficult to keep her hands at her sides when his dark eyes narrowed and bore into her.

Colin's glance never left her face, yet he saw all of her. Mercedes's hair framed her face softly, secured only loosely by the red grosgrain ribbon. That touch of color contrasted starkly with the virginal white of her simple nightgown. The cotton fabric lay lightly against her skin, not transparent, but suggestive all the same of the slim curves beneath it. Her nipples were pale as the blush on a rose, the tips extended like buds of the very same flower. The rise and fall of her breasts was gentle as she breathed shallowly under his hooded scrutiny.

She was without slippers. One bare foot nudged the other, turning the delicate ankle out. Colin saw the nervous movement was prompted by a burst of shyness, as if she would in the next moment run from him.

"Come here, Mercedes," he said lowly.

She had no doubt it was a command. The space that separated them loomed greater than any distance she had covered thus far this evening. He held out a hand, palm up, and she found herself walking toward him. She was propelled into his arms by a force outside her control, raised on tiptoe by a cushion of air, and held against him as though bound.

His mouth was hard on hers. Urgent. Seeking. Almost a punishment. It was only when she returned the full measure of his passion that his lips gentled and softened. He tasted her mouth now, savored it, ran the edge of his tongue along the sensitive underside of her lip and across the uneven ridge of her teeth. She opened to this sensual assault, pressing herself closer.

Her breasts flattened against Colin's chest. The gold buttons on his waistcoat imprinted themselves on her skin. Mercedes's arms looped around his neck and she drew herself up. His hands closed over her waist, supporting her.

"You're standing on my toes."

She could feel his words as a whisper on her own lips. "What?"

Colin's hands tightened and he raised her easily. "My toes," he said softly. "You were standing on them."

Not enough space separated their bodies for Mercedes to look down and see the truth of it. She believed him. "I won't do it anymore." It was a breathless promise.

He set her down on the tip of his boots again. "I don't mind." He kissed her again and felt her bare toes curl to gain purchase.

All of her responded to the pressure of his mouth. She was as light and supple as a willow, arching beautifully as delicious sensation pulled her taut.

He cupped her bottom, pulling her closer until her warm cleft cradled him. Her fingers pressed whitely into his shoulders when she felt the hard length of him against her thighs. Her faint gasp was caught by his mouth. His palms covered her, rising to the small of her back then falling again. This time she placed herself in the cup of his hands and when he lifted her against him there was no gasp, only a hum of pleasure that tickled his lips and sent a fiery shudder to his groin.

Mercedes's fingers threaded in Colin's bright hair. Even in the murky shadows cast by the lamplight its flaxen brilliance would not be dimmed. Silky strands of it were twisted around her fingers. She brushed his nape with the tips of her nails and felt his reaction strike a chord in her as well. In the beginning she had imagined she was the spider and he was the fly. Now she was not so certain who owned the web or if it was even important anymore. They were both caught in it.

Colin broke the kiss. Mercedes lowered her head and rested her brow against his shoulder. He could hear her light breathing and feel the steady thrum of her heart. She turned her face to the side and lay her cheek flat on the lapel of his jacket. His mouth lightly touched the crown of her head. He held her loosely now, the need to pace himself governing his responses.

Was it finished? she wondered. She felt shaky and light and strangely restless. His kisses had nearly devoured her and now. . . . Mercedes raised her face. She couldn't know that the color of her eyes was like smoke and the centers were nearly as large and as black as the ones that mirrored her gaze. When she lifted her mouth to his, Mercedes was not thinking only of the papers that lay beneath Colin's bed, waiting to be discovered if she should falter. There were other reasons, intimately selfish ones, that prompted her to act as she did.

Colin returned the kiss only lightly.

She stared at him, puzzled. "Is it because I'm on your toes again?"

He shook his head. "It's because if you touch me I'm likely to come out of my skin." Her eyes grew wide at this and he was reminded that for all her siren's ways she was really an innocent. "It's a compliment," he told her.

"Oh."

It was only a soft expulsion of air, yet it had the impact of the stamp of her mouth on his. "God," he whispered. Nothing could prevail upon him to stop now. He lifted Mercedes and bore her down on the bed.

The change of positions altered her perceptions. Even standing on his toes she believed she had been on equal footing. Now, stretched beside her, he loomed more largely. The weight of him could be felt across her legs where he covered them with his thigh. His hands had caught her wrists and pinned them back lightly. As gentle as the pressure was, she could no more escape it than she could iron manacles.

He buried his face in the curve of her shoulder. There was only a faint arcing mark left by the tail of the earl's quirt. The damp trail made by the edge of his tongue was hotter on Mercedes's skin than her memory of the whip's slash and sting. She cried out, arching with the ache his touch opened in her. "Colin," she said.

He brushed the corner of her mouth with his. "Say it again."

She didn't hesitate. "Colin."

His mouth descended to the curve of her neck. His teeth found one tail of the scarlet ribbon and he tugged. Colin released her wrists so his fingers could slip into her hair. The fragrance of lavender tempted him.

Mercedes held her breath as his fingertips slipped past her temples and brushed her cheek. The touch was reverent. Adoring. He sifted through her hair, raising thick locks of it then letting it cascade around his fingers and past his wrist.

Raising himself on one elbow, Colin nudged the straps of

Mercedes's shift over her shoulders. His hand traced the length of her collarbone. He bent to kiss the hollow of her throat.

The material hovered at the level of her breasts. He pushed it out of the way.

The sight of his mouth lowering over her nipple was dizzying. But what he said robbed Mercedes of all feeling.

"How much is it costing me to lie between your thighs?"

Eight

Mercedes pushed at Colin's shoulders. His lips only grazed her breast. She twisted and tried to remove herself from the arm and leg that pinned her. His casual hold tightened but he raised his head and looked at her. "Why did you say that?" she whispered.

He didn't answer, but studied her instead. Lamplight washed her features, highlighting the pared shape of her nose and the perfect curve of her mouth. Her chin was raised slightly but the effect was only to offer the slim length of her neck up for his punishment or his pleasure. He considered throttling her. What he did was kiss her.

Colin's mouth touched the base of her throat. His tongue dipped in the hollow. He felt her small gasp as a vibration against his lips. Her fingers fluttered on his shoulders and she pushed but there was no real force behind the movement. His kisses slipped lower, tracing the length of her collarbone, then sliding to her breast. He captured one nipple and sucked.

Mercedes's breath caught as sensation spiraled through her.

It was only when he felt her arch beneath him that he lifted his mouth. "You haven't answered my question," he said.

For a second time she went rigid beneath him. It lasted only a second. Her hands came up and she hammered his chest and shoulders so that he had no choice but to pin back her arms. Mercedes's heels ground into the mattress for leverage and she pushed herself up, almost dislodging him as she twisted. This near success gave her reason to try again. And again.

Colin only had to wait her out. In the end she had not so much surrendered as simply been exhausted. Her breathing came harshly to his ears but she had managed to compose her features. Only the small vertical crease between her finely drawn brows exposed her distress. There was no expression save watchfulness in her clear gray eyes.

"Don't insult me," he said in a low voice.

"I don't know what you mean."

Colin tightened his grip on her wrists. It was only when he saw her wince that he realized what he was doing. The pressure was eased immediately but he didn't release her. "Don't do this, Mercedes. Tell me."

Her throat was clogged by the unfamiliar ache of tears. There was nothing she could have said in that moment.

Taking her silence as refusal and her dry-eyed stare as defiance, Colin swore softly. "Must you ever have your back to the wall?" he asked. "I *saw* you putting the ledger away and all that came after that."

Mercedes turned her face from him. She could not hold back her small despairing cry.

"Does that make it easier for you to admit what you've done?" Colin said. He let go of her wrists and eased himself beside her, taking her face lightly in his hands. With the gentlest pressure he made her look at him. His thumb traced the underside of her lip. Her silky hair brushed the back of his hands like gossamer threads. Colin's voice was quiet, husky. "The only thing that's changed is that you know I know."

She bit her lower lip. His mouth on hers made her stop. He kissed her once. Twice. Then a third time, more deeply, searching for the response she had given him before. Her lips softened slightly, parted. The tip of her tongue touched his before he withdrew.

"Mercedes?" He said her name quietly, attaching no further demand. She would know it was there whether he said it or not.

"Two thousand pounds," she said. She stared at him, waiting

for a reaction: a gasp, a shout, an epithet. Something. There was nothing. Colin didn't so much as twitch.

"Very well," he said. He released her, sat up, and levered himself to the edge of the bed. Upon getting out, he scooped the two pieces of paper from beneath the bed and carried them to the desk. Her raised the lid, removed the ledger, then made a notation in the tally of accounts for two thousand pounds. "Should I make this draft to you?" he asked.

Mercedes was sitting up now. She had lifted the straps of her shift to cover her breasts but somehow it still didn't seem enough. Reaching for one corner of the coverlet, she brought it up to shield her. "Ashbrook and Deakins."

Colin made the note then closed the ledger. He put it and the crumpled letter away. He jabbed his pen once in the inkwell before he smoothed the blank, watermarked draft on the desktop. His hand moved quickly across the paper, the writing heavy and bold with no flourishes or elaboration. "And these gentlemen would be . . ." He let his sentence trail off purposefully.

Mercedes recalled what her uncle had said, but it made no sense to tell Colin they were merchants. What could she ever show that two thousand pounds had purchased? "They're solicitors," she said. It was a safer answer because she would not have to produce anything. What was the outcome of contact with any lawyer save for mountains of paper, all of it stamped with the peculiar language of the legal trade.

Colin nodded and continued writing. "The address of their office?"

Mercedes gave him the location of her uncle's London townhouse. The lies settled uncomfortably in the pit of her stomach as she watched Colin write.

He signed his name with a few spare lines and laid aside the pen. He looked at the draft a moment longer before he turned to Mercedes. "Do you want to see it?" he asked.

She shook her head. "I trust you," she said. Mercedes ducked her head when she felt the sharp edge of his narrow, derisive smile.

"Would that I could say the same of you."

It struck her then that he was not so scornful as he was resigned, perhaps even sad. She spared him a glance but the dark
eyes were implacable and it was easy to believe she had mistaken
or misinterpreted his tone. Mercedes moved to the edge of the
bed. "I'll go now," she said quietly.

"No." Colin removed his jacket and slung it over the back of
the chair.

"No?"

He began to unbutton his waistcoat as he approached the bed.
He stopped only when he stood directly in front of her. Her face
was raised to look at him. "You could have asked me for the
money," he said. "I don't know what I would have said, but you
could have asked. You didn't. You chose to steal from me instead."

There was no defense she could offer. That she had been
stopped from committing the act was all Colin's doing. Her grip
on the coverlet was white-knuckled now.

He reached out and touched her face. His fingertips brushed
Mercedes's pale cheek. "You offered yourself up to hide your
deceit."

Mercedes would have looked away but Colin's own glance
was compelling.

"You were willing to share my bed to cover your crime." He
paused. His fingers drifted away from her face and slipped into
her hair. "I'm willing to ignore your crime as long as you share
my bed."

She didn't move away from his touch. The movement of his
fingers at her nape was gentle. She could have easily turned her
cheek into the palm of his hand. Her voice was grave, her gray
eyes intent. "Then I'm to be a whore for you."

"Whores are for an evening," Colin said. "Two thousand
pounds is a great deal of money. For that you'll have to be my
mistress."

A light shudder caught Mercedes unaware. It could have been

his words. More likely it was the pass his thumb made along the underside of her jaw. "I don't—"

He stepped slightly to one side so she could see the desk and the paper upon it. He watched her eyes shift in that direction. It wasn't necessary to say anything else. The threat would have been ugly if spoken aloud.

Mercedes looked back at Colin. Her mouth parted but she had no voice.

He sat beside her on the edge of the bed. The coverlet she held so tightly was lowered slowly between them. His fingers nudged her until she was looking at him again. Beneath the heel of his hand he could feel her pulse racing. He bent his head and kissed her lightly, tasting the warmth of her softly parted lips. "Shall I tell you what's really different?" he whispered against her mouth.

Mercedes wasn't certain she wanted to hear. She was being lowered back to the bed. Supported by his hands, she felt weightless. There was a sense of detachment, as if the things that were being done to her were being done to another, as though she were only a witness to the mouth that covered hers or the fingers that lowered the straps of her shift.

"What's different," he said lowly, "is that there are no pretenses left. You can't tell yourself that you're in my bed to serve some other purpose. You can't fool yourself that I don't know why you're here. You can't pretend that my mouth on yours means I'm halfway to falling in love with you."

His perception was sharper than the dagger he carried in his boot. The cut of it was deeper. Mercedes gasped at the pain he could inflict with words. A moment later her breath caught again, this time because his mouth touched her breast, and where she felt the deepest ache there was suddenly the damp edge of his tongue, laving her, licking at the wound.

"It was fine with you," he said huskily, "if I was the one deceived. You didn't mind feigning some interest, acting as though you really wanted me. If I was half-witted enough to believe you might desire me, better yet, that you might actually be in love with me, you would find more pleasure in it."

"No." It was a desperate sound, softly spoken then extinguished by the pressure of his mouth on hers.

The kiss was deep and hard, like a battle engaged. Mercedes met him measure for measure. Aroused, she became arousing, taking the fullness of his passion and turning it back on him. She arched beneath him, not to escape the weight of his body but to feel the strength of him at her breasts and hips and especially at her thighs.

The gown was stripped from her. A sliver of lamplight bathed her shoulder. She lowered her eyes, not to shield her glance, but to watch Colin as his lips trailed between her shadowed breasts. He sipped her skin before her nipple was covered by the hot suck of his mouth. Her fingers threaded in his bright flaxen hair and when her heels found purchase in the mattress it was to make herself more open to him.

The back of Colin's hand brushed her side from breast to hip. It lifted again and settled at the curve of her waist then trailed along her abdomen. Her skin retracted beneath the calloused pads of his fingers. When he raised his hand it retracted again, this time in anticipation of the contact. She was exquisitely sensitive to the lightest touch, and when his hand slipped between her thighs he wrested a cry of pleasure from her.

Levering himself on one elbow, Colin watched the play of emotion on her face as his fingers continued to search and stroke. "Look at me," he said when she would have turned away. "I want to see your face."

Even now she couldn't blush. Mercedes tried to move away but found herself rising to meet his intimate caress instead. She could feel her own fiery heat against the warmth of his fingers and when he slipped one inside her she felt her damp response to his entry. A cry hovered on her lips and she held it back, the restraint causing the ache in her chest to deepen.

"You can say it," he whispered, bending closer. The movement of his hand was insistent now, the rhythm purposeful. He bound her with the knowledge that as soon as he wished, it would be his body filling her this way. "You can say anything."

Not anything, she thought. "I could learn to hate you," was what she said.

He smiled then, that narrow, maddeningly enigmatic smile that could have meant everything or nothing. He laid that smile upon her mouth until he drew out another response. Then he watched her as the thrust of his hand and fingers pressed and quickened and she met the caress with the lift of her own body.

Her fingers curled in the sheet under her. Her breasts ached for the pressure and suck of his mouth. Tension pulled her so that her skin was taut as she arched and stretched her neck and back. The heat that was coiled like some steel spring straight from the furnace began to unwind and slipped through her veins in its molten state, raising her temperature until the room seemed cool in comparison. The shiver became more than that as she was mounted by pleasure.

Mercedes cried out, weightless again as she was raised by a new, frighteningly more powerful sensation. It licked at her skin and swelled her breasts. The slender length of her legs tightened as she was buffeted, then carried by the waves of heat and light. Everything that had come before was in preparation of this and she was helpless to do anything but ride it out.

When it was over she lay very still. She was heavy now, heavier than she had ever been in her life, weighed down by the slumberous aftermath of pleasure and the enormity of what had been done to her. The ache was back, not in her chest this time, but in her throat. It was difficult to muster the words, impossible to manage dignity. "Are you through with me?"

Colin didn't hide his dry amusement. "Hardly."

He kissed her at his leisure, tasting, sipping. His lips touched the backs of her closed eyes, her cheeks, her jaw. He placed kisses at the base of her ear and along the sensitive cord of her neck. His tongue made a damp line to the hollow of her throat before he slanted his mouth over hers again.

Only when he felt the faint stirrings of a like response did he raise his head. Sitting up so that he blocked her path out of the near side of the bed, Colin divested himself of his clothing. He

would have welcomed her hands on him, helping him do what
he was entirely capable of himself, but she didn't offer and he
didn't insist.

When he was naked he stretched out beside her. Her hip
pressed against his hard groin and Colin's body reacted instinc-
tively, thrusting against her. Mercedes closed her eyes but she
didn't move away.

"Don't do this," he said, brushing his lips against her shoulder.
"Don't make this a sacrifice. This isn't against your will."

She would have liked to deny it, but he was right. She had
named a price and he had paid it. She owed him this. Earlier she
had been willing to do anything to gain freedom from her uncle;
what galled her was that she would win it from one man and
come to know tyranny from another. Mercedes opened her eyes
and saw Colin watching her closely. "No," she said finally, softly.
"It's not against my will."

She raised her arms and laid her hands on his shoulders. Her
fingers threaded at the nape of his neck. His flesh was firm and
warm. She drew him down then raised her face in the last instant
and initiated the kiss.

There was strength in the way he held her, still more in the
way he held back. Mercedes's fingers flicked at the bright tufts
of hair at his neck then her hands spread apart and ran along the
breadth of his shoulders. His fair hair was in contrast to the
bronzed patina of his skin. Weeks and months on the *Remington
Mystic*, shirtless in the saltspray, had lent his skin a sun-kissed
color that even an English summer couldn't fade. Her hand was
pale in comparison, slight and delicate against the corded muscles of his back and arms.

Her nails were drawn lightly along his chest. His belly was
hard and flat and his waist tapered to narrow hips. She touched
the back of his thighs once then raised her hands again. He drew
them back and she caressed the firm curve of his buttocks in her
palms. Groaning softly, he pressed against her.

His legs were strong and lean and covered with flaxen hair
even lighter than that on his head. The texture was somehow both

rough and silky and wonderfully different from her own. She rubbed her foot on his calf slowly, liking the heat and friction and the shudder that vibrated his body first, then her own.

It was then that Colin separated her thighs with his knee. She cradled him as he lay with more of his weight against her. His breath came more harshly but there was no hurry in his movements. When he raised himself she missed his warmth. Her knees were lifted and pushed backward as she was positioned for his entry. She clutched his arms and then he was pressing himself into her.

The first thrust brought pain. With the second there was only a sense of fullness. He waited after that, letting her feel all of him inside her. She was tight, surrounding him like a warm leather sheath. Her muscles contracted, then accommodated, and when he pulled back she tried to hold him, making the withdrawal exquisitely pleasurable.

She knew the rhythm. It had been taught to her by his hands and fingers. She moved with him now as he ground against her. He came forward and was embraced by her thighs and captured by her knees. His breath was hot on her breast but the edge of his tongue was hotter, and sparks skittered along Mercedes's skin.

Each thrust was hard and sure until pleasure was in a moment of overwhelming him. She felt his rhythm change and the strokes become more rapid and shallow and it was then that the bud of heat in her own belly burst open and she was flooded with his seed.

He was the first to move. Sliding off the bed he went to the dressing room and washed himself. When he came back he was carrying a basin of water and a towel. Mercedes had drawn a sheet over her but now he pushed it back. She tried to turn away but he brought her to him again. There was no expression on his face as he dampened the edge of the towel and laid it between her thighs. It came away tinged with her blood as his penis had been.

"You were a virgin," he said without inflection. "I wasn't sure."

Another thrust, she thought. Once again it was more painful than anything he had done to her body. She placed her forearm over her eyes while he bathed her as if it could make her invisible to him and herself. When he was finished, she asked, "May I have my shift?"

He handed it to her and she slipped it over her head, but when she would have risen to leave the bed, he laid his hand against her shoulder. He didn't have to press. The resistance of his palm was enough.

"I want to go to my room now," she said.

"No." He offered no explanation, but put the basin and towel on the floor then slipped in bed beside her. With simple direction—a touch on her knee, another on her shoulder—he brought her to curve her body against his so that they lay like spoons in a velvet-lined drawer.

Colin never slept long and he never slept deeply. It had been his way since the first days at Cunnington's Workhouse when he learned that the older boys often wanted something at night from the younger ones. He had fought them away then, even when he didn't know what or why he was fighting. Those answers came later when Jack Quincy took him aboard the *Sea Dancer*. His favored status with the captain and Quincy's watchful eye weren't always enough to protect him. There were men among the crew who saw it as a challenge. It was still early in the voyage when Colin was pinned to the wall of the armory while another young sailor was raped. His two abductors satisfied themselves with their other victim and let Colin go. The threat that they would enjoy him in the same manner was never spoken. Even at that young age Colin sensed it was because it made them savor the cat and mouse game that followed.

They never trapped him again. One man was lost at sea in a wild North Atlantic storm. The other died of food poisoning. The victims themselves never suspected Colin. Certainly no one else did.

Colin had no reason to expect he would sleep well this night but he was reluctant to leave his bed. The prospect of lying beside Mercedes, having her curled against him when she had been so recently joined to him, was curiously comforting. He imagined watching her sleep or listening to her gentle breathing. It was outside all his experience that exactly the opposite could happen.

The lamp had extinguished itself before Mercedes eased out of Colin's light embrace. After he fell asleep she had turned toward him and rested on her side while she watched him, and remained like that for a long time, her attention caught by the unguarded boyishness that crept into his features while he slept. Gone was the narrow, enigmatic smile and the cynically arched brow. His jaw was relaxed, his lips slightly parted. A lock of yellow hair had fallen across his forehead. Twice she pushed it back and twice it slipped forward. In the end she let it lie there. His lashes fanned his cheeks and on close inspection she saw that the tips were darker, like the end of a golden brush dipped in black lacquer.

Mercedes cast a last look over her shoulder as she stood at the desk. Colin was still sleeping soundly. She picked up the draft he had drawn for her and hurried for the door. Upon waking there would be no hint of the youth she saw now. Not for the first time that night, she wondered how the child had become the man.

Except for a light dusting, the earl's room had not been touched since his disappearance. She found two valises at the bottom of his wardrobe and packed them quickly, distributing his clothing evenly between them. Rather than return to her own room to dress, Mercedes chose a pair of trousers, shirt, and jacket from among her uncle's things and slipped them on. Using a neckcloth as a belt, Mercedes was able to keep the trousers around her waist. She gave the jacket cuffs two turns to raise them to wrist level then she coiled her hair and stuffed it under one of his hats. No one would mistake her for the Earl of Weybourne, but from a distance at least, she thought she would pass as a man.

She carried a pair of his boots with her to the pantry, along with the valises. Her feet were too small to wear the things without clopping around on the hardwood floors like a horse in the paddock. Mercedes didn't put them on until she had selected bread, fruit, and cheese from the larder and packed it away. She had known at the outset that she was not going to bring him any liquor. As a rebellious gesture it was small, but it gave enormous satisfaction to thwart that request. When she packed his dueling pistols, she took another for herself. Primed and loaded, it was tucked into her trousers.

From abovestairs she heard the enormous hall clock chime the third hour of the morning. She hadn't known it was so late and realized that for some portion of the night she had slept in Colin's arms as he had slept in hers. Had he woken even once and watched her? Had her features been stamped with the same vulnerability as his? She could only hope it hadn't been so. The thought that it may have been otherwise did not bring her any pleasure. She needed to show Colin strength, not weakness.

Mercedes hefted the valises and headed for the rear door of the manor. Had she been able to ride, the trip to the abandoned cottage would have taken but ten minutes. Hampered by the weight of the valises and the ill-fitting shoes, she was still walking at the end of thirty.

The cottage was deserted when she arrived. Even though her uncle had told her to expect it, Mercedes still peered into the deep shadows anticipating him to surprise her. She didn't waste time wondering if he would come while she was there. Folding the draft neatly into thirds, Mercedes left it lying on top of a loaf of bread in one of the valises.

Her feet were blistered by the time she reached the manor. She removed the boots as soon as she was in the door and stared down at herself in dismay. She would be hobbling around in her own shoes for days if she didn't care for herself.

Once in her bedchamber, Mercedes quickly removed her uncle's clothes and stuffed them into the bottom of her wardrobe. She dropped the pistol into one of the boots and put them away as well. It would be a simple enough thing to return them later. The bath that had been drawn for her was completely cool now but Mercedes stripped out of her shift and slipped into it anyway. It was not just her feet that hurt but also her inner thighs where the loose trousers had rubbed her tender flesh. And then there was the ache more deep inside her that the water could not soothe or heal, the ache that made her aware she had taken a man into her and that she could take one again.

One man.

Colin Thorne.

Mercedes leaned back against the lip of the tub and closed her eyes. It was only when she heard the click of the door that she realized she had neglected to lock it. The man who moments ago had filled her mind's eye was now filling the doorway.

"Washing all of my touch away?" he asked.

Wide-eyed, Mercedes shook her head. Although Colin's question had been delivered almost impersonally, anger simmered in his tone. She hunched forward in the tub, drawing her knees to her chest.

Colin came toward her, not bothering to shut the door. He knelt beside the tub and dipped one hand in the water. "You must have been anxious to bathe; this water's ice cold."

"Please," she said softly. "Just go."

Scooping a handful of water, Colin raised it to the level of Mercedes's bare shoulder. "It won't do any good, you know," he told her. "I'll want to touch you again." He tipped his hand and let the water slide out of the cup of his palm.

Mercedes shivered, reacting equally to the water and his words.

"Stand up," he said.

"The door's open. Someone could—"

"You and I are the only ones awake."

"At least turn back the lamp."

Colin got to his feet and went to the bedside table. When he had done as she asked he made his demand again. This time Mercedes stood. The only sound in the room was her shallow breathing and the intermittent splash as droplets fell back to the surface water. She made no move to step outside the tub, but stood there, not so much shivering any longer, but trembling.

Colin gave her his hand. He was surprised by her firm grasp. It was as though she needed his assistance to take the next step. When he held out Mercedes's nightshift, she merely raised her arms and allowed him to slip it over her head. It fell around her like a cloud but where it touched her damp flesh it clung like mist.

Lowering her arms, Mercedes swayed slightly on her bruised and blistered feet. Colin couldn't know that the movement toward him wasn't meant as an invitation, yet when he took it as such, Mercedes didn't correct him. She let herself be lifted off her feet and cradled against his chest. One of her arms even came up and slipped around his neck. She let her head fall against his shoulder as he carried her out of the bedchamber, and when they stood in the hallway it was Mercedes who closed the door to her room.

Colin carried her through two wings and the landing without breaking stride or straining his breath. Inside his room, he lowered her on the bed and followed with his own body.

His hands held her face still, his fingers buried in her thick hair. "Don't do that again," he whispered against her mouth.

"What?" Her lips brushed his.

"Leave me." The answer was not freely given, but rather torn from him so the sound of it rasped in his throat. Then, regretting what he could not control, his mouth came down hard over hers.

As a kiss it began as more punishment than pleasure. His lips ground against hers, taking her breath. His tongue forced its way past the ridge of her teeth and speared her mouth. Even though Mercedes didn't fight him, his hands tightened on her face and kept her captive.

She was the one who changed the tenor of the engagement. Her mouth softened. Her fingers slid around his neck and threaded through silky strands of his flaxen hair. The tips of her nails stroked him then lightly scored his naked back along the length of his spine. At the waistband of his trousers they dipped inside and circled his waist.

It was Colin's sharp intake of air that finally broke the kiss. His breathing was harsh and it sounded loud in the still room. The pressure in his fingertips eased and he released Mercedes's face, tangling his fingers in her spill of dark hair instead. There was too little light in the bedchamber now for Colin to make out her features, but he could not feel anything but supplication in her slender form.

"Mercedes?"

It was the tentative way he said her name, the way he asked the question without using any other words, that Mercedes responded to. Likewise, with a single word, she was able to give him everything he wanted. "Yes."

Mercedes was not so emboldened that she could help Colin off with his trousers, but she sat up on her knees and raised her shift to the level of her hips before he caught it and took it the rest of the way. Both articles of clothing were allowed to slip unnoticed over the side of the bed.

She came in his arms then and her breasts, with their swollen and excited peaks, were flattened against his chest. Between them, flush to her flat belly, was the hard length of his shaft. He cupped her bottom, raising her so she could feel him even more intimately against her. Her thighs straddled him while her arms wound around his shoulders. Colin lowered her back to the bed, his mouth on hers as he entered her.

He swallowed her small moan, then as he began to move inside, her hum of pleasure. He kissed her neck, the curve of her shoulder. His lips grazed her breasts and his tongue flicked her nipple. She was supple in his arms, pliable, moving with him, rising and falling to counter each plunge of his hips. He was inside her but she was under his skin. He had no words to tell her or himself that she had become necessary to him. He had only this: his mouth on her skin and the hard thrust of his body.

Mercedes sipped the air as she was rocked back by the joining of their bodies. Her head was thrown back, her throat exposed in a slender arc. Her palms slid along Colin's shoulders. Muscles bunched beneath her fingers. The rise of heat between her thighs was intense as he moved against her. Sometimes he would touch her in just a certain right way and she would feel tiny bursts of heat skim the surface of her skin. The moment would pass, then come again, stronger the next time but still elusive.

It was only at the very end that pleasure became flesh and sinew deep. Mercedes felt the tug on her tendons as she was stretched taut by the steady thrust of Colin's body. Her fingers curled against his arms. Her belly rippled when the force of tension snapped. She felt herself contracting all around him.

Colin felt it, too. It was all he needed to allow himself his own release. The shudder that had begun in her was absorbed by him. He arched, pushing himself deeply into her one final time before he came.

Moments later, with the raw sensations of pleasure still lingering, Colin withdrew and moved to one side. He raised the sheet to cover them, and this time Mercedes required no direction or urging to stay cradled in the curve of his body. "I'll wake you before first light," he said.

He fell asleep with one hand on her hip.

Mercedes was sitting at the breakfast table the next time he spoke to her. She wasn't alone. Britton and Brendan and Sylvia were there. Only Chloe was later to rise than he was. Colin helped himself to a soft-boiled egg, fresh bread, and several tomato slices at the sideboard before he sat down. "Good morning," he said. It was a greeting to everyone but his eyes alighted last and longest on Mercedes.

It was not Mercedes who answered, but Britton. "G'morning, Captain," he said happily. He sopped up some more gooey yellow from his egg with a finger of bread, then popped it into his mouth. He didn't wait to swallow before he spoke again. "You almost left it to too late." At best this announcement was garbled. Under Mercedes's stern eye he gulped.

Brendan didn't wait for his brother to clear his throat. "What he means," he explained with an air of importance, "is that if you'd come down any later, we'd all have been gone."

"Oh?" Colin tapped the eggshell with the side of his spoon.

The subsequent, satisfying crack punctuated his question. He saw Mercedes start at the sound but she remained silent and seemingly uninterested in anything save her plate.

Sylvia turned her bright smile on Colin. "Mercedes says we're all to accompany Chloe to Glen Eden. Remember? Chloe's going to stay with Mr. Fredrick's aunt for a few weeks." When she wasn't able to raise a response from Colin she prompted, "Chloe's intended? The vicar?"

"Yes," he said finally, slowly. "I remember. I didn't realize that today was the day." That at least explained Chloe's absence from the table. She was no doubt in her room selecting clothes and supervising their packing. That meant that he was indeed the last one up this morning. "I didn't know it would be an excursion for all of you." This time he looked so intently in Mercedes's direction that no one else dared to answer.

It was the lengthening silence that made her look up. She met his implacable dark eyes squarely and offered with no defensiveness or guile, "I thought the twins would enjoy the ride and Sylvia wants to see that her sister is safely settled. Ben has already prepared the carriage and Henry will drive us. We're to leave after breakfast. As Britton attempted to tell you, you almost left it to too late."

"Then I'm invited on this trip?" he asked.

"Of course," Britton and Brendan chimed together.

"Oh, yes," said Sylvia.

"As you wish," was Mercedes quiet reply. She bent her head and applied herself to her breakfast.

Cool civility marked Mercedes's demeanor throughout the day. Otherwise Colin found her unchanged. From time to time he would catch a glimpse of her profile as he rode along beside the carriage. She was a remarkably lovely woman even when she was gravely thoughtful, but when one of the others made her smile, she was radiant.

Chloe's fiancé welcomed them at his aunt's house in the village of Glen Eden. They had luncheon in the garden and spent the afternoon walking leisurely along the cobbled village road to the outlying estate. Mercedes and Sylvia kept Mrs. Fredrick's company, while Colin stayed apace of the twins. Chloe and the likable vicar followed the group more slowly, their hands brushing ever so slightly as they walked.

It was dark by the time they returned home. Sylvia was already missing her sister and retired immediately to her room. The twins yawned deeply, not even raising a protest when Mercedes pointed them up the steps. She watched them sluggishly meet the challenge of the grand staircase then disappear around the corner of the landing. She and Colin were alone at the foot of the stairs when she turned to him.

"Will you be wanting me this evening?" she asked.

He didn't answer immediately. For all the inflection or interest in her tone, she may as well have asked if he wanted sugar with his tea. Colin reached up to brush back a strand of hair that had fallen along her cheek. She shied away.

"Not here," she said. "Never here."

He let his hand fall slowly back to his side. "What goes through your mind, Mercedes?"

"I don't know what you mean."

She probably didn't, he thought. "Yes," he said at last. "I'll want you this evening."

Mercedes was waiting for him when he came up from the library. It was a cool night and she had laid a small fire in the fireplace. She sat curled in a wing chair, facing the flames to absorb their warmth. Her hair was bound loosely by a black ribbon this evening and her white lawn gown was edged with lace across the bodice.

She started to rise as he entered the room but he motioned her back. Her bare toes peeped out beneath the hem of her gown. He watched her cover them before he unbuttoned his jacket and shrugged out of it. He let it dangle at the end of his hand. His shirt was very white against the dark gray waistcoat. "Have you been waiting long?" he asked.

"Not long, I think." A few minutes or a few hours, it had been an eternity. Her eyes followed him as he crossed the carpet with a soundless tread and dropped his jacket on the back of the chair opposite her.

Colin unfastened the gold studs in his cuffs and laid them in a blue Wedgwood box on the table. He rolled up his sleeves then picked up a poker at the fireplace. Out of the corner of his eye he saw Mercedes flinch. He looked down at the poker then back at her. Puzzlement gave way to understanding. "My God," he said softly. "He hit you with this."

Ashamed, Mercedes ducked her head and stared at her hands in her lap.

Colin didn't pursue the topic. He stabbed at the fire instead, shooting sparks up the flue so that embers popped and crackled. When a measure of his anger had subsided, he dropped the poker in its black iron stand. He remained at the fireplace, one arm resting on the mantel. "Look at me, Mercedes."

She raised her face slowly.

"Do you imagine I'm going to beat you?" he asked.

She shook her head.

"Or flay your skin with a whip?"

Of its own accord, her hand came up and touched her neck. "No," she said on a thread of sound. "I don't think you'll do that."

Colin wasn't certain he could believe her. She had pressed herself back into the chair sharply the moment he'd raised the poker. "I mean it," he said. "I would never hurt you."

In Mercedes's mind she heard the sentence differently. *I would never hurt you like that.* To her way of thinking, the addition of the last two words made the statement true. He had already said things to her that stung as deeply as if he'd taken a strip off her skin.

Colin watched her closely but in the end he had to be satisfied with her silence. He raked back his hair in a weary gesture. "Go to bed, Mercedes," he said quietly. And when she looked at him, bewildered by this order, he realized she had misunderstood. "My bed."

Confident of her compliance, Colin picked up his coat and

disappeared into the adjoining dressing room. He didn't hurry
his undressing or his ablutions, giving her ample time to fall
asleep. He couldn't know that the waiting was an agony for her.
She felt as though she were a single nerve ending by the time he
joined her.

Colin felt her stiffen as he slipped into bed beside her. Her
uneven, shallow breathing made it impossible for him to even
pretend she was sleeping. He raised himself on one elbow and
touched her shoulder, turning her gently so that she lay on her
back. His body blocked the firelight, casting her face in shadow.
Even so, he could sense apprehension in her large gray eyes.

He drew a lock of dark chocolate hair forward. The tension
in her slender frame was so great she fairly vibrated with it. Colin
leaned into her and kissed her softly on the mouth. "I only want
you beside me in bed tonight," he said quietly. "I'm not going
to touch you."

Mercedes was afraid to lower her guard. She studied him warily, her eyes darting over his face, searching out the lie.

"I shouldn't have taken you a second time last night." He felt
her uncertain glance but before she could frame her question he
went on, "I saw you take Mrs. Fredrick's arm this afternoon. It
was clear to my eyes at least that her walk was less troubled than
yours."

Mercedes turned sharply away from him and pressed her fist
against her mouth to keep from crying out. Tears sprang to her
eyes and her shoulders heaved. She felt her hand on his arm but
she tore away from his touch. Her relief that he did not pursue
the contact was so great that it tore a shudder through her.

Not for the world did she want him to know the suppressed
sob that wracked her body was laughter.

It was much later, when she heard his steady and even breathing, that she trusted herself to turn over. He wouldn't have
thanked her for her laughter any more than he would have understood it. Mercedes raised her right hand and lightly touched
his temple with her fingertips. His bright hair was as soft as

down and beneath the pads of her fingers she could feel his beating pulse.

His assessment of her condition had been so skewed by his manly perceptions, that she found she could not be angry with him. In an odd way, it was endearing. He had seemed very human to her in that moment, apologetic and hesitant, but not without an edge of male conceit. He must have imagined himself to be inordinately proportioned to have been the cause of so much of her discomfort. He wouldn't have thanked her for pointing out it was her blistered feet causing her ungainly walk, not anything he had done to her.

She knuckled her mouth again to stifle a low chuckle. It was true that she had felt an ache there most of the day, but it was never painful. Quite the opposite, and it had driven her to distraction to have the memory imprinted clearly in her mind and stamped indelibly between her thighs.

Mercedes index finger traced his jaw from temple to chin then laid her hand against his neck. She moved closer, careful not to disturb him. Her fingers drifted to where his nightshirt was opened at the throat. He didn't stir when she stroked his skin lightly and she was struck again by the realization that his sleeping pose was not half so arrogant as his waking one. It gave her courage.

Mercedes let her hand slide across his chest and rest on his shoulder. She pressed a kiss at the base of his throat. Her knees drew forward and bumped his and she made herself go still, holding even her breath, while she waited to see if he would move. She was emboldened when the cadence of his sleeping rhythms didn't change.

Gingerly, Mercedes stretched one of her legs out along the length of his. The tails of his nightshirt were raised higher than his knees and his skin was pleasantly warm against hers. She rested just that way for a moment, breathing deeply of his male scent, appreciating the angles and textures that made him different from her, intrigued by the way her body could be tucked so neatly beside his, without discomfort or strain.

Her hand moved from his shoulder to his thigh. She fingered the edge of his shirttail, tracing the hem at first, then the skin just below it. Gradually her fingers moved under the shirt. Her palm grazed his flank and the curve of his buttock. She let her hand fall forward.

Now she felt Colin stir. Not with his whole body, as Mercedes had been anticipating, but only with that part that had been joined to her. Her first instinct was to retract her hand and indeed, she was almost free of the tangle of his nightshirt when curiosity won out over common sense. Mercedes's fingers rose again and this time curled around the thick, hard length of him. The pulse of his body beat strongly here and the flow of blood made the shaft hot and heavy. It angled away from his thighs as if seeking entry between hers.

Mercedes felt a tug deep in her womb. Her body's response caught her off guard. Until this moment she could have said honestly that she was only satisfying a curiosity, not gratifying some carnal pleasure. Now she was conscious of her swollen breasts and the aching tips that would have been soothed by the suck of Colin's mouth. There was a dampness between her thighs that she understood was her body's way of preparing for his entry. Then there was her own breathing. In contrast to the steady rise and fall of his, Mercedes's came rapidly and sounded strained in the quiet bedchamber.

Guilt mingled with the rush of sensation and overwhelmed her. Mercedes withdrew her hand quickly and turned away, curling on her side with a pillow caught close to the chest.

With great effort, Colin remained as he was. He had been sleeping when Mercedes began her first, tentative explorations, but by the time she had pressed her mouth to his throat he was very much awake. At first he had been amused by her actions, then moved, and finally maddened. He doubted she could appreciate the restraint he had shown through his pretense of sleep. Had she been less naive, she would have known that he could have only held himself back by conscious will. Had he really been sleeping she would have found herself flat on her back, her thighs open to him, while he satisfied himself in the netherworld between dream and reality.

He waited until he was certain she was asleep before he slipped his arm around her waist and drew her close. It was only then that Colin could ease into sleep himself.

Mercedes allowed herself to be persuaded to attend a horse auction at Tattersall's the following day. She suspected Colin knew she wasn't proof against the twins and had put them up to asking her to go. He must have also known she wouldn't have accompanied him to London alone.

Although they had discussed the need to restock Weybourne Park's stable with prime horseflesh, it was decidedly low on Mercedes's list of things to be accomplished. A good stud and healthy mares would be outrageously expensive to purchase as well as maintain. When she wondered aloud if he could afford it at this juncture he shot her a sideways glance and asked if she had other plans for his money.

It was not the most propitious beginning for the trip but Britton and Brendan cut through the tension with their antics and good spirits. Mercedes began to believe that Sylvia had made the less wise decision by choosing to remain at the manor.

Once they arrived at the horse market, Mercedes elected to stay in the carriage. The twins' pleas were of no consequence now and when Colin saw she was quite adamant in her decision, he shooed the boys away.

"Shall I have Henry take you elsewhere while I conduct this business?" Colin asked. He stood just outside the carriage, reluctant to leave her unattended. There were few women at the market and he had not considered what might be made of her presence on his arm, even in the company of her young cousins.

"No," she said. "I'll be fine here where I can watch people coming and going. There's no need for me to be in the thick of it." Mercedes leaned forward on the padded leather bench toward the open window of the carriage. "And I know Henry wants to get down from the driver's box and see the animals as well. You won't be disappointed by listening to his counsel. He knows a great deal about good horseflesh."

Colin nodded. He turned to go, then stepped back again. "I didn't mean for this to be a painful or insulting exercise for you," he said quietly. "I thought if you could be persuaded to stay at my side, you would see you have nothing to fear." Before she could reply, Colin turned on his heel and headed across the yard in the direction of the twins. He called out to them and they came up short, fairly dancing in place until he reached their side and could accompany them safely to the stalls.

Mercedes watched them until they disappeared in the milling crowd. The carriage was jostled as Henry climbed down from the box and hurried off to the stalls. She chastised herself for being so weak-kneed. Wasn't it time she confronted her fear, now when Colin had offered his protection? The thought of that brought a rueful smile to Mercedes's lips and her fingers wavered uneasily on the handle to the carriage door. He couldn't have known that standing at his side would have raised almost as many unsettling emotions as standing next to the horses.

Even as she thought it, she realized she would have to face it. Mercedes twisted the handle and opened the door. She had stepped onto the foot plate when she was roughly unbalanced by a pair of hands on her waist and thrust back into the carriage.

Marcus Severn followed her in, closed the door, and tapped his walking cane against the roof. The carriage wavered slightly as a driver mounted the box and took up the reins. Mercedes was pitched back against the leather cushions when the horses were whipped smartly and bolted forward.

She lunged toward the door but Severn blocked her with his hand. Instead of pushing her away, he grasped her upper arm and yanked her toward him. Mercedes fell across his lap and was caught between his body and one corner of the carriage. She raised her hands defensively. Had he been intent on hurting her she knew the gesture would have been useless.

Severn did not come any closer, however. He smiled instead,

watching the play of emotion on her face. "I wonder if you're more angry or fearful," he said thoughtfully, without inflection. "No matter. I suppose before the day is out I'll give you cause to be both."

Nine

In spite of his words Marcus Severn knew he did not have all day. Pity that, he thought as Mercedes's chin came up. She didn't have the good sense to cower. With time on his side he could have made something of the challenge.

"Where are you taking me?" Mercedes asked.

Severn's answer was to pull the blinds and block the view and the sunlight. The interior of the carriage was cloaked in dusky shadows. Slivers of summer sun cut through the gloom as the vehicle bounced on cobbled streets and the blinds were jarred. Each flash had the searing brightness of lightning, and twice Mercedes was blinded as she tried to stare him down. Severn's well-shaped mouth lifted at one corner and he tapped her lightly on the cheek, mocking her as if she were a child. His smile deepened when she raised her palm to cover the place where he had touched her. It pleased him to think she had felt his touch as a slap.

"We're going for a ride," he said. "Nothing more. Did you hope there would be?"

Mercedes's calves were lying across his lap. The poplin skirt was pushed almost to her knees by her tumble and now Severn's hand lay heavily across her stockinged legs. He kept it there without moving, but when he glanced down his eyes made the journey from her ankles to knees. Mercedes could not quell her shiver.

"You're very quiet," he said casually. "I suspect you're as surprised by my presence as I was by yours. Tattersall's is the last place I expected to see you. Does the captain not know about your fear of horses or does he just not care?" He looked back at her. "Never mind. It isn't important."

Mercedes tore her legs from his grasp and pushed her gown over her knees. She managed to elude him as she pushed out of her corner and swayed forward to the opposite bench. Twisting, she landed on the thickly padded cushions with her legs tucked modestly under her. Her eyes darted toward the carriage door then back to him.

"There's no need to throw yourself out," he said, amused. "Or do I mistake your thoughts? Perhaps I'm the one you wish to toss to the street. Either way, it would raise eyebrows. Do you really wish to call attention to yourself?"

"I wish to return to Tattersall's," she said.

He nodded. "In time. I promise I won't keep you long. I have no plan to steal you away from your captain, though the thought crossed my mind when I saw him standing beside the carriage. The two of you looked very intimate." One of Severn's brows was raised now. He managed to cover deep feeling with an expression of mild interest. "I wonder . . . is he crawling between your thighs at night?"

Mercedes paled but she said nothing.

"He'll only be here another three weeks," Severn said. "How will you manage when he's gone? I've made inquiries about the twins, you know. If Weybourne's body isn't found, or if he doesn't come forward, I may sue for guardianship of the boys. They're my cousins, after all, the same as yours. Our kinship may be more distant, but some people would consider it my duty to take them in hand."

"You couldn't," she said. To Mercedes's own ears she sounded panicked. She drew in a settling breath and repeated the words, more calmly this time. "You couldn't. I'll be granted custody. Everyone knows I've raised them."

"And soon . . . perhaps . . . everyone will know what a slut you are." He watched her fingers curl in her lap but they remained there. He noticed the line of her shoulders change as she slumped forward a little. Her chin lowered as if the effort to hold it up had suddenly become too great. "I see I have your attention."

"What do you want, Severn?" she asked dully.

"Tell me where Weybourne is."

Mercedes's head snapped up. It was the last request she had expected him to make. "I thought you believed he was dead."

"It's been three weeks. I'm realizing I should plan for any eventuality. If he's alive he would have come to one of us for help. He hasn't approached me; that means he went to you."

"You're wrong," she said. "He would never ask me for anything. He knows I'd go to the authorities."

"Would you?" asked Severn, watching her closely. "I wonder . . ."

"Believe anything you like," she said carelessly. "But I can't help you. Even at the risk of my own reputation."

Severn was thoughtful. A muscle worked in his sharply defined jaw. "Even at the risk of losing the twins?" he said after a moment.

Mercedes didn't answer immediately. She knew a little about bluffing and it seemed to her that too quick a response would show her hand. Severn had to believe she meant what she said. "Even then," she said finally, heavily, as if the words had weight and were lifted from her with difficulty. "I can't help you."

Severn stared at her for a long time. His eyes darkened as his anger simmered, then boiled over. Without warning, his hand snaked across the distance that separated him from Mercedes. His fingers tightened on her wrist before she could pull it away. He hauled her effortlessly onto the seat beside him and pinned her in the corner, bracing his arms stiffly on either side of her shoulders. Severn leaned toward her until their mouths were almost touching. "This isn't settled," he said quietly, between tight lips.

Mercedes was careful not to recoil. "Why is it so important to you?"

"Can't you guess?" He lowered one of his hands and touched

her cheek lightly with the back of his hand. His eyes roamed her face, studying her for a reaction.

"It's not because of me," she said.

"You don't place a high enough value on yourself."

Mercedes ignored that. "And it's not about the Park."

"Don't fool yourself into thinking I don't want the Park," he said.

"I don't think my uncle has been such a good friend to you," Mercedes said. There was a flicker in Severn's eyes and she knew she had finally hit upon it. "Has he betrayed you in some way, m'lord? Is that why you want to know where he is? So you can get some of your own back?"

Severn's hand left Mercedes's cheek and closed around her throat. He squeezed just enough to make her struggle for a breath. When she tried to pull away, he held her tight. "You would do well to keep your thoughts to yourself," he said.

It was an effort to speak. "You're going to mark my skin."

"Afraid the captain will see?"

"You should be."

He shook his head but his grip eased slightly. "That's the last thing I fear. Don't mistake me for Weybourne."

Mercedes recognized the truth there. Severn would welcome the opportunity to be rid of Colin Thorne and there was no better way to initiate a challenge than through her. When Severn saw her at the market he had seized on a chance to set that in motion. He wanted to leave his mark on her and he wanted Colin to know that he'd done so. In any match against the Yankee, Marcus Severn was confident of his ability to emerge the victor.

Severn squeezed one more time, choking off Mercedes's half-formed response, then he removed his hand slowly, letting it drift across her bodice and fall into her lap. He covered her fingers with his palm. "I wonder what he'll make of that?" he asked idly.

Tapping the roof of the carriage again with his walking stick, Severn directed the driver back to Tattersall's. "Perhaps he won't have missed you," he said. "You may be on your way home before the bruises show."

Mercedes remained silent, giving him no easy excuse to touch her again. When they reached the horse market, Severn opened the shades and twisted the door handle. Almost as an afterthought—though Mercedes had come to learn that nothing Marcus Severn did was an afterthought—he bent forward and kissed her cheek.

"I'll look forward to hearing from your captain," he said, smiling openly now. "Good day, Sadie."

The interior of the carriage was warm. In spite of that, Mercedes shivered.

On the return to Weybourne Park, the twins slept on either side of Colin. Their fair heads rested against his arms like exquisitely matched bookends. As much as Mercedes would have liked to have them close to her, she appreciated the opportunity for her eyes to linger on them without fear they would chafe at the attention.

Britton and Brendan were quite exhausted. Colin had seen to that. Following his business at Tattersall's he took them to the riverfront and arranged for a tour of the *Remington Siren*, a clipper of the same line as his own *Mystic*. The twins' excitement was difficult to contain as they were given the freedom of the ship, but when Mercedes protested that they might get underfoot, Colin was unconcerned. He let them, one at a time, climb into the rigging with him while Mercedes stood on deck and tried not to imagine cracked skulls and tiny broken bodies.

Britton's appetite for knowledge was insatiable and Brendan always had a question to follow his brother's. Colin answered everything in clear and simple language so that even Mercedes, who knew much less than the boys, began to form a picture of the clipper's cutting edge through the water. There were jibs and halyards and topsails, staysails, and mainsails. There were masts and lines for all the sails and cross-wise beams called gaffs and yards and booms. It was a dizzying array of mechanical parts, of blocks and tackle, of rudders and wheels, all of it brought into a harmony of movement with the wind and water under the command of one man.

Mercedes looked at that man now. He was resting with his head leaning back against the plump leather upholstery, his strong neck exposed by the tilt of his chin. His eyes were closed but she knew he wasn't sleeping. There was still tension in the line of his jaw and none of the unguarded boyish expression she associated with the moments of his deepest sleep.

They had shared little conversation since Tattersall's. For much of the day Colin had been the teacher, directing answers to the boys and communicating to her through them. Even during dinner, which Colin had brought from a local tavern and served in the captain's cabin aboard the *Siren*, she was aware he had little to say to her. She wondered at what point Severn's prints on her throat had become visible and what Colin made of them.

Brendan's head lolled forward heavily and he sighed softly in his sleep. Colin drew up the boy's legs so they rested more comfortably on the seat and eased Brendan's head onto his lap.

"You're very good with them," Mercedes said. She had noticed it often enough, but it was especially true today when the twins were carried away with the excitement of a London adventure. Colin's command of them was so easy and effortless that they had no idea he kept them on a short leash. "They enjoy the attention you show them. I hope you—" She stopped short as Colin lowered his head and looked at her squarely, almost as if he knew the direction of her thoughts.

"Yes?" he drawled.

She may as well say it aloud. He knew she'd been thinking it. "I hope you don't mean to use them as a way to get to me."

"It occurred to me," he said. "Once."

"And now?" she asked softly.

Colin shrugged. "Now I like them better than you."

Mercedes felt herself being pinned back into her seat by his dark eyes. "I see," she said lowly.

"I doubt it." Colin ruffled Brendan's hair. The boy didn't stir. "I had brothers, not twins like this pair of young ruffians, but two of them just the same."

"You told me you have no family."

"And I told you the truth," he said. "I don't know where either of them is and I haven't known for twenty years."

"Twenty years," she whispered, frowning. "But you would have only been Britton and Brendan's age then."

"About that. Decker was four years younger. Greydon was a babe in arms. They may be dead for all I know." In spite of his wish to say this last carelessly, his voice was quietly strained. "It was a long time ago."

Not so long that he had become indifferent, Mercedes thought. A shutter closed over his expression and his polished obsidian eyes were once again unreadable. "I'm sorry," she said. And she was.

Colin looked down at the boy sleeping beside him, then the one in his lap. "So am I," he said softly.

Mercedes watched him turn his attention to the window and understood the subject was closed. This glimpse of his past was the most personal information he had ever offered and already it appeared he was regretting it. What did he imagine she would do with it? She wanted to ask him about his parents and how he had come to be separated from his brothers, but he obviously had no intention of sharing it. Perhaps the real surprise was that he told her as much as he had.

Mercedes unfastened her bonnet and laid it on her lap, smoothing out the pale pink ribbons between her thumb and forefinger. "I saw Severn at Tattersall's today," she said.

Colin's eyes remained remote. "I know. He came up to me during the bidding and made a point of telling me."

Her fingers stilled on the ribbons. "Why didn't you say anything before now?"

"Why didn't you?"

"It would have spoiled the day," she said. "The boys didn't deserve that."

A single brow arched skeptically. "Is that the only reason?"

"I didn't know what you would do."

"Do?" he asked. "Why would I be moved to do anything?" His eyes fell deliberately on her throat and he watched her hand come up slowly to cover her neck. "Oh, you mean because Severn tried to throttle you. Did you tell him I'd call him out for that? Is that why you let him do it?" He smiled narrowly. "I'm aware of Severn's reputation with a pistol. I have been since Weybourne named him as his second. There are easier ways for you to get rid of me, Mercedes. You know where I keep my dagger. Feel free to use it, unless you've lost your stomach for it."

Mercedes frowned and her gray eyes clouded. "What are you saying?" she asked. Her voice rose in proportion to her incredulity. "You actually believe that I concocted some scheme with Severn to force you to issue a challenge?"

"Didn't you?"

Silence settled between them as Mercedes considered what she might say. If she could make Colin believe her, what purpose would then be served by the truth? It could indeed bring about the exact end that Severn wanted, the very end that she wanted to avoid. At last she sighed, her decision made. Her eyes darted away guiltily.

Beyond the carriage dusk was settling over the countryside. Blue-gray light brought the rows of larch and copper beech along the road into dark relief. Cottages set back among the trees were visible by the lanterns marking their windows. Mercedes wondered what it might be like to live in one of them, what problems might face her if she were not the daughter of an earl and trying to hold onto a birthright that no person or law recognized.

"It seems your cynicism is justified again," she said finally. She darted a glance in his direction but did not meet his eyes. "Was I so easy to read?"

"No more than usual." Colin's tone held no boast, rather it was marked by a weary flatness. "I know you have no liking for Severn. That you were willing to join forces with him speaks to your eagerness to be rid of me." He raked back his hair. "I've seen you with Severn. If he was close enough to you to put his hands around your neck, then it's because you allowed it. I know you're capable of defending yourself or at least calling out for help."

"Severn told you what he did?" she asked.

"He hinted that something occurred between the two of you. He would have had me believe it was sexual." His eyes lowered to the bruises on Mercedes's throat. "Perhaps it was. I've heard that choking heightens the moment of pleasure." Colin looked at her frankly. "Does it?"

Mercedes ducked her head and stared at her hands. Her fingers twisted her bonnet ribbons.

"Does it?" he asked again.

There was an ache behind her eyes that blinking could not ease. "Go to hell," she said quietly.

"I probably will."

Mercedes stopped fingering the ribbons. "I didn't suspect Severn's idea would work."

"Severn's idea?" Colin asked. "I thought it had more of your stamp."

"I would have planned it. With Severn it was born of opportunity. He miscalculated badly."

"Oh?"

"It could only have worked if you cared what was done to me. It didn't seem likely that you would."

"Yet you went along with it."

Mercedes shrugged. The pressure in her chest was easing slightly. It shouldn't have mattered what he thought of her, yet she knew the pressure was there because it did. "As you pointed out," she said, meeting his gaze for the first time, "I'm desperate to be rid of you."

Colin carried both boys up the stairs and helped Mercedes get them ready for bed. Between them they thanked him a dozen times for their London adventure before finally nodding off. Mrs. Hennepin caught Mercedes and Colin in the hallway between rooms and offered a light repast. They both refused. After the twins were tucked in their separate beds, Colin escorted Mercedes to Sylvia's room. He poked his head in long enough to bid her good evening, then ushered Mercedes inside.

The library had a selection of brandy, whisky, and port in crystal decanters. Colin poured three fingers of each into separate tumblers and lined them up on the desk. Easing himself into Weybourne's leather chair, he swept up the first tumbler in his palm and raised it in a mocking salute as if Mercedes were present. "Next time," he said softly, "use the goddamn dagger."

Upstairs, Mercedes finished her *tête à tête* with Sylvia and slipped quietly into her own bedchamber. The only good thing to come of Severn's interference was that she wouldn't be expected to share Colin's bed. At least it seemed like a good thing until Mercedes crawled into hers alone. When had her four-poster ever seemed so enormous?

She stretched out under the covers, first on her left side, then the right. She tried drawing her knees toward her chest, with and without hugging a pillow. Lying on her back, she waited for her eyes to adjust to the darkness, then looked for recognizable shapes in the shadows on her ceiling. Turning over, she buried her face in a pillow and dug her toes into the mattress. Finally admitting defeat, Mercedes sat up, lighted the lamp beside her bed, and picked up the book that had bored her to sleep on any number of nights. It was only when she had doggedly read the same page three times with no accompaniment of yawns or comprehension that she tossed the volume down.

Mercedes shrugged into her robe, cinched it at the waist, and padded softly to her door. Hot milk was the answer. She didn't know why she hadn't thought of it right off.

There was a muted band of light slipping out from under the library doors that drew Mercedes's attention. She paused, wondering if it was indeed Colin inside the room, or if the lamps had been left burning unattended. Mercedes laid her hand on the door, then retracted it, and continued on her way to the kitchen, telling herself she didn't care for the answer one way or the other.

The kitchen was deserted. Mercedes poured milk into a sauce-pan and fired up the kindling in the brick stove. She sat on the edge of the old oak table, her bare feet resting on the seat of one of the chairs, and waited for the familiar fragrance of warming milk to rise from the pan.

"Do you think I might have some of that?"

Mercedes swiveled around so quickly that she almost was un-seated. She grabbed the edge of the table with one hand to steady herself, while the other was raised to her heart as if to keep it in place.

Colin was standing just inside the doorway. He was leaning against the wall but the pose was not precisely casual. It took Mercedes a second glance to understand that her visitor was in need of some physical support to remain upright. His bright hair was raked back, but not neatly. It was a cross thatch of indecision where he had first pushed it one way, then another, then yet another. The sharp, usually impenetrable black eyes were a little flat now, a little dull. The narrow smile was no longer in evidence as the effort would have been too much. Instead, the corners of his mouth were turned faintly downward. He looked rather dis-concerted as he glanced around the kitchen. When his glance alighted on her again, he seemed both hopeful and apologetic.

Mercedes wasn't moved. "You're drunk," she said flatly.

Colin considered her observation. His head was muzzy, the floor was listing, and his tongue was thick in his mouth. "I be-lieve you're right," he said pleasantly.

"I know I am," Mercedes said. "I've seen enough of it." She eased herself off the table and pushed a chair toward him. "Sit here, before you fall."

Colin made a point of studying the wall that was supporting his lean frame. "This seems sturdy enough."

Mercedes gave the chair a little shake. "Sit!"

Weaving forward on unsteady legs, Colin twisted the chair

around and straddled it, dropping like a stone at the last moment.
His salute was clumsier than it was smart.

"You don't need any warm milk," she said, moving to stand
at the hearth. "Like as not, it will make you sick. How much did
you drink?"

Colin held up three fingers.

"Three fingers?" It wasn't so much, Mercedes thought. The
earl could easily finish a decanter with less effect to himself than
Colin showed from a single tumbler. Sighing, she shook the
saucepan. Milk sizzled against the hot edge. "Perhaps a better
question is *what* did you drink?"

"I believe the first was brandy."

"The first?"

"Then whisky."

Mercedes began to understand the problem. "You had three
fingers of whisky as well?"

"And port for a chaser."

"Port?" She pulled a face. "With the brandy and whisky? You
followed them with port?"

Colin's arms were folded across the top rung of the ladderback
chair. He rested his chin against them and nodded. His smile was
sheepish. "You think it was foolish?"

"You're too drunk to know how foolish," she said. Mercedes
could not quite hide her own sly smile. "But on the morrow
you'll learn it well enough. A sore head will be the least of your
worries." She took the saucepan off the stove and poured the
scalded milk into a mug. Sipping it gingerly, Mercedes watched
Colin over the rim of rising steam. His lids were lowering and
his handsome features contorted comically as he tried to stifle a
yawn. She should leave him here, she thought. He would be able
to add a stiff neck and aching back to the pounding that would
visit his head in the morning.

Mercedes sighed. "Come along," she said. "I'll help you find
your way to your room."

It wasn't as easy as she might have hoped. Colin's arm lay
around her shoulders heavily and she had to thrust her hip against

his thigh to support him. Their graceless gait got them down the
hall in fits and starts but the grand staircase loomed before them
as their biggest challenge. Halfway to the top Colin decided he
wanted to sit down. This was communicated to Mercedes in the
most elemental way: Colin simply twisted beneath her arm and
let his long legs collapse like a house of cards. Mercedes counted
herself fortunate not to be under him or across his lap.

"Oh, no," she said, looking down on the ruffled crown of his
bright hair. "There's no resting."

Colin glanced up. His mouth was shaped by an impish, youthful smile. He clasped her outstretched hand and tugged once.
There was only the faintest resistance before Mercedes's legs
folded and she was sharing the step with him. "No resting," he
said confidentially. "Sometimes I just sit."

Mercedes let it pass. She supposed it made sense to him. Neither did she object when he looped his arm through the crook of
hers. It took her a moment to realize that she was no longer
supporting him, but that her shoulder lay lightly against his and
she was leaning into him. Out of habit she started to pull away.

Colin exerted the smallest pressure to bring her back to him.
"If I can sit," he said, "you can lean."

"All right," she said after a moment. "Just as long as there's
no resting."

His smile was a trifle crooked as he accepted her concession.
It faded slowly when he turned away and other thoughts occupied
him. He was quite comfortable with the silence and it was a
pleasure to him that Mercedes felt no need to fill it with chatter.
They could have been on the river bank, he with his line in the
water, she with a book in her lap. There was a note of quiet
resignation in his voice when he finally spoke. "I'm going to
have a very sore head in the morning, aren't I?"

Mercedes couldn't help smiling to herself. So much for sup-
posing Colin's thoughts had been running a deep course. "Yes,"
she said. "I think I mentioned that earlier."

"Must be where I heard it."

Her grin deepened. "You don't drink often, do you?"

"No. Not like tonight. Never seems like a good idea."

"Then why tonight?"

"Seemed like a good idea."

"Oh." To hide her unease, Mercedes smoothed the material of her gown over her knees. She looked back over her shoulder at the steps left to climb. "Perhaps we should go." When she turned again it was to find Colin's mouth very near her own. He was watching her closely, his dark eyes holding her as steadily as he might have with his hands. If she spoke now her lips would brush his. Mercedes's lungs ached with the breath she was holding. In her lap her fingers clenched.

Colin lifted his head and the moment was over. His narrow smile held a hint of regret but there was no apology. He stood, pulling Mercedes to her feet. Upright now, he wavered unsteadily. She was instantly available to him, offering her entire body as a crutch. He glanced down at her as she fitted herself against him. When Mercedes brought his arm around her neck and gripped his hand so that it lay close to her breast, it occurred to Colin that she delighted in practicing sweet torture. But when she lifted her face, her gray eyes were merely grave, not guilty, and he was reminded that she had little sense of herself as someone desirable.

"Are you quite certain you're ready?" she asked.

"You have no idea how ready," he said. When she frowned uncertainly, he sighed. "Lead on, Mercedes."

They made it to Colin's room without stopping, but Colin only made it as far as the wing chair before he sat down.

"I don't think you want to sleep there," she told him.

"I do." He was making himself comfortable, slumping against the brocade back and stretching out his long legs. He folded his arms across his chest then shut his eyes.

Mercedes studied him a moment. Colin's head was already listing at an odd angle that would cause him grief in the morning. And no man's back could curve at such an unnatural angle without pain upon straightening. He would be sorry in the morning for having ignored her advice. She could walk away now and know she had given her best effort to make him see reason.

She sat. Her back rested narrowly against the chair and her shoulder brushed his leg. Her own knees were drawn up toward her chest, her robe and nightgown spread out around her like a bell. She stiffened a little as Colin laid his hand on her shoulder. His thumb made a pass along her neck just where Marcus Severn's fingerprints blossomed on her pale skin.

"Do you believe in keeping promises?" he asked.

The question surprised Mercedes. His hand on her neck distracted her. "I don't think I understand," she said carefully.

"Do you believe in keeping promises?" he repeated.

It was hardly any clearer to her the second time. The question wasn't difficult, but why was he asking it? "Well, yes," she said slowly. "It's a point of honor, isn't it?" She tried to turn to see him but his hand kept her looking straight ahead.

Behind her, Colin nodded gravely. "That's what I thought." His fingers slipped into Mercedes's hair. The pins that held it in place loosened under his gentle urging. He sifted through the strands, letting them slip over his fingers as if they were liquid.

His attention confused Mercedes. Her breath became shorter and harder to draw as she waited for his hand to tighten in her hair and yank on her scalp. It was her experience that tenderness was the precursor to some pain. Anticipation was often more cruel than the reality. She willed him to have done with her.

"And promises to oneself?" he asked. His fingers drifted to the nape of her neck. "How do you figure those?"

Words seemed to be frozen in her throat. "I . . . I don't know what you mean," she said. A shiver ran the course of her spine as the rough pads of his fingers drifted over her skin.

"Is it still a point of honor to keep a promise to oneself?" His hand was buried in her thick hair again. Tendrils of bittersweet chocolate poured through his splayed fingers.

It was almost as if he were speaking to himself, Mercedes thought, as if he were asking the questions aloud to hear himself think through the answers. "Honor starts with oneself," she said softly. His hand stilled in her hair. Mercedes tensed, raising her shoulders to ease the pain she was certain was coming.

Colin sighed. "I thought we might be of one mind on that point." He let his hand fall back to his lap.

Mercedes waited. Her shoulders ached from holding them so stiffly. The back of her neck was cramped and her heart was thumping uncomfortably hard in her chest. She swiveled her head slowly to look at him. There were no visible lines of strain cutting across his forehead or narrowing his mouth. He appeared as relaxed as anytime she had seen him sleeping, yet Mercedes could sense by his breathing that he was still awake. When she started to move away his eyes opened immediately.

"You're very skittish this evening," he said, studying her with his implacable dark eyes. "Is there somewhere you're supposed to be?"

"I . . . no, there's nowhere." She regretted her slight hesitation as it caused her to be regarded with more scrutiny. "That is," she corrected. "I'd like to go to bed."

Colin was instantly agreeable. "Of course." He pushed himself to his feet, drew Mercedes to hers, and gave her a gentle nudge in the direction of the bed.

"I was thinking of my own bed," she said.

"I wasn't."

Mercedes gave him an uneasy, over the shoulder glance. "Very well." She turned away, bent her head, and began to loosen the belt of her robe. She would have allowed it to fall to the floor but Colin caught it and folded it carefully over the back of the desk chair. He watched her turn back the covers on his bed. Instead of crawling in, she perched on the edge, her heels resting on the frame. He was not so many sheets to the wind that he couldn't see the lines of apprehension that defined her every feature.

Unnerved by his steady regard, Mercedes's chin came up. "Have done with it," she said flatly.

Colin's brows lifted and his eyes took on a certain blank look that could not be feigned. "Have done with what?" he asked.

She raised her hands helplessly, struggling to find the words. "With whatever you're going to do."

"I'm going to get undressed."

When Mercedes's hands dropped back to the bed her left one fell on the pillow. No thought was involved as her fingers curled around the corner. In a swift, swinging motion she tore it free from the sheets and let it fly in Colin's direction.

Surprise, more than the whisky, port, and scotch, was responsible for Colin's staggering step back. He caught the pillow against his gut and steadied himself before he threw it toward the foot of the bed. "What was that in aid of?" he asked, standing his ground. "Are you trying to provoke me?" Even as he heard himself ask the question, he knew the answer. The blank look in his eyes faded and they sharpened with understanding. His voice lowered as he spoke, this time to himself, "Of course, you were." Colin's head tilted to one side as he skimmed Mercedes's wide eyes and pale face. "Why, Mercedes? What do you want?"

Her fingers tightened on the edge of the bed. She spoke in a burst of staccatos. "I want it over with."

Colin recognized the alcohol *had* made him thick-headed. "I'm not going to hurt you," he said. "That's what you've been expecting, isn't it? That I'm going to punish you for that bit of bad business with Severn this afternoon."

Mercedes was not convinced. "Aren't you?"

"I told you once that I would never hurt you. Have I given you reason to think I might change my mind?"

There was an ache in her throat that made it difficult to speak. The same ache spread and became a stinging sensation behind her eyes and a throbbing in her temples. She felt the press of tears and blinked them back. The lump in her throat was swallowed hard. "What then was all that talk of promises?" she asked. "Are you a man who keeps or breaks them?"

Colin felt her question as a blow. Had she hit him with her fists, he could not have felt it more keenly. "I was speaking of other promises," he said. "It had nothing to do with you."

"It has *something* to do with me," she contradicted. "Else you wouldn't have made a point of saying it in front of me. You meant to make me wonder at your intentions. And if you have to ask yourself if promises should be kept, then why wouldn't I be concerned that you might not honor the ones made to me?"

Colin stared at her for a long moment while silence filled the space between them. He could see what it had cost her to speak so plainly. Where her fingers clutched the edge of the mattress, her knuckles were white. Her gray eyes shone with a wash of unshed tears. The cascade of dark hair along her shoulders shimmered with the faint trembling of her tightly held frame.

What she suggested he had done was nothing short of cruel. He had asked her to sit beside him because she quieted him in a way only the sea ever had. He recalled laying his hand on her shoulder, touching her neck, her hair. Her skin was achingly soft beneath his fingers and her hair was like silk. There was comfort to be drawn from the steadiness of her pulse along the fragile cord of her throat. And all the while he was taking pleasure from her presence, she was waiting for the first blow. The anticipation would have been an agony.

"You're wrong about me," he said at last. Colin turned on his heel and stepped into the dressing room.

Mercedes picked up the pillow at the foot of the bed and held it against her. He hadn't raised his voice. He hadn't threatened. He hadn't lifted a hand against her. Still, she had the sense of being beaten down, this time by the weight of her suspicions and mistrust.

Mercedes glanced at the door. She could leave. She knew she could and she knew he wouldn't follow—not tonight, not when she had accused him of deliberately playing to her fears. Did she want to leave? That was a question she had been avoiding, less certain of herself than she was of Colin. It was far simpler to think about what he wanted.

She listened to him moving around in the dressing room, the sound of him washing his face, cleaning his teeth, removing his clothes. She heard him swear softly as he stubbed his toe. This was followed by an intermittent thudding as he hopped on one foot. For reasons she didn't entirely understand, it was the hopping that made up her mind. In his inebriated state, he couldn't have managed it with any grace.

Mercedes was lying on her side facing the far wall when Colin entered the bedchamber. He was wearing a pair of drawstring drawers that rode low on his hips and nothing else. He paused at the bedside to turn back the lamp, then raised the sheet and crawled in. She hadn't lingered on his side of the bed long. The sheets were still cool. He stretched out on his back and cradled his head in his hands. He listened to her breathing and knew she had been waiting for him.

"I'm sorry," she said.

"You don't have to be here," he said.

They spoke simultaneously and neither quite heard the other. Mercedes turned over so she could face him. "I'm sorry," she repeated.

"I said, you don't have to—"

"No, I didn't mean that I didn't hear you. I mean I'm sorry that I misjudged your intentions." She fell silent but Colin didn't answer her apology. "You don't know what it was like with my uncle," she said.

"No, but I'm learning a little more every day."

"I don't want your pity."

"I didn't think you did. I imagine that if you could help yourself, you wouldn't give me any hint of the dark side of his nature." Colin's short laugh was without humor. "To say he has a dark side suggests there's something redeeming about the other half. From what I've observed, the Earl of Weybourne made a thorough job of being a bastard."

A small smile tugged at Mercedes's mouth. "Now you've insulted bastards everywhere."

Colin glanced at her, surprised. "So you don't always come to Weybourne's defense."

"Not always," she said quietly. "I suppose I'm hating him a little more these days. Just when I think he's out of my life, something he's said or done comes back to touch me."

"Like tonight."

She nodded. "Your drinking . . . I didn't know what . . ."

"And when I asked you to stay with me . . ."

"You didn't ask," she corrected him.

"No, I didn't, did I?" Colin fixed his eyes on the ceiling. "That's what I was trying to tell you when I came in. I want you to know that you don't have to be here."

"I know."

"Then you're here because you want to be."

"I didn't say that," she said.

Colin's eyes darted from the ceiling back to Mercedes. He could make out the serenity of her expression even in the darkness, but there was something else, something she was holding back that made her lower her lashes and avert her eyes. "Then why?"

She regarded him steadily now. "I'm here because I know it's where you want me to be."

Colin raised himself on one elbow. "I'm not sure—"

"I am." She raised her hand and placed two fingers against his mouth. "Don't say anything. Just accept it. I have." Her hand slid over his cheek and her thumb traced his lower lip. She watched him closely, drawing him nearer with her eyes and the parted invitation of her own mouth.

Colin bent his head but it was Mercedes who initiated the kiss. She laid her mouth across his and tugged gently on his upper lip. Her tongue slipped along the sensitive underside. Groaning softly, Colin rolled Mercedes onto her back. Her fingers were in his hair, dipping into the thick thatch at his nape. Her nails drew lightly across his scalp and his entire body contracted as sensation swept the length of him.

She deepened the kiss, thrusting her tongue in his mouth, tasting the hint of alcohol that remained. She stole his breath. Her hands moved down his neck and across the broad beams of his shoulders. She lightly scored his arms with her fingernails and raised another shiver under his skin. Mercedes felt her breasts swell, the nipples harden to tiny stones, then she moved under

Colin, letting him feel the changes in her body against his naked chest.

She raised her knee. Her nightshift rode to her thigh. Colin's palm was warm and getting hotter as he let it trail from knee to hip and back again. On the third pass her hips lifted of their own accord as the need to have him there, moving intimately between her thighs, overwhelmed her.

Mercedes let her fingers slip along the edge of his drawers, dipping just below the material a time or two, lingering long enough and with enough carnal intent so there could be no mistaking she meant to do it.

The straps of her nightgown were pushed past her shoulders. Colin's mouth touched her neck, her shoulder, then sipped at the skin at the base of her throat. He drew a whimper from her and felt her arch beneath him. He sucked her nipples through the thin cotton nightshift. The damp abrasion of his tongue on the material caused her to cry out.

He covered her mouth with his again. His hips pressed against her and they rocked together, restrained only by the barrier of their clothes.

Mercedes pushed at his drawers. He lifted her shift. Her hands slipped between their bodies and she grasped and guided him into her. His sharp thrust secured them but not as much as the arms she slid around his back.

Watching Mercedes closely, Colin held himself still. She returned his look from eyes that held only a hint of gray at the rims. Dark black centers mirrored his wanting. Her lips were soft and damp and parted. The first faint flush of desiring colored her cheeks.

Restraint tightened Colin's body and lent his voice a raspy edge. "Tell me this is because you want it," he said.

Mercedes caressed the length of his spine and felt the involuntary thrust of his body against hers. Her body contracted around him and when she saw the effect, the next contraction was by her will.

Colin was not proof against this pressure but he held himself back long enough to make his demand a second time. "Tell me," he said.

Mercedes moved under him, raising her hips to begin what he was denying them both. When his head lowered, she whispered against his ear. "I want what you want."

It was not the answer he had asked for. It was all she was willing to say, and his choices were two: he could accept it or he could leave her.

Colin did not think he could leave her.

Mercedes cradled him as he rocked her with the force of his thrusts. She could not make him raise his voice, or threaten her, or lift a hand against her, but she could bring him to this edge where his body was pressed hard to hers and where she finally had to yield to him.

Her hands dropped away from Colin's back and found purchase in the sheets. At the point of their joining there was heat that was spreading across her skin. She felt it in her fingertips, in her breasts, in her belly, and where she touched him he felt it, too.

"It's not supposed to be a punishment," he said against her mouth. "Never that."

She gasped a little at his perception. "I don't—"

He kissed her hard to cut off the lie. "Yes, you do," he whispered. "It's exactly what you think." Now when he held himself still it was Mercedes's voice that rasped as she called out his name. Colin kissed her again, gently this time, and said softly against her lips, "It's not being done *to* you, Mercedes, but *for* you."

Ten

Sleep eluded Mercedes. Her limbs felt languid, her lashes heavy, in the aftermath of Colin's loving. She was deliciously sated, warm and comfortable in the large bed. Colin slept beside her, one arm thrown over her waist and his leg flush to hers. His breathing was even, the regularity soothing as the ticking of a clock. Mercedes thought it was impossible to be more replete.

Her mind was the thing on edge, a tangle of thoughts so twisted she envisioned a skein of yarn she could never unravel.

Colin's voice came to her again, soft and faintly challenging, "It's not being done *to* you, Mercedes, but *for* you." She had stiffened then, struck by the realization that an act she had vaguely considered selfish, could be done in the spirit of giving. He hadn't given her time to think more than that. His mouth took hers again and the thrust of his body filled her deeply. She held him close, not wanting to have him apart from her for even a moment. Her breasts were achingly sensitive to his touch and she arched to prolong the contact and friction of their flesh.

Heat that had blossomed between them danced along the length of her limbs and she took short breaths, sipping the air, as Colin surrounded, held, and joined her. Tension kept her body taut and at the moment of coming she tried to hold back her inarticulate cry of pleasure. Colin did not let her keep it to herself and laid his mouth on her breast, tugging gently so that the cry spilled from her.

There was satisfaction for him in her surrender. His movements quickened and the contractions of her body pulled him over excitement's edge. He buried his face in the curve of her neck and filled his lungs with the fragrance of her hair and skin. When he began to shift his weight off her, she stopped him and kept him close to her awhile longer.

They said nothing. They felt the quieting of their hearts and the ease of each breath. The sheets rustled as Mercedes adjusted their cocoon. There was no other sound in the room and the silence took on a certain weight and comfort, like another blanket to cover them.

Colin had fallen asleep then. Mercedes had not.

She turned on her side toward him and nudged Colin's leg aside. Moving his hand from her waist, Mercedes sat up. She leaned against the headboard with her shoulder, her legs curled to one side. Colin didn't stir.

Mercedes studied the shadowed profile of his face, the strong lines that were softened slightly by sleep. Reaching out, she let her fingertips trace his hairline from temple to temple, sweeping lightly across his forehead and pushing back a heavy lock of sunshine-bright hair.

He was an astonishingly handsome man. His features weren't refined or classically molded in the way Severn's were, but there were firm, patrician lines that lent him a certain authority even in sleep.

The backs of Mercedes's fingers brushed his cheek then lay without pressure against his neck. She could feel his pulse, faint and steady. Her fingers trailed along his shoulder. His skin was warm. She laid her hand on his chest and kept it there.

Colin didn't wake until Mercedes left the bed. He knew himself to be a light sleeper as well as requiring little of it. This sensation of rising from deep, almost drugged sleep was new to him. He opened his eyes only a fraction, just enough to watch her progress from the window where she had been standing to the wing chair where she curled in one corner. Her light cotton shift gave her a wraith-like appearance. When she moved she seemed no more substantial than mist rising from the sea.

"Are you going to sleep there?" he asked.

Mercedes gave a start. His voice was deep and faintly raspy and it was exactly that voice that had whispered in her ear while he held her so intimately. The memory was suddenly so powerful she could actually feel him inside her, holding himself still while his mouth and hands drew another response from her. The shiver that coursed through her was one of pure pleasure.

Colin raised the covers. "Come here," he said. "You're cold."

She didn't deny it. To do so would have forced her to tell him about the pinwheel of sparks that had just skittered across her skin and the bone-deep heat it had left in its wake. Mercedes rose from the chair and crossed the room in a delicate, graceful glide of which she was perfectly unconscious. She slipped under the covers that were lifted for her while Colin moved over to make room.

It wasn't until she was beside him that he wondered if she wanted to be there. "You can go to your own room," he said rather stiffly, rising up on one elbow. "If you want."

His less than gracious offer raised a small smile. "No, there's time for that later. I can be back in my room before morning. It's only half past three."

Colin was struck by how long and how deeply he had slept. The last thing he remembered was slipping his arm around Mercedes's waist and the natural curving of her body to his. He tucked a lock of dark hair behind her ear and asked quietly, "Have you slept at all?"

"A little, I think. Off and on." Mostly off, she thought, but she kept this to herself. "I didn't mean to wake you. In fact, I was trying to avoid it. I was restless so I left the bed."

He knew the kind of restlessness that could keep a body awake for hours on end. Until Mercedes came to his bed he had never known there was respite for it. "Can I get you something?" he asked. Colin remembered her earlier trek to the kitchen. "Warm milk?"

Mercedes shook her head. "No. I'm fine." She hesitated, her eyes darting over his face.

"What is it?" Colin asked.

"Nothing," she said. Again there was a hesitation. "It's just that . . . no, nothing."

Both of Colin's brows kicked up and he let a lengthy silence do the talking for him.

"Well, I've been wondering what you meant earlier . . . about the promises . . . about keeping them." Mercedes noticed the change in him immediately, the shuttered expression, the guarded look. The lines at the corners of his eyes deepened and where his body touched hers, she could feel his tension. "I didn't think you'd want to tell me," she said.

"I had too much to drink."

Disappointed, she nodded. "I thought it would be something like that."

Colin sighed. "None of it was about you."

"I know. I believe you." She glanced at him again, her dark eyes uncertain. "But if it wasn't about me, I wondered, you know, who it might be about."

Colin lay on his back. The last thing he expected was for Mercedes to move closer and place her head on his shoulder. Her arm rested lightly on his chest and the fabric of her nightgown was soft against his skin. She was warm and smooth and restful. Unlike him, her silence was completely undemanding.

"They came for the baby first," Colin said at last. He knew he had captured her complete attention. In a low, steady voice devoid of most inflection or feeling, he told Mercedes about Decker and Grey and Cunnington's Workhouse. There were some things he kept to himself—the mindless cruelty of the older boys, the abuses he witnessed and was almost a victim of, and how he had nearly starved himself to make certain his brothers had enough to eat. He knew Mercedes was not naive about the conditions in workhouses like the one the Cunningtons operated. The few questions she asked proved that she was quite able to elaborate on descriptions when he did not.

Colin's account was finished in the same tone it had begun, as if he were offering information that had no bearing on the child he was or the man he became. "The promise wasn't really made to them; they were too young to understand. I made it to myself. I promised I would find them and we would be together." His low laughter was filled with self-mockery. "I didn't realize then what a task I had set for myself. When Greydon's new mother said she didn't care for his name, it didn't mean anything to me, but after searching these past ten years, I have to believe his name was changed. He could be anybody and called anything."

"And Decker?"

"I think he was adopted by French missionaries but I've never been able to verify it. I've been to ports in the South Pacific and I've made inquiries through French missions. I've even looked at manifests and passenger lists of ships that were lost around the same time he was taken, but there's never been so much as a thread to follow."

Mercedes ached for him. She said nothing because words were inadequate. She had no words for the hurt in her heart and no words that could heal the hole in his.

The first splash against Colin's skin was like a scalding raindrop. It was quickly followed by another. With the third drop he identified the source. "Mercedes?"

She didn't lift her head or acknowledge her name.

"You're crying." He had never seen her cry. Even when he thought she had cause to do so, she invariably seemed to swallow her hurt and her tears. He had seen her gray eyes glisten with the evidence of her pain or anger, but she had never let him, or anyone—if the stories he heard were true—see her cry.

Now she was crying for him. Colin was moved powerfully by this gift, just as he was by her rare and beautiful smile. His fingers threaded in her hair and the fragrance of lavender and musk was lifted in the air. He bent his head and laid his lips against the crown of her dark hair.

"I gave each of my brothers one of our mother's earrings," he told her quietly. "She had entrusted them to me before she died. They were very old and valuable, a gift from my father to her and they had been in the family for generations, presented by the queen."

Mercedes pulled at one corner of the sheet and tried to surreptitiously wipe her eyes. She was thankful that if Colin noticed, at least he didn't comment. Her voice, however, was still thick with unshed tears. "The queen?" she asked. "Do you mean Anne or Mary II? That would make them more than a hundred years old."

"The earrings are nearly twice that," he said. "I was speaking of *the* queen. Elizabeth. I believe they were made for her as a coronation gift. If memory serves, that would be 1558." He enjoyed watching Mercedes try to take in this information. She was sitting up now, reaching for the bedside lamp to light it. When she'd done so, she held it aloft a moment, staring at him as if she'd never seen him before.

Mercedes's brow was furrowed and her mouth was pulled to one side as she considered what he'd told her. "You have earrings that were given to someone in your family by Queen Elizabeth?" she asked with no small amount of skepticism.

"Had," he corrected. "I *had* the earrings. Now Grey and Decker have them. And they were given to my great-great-great grandfather for some service he performed for his queen."

Mercedes replaced the lamp on the table. "Then you're English," she said slowly.

He laughed a little at that. "Most Americans were," he said, "at one time or another, but it's not a point we dwell on."

"No," she said. "I mean *you're* English."

"Not any longer."

"But you were *born* here."

"I thought you knew that."

"How would I know?"

"Most people can tell by my accent."

"You speak like a Yank."

"To Yanks I talk like a bleedin' Limey." Colin cradled his head in his palms and watched Mercedes. For reasons he didn't understand, she seemed taken by this information. "Is it so important?" he asked.

"No," she said quickly. Then, "Well, yes, it is." She looked down at her hands, wondering how to explain, and back at him when she found the words. "It's about Weybourne Manor you see. I didn't think I minded that it would become the property of an American. I didn't think I could be so small about it, but I suspect I was, because now that I know you're English, well, it's something of a relief to me."

"And it doesn't hurt that I once held a pair of earrings that were worn by the queen."

His dry tone mocked her but Mercedes entered into the spirit of it. "It never hurts to have royal connections," she said haughtily. "The Leydens were particular favorites of Queen Elizabeth, and I believe she took one Earl of Weybourne for a lover."

"Yes, but did he get to keep her earbobs?"

"Better," Mercedes said, her eyes flashing mischievously. "He got to keep his head."

Colin's deep laughter rumbled in his chest. He pulled her down and kissed her winsome smile away. He might have been able to do more than that except her curiosity was piqued and questions kept slipping in between the kisses.

Mercedes lay on her stomach beside him, supported by her elbows and a pillow she had folded and stuffed under her chin. Chocolate-brown hair framed her face and spilled over her shoulders. In contrast to the Madonna-like aura that surrounded her, Mercedes's features were seriously composed. Her wide gray eyes regarded Colin gravely and there was a small crease between her brows where her forehead puckered.

"Tell me about the earrings," she said. "They must be singular if they were fashioned for the queen."

"They were pearl studs with a raindrop of pure gold dangling from them. The letters ER were engraved in script on each drop and the pearl stud was set in a gold crown. I'd know them if I saw them again."

"Elizabeth Regina," Mercedes said, awed. "How did you manage to pass them to your brothers?"

"When I held Grey for the last time I turned my back and slipped one between his gown and his blankets. I placed the other in Decker's pocket the morning he went to meet his new parents. Decker would have recognized the earring as one our mother wore. I have no idea what the couple who took Grey made of what they found in his blanket, or if they even found it." Colin drew in a breath and exhaled slowly. "At eight I knew that I may never recognize my brothers again. The earrings are the only link I have to them." His laughter was quiet, even a little sad. "And it's not likely I'll come across them wearing one of the queen's bobs."

Mercedes had thought the same thing but she hadn't the heart to say it. "Do you really think if you quit searching now it will be breaking the promise?"

Colin didn't answer right away. He stared at the ceiling, watching shadows chase light as the bedside lamp flickered. "It will be giving up," he said at last. "It will be admitting I failed at the only thing I ever set out to do."

"Failure?" Mercedes asked. "At the only thing you . . . but what about the records you set in your clippers, the wagers you've won? You've had men at your command and a fleet of ships for your use. Weybourne Park is yours. How can you say you've never set out to do anything save find your brothers?"

It was in Colin's silence that Mercedes finally grasped the answer. "It was never about the sea," she said softly. "The ships . . . your career . . . the Remington line . . . it's always been about finding Decker and Grey."

She realized then how little she had ever known about him, more than that, she realized how little she understood him. Mercedes had imagined the sea was his life, the clippers, his love, and now she saw that they had only ever been a means to an end.

"I would have gone with anyone," Colin said. His glance dropped away from the ceiling and found Mercedes's light gray eyes watching him. "Just to get away from Cunnington's I believe

I would have gone with the devil himself. I was fortunate it didn't come to that. Jack Quincy was a better bargain. Not that he gave much for my chances of making it through that first voyage. He told me later it was why he kept a close eye on me. He expected me to keel over and he didn't want me slipping overboard. I think he had plans to return my body to Cunnington and demand his money back."

Mercedes's eyes widened. "You're not serious."

Colin merely raised one brow.

"I think he *was* the devil," she said, appalled.

"Jack was practical. He worked hard and he didn't get where he was by squandering his money or that of his captains. It wasn't a square-rigged clipper that took me from London to Boston. In those days it was a three-masted schooner and she rode the waves hard. We carried a full load of cargo and no passengers. The captain of the *Sea Dancer* was John Remington himself. He fell ill on the voyage to London, laid low by the same fever that killed his cabin boy. Jack came to Cunnington's looking for a nurse-maid."

"And he took you."

Colin nodded. "I promised to return what he paid Cunnington for me with interest."

"He must have fancied that."

"I think he did."

"You survived the voyage."

"Yes," he said. "I survived." He had no intention of telling her how he survived or that lives had been taken to save his own. "Quincy kept watch and Remington took a liking to me. It was easier to stay alive than I first thought. The food was better and more plentiful. There was exercise in the guise of hard work, but there was also fresh air and sunshine and an almost endless sky."

"And you had your promise to keep."

Colin smiled faintly and pushed back a heavy lock of hair that had fallen over her shoulder. She was beginning to understand. "I'm certain that had a lot to do with my tenacity." He let his hand fall back. "When we arrived in Boston Mrs. Remington

was waiting at the dock to meet her husband. She had her newborn daughter in her arms. The captain hadn't even seen his child
yet. You can imagine there was a great deal of excitement on the
wharf. No one really knows how it happened—there were as
many different versions as there were witnesses—but everyone
always agreed on the ending. Mrs. Remington took a spill off
the gangway and she and her daughter landed in Boston Harbor.

"The captain never hesitated. He dove right in after his wife.
Her skirts and petticoats pulled her down deeper and faster than
you can imagine—unless you've taken a dive like that yourself?"

Mercedes shook her head. "What about the baby?"

"Captain Remington came up with his wife and his daughter's
blankets, but no daughter. I suppose I was the first one to realize
they didn't have the baby between them. That's why I jumped in.
Jack always said he missed me before anyone missed the baby.
He wondered what the hell I was doing. By the time he understood, I was bringing Jonna to the surface."

"Jonna," Mercedes said softly, more to herself than to Colin.
"Jonna Remington. You write to her. I've posted letters."

"I *work* for her," Colin said.

Mercedes blinked. "You mean she owns the line?"

"That's what I mean."

"But she must only be Chloe's age."

"A year older."

"But surely she doesn't manage it," Mercedes said.

Colin's mouth pulled to one side in a narrow, lopsided grin.
"I confess to finding your disbelief a surprise. How long have
you been managing Weybourne Park?"

"It's not the same thing."

"It's very much the same thing. Only Jonna's had more help
than you. There's no one she's ever had to fight for her inheritance. The Remington Line became hers when her father died.
She was fifteen at the time."

"Her mother?"

"Like your Aunt Georgia, she died in childbirth when Jonna
was six."

"I never imagined you worked for a woman," she said slowly.

He laughed at that. "Your entire *country* works for a woman, and she's younger than you."

"Only by a year or so," she said with some asperity. "And you can't compare Queen Victoria to Jonna Remington."

"I know. Jonna doesn't have to put up with Parliament." He heard Mercedes sigh. "You're really quite amazed, aren't you?"

"I suppose it's not flattering to my own sex, but yes, I am. For a woman to manage a business . . . it's just not done."

"It's that sort of thinking that entailed estates and helped you lose Weybourne Park," he said, giving no quarter. "You can stand on ceremony too long. Eventually it crumbles under your feet."

"You're not English at all, are you?" she said after a moment. "You're a thorough Yank."

Colin's grin was spontaneous and rakish. He didn't know that it took Mercedes's breath away. "Through and through," he said. "I have been since the day I fished Jonna out of Boston Harbor."

"Did the Remingtons take you in?"

"Not exactly. I didn't live at the house, if that's what you mean."

Mercedes had the impression that it had been Colin's decision. She imagined him as he must have been at eight, thin and reedy, with great dark eyes in a narrow face. *She* would have taken him in. For saving her baby she would have raised him as her own.

"But they showed they were grateful in other ways," Colin went on. "Mrs. Remington made certain I was schooled. I was the only member of the crew with my own tutor. I wasn't always happy about her manner of saying thank you, but she was not someone you could refuse. Jonna takes a lot of her stubborn will from her mother."

"What else did they do for you?" Mercedes asked.

"I never wanted for clothes or books or spending money. I earned a decent wage for my work, but there was always something extra put aside for me. I never suspected how much until Captain Remington passed away. He made me an investor in the line."

"So when the business was doing well—"

"I was doing *very* well," he finished for her. "Jack gave up command of his ship to help Jonna run the line and I took over as master of *Liberty*. When Jonna built her first clipper I was named its master."

"*Mystic*?"

"No, the first was *Charlotte Reid*, after her mother. I took her out for two years and across three oceans. I only gave her up because Jonna and Jack had something faster for me. That was two clippers ago. I've only been at *Mystic*'s helm for eight months."

"Each one faster than the one before."

"That's what they ask me to prove."

"And so you make wagers and break records."

"I break records because there are always people who don't believe I can. I make wagers because someone will pay to see me fail."

"You've made a fortune, haven't you?" she asked.

"Some would say so."

"What would you say?"

Colin's dark eyes narrowed as he studied her, trying to gauge her interest. "Are you planning to write another bank draft?" he asked.

Not looking at him, Mercedes sat up and smoothed out her pillow. She leaned over to the lamp and turned it back. The light flickered once and then was gone. She welcomed the darkness that obscured her pale face and regretful glance. "I know I deserve that, but I wish you wouldn't make mention of it again. I think you forget my presence in this room is the payment you asked for. It will cost you something additional to tear a strip off my flesh."

"Mercedes."

She had managed her speech with dignity but her composure was threatened by his use of her name. "And don't patronize me." She was grateful he didn't deny it or respond in any other way. When she was certain the subject was closed, Mercedes lay down again. She curled on her side facing him and drew her knees close to her chest. Mercedes counted five chimes as the entrance hall clock announced the hour. "Can you believe it's so late?" she asked softly. "I'll have to go to my own room soon." But she made no move to do so. There was pleasure in lying close to him and she was reluctant to deny herself. "You know," she said, "in all the things you've told me, you never once mentioned how it was you and your brothers came to be at Cunnington's. What happened to your parents?"

There was no answer.

"Colin?" Mercedes frowned and lifted her head. Her eyes narrowed on his face. "Captain Thorne?" Sighing, she dropped back to the pillow and moved closer to him, slipping one arm across his chest. She felt his steady heartbeat against the underside of her elbow. "I'm glad one of us can sleep," she murmured, snuggling. "I wish it were me."

Mercedes was the last one at breakfast the next morning. The twins and Sylvia were finishing their meal while Colin was at the sideboard, helping himself to a second portion.

"I'm sorry," she said, closing the pocket doors behind her. Guilt caused her to avoid making eye contact with anyone and nervousness made her state the obvious. "I overslept."

Sylvia looked longingly at the second plate Colin was bringing to the table. It took an effort to put her own fork aside. "Captain Thorne said you might decide to have a lie-in this morning."

The most interesting thing, Mercedes thought, was that she would have been lying in her own bed. She couldn't say how Colin managed it without waking her—she had no recollection of ever falling asleep—but when she opened her eyes, she was back in her room. "Did he?" she said coolly.

"You had a full day yesterday, didn't you?" said Sylvia. "I shouldn't wonder that I'd take my breakfast in bed the following morning."

Mercedes noticed that Colin was calmly eating. She looked

at him sharply, searching out some small smile that would hint
at his laughter, but she could see nothing. At least he didn't appear
to be enjoying her discomfort. "And you certainly may," Mercedes said pleasantly. She went to the sideboard and began to
serve herself. She chose a large portion of eggs and tomatoes,
three fingers of warm bread, and half a dozen orange slices.
Britton held out her chair as she came to the table.

"I say, Mercedes, Brendan can help you with that plate." He
grinned at his brother. "Brendan, fetch Mr. Hennepin's wheel-
barrow."

Mercedes gave both boys a crossways glance and sat down.
"There's nothing wrong with a healthy appetite," she said.

Britton slid back into his chair. He was prepared to make another aside to his brother but he intercepted a quelling look from
Colin that subdued him. He folded his hands neatly in his lap
and waited until he was spoken to.

Mercedes, who had missed the exchange between Colin and
Britton, wondered at her young cousin's sudden calm. "Are you
feeling quite the thing, Britton?"

"Yes."

This short reply did not allay Mercedes's concern. "Are you
certain?" She laid her fork aside and leaned toward him.

"He's fine," Sylvia said, giggling. "Captain Thorne just gave
him a look that would make smarter men walk the plank. Isn't
that right, Brit?"

Brendan laughed and pointed gleefully at his brother. "She
called you stoo-pid."

Britton pulled a face at both of them but he didn't rejoin.

"My, oh my," Mercedes said, amused. "Do you mean it only
takes one look from the captain to make you sit still in your
chair?"

"*And* keep his trap closed," Brendan said helpfully. For this
comment he received the same quelling glance that had brought
his twin to order. He ducked his head guiltily and stared at his
plate.

Mercedes caught this second glance. She had to agree it was

a powerful motivator. "I see," she said wisely. "I shall have to ask Captain Thorne to teach it to me."

Colin paused in raising his coffee cup. "It helps if you've already bargained a bit with them."

"Bribery," Sylvia said. "That's what he's talking about. He told the twins he'd help them make a ship they could sail at the pond. But I think they have to behave themselves."

Mercedes looked from one boy to the other. "Bargains or bribery," she said, shrugging. "Apparently it works."

Britton grinned. "I know I like it better than a fist in my ribs."

Mercedes's face drained of color.

Brendan kicked his brother under the table. "What did you have to say that for?"

Grimacing as Brendan's foot connected solidly with his shin, Britton said defensively, "Well, it's true. And you know it, too. We're all agreed things are better since the captain came. I don't see the point in not saying so."

Mercedes laid her hand on Britton's shoulder. She could feel everyone's eyes on her, including Colin's. "You're right," she said quietly. "There's no point in not saying so." Standing, Mercedes let her napkin drop on her chair. "If you will excuse me." Without waiting for a reply, she hurried to the doors.

Britton looked blankly around the table. "What did I do?"

Brendan rolled his eyes while Sylvia sighed heavily. It was Colin who answered him. "I think Mercedes took her job to look after you and protect you very seriously. You just reminded her that she wasn't always successful."

Britton's mouth sagged. Tears came to his eyes. "But I didn't mean to hurt her. I would never—"

"She knows that," Colin said. He stood. "If you're done with your breakfast, you and Brendan should go see Mr. Hennepin about some wood and tools. Sylvia, could you find something we could use for a sail?"

She smiled, pleased to be asked to help with the project. "Of course."

"Good. Give me thirty minutes and I'll meet you at the stable. We can work there."

Colin found Mercedes outside. He almost missed her the first time he stepped onto the flagstones at the rear of the house. It was the flash of her pale rose gown among the darker greens of the arbor that caught his eye. She stepped out from under the canopy of leaves when she saw his approach.

"You didn't have to follow me out here," she said. She began walking along the path that meandered through the garden. The sky was clear, almost endlessly blue from treetops to the horizon. The fragrance of summer flowers, fresh and sweet, was part of the air she breathed. "I don't need—" Mercedes stopped, frowning. She sniffed. "Do you smell that?" she asked, turning to Colin. "It smells like—"

"Smoke." He turned three hundred sixty degrees, scanning the grounds and the sky for some sign of what he smelled. "I don't see anything." The sky above the manor was as serenely blue as anywhere else. No clouds billowed from the chimneys. There were no cries of alarm from the stable and no flicker of flames along the roof. "It's fainter now," he said. "I can barely make it out."

She nodded. The odor was lifted away by the morning breeze and a moment later it was as if it had never been. "I wonder what it was."

Colin was no longer concerned about that. Mercedes was already walking away. He caught up to her and matched his natural stride to her smaller steps. "Britton feels terrible," he said.

"He shouldn't. He spoke the truth."

"You couldn't always protect him from the earl."

She couldn't speak so she shrugged.

"Mercedes, you did more than anyone could expect."

She glanced at him. "I expected more." The words were choked and she swallowed hard. "I promised my aunt more." Bending, she plucked a stray daisy along the border of greenery. She twirled it between her palms as she walked. "Anyway, as

Britton said, things are better since you've come to Weybourne Park."

"He only meant that the earl's been gone since I arrived. That was bound to improve things."

Mercedes stopped and looked up at him with clear gray eyes. "No, that isn't what he meant. The earl's been away before and it's never been like this. We've always lived with the anticipation that he would return."

"He still might."

"No." She shook her head. "Not this time."

"You seem sure."

"I can't live my life thinking about it any other way." Mercedes turned away and began walking again. "Neither can my cousins."

"You know I wouldn't let—"

Mercedes held up her hand, cutting him off. She smiled briefly but there was no joy in it. "What I know is that you won't always be here. It's better to go on believing that he won't return, rather than rely on your protection."

Colin opened his mouth to object, then thought better of it. He didn't know that he *could* object.

Changing the subject, Mercedes said, "It's good of you to take so much time with the boys."

"I have the time," he said. "After all, I hired myself a very competent manager."

This time her smile was fulsome as she gave him a sidelong glance. "Yes, you did. And she's dallied overlong feeling sorry for herself. Perhaps she'll see you at—" Mercedes's smile faded as she heard her name being called. It came to her twice, like an echo, but with none of the pleasant reverberation. These voices were strident and urgent. She and Colin turned simultaneously toward the source of the cries.

The twins were running from the house at breakneck speed, one trying to get ahead of the other. They arrived toe to toe in front of her and stopped so sharply they rocked forward on the balls of their feet. Colin had to put his hand out to keep them from bowling Mercedes over.

"She's not a nine pin," he told them dryly.

If they understood his comment, they weren't moved to apologize. Breathlessly Britton began, "Mr. Thayer's come to see you."

"And Mr. Patterson," Brendan added. "The sheriff."

"I know who Mr. Patterson is," Mercedes said. She wasn't certain why the boys were so excited. A visit from either man was unusual, but not without precedent. "Then I shall see them both. Thank you for bringing it to my attention."

Fairly dancing in place, Brendan blocked her path as she started forward. "You don't understand," he said hurriedly. "They've come together. There's been some sort of accident."

"What in the world?" she said softly. She looked at Colin. His bewilderment was as plain as hers. Mercedes couldn't help wondering aloud, "One of the children?"

"I heard them tell Mrs. Hennepin it was something about a fire," Britton said helpfully.

Colin pulled both boys aside by their collars so Mercedes could get by. She almost knocked them over anyway.

"We're not nine pins, you know," they called after her.

Colin gave them a shake. "Very amusing," he said in a tone that let them know it wasn't. He released them. "The ship will have to wait, but you still might want to get the wood."

"It's all right," Britton said philosophically. "This is rather exciting." He was treated to another of Colin's quelling glances. "C'mon, Brendan. Let's go find that plank now."

Colin permitted himself a small smile as the boys took off at a run for the stables. "You've done fine by them, Mercedes," he said to himself. "Better than even their mother could have expected."

Colin found Mercedes in the library with her tenant and the sheriff. He greeted both men solemnly, but turned to Mercedes for an explanation.

"The children are fine," she said. Her hands were folded in front of her and the only sign of her agitation was in her white-knuckled grip. "The fire was in the cottage closest to the Thayers.

It's been vacant for several years. That's why—" She hesitated and looked at Mr. Thayer. "Please, you tell him what happened."

The tenant farmer had no liking for center stage, but he couldn't refuse Mercedes. He clutched his hat and shifted his weight from one foot to the other. "My wife rose to feed the babe," he said. "Sometime after midnight, it were. She saw the flames in the neighboring cottage and called to me. I roused the children and we went with buckets but there was nothing to save. The best we could do was let it burn itself out and make sure the fire didn't spread to our own place or the fields." His gaze wavered and he looked to Mercedes uncertainly.

"I'm sure you did the right thing," she said.

This small encouragement helped him continue. "I talked it over with my wife and we both agreed there was no need to let you know what happened until morning. There wasn't anything you could do, and with the cottage being empty and all . . ." His voice trailed off and he stared at the floor. "Well, this morning I got to thinking about how the fire started. I was worried about the children, you see. Sometimes they play over there." He shot Mercedes a quick glance. "I tell them they're not allowed but—"

"Yes," she said. "I know how children do."

He nodded. "I wanted to be sure they hadn't been the cause— else I'd make them come tell you themselves—so I went over this morning and poked around a bit, just to see what I could. The embers were still hot but I managed to move a few rafters." Mr. Thayer looked at Colin squarely. "I found a body, sir. That's why I went to get Mr. Patterson."

"They think it's the earl," Mercedes said quietly. "His body is burned . . ." She sat down on the edge of the chair behind her.

Colin went to the walnut table that held the decanters of liquor. He splashed a tumbler with whisky and handed it to her. "Drink it," he said when she hesitated. "These men won't think worse of you for it." To prove it to her he offered drinks to Patterson and Thayer and they both accepted. "If the body is badly burned," he said to the sheriff, "what makes you think it's Weybourne?"

Randall Patterson was in his early fifties, a contemporary of the earl but certainly not of the same circle. He owed his position as county law officer to Mercedes's father and he managed to keep it after power and influence changed hands by the fact that the present Earl of Weybourne had little interest in local politics. He was a slim man, almost gaunt, with a shock of gray hair at his temples and at his nape. The crown of his head was as smooth as a glass globe. His thick, wiry eyebrows were raised slightly as he spoke. "We found something next to the body that we thought might help settle the matter," he said. "I'm hoping Miss Leyden can identify it."

Patterson set his drink down and slipped one hand into his coat pocket. His palm covered the object until he had it completely free. There was no flourish in the gesture as he held it out for Mercedes to see.

Fire had tarnished the silver flask. There were fingerprints in the soot where it had been handled by Mr. Thayer and the sheriff, and the cap of the flask had melted to the neck. Still, Mercedes had no difficulty identifying the object or remembering where she had seen it last. She stared at it, unable to speak.

Colin removed a handkerchief from inside his pocket. "May I?" he asked Patterson.

"By all means." He passed the flask to Colin and wiped the tips of his blackened fingertips with his own handkerchief.

Colin **stu**died the flask, wiping away the soot along the gold-banded bottom. There were no engraved initials to identify the flask as his, but he recognized the small dimple in the band, put there by a wayward fist in a tavern brawl. It was hard to believe there could be another just like it. Frowning, Colin looked at Mr. Thayer. The farmer wouldn't meet his gaze.

He started to hand the flask back to Patterson but Mercedes came to her feet and took it from him. "I think you'll see that it's—"

"Yes," she said, stopping him from saying another word. "I do see. It's the earl's." She gripped the flask in the handkerchief. "Of course I recognize it." Her hands trembled as she turned it over. "This is it?" she asked. "This is all you found?"

Patterson and Thayer nodded in unison. "If you're certain it belongs to your uncle," Patterson said, "then I think we can safely say it's his remains in the cottage."

Colin's eyes darted from Mercedes to Thayer and back again. It was on the tip of his tongue to ask her if she was quite certain of her answer, but Patterson interrupted him.

"It would be helpful if you could actually recall seeing him with the flask," the sheriff said.

Mercedes's smile was rueful. "It would be harder to recall him without it," she said, then she looked apologetic. "I'm sorry. I shouldn't have . . ." She forced another smile and leveled her clear gray gaze on the sheriff. "But yes, I know he had it when he set out to meet Captain Thorne. That's the last time I saw him."

Patterson nodded. He held out his hand for the flask.

"I'd like to keep it," she said. "After all, it was my uncle's."

"I'm afraid I can't let you. I may need it as evidence."

"Evidence?" Mercedes asked. "Why is it evidence? I've already identified it as the earl's."

Patterson took it from her, wrapping it in his own handkerchief this time, and slipped it into his pocket. "One can never tell what will be needed in a murder investigation."

Mercedes blinked. "Murder? But surely you don't think the fire was started on purpose?"

The sheriff rubbed his pointed chin with the back of his hand. His gaze wandered from Mercedes to Thayer, then to the shelves of books, and finally settled, quite deliberately on Colin. "I think that's the one thing I *can* say with some assurance. Would you agree, Captain Thorne?"

Colin didn't flinch from the thoughtful gaze turned in his direction. "I don't think I know enough to agree one way or the other."

"The fire makes it impossible to know how long the earl's been dead."

"I don't understand," Mercedes said. "I thought the fire killed my uncle."

Patterson shook his head. He answered Mercedes's question but he remained looking at Colin. "There would have been no reason to shoot him if that were the case." He reached in his other pocket and held up a lead ball between his thumb and forefinger. "I apologize for not telling you sooner, Miss Leyden, but this would be the other thing we found."

Mercedes's fingers twisted the handkerchief in her hands. "What are you saying? The earl was shot?"

Colin's smile was grim. "That's precisely what he's saying. And I imagine I'm a prime suspect. Isn't that right, Mr. Patterson?"

"Afraid so."

"Am I under arrest?"

"No." He paused. "Not yet."

Mercedes took a step forward. "You're wrong, Mr. Patterson. Captain Thorne had nothing to do with my uncle's death. That cottage was searched the morning of the duel and the day after, as well. Mr. Thayer says his children play there and they've never reported seeing my uncle around. Surely they would have come forward if they had stumbled upon his body." She looked to the farmer for support.

He nodded. "That's right. None of us saw anyone."

"Or heard anything," Mercedes prompted.

"Not a sound," he said quickly.

Patterson listened patiently. "I didn't say the murder took place there. It's only where the body's been found."

Mercedes's heart was hammering in her chest. "You've got this wrong," she said sharply. "Captain Thorne has been here, with one of us, since his arrival at Weybourne Park."

The sheriff cleared his throat and ducked his head apologetically. "Your defense of the captain is noted, Miss Leyden, and it weighs heavily, given the fact that it's your own uncle who's the victim here, but you can't account for Captain Thorne's whereabouts day *and* night." He watched her carefully. "Can you?"

Despair clouded Mercedes's eyes. She glanced at Colin helplessly.

Colin wasn't looking at Mercedes. His mouth had thinned. A muscle worked in his jaw. His darkly cold glance was boring into the sheriff. "Of course she can't," he said tautly. "And a gentleman wouldn't have asked her. You will *not* disrespect the lady again."

Patterson did not back down from Colin but he did make a short bow to Mercedes. "I beg your pardon. I meant no disrespect. I believe a point had to be made."

"Then you will make your point to me," Colin said, giving no quarter.

The sheriff straightened and made the small concession. "As you wish."

"I want to see the body myself," he said.

"It's still at the cottage. We haven't removed it." To Mercedes, Patterson said, "You'll want to send someone to see to the earl."

"I'll go myself," she said.

All three men answered simultaneously. "No!"

Mercedes gave a start at the force they put behind their response. Even Mr. Thayer managed to show some real heat.

"It's no place for you," Colin said. "Send Mr. Hennepin and Fitch. They can fashion a box quickly for the remains. You can decide what you want to do once he's returned here."

Mercedes recognized the futility of arguing. They all thought she was quite mad for even suggesting she wanted to go. None of them understood that until she saw it with her own eyes, she couldn't believe it was true. She nodded slowly. "I should call the staff together . . . and my cousins." It was difficult to think clearly. Her tongue felt thick in her mouth and the edges of her vision were becoming obscured. "Chloe's with the vicar. She'll have to be told . . . her wedding . . ."

Colin put his hand on Mercedes's elbow and made certain she was sitting before he rang for Mrs. Hennepin. "If you men will wait for me in the hall, I'll be with you in a moment."

Mr. Thayer was on his way to the door immediately. Mr. Patterson followed at a slower pace. He glanced over his shoulder once before he left the room to see Colin solicitously place Mercedes's drink in her hands again. Their fingertips brushed. The touch seemed to linger. The sheriff stepped outside, wondering what he should make of that.

Colin pushed the tumbler toward Mercedes's lips, let her sip, then set it aside. He straightened and looked down on her. "That's a credibly dazed look you've shown them. I shouldn't wonder that they're convinced of your innocence." He cupped her chin and raised her face to him. "But I'll be damned if I know how you could have gotten the rope any tighter around my neck."

Eleven

Wallace Leyden, the Right Honorable the Earl of Weybourne, was laid to rest two days later. Word of his death had reached all the way to London even before the *Times* printed the obituary. Mourners began arriving at Weybourne Park early in the morning. Chief among those feeling the loss were creditors and friends to whom Weybourne owed money. Marcus Severn was there with his father. The old earl needed his cane and his son's assistance to get around, and Marcus was solicitous and attentive. Mr. Patterson attended, standing in back of the gathering while scripture was being read and observing the group without seeming to.

Tenants came to pay their respects. They shuffled past Mercedes and Weybourne's children slowly, murmuring their condolences. None of them voiced the questions they had about their own futures or the future of Weybourne Park.

Colin's man of affairs also arrived. The solicitor came without being summoned, in response to what he knew would be a legal tangle once he learned of the earl's passing. Mr. Lawrence Abernathy remained quietly in the background, offering his counsel to Colin beyond the watchful eye of Patterson and Marcus Severn.

There was no official mention of murder but rumor ran true to form, spreading among the peerage with the conscience and speed of a brushfire. Mercedes had little doubt as to where the gossip mill got its grist. She had only to watch Severn move among the mourners, dropping a word here and there, always without seeming to accuse or pass judgment. After he moved on, however, she observed the furtive glances in Colin's direction and the whispered asides.

Of Colin, she had seen little. After returning from the burned out cottage, he offered to take the carriage to Glen Eden and return with Chloe. Sylvia went with him, leaving Mercedes to manage alone with the twins underfoot. Britton and Brendan were quiet upon hearing the news. They exchanged looks, not certain what they should say, then broke Mercedes's heart by offering their sympathies to *her*.

Sylvia wept softly when she was told and she wept again with her sister at Glen Eden, but by the time they returned to Weybourne Park they had put most of their mourning behind them. They were sensible of the need to show the correct public face and were properly subdued while greeting guests and accepting condolences.

Mercedes went through the motions mechanically. She heard half of what people said to her and dismissed half of that. Over and over again she tried to catch Colin by himself, to explain, to say something that would make him understand that it had never been her intent to incriminate him. After several attempts, both obvious and subtle, she realized that he was purposely avoiding being alone with her.

It was easy for him to do. The legal affairs of Weybourne Park occupied him with his solicitor and he made himself available to Chloe, Sylvia, and the twins. He also spoke to Mr. Patterson at length and Mercedes knew that he had produced the lacquered case with his dueling pistols for the sheriff to examine. Colin never drew her aside to tell her what was discussed. At night she slept alone.

The earl's will was read on the afternoon following his internment. Mr. Gordon, a small, stiff man with a stentorian voice, had managed Weybourne's personal affairs for thirty years. He was particular to gather only those people who were named in the earl's will. It was a small group that met in the library. In the drawing room Colin, his solicitor, and Mr. Patterson waited to hear the outcome.

Mr. Gordon stood behind the earl's desk, smoothing the creases in the document in front of him. Marcus Severn and his father sat in chairs closest to the solicitor so the earl could hear. Chloe and Sylvia each had one of the boys in hand on the small sofas moved into the library for the reading. Mercedes sat behind them all, pale but composed, in the large wing chair at the back of the room.

Mercedes wished herself elsewhere. The reading was a matter of form, more than a matter of import. It did not matter what gifts her uncle bequeathed, he had no assets to pass on. There was no guarantee that the creditors could all be paid, and there was still Colin's claim against the estate to consider. The only thing of value as far as Mercedes was concerned was the title itself, and she supposed Severn had brought his father to make certain it came to them.

"I wish to get to the heart of this matter," Gordon announced in his strident voice. "I have a document here, signed and properly witnessed, which arrived in my office five days ago. Although I did not draw up the document, I find the language is all in order and there can be no doubt of the late earl's intent. This addendum modifies Weybourne's earlier will and exists as the only such modification to come to my attention." He paused to look at the family members and to allow this information to settle on them.

Mercedes had barely taken in the import of this news when she was faced with Severn's hard and critical look. He turned in his chair and stared at her, raking her face for some clue. She managed to school her features and maintain a serene presence though she had no idea what she could expect. When the girls glanced back uneasily, she smiled faintly and shook her head, reassuring them as best she could.

"Well," Gordon said at last. "If no one can produce another document to supercede this one, then I will continue." He smoothed the papers again, adjusted his spectacles, and began.

Utter silence met him at the end.

Severn's father was the first to speak. He stood, grasping his

cane firmly, and said, "That's it, then. Weybourne finally did
right by his family. Damn me if thought I'd live to see it." He
touched Marcus on the shoulder. "Let's go, son. There will be
enough for the others to do without us being in the way."

Marcus came to his feet. He glanced back at Mercedes. "But
perhaps Mercedes will want my counsel," he said. "I believe
Wallace would want me to advise the family. It's not as if the
child—"

The earl turned slightly so he could see Mercedes better. She
was still looking rather stunned by the developments. "Is Marcus
right, my dear? Will you be wanting the benefit of his counsel?
He has a good head on his shoulders."

Mercedes saw Marcus flush at his father's off-handed compliment. Nervous laughter tickled her lips and she pressed them
flat to hold it back. "I'm grateful for the offer," she said graciously. "But I am confident that Mr. Gordon can guide us, and
I would feel better if Marcus were to accompany you back to
Rosefield."

The earl nodded. He held out his free arm for his son to take
and then hobbled to the door. At the point of leaving he paused
and, eschewing Marcus's help, he went to Mercedes. She was on
her feet immediately and accepted his parting kiss on her cheek.
"You're a good girl, Mercedes. Always thought so. Hope it goes
well for you. Can't say that I ever wanted the Park."

"I understand," she said. "And thank you. I appreciate your
coming." She led him back to Marcus and opened the doors for
them. There was no one in the entrance hall when she looked out
and she could only assume that Colin and Mr. Abernathy had
retired to one of the drawing rooms. She could imagine that the
sheriff had joined them. After leaving Severn and the earl in the
good hands of Mrs. Hennepin, Mercedes returned to the library.

"What does it mean?" Britton wanted to know as soon as she
closed the doors. "Sylvia says I'm to be the earl."

"That's right," Mercedes said calmly.

Britton's mouth was pulled to one side and he crossed his arms solidly in front of him. "Well, I don't think I want to be. What about Brendan? Is he an earl, too?"

"No. You're the first born son, so the title's yours."

Chloe sighed. "We've tried to explain."

"I'm sure you have. Britton, you've understood this for some time. I'm not sure what your real concern is."

"Well, everyone—even Sylvia—said he wasn't our father, but now he is. Or was, because now he's dead."

Mercedes laid a hand on his narrow shoulder. "I see," she said gently. "It's quite a lot to take in."

"Yes, it is, rather."

Britton's air of perfect gravity brought a smile to Mercedes's lips. "Mr. Gordon, you mentioned this addendum to my uncle's will came to your notice five days ago."

"That's correct," he said stiffly.

"And it's dated?"

"Why, yes. For the previous day."

"And you located the persons who witnessed my uncle's wish to recognize his sons?"

"I did." He cleared his throat. "It wasn't easy, I can tell you. Not the usual sort, but they appeared reliable."

"Who were they?"

"A Mr. Ashbrook and a Mr. Deakins," he said. Mercedes wavered slightly on her feet. Mr. Gordon skirted the corner of the desk, concerned. "Are you sure you're quite all right?"

"No . . . I'm mean, yes . . . I'm fine." She felt Sylvia and Chloe regarding her pale face closely. "I think, if you don't mind, I'll sit down again." Britton immediately slipped out from under her hand and offered his seat. "Can you tell me something about Ashbrook and Deakins," she said, recovering her composure. "I believe you said they were not the usual sort. What did you mean?"

"I mean they weren't in your uncle's circle of friends. Mr. Ashbrook is the proprietor of a tavern on the waterfront and Mr. Deakins books passages for the Garnet line."

"Didn't you find that odd?" she asked. "Why did my uncle ask them to witness this change in his will?"

Gordon's eyes slipped from hers to the other family members. He returned to Mercedes, consternation tightening his already stiff demeanor. "Are you quite sure—"

"You may speak in front of them," she said. "They're his children."

"Well," he said shortly. "I admit I assumed Weybourne was making plans to leave the country."

Mercedes nodded. "My thoughts also. Mr. Gordon, I'd like to invite Captain Thorne, his solicitor, and Mr. Patterson our sheriff to hear this piece of news. Sylvia. Chloe." They were on their feet before she had finished, taking the twins in hand and removing themselves from the library. "If you'd be so kind, Mr. Gordon, to ask the others to attend us now."

When the group was assembled Mercedes offered a brief introduction. "I think you will be interested in what Mr. Gordon has to say—especially you, Mr. Patterson."

The sheriff greeted Mercedes with a solemn nod, indicating he was willing to listen.

"Please, Mr. Gordon. Just as you explained it to us."

The solicitor pressed his spectacles firmly on the bridge of his nose and began by rereading the addendum to the earl's will.

Colin's attention was not on the reader or his reading. He sat back in the wing chair previously occupied by Mercedes and studied her through his hooded glance.

She was sitting alone on the small sofa now, her hands folded quietly in her lap. There was less tension in her than he had seen in the last several days. Her gray eyes were clear again, not clouded with anxiety. Her brow was smooth and she had ceased worrying her lower lip. There was a faint wash of color in her cheeks, quite a contrast from the pale-as-salt complexion he had observed since she was first confronted with the earl's death.

Her black mourning clothes outlined her slender frame with a severity that was not unbecoming. Rather than weigh her down, the yards of material highlighted her form, making Colin think of his hands on her body more often, not less.

Colin had set himself the task of avoiding her. It was far easier to do than to stop thinking about her. He had to pretend he wasn't aware she wanted to talk to him, that he hadn't seen her try to catch his eye. He knew she wanted an opportunity to explain herself but he wasn't interested. When the anger finally left him, what he felt was betrayal . . . and loss.

She had handled herself admirably these last few days, taking charge of the arrangements for her uncle's funeral, allaying the fears of the staff, and answering questions that were put to her almost endlessly by her cousins about their future. He knew she had to be more uncertain of what the future held, yet there was never any hesitation in her voice. She talked about Chloe's wedding and the twins' schooling and Sylvia's Season as if nothing had changed.

He wondered how she thought he would honor his promises swinging from a rope.

Colin had not been able to acquit himself in the eyes of the sheriff, but no charges had been leveled. There were still the matters of a weapon, which had not been found, and timing, which was difficult to evaluate. Colin could give a good account of his whereabouts and have it verified by a number of different people. But with the time of death not really known, his alibis carried limited weight.

Looking at Mercedes now, he wondered that she could be so composed. It seemed to him that her uncle's sudden change of heart did not have any impact on her bearing. Perhaps his recognition of the twins was not so sudden, or at least not a surprise. If that were the case, then she had set it up beautifully. Once he was accused of Weybourne's murder, he would lose his claim on the estate and the Park would be in Britton's hand, and until he reached his majority, in Mercedes's capable—if slightly blood-stained—ones.

She was cunning. He would give her that.

Colin leaned back in his chair as Gordon droned on. Mercedes's profile was beautifully clear. He traced it with his eyes from her hairline to the base of her throat. As if she felt him watching her, she turned.

He did not look away and he noticed she did not have the grace to blush. She never did. Instead he saw tension run a course through her, first her head as it retracted and the chin came up, then the shoulders as they were braced. She drew in a breath, her torso stiffening as though receiving a blow, and her hands tightened in her lap. Her legs trembled at the strain of having her feet so firmly planted. And finally, in the moment before she turned away, he saw pride bring a certain chill to her clear gray eyes, leaving them quite capable of frostbite.

Colin wondered what the others would make of it if he crossed the room, pulled Mercedes to her feet, and laid his mouth across hers, because, perversely, it was the very thing he wanted to do right now.

Instead, he ran one hand through his hair, stretched his legs in a casual, even bored, posture and gave his attention back to Mr. Gordon. The solicitor had paused and was looking expectant.

"Thank you, Mr. Gordon," Mercedes said graciously. "You've explained the content of the amendment to my uncle's will thoroughly. I would like you to go over the dates of the changes, if you please."

Mr. Gordon nodded. "As I explained to the family," he said, "the earl made these changes only recently. I received this document five days ago, it being duly signed and dated the previous day."

Mercedes's head swiveled in Mr. Patterson's direction. "My uncle's body was discovered in the morning three days ago and we know it was there when the fire started some time after midnight. Mr. Gordon has proof that he was still alive a little over forty-eight hours before that event. That narrows your time of death significantly, doesn't it?"

Mr. Patterson did not respond quickly. His brow furrowed over his deeply set eyes as he considered the information. "Yes, it would appear so," he said carefully. "There were witnesses, I suppose." Now he looked to Mr. Gordon for confirmation.

The solicitor's mouth flattened. "Certainly," he said coolly. "I would have hardly presented this to the family without verifying it. I spent no small amount of time or money in locating the witnesses. I am able to say unequivocally that I consider them to be reliable."

"Their names?" Patterson asked.

"Ashbrook and Deakins."

Mercedes had turned to watch Colin's reaction. Recognition of the names was in the faint narrowing of his eyes and nowhere else. If she hadn't been looking, she would have missed it.

"You'll have addresses," the sheriff said to Gordon.

"Of course, though I must say I don't know why you require them. I can assure you—"

Mercedes interrupted. "No one is doubting that you've conducted this all quite professionally," she said. "But there are some questions surrounding my uncle's death that require answering. I believe Mr. Patterson would find it helpful to speak to Mr. Ashbrook and Mr. Deakins." She indicated the sheriff with a gentle nod of her head. "And if you can confirm to your satisfaction, Mr. Patterson, that my uncle was indeed alive five days ago, then you no longer have any cause to suspect Captain Thorne of wrongdoing. His whereabouts in that forty-eight hour period can be accounted for with complete assurance."

Mercedes stood. As she did, the men also came to their feet. Though she did not look in his direction, Mercedes was only aware of the towering presence of Colin Thorne. "I am speaking of the entire forty-eight hours," she told Patterson pointedly. "Day *and* night."

Leaving them to make of it what they would, careless of her own reputation, Mercedes swept from the room.

Colin had to wait until Patterson, Abernathy, and Gordon had all departed and Chloe, Sylvia, and the twins had gone to bed.

After her announcement in the library, Mercedes had retired to her room and made herself unavailable to anyone save the maid who took her meals. He had placed a note on her luncheon tray but when it went unanswered, he did not try again.

Colin was conscious that the north wing was occupied by more than just Mercedes when he knocked on her door. He was careful to keep his voice low.

"I know you can hear me, Mercedes," he said. "I don't believe for a moment that you're already asleep." He could hear her moving around the room but she didn't respond. "I won't talk to you through this door much longer. And that doesn't mean I intend to give up, lest you miss my point."

"Don't you dare threaten me," she whispered harshly.

Colin's palm lay flat against the door. He could feel it vibrate as she braced her shoulder to the other side. "Open up or move aside."

"Go to hell."

He smiled. She definitely sounded as if she meant it. "Very well. But remember, I gave you a choice."

Mercedes didn't believe he'd do it, not at the risk of waking her cousins. Still, she laid her back fully against the recessed door panel, dug in her heels as best she could, and braced herself for the first shock of Colin's body slamming against the wood.

Colin took a key from his inside vest pocket and inserted it. He gave the door handle a quick twist and pushed. Mercedes's bare heels bounced and slid along the hardwood floor as he overcame her resistance.

She gave up, removing herself so suddenly that Colin would have fallen into the room if he hadn't been expecting it. She turned on him angrily. "You had a key!" she said accusingly.

He made a point of dangling it in front of her before he dropped it back in his pocket. He asked pleasantly, "Did you think I would break down the door?"

Mercedes glared at him. It was precisely what he had wanted her to think. She cinched the belt of her robe tighter. Her unbound hair had fallen forward over her shoulders. She pulled it to one side and made a thick plait with nimble fingers, binding it and tossing it behind her back. "What do you want?" she asked with ill-grace.

"Do you doubt I mean to talk to you?" he asked. She gave him a sour look. "The trouble is," he went on, "you've been avoiding me."

"I wanted to speak to you on any number of occasions these past three days. I believe you're the one who's been avoiding." Mercedes turned away from him and walked to her nightstand where she picked up the book she had been reading. She did not know he had followed her until she felt his hand on her shoulder. Spinning around, Mercedes jammed the hard edge of the leather-bound volume into Colin's gut.

Surprise made him take a step back. He released her shoulder, grunting as she came at him again, jabbing harder this time, all her angry energy bound up in every thrust. "Leave—my—room—now," she bit out, each pause punctuated by another jab.

Colin sucked in his breath, bent in the middle, and was able to avoid her last ram. He grasped her wrists, held them tight, and managed to make her drop the book. It thudded to the floor between them. Colin kicked it aside and it skidded under her bed. "If you're quite through with your temper tantrum," he said softly, "I'll let you go."

Angry for being named a child, she behaved as a child, struggling to pull away from him even when she knew his superior strength would hold her fast.

"Mercedes," he said softly. "Talk to me."

"I hate you."

He nodded. "In your place . . ."

"You thought I deliberately set out to frame you. Admit it," she challenged him, her voice rising. "You thought it was a plan to get rid of you."

"You said as much yourself once," he reminded her. "You plotted with Marcus before looking for a way to be rid of me."

Mercedes stamped her bare foot in frustration that her earlier lies had come back to thwart the truth now. "Believe what you will," she said coldly. "I want no part of you any—"

Colin gave her a small shake. "Have a care, Mercedes, you'll wake your cousins."

"I don't care," she said recklessly. "How long do you think it will be before they learn I've been your whore?" She saw him recoil at this description of herself and by implication, of what had passed between them. "Unless you're telling me that those gathered in the library mistook my meaning?"

Colin let her wrists fall. It was not a surrender on his part. It freed up his hands to throttle her. He raked back his bright hair and shook his head. "I don't believe anyone misunderstood you. I also believe it will be kept confidential. There's nothing to be gained through repetition. Mr. Abernathy and Mr. Gordon would choke on the words before they'd say them aloud. If your cousins and the staff are alerted to our—" He paused, seeking the right word. "Our *relationship,* then it's because you acted the town crier a moment ago." He gave her time to let that sink in. If she was chastened, she made a good show of hiding it.

Mercedes's expression was unrepentant. "I suppose you have some place in mind where we can talk," she said.

"My room."

"Now *there's* a surprise."

"Do you have another idea?"

"Downstairs," she said. "Anywhere will do."

"Very well. The forward turret."

At another time she might have smiled at his use of a ship position to describe the location of the north tower room. "I said belowstairs."

"And I believe we can be certain of no interruptions and have no fear of being overheard in the tower room." His choice surprised her. She would have preferred the more formal surroundings of the library or the stately appointments of the gallery. Even the conservatory would have been preferable with its flowers and greenery to the familiar setting of her childhood fantasies. "You recall it's not furnished," she reminded him.

"You have some objection?"

"No. That's fine." Better, in fact, she thought. She would not have to concern herself with fending off a seduction. The most she would have to worry about was being tossed out a window.

Colin caught the small smile that momentarily changed the shape of her mouth. "Something amuses you?"

"It was nothing." She brushed past him and stepped into her slippers. Curiosity won out. Mercedes glanced over her shoulder and asked, "If it's a woman who falls out of the crow's nest, do you still cry man overboard?"

"Yes," he said. Colin opened the door for her. "And, Mercedes, you really shouldn't tempt me."

Mercedes had a sense of peacefulness the moment she came upon the northern turret. Holding an oil lamp aloft, she entered her childhood sanctuary almost eagerly and quickly climbed the steep and narrow spiral of stairs to the small room. When she reached the top she discovered there was no need for the lamp. The full moon was bright enough to cast her shadow and illuminate the panoramic landscape of Weybourne Park.

Mercedes extinguished her light. Colin, who was still at the bottom of the stairs, complained about the sudden darkness but Mercedes barely heard it. She turned slowly, taking in the scene from each of the tower windows as if she were studying paintings in a gallery. The meadow and pond, the gardens, the woods, the fields, the distant cottages, all of it was opened to her in a single, breathtaking glance.

When she completed her rotation she came face to face with Colin. He was standing almost at the top of the stairs, his features without expression, his body still, and she knew that his eyes had never once strayed to the windows. He had been watching her.

Uncomfortable with his silent scrutiny, resentful of his intrusion, and irritated with herself for forgetting—if even for only a few moments—why she had come to this room, Mercedes felt her hackles rise. Her tone was immediately impatient. "Say what you think you must."

Colin took the next step and immediately towered over her. He gave her full marks for not backing away. "I'll take that," he said, reaching for the extinguished oil lamp. "Before you drop it." The lamp's slight bobble was the only visible indication that her nerves were stretched taut.

Mercedes didn't try to hold on to it. When he turned away to set it on one of the narrow window ledges, she backed up the few steps necessary to give her breathing room.

"Do you regret agreeing to come here?" he asked, facing her again. Colin noticed the distance between them had suddenly increased but he was wise enough not to mention it. "With me?"

"No." She wondered if he could see through her lie. "But I would prefer that you come to the point. My feelings are of no consequence one way or the other."

"Then we're agreed on that," he said, watching her carefully. Colin could see that she was put off balance by his lack of protest. He crossed the small room and stood in front of one of the large windows, his back to Mercedes. He stared out for a long time, letting silence further erode her fragile wall of composure. "I think you better start with the flask," he said finally. "Why did you tell Patterson and Thayer that it belonged to your uncle?"

Mercedes's arms hung at her sides. It was an effort not to cross them in front of her defensively. "Not for the reasons you apparently thought," she said coolly. "It was never my intention to make it seem you had something to do with his death. Quite the opposite, in fact."

Colin turned, his eyes narrowing slightly. He said nothing, but he could see Mercedes felt the full burden of his suspicions. Her shoulders stiffened, bracing to accept the weight.

"Didn't it occur to you that if you admitted the flask was yours, you would *then* be implicated?"

"No," he said. "It didn't. And do you know why?" He paused a beat though the question was strictly rhetorical. "Because *I* wasn't the last person to have that flask in my possession. I wouldn't have necessarily gone to the lengths you did to protect poor Mr. Thayer, but neither would I have given him up to the sheriff without talking to him first."

Mercedes blinked. "Mr. Thayer?" she said softly, bewildered by Colin's conclusion. "What has he to do—"

"I can appreciate," Colin went on, "that when the flask was presented to you, you saw an opportunity to be rid of your uncle. You already knew he had left the country, but you were probably sworn not to tell anyone. By identifying the flask as Weybourne's you as good as identified the body. You certainly satisfied Patterson. And as a result of Weybourne's declared death you were able to have his will read. You were probably the only person today who *wasn't* surprised to hear your uncle had written new instructions. I can imagine that you struck a hard bargain with him, Mercedes."

She shook her head, slightly dazed by Colin's construction of the events. "I don't know what you mean."

"Please. Do you take me for such a fool? You paid him off with my money. Ashbrook and Deakins, remember? The only thing I don't know is the identity of the man Mr. Thayer murdered. I saw the body, Mercedes. Those charred remains could be anyone. Anyone, that is, except your uncle. I'm quite confident he's enjoying himself immensely somewhere at my expense."

Mercedes was sorry she had not insisted upon another setting for this confrontation. Any room with chairs would have done. She was feeling a strong need to hit him over the head with one. "You've worked this all out by yourself," she said with a touch of irony. "Of course you have. You wouldn't speak to me these past few days. And why bother? I couldn't possibly have an explanation that would be at odds with yours. Frankly, I'm surprised you've decided to speak to me at all. I'm finding it harder and harder to believe you might be willing to entertain another scenario."

Colin's eyebrows lifted slightly. His tone was dry and faintly challenging. "Entertain me."

Mercedes's chin came up. "You're assuming Mr. Thayer was

the last one to have the flask because I told you I gave it to him. The person I gave it to was my uncle. He waylaid me on the way to the Thayers' cottage and made short work of the flask's contents. You were correct that he wanted money. He had every intention of leaving the country. Only I know my uncle. He would be back to cause problems when his funds ran low. It occurred to me that with his penchant for gambling he might not make it to his next port with money in his pocket. That would land him back at Weybourne Park wanting more." Her voice took on a bitter, resigned quality. "Always wanting more."

Now Mercedes crossed her arms in front of her. It was a protective gesture, not defensive. "I agreed to meet his price of two thousand pounds. You know how I did that and what it's cost me. I showed him the draft before I killed him. He was so taken with his success that he didn't see the pistol. It was over rather quickly, I'm afraid. I had imagined making him suffer, but in the end I had no stomach for it. I hid the body. I wasn't prepared for it to be discovered just yet."

"The will," Colin said.

She nodded, pleased he understood. "Exactly. It was much easier than you might suppose. Mr. Gordon would be surprised to know that the signature he verified as my uncle's was done by my hand. It's a skill I had to perfect in order to manage Weybourne Park in my uncle's absence. It proved more valuable than I could have ever expected."

"And Ashbrook and Deakins?"

"They're exactly who Mr. Gordon supposes them to be, though perhaps less reliable and honest than appearances would suggest. My uncle owed them both money, Mr. Ashbrook for his lodgings and Mr. Deakins for his passage. Neither man balked at signing the document I drew up when I offered them such handsome interest on the amounts they were owed."

"But they're located in London. How did you—" He stopped because he realized the answer on his own.

"Tattersall's," he said softly. "You left with Severn."

"I couldn't very well drive myself."

"So Severn knows."

"Hardly. He wouldn't have approved at all. He wanted the title, remember?"

"Then how did you manage it with him in tow?"

Mercedes gave Colin a steady look. "I'm finding when a man is sniffing after my skirts he's not looking where he's going."

Colin smiled narrowly but his dark glance was cold.

Mercedes's own icy anger was a match for his. It drove her to finish her tale. "Once I had the will signed and witnessed it only remained for me to allow the body to be discovered. I didn't think it could be accomplished so quickly but you presented me with the opportunity that very night. I've noticed you're not so light a sleeper after you've pleasured yourself." She was satisfied to see Colin's head jerk slightly at this observation, confirming what she knew to be true. "I slipped out of the manor, moved my uncle's body to the cottage, and started the fire. I hadn't considered that his body might be burned beyond recognition. The flask provided an answer to that. It would have ruined everything if I couldn't have convinced Patterson that the murdered man was the Earl of Weybourne."

Mercedes waited a moment, collecting her thoughts and watching Colin take it all in. "Now Britton has the title and you'll have the estate. I will advise him not to fight you for it. I'll be able to continue to manage Weybourne Park without fearing my uncle's interference. I think it's been concluded satisfactorily. We've all gotten what we wanted. I believe I was successful in turning suspicion away from you this afternoon, so you'll be quite free to enjoy the spoils of my success."

Mercedes extended her right hand and indicated the expanse of Weybourne Park with an unconsciously graceful gesture. "It's all yours," she said softly. Her hand dropped to her side and she stood before him without defenses, her posture somehow suggestive of an offering. "All of it."

There was no mistaking what she was giving him. Colin's dark eyes shifted to the moonlit grounds of Weybourne Park then back to the wash of blue and silver light on Mercedes's face. He could have both. They were his.

He shook his head. "No," he said. "I don't want any of it." He saw her stiffen as if he'd struck her. "It's yours if you want it. The price you paid is too steep for me."

"What price?" she asked. "My uncle's life?" Her short laughter held no humor. "You were quite willing to kill him."

"I was challenged," he said.

"Are you reminding *me* about proper form?"

"No," he said tiredly. "I wouldn't presume to do that." Colin raked his hair back in an absent gesture. "I really did want to be convinced of another explanation," he said at last. "This isn't the one I wanted to hear."

"Even when it confirmed everything you've been thinking these last few days?" she demanded. "Especially since you heard the revelations of this afternoon. Don't you take any pleasure in being right?"

"Not this time."

At her side Mercedes's hands clenched into tight, white-knuckled fists. "You can't know how much I despise you," she said coldly. Turning sharply on her heel, Mercedes started down the steps.

Colin crossed to the top of the stairs and made a grab to stop her. She ducked to avoid his hand and vaulted the next three steps by bracing herself between the walls and jumping. She stumbled a bit on the landing, righted herself, then launched herself again. Mercedes reached the door well ahead of Colin and yanked on the handle.

It didn't budge. Cornered, she turned on him just as he cleared the last step. "Unlock it," she said sharply. "Unlock it or I swear I'll start screaming."

"As if that would help," he said under his breath. He put out his hand and watched her jump out of the way. "I'm trying to get to the door, not touch you." He rattled the handle and pulled. Nothing happened.

"Use the key."

This time Colin gave her a quelling look. Its impact was minimal in the stairwell where the moonlight couldn't reach. "I don't have the key," he said. "I didn't lock the door."

Mercedes pushed his hand aside and tried again. "It's stuck," she said. "It must be." She thrust her shoulder into the door. Her effort bruised her but it didn't budge the door.

Colin picked Mercedes up by the waist and put her on the step behind him. "Stay there," he said. "And let me try. If you move I swear I'll use you as a battering ram."

Because his threat sounded reasonably sincere, Mercedes remained still as stone. Colin pushed and pulled at the door. Neither action was effective. "It's not stuck," he told her. "It's locked."

"How could you?" Her tone was both accusing and forlorn. Mercedes dropped to sit on the stairs under her.

Colin glanced over his shoulder. "I didn't do this. Why would I?"

"To torment me."

"A minute ago you were offering yourself to me. The only one likely to be tormented by this situation is me."

Mercedes was glad for the shadows in the narrow stairwell. She didn't want him to know how cleanly he had found his mark. "What do we do now?"

"Screaming might help."

She gave him a sour look. "No one can hear."

"So it was an idle threat."

"Not entirely," she said sweetly. "It would have tormented you." Without waiting for his reply, Mercedes came to her feet and went up the steps. There was nothing for it but to claim space on the floor and wait to be rescued. She heard Colin follow but she didn't glance in his direction. "If this is the work of one or both of the twins, then they're bound to feel guilty before too long and let us out."

"My thought also."

Mercedes nodded. Her head jerked up as she was struck by a possibility she hadn't considered before now. "What do you think they might have overheard?"

Eavesdropping had already occurred to Colin. "Everything. Any part of it. Or nothing."

"Well, thank you. That's reassuring." She sighed. "Do you think I was believed?"

"It was a convincing confession."

"But *you* know it's not true."

"I do now."

Mercedes said nothing for a moment. She regarded him frankly and said exactly what she was thinking. "You found it very easy to believe the worst of me."

"You told a good story."

"No. I merely told you what you expected to hear." She sighed. "You may not have wanted to hear it, but it didn't stop you from believing it."

"You're right, it didn't." Sitting opposite her, much the way he had with Aubrey when he and his second in command had been trapped in the very same room, Colin drew up his legs to his chest. "It's difficult to mount a defense for myself," he said. "The only thing I can tell you is that I knew *I* didn't kill anyone. And if I didn't . . ."

"Of course I must have."

"I presented Mr. Thayer as a possible suspect," he reminded her.

"That must have stretched your powers of deduction," she said smartly. "Especially when I was so clearly your first choice as the murderer."

Colin refused to be engaged. "If I can't end this with an apology, perhaps you can end it with the truth."

"I haven't heard an apology," she said. Silence followed. Mercedes felt it as a pressure in her chest. She struggled not to fill it with the sound of her own voice. Clearly Colin was not used to having anything to apologize for.

"I shouldn't have provoked you," he said at last. "When I asked you to entertain me, you took that as a challenge and proceeded, in your own way, to do just that. I deeply regret pushing you to that pass. As for believing what I did, there's nothing I can say. I didn't judge you harshly for what I thought you'd done. I even understood it. Your confession couldn't have been safer if you had told it to a priest."

"You refused the Park," she said. "And you refused me."

"Because the offer was for my silence," he said. "You were trying to buy me off. And you were hoping I would accept the offer so you could throw it all back in my face."

She shook her head. "I was spinning out the tale as it occurred to me. I hardly knew what I was saying."

"You knew."

Mercedes found she could no longer hold his darkly mirrored gaze. He had hit upon the truth so accurately that it was she who felt the need to apologize. It had been calculating *and* petty. "You're right," she said. "I'm sorry."

He smiled a little at that. Her head was still turned away. Her fingers were absently smoothing the material of her robe over her knees. One of her slippered feet was nudging the other. The hastily braided rope of hair was hanging over her left shoulder and the thick lock at the end curled at her breast. "Mercedes?"

Her eyes shifted in his direction. "Yes?"

"I love you."

She simply stared at him.

"Did you hear me?"

She nodded.

"Did you understand?"

She nodded again.

"All right." Colin had no expectations. He cocked his head in the direction of the stairwell. It did not appear that rescue was imminent. "I'd like to hear the truth now, if you please. Not what you think I believe or what you think I want to hear. Just the truth as you know it."

It took Mercedes a moment to clear her thoughts. At first she thought he wanted the truth about her feelings toward him. When she realized he was only asking about the events surrounding the earl's death, she was visibly relieved. As if he could guess the nature of her thoughts, Mercedes saw one corner of his mouth rise in a slim, amused smile.

"What I know will hardly satisfy you," she said. "My uncle did indeed cross my path on my way to the Thayers. He took the flask from the things I was carrying and never returned it. He asked for money which I promised to provide. He was the one who suggested Ashbrook and Deakins. I really thought those were names pulled out of thin air. I had no idea these men might exist. I did ask him to consider recognizing the twins as his heirs, but I recall that he struck me for my impertinence."

Colin heard no self-pity or bitterness in Mercedes's tone. It was stated simply as fact.

"That same night I was able to return to the cottage with the draft you signed for me."

Thinking back, Colin remembered waking and discovering she was missing. He had found her in her own room, soaking in the tub. "Was your uncle there when you went back?"

"No. I never saw him again. As far as I knew his plans were to leave the country. He wouldn't tell me where he was going. He had some idea that you might follow and he had no desire to live his life looking over his shoulder." Although Colin made no comment, his expression led Mercedes to believe he and the earl were finally of one mind. "The first I knew that there had been any foul play was when I was presented with the evidence by Mr. Patterson."

"Then you believe your uncle is dead?"

"Yes." His question surprised her. "Of course. He had the flask."

"He may have simply left it behind. It doesn't conclusively identify him."

"In my mind it does. The flask wasn't there when I returned to the cottage. I looked for it because I wanted to refill it and present it to Mr. Thayer. I suspected that someday you might ask him if he enjoyed his brandy."

"And he would have looked at me blankly."

She smiled softly at that. "Not so different from his usual expression, I know, but you would have been suspicious."

"He would never have betrayed you."

"I know, but it wouldn't have sat well on my shoulders." She picked up the end of her braid and idly stroked the tip. "You thought I was covering for him in front of the sheriff."

Colin didn't deny it. "It's the sort of thing I've come to expect from you. Defending those who can't defend themselves. I figured you thought I could take care of myself against the charges."

"I wanted to explain," she said quietly. "You didn't want to listen."

"I was angry."

"You didn't trust me."

"I thought I trusted you, too much."

It helped her understand how it had been for him, the full measure of betrayal that he must have felt. Yet she remembered that when she would have offered herself as his alibi to Mr. Patterson, Colin would not let her speak. Instead he had chastized the sheriff for suggesting that she could account for his whereabouts at night. She suspected he would have done something similar this afternoon if he had known she was going to announce that she was his mistress.

"Tell me about Ashbrook and Deakins," Colin said.

"I learned who they were when Mr. Gordon told us about the earl's changes in his will. I asked for you and your solicitor and Mr. Patterson to be brought in to hear it as soon as I understood the significance."

"You didn't have to tell them you were my mistress."

"I think I did. It cleared your name, didn't it?"

"And muddied your own."

She shrugged.

"Why did you do it, Mercedes?"

She didn't answer the question but asked one of her own. "What you said earlier. Did you mean it?"

He had said a lot of things, all of them earlier. Still, Colin had no difficulty discerning her point of reference.

Mercedes prompted, "You didn't say it because you thought it was what I wanted to hear, did you?"

"*Is* it what you wanted to hear?"

"I . . ." Her voice died away.

Colin took pity on her. "I said I love you because it's the truth."

She nodded slowly and considered this in silence.

"What are you thinking?"

Mercedes couldn't quite meet his eye. "That there might be a better way to pass the time than talking."

Twelve

They were rescued shortly after dawn. Mr. Hennepin saw them as he was approaching the stables. "Like lovebirds, they were," he told his wife later. "The two of them just sitting out on the roof, arm in arm. Her head gentle on his shoulder. And I thought they weren't even speaking."

Mrs. Hennepin had smiled indulgently at her husband. "What did they say they were doing out there?"

"Star gazing."

Ninety minutes later Mrs. Hennepin was still humming softly to herself as she set out dishes on the sideboard.

Colin and Mercedes were the first to arrive in the breakfast room. They were both aware of the housekeeper's frequent glances in their direction and the happy, knowing grin she couldn't quite tamp down. When Mrs. Hennepin left they looked at each other from opposite ends of the table, their complacent smiles mirrors of one another.

The twins elbowed their way through the doors until they saw the room was already occupied. They made a show of good manners as they stopped jostling for position and walked to the table with matching solemn strides and grave faces.

Britton scooted into his chair, his eyes darting between Colin and Mercedes. "I say, could you share the secret? It's rather bad of you to leave us out."

"No," Colin said. "We will not share."

Brendan noticed that for some reason this made Mercedes's smile deepen. He caught his brother's eye, made a quick nod in

Mercedes's direction, and communicated his thoughts on the matter without saying a word. The fact that this silent exchange was completely overlooked by Mercedes, who was usually quick to notice such things, merely confirmed the boys' suspicions that something was afoot.

Sylvia and Chloe were still yawning as they walked in for breakfast, Chloe with only a bit more delicacy than her younger sister. That the twins didn't make some comment about their open mouths being fit for fly catching, alerted them to the altered atmosphere. It didn't take them but a moment to see that the real change was between the head and foot of the table. Ducking their heads to hide their satisfied smiles, the girls still communicated with each other by a series of under the table nudges which were only slightly more sophisticated than the kicks usually passed between Britton and Brendan.

Mercedes smoothed her napkin in her lap. "There seems to be quite a bit of restlessness," she said to no one in particular. "Did everyone sleep well?"

This comment caused some consternation among the gathering. Colin alone was at ease. He watched them closely as they ceased moving while managing to cast furtive, questioning glances at one another.

Colin leaned comfortably back in his chair, his head tilted slightly to one side as he regarded Mercedes. She was looking back at him with something of the same question in her eyes.

"Perhaps they're all guilty," she said.

"It occurred to me also."

This raised a general murmur of alarm from the others. "Guilty of what?" Sylvia wanted to know. "I'm sure I didn't do anything," Chloe defended herself. "If I did, I'm sorry," Britton offered hurriedly. Brendan pulled a face and whispered miserably, "They already said what I wanted to say. All the good excuses are taken."

Mercedes had not expected to hear so many protests of innocence. She was inclined to believe they were all in it together. "What do you think, Captain Thorne?"

"They're a sorry lot, but loyal. We may have to use torture."

Chloe sat up straight. "Torture! What does he mean, torture?"

Sylvia was eyeing the twins sternly. "What have you two done now?"

"It mightn't be us," Britton said.

"That's right," Brendan chimed in. "It might be you."

Colin tapped the bowl of his spoon on his juice glass to silence the gallery. "Last night Mercedes and I were locked in the north tower room," he told them. "This is my second experience with that trick. You'll understand why I might be skeptical of all these protests."

Four pairs of bewildered eyes turned in Colin's direction.

"They're innocent," Colin announced.

Mercedes's glance was amused. "What happened to torturing them?"

"I find I haven't the stomach for it."

Mercedes felt the pressure of all those stares turned on her. "Oh, very well," she said.

There was a collective sigh of relief.

"But I remain unconvinced," she added, regarding each one of them pointedly. "My experience with the four of you goes back much further than the captain's." Mercedes was somewhat dismayed to realize that not one of them seemed overly concerned.

It was much later that day before Mercedes had an opportunity to speak to Colin alone. She had spent the morning with Chloe as they reconsidered plans for her wedding. The observance of mourning had to be weighed against all they truly felt in their hearts. Mercedes had her luncheon with Sylvia who she was aware had been keeping to herself for some weeks. It did not require a great deal of perception to see into the young woman's heart and recognize she was pining for Aubrey Jones. Mercedes didn't remind Sylvia that Aubrey was virtually a stranger and that he had no roots in England. She merely listened, offering no judgment, and Sylvia was much heartened by the time spent together.

The twins were tutored on matters of math and geography in the afternoon. Still later there were accounts to oversee and tenants to talk to. It was on her way back to the manor from the cottages that she saw Colin walking toward the woods with a fishing pole resting on his shoulder. She veered from her course and followed him instead.

He was wading into the stream when she came upon him, and he didn't hear her approach. Mercedes stood on the bank and watched Colin cast his line. It arced over him like a whip of sunlight, a single undulating curve until it was snapped taut by the water and Colin's pull on the rod. He was barefoot, standing amid the rippling, bubbling water with his trousers rolled up to his knees. The cuffs were already damp from the spray. His jacket lay on the bank with his shoes and stockings, but Colin still wore his vest. The silver threads running through the blue-gray fabric looked as liquid as the water flowing past his ankles.

His hair was a bright helmet, reflecting sunshine as he tilted his head and watched for movement along his line. He squinted against the brilliant, diamond-like surface of the water. For no reason that Mercedes could see, there was a slender smile lifting the corners of his mouth.

She called to him and he turned. His smile deepened. "I was thinking about you," he said.

That warmed her. She sat down on the bank and took off her shoes and stockings and dangled her feet where they could be cooled by the rushing water spray. "Are you going to share those thoughts?" she asked after a moment.

"No," he said, glancing over his shoulder. He cast his line again. "I don't think so."

She didn't mind that he had his secrets. Mercedes leaned back on her elbows. "Would you care to share your thoughts about my cousins?"

"I really don't think they locked us in, Mercedes."

"I don't know what I think anymore. I've spent all day with them. They're not like you, Colin. They've never been able to keep a secret."

"So you didn't ferret the truth out of them."

"That really wasn't the point of being with them, but it did occur to me that one of them would let something slip." She shook her head, still wondering at their silence. "Nothing. Not a word. I'm afraid I'll have to agree with you."

"That *is* something to fear," he said dryly.

"You know what I mean."

Colin reeled in his line and waded to the bank. Tossing the rod on the grass, he sat beside Mercedes. She looked deliciously relaxed, like a slender reed turned gently by the wind and the sun with no care but to enjoy both. He bent his head and kissed her.

Her lips were damp, her mouth warm. She responded sweetly, without haste or pressure. It was a slow, languorous exploration, an appreciation of the tastes and textures that made them the same and different. Her tongue swept along the edge of his upper lip. She kissed the corner of his mouth.

He laid his hand on her breast. Beneath the fabric of her gown he could feel her flesh swell. She arched ever so slightly, filling the cup of his palm. His mouth touched her just below her ear. She lifted her chin and exposed the long line of her throat. He kissed her jaw, then the pulse in her neck.

The fragrance of the thick damp grass mingled with the fragrance of her hair. Her elbows no longer supported her as she stretched languidly beneath him. Her arms circled his neck and the shadow cast by his head cooled her face.

"This is what I thought you had in mind last night," he whispered against her mouth.

Her smile was serene. "I know." Silent laughter brightened her eyes. "But you enjoyed star gazing, you know you did."

"The moon was too full."

"We had a spectacular view."

"We were on a rooftop."

"It was like a crow's nest."

"Crow's nests don't incline forty-five degrees except in Atlantic storms."

"It was lovely."

"You were lovely."

Mercedes felt heat rush to her face. She welcomed the mouth he laid across hers. They kissed for a long time, unhurried but not without hunger. It was Colin who eventually pulled back and sat up. Mercedes stayed where she was, trying to regain her measured breathing. She stroked his back.

"Will you come to my room tonight?" he asked.

She nodded. "Of course."

"Because you know I want you, or because you want to be there?"

Mercedes's hand stilled on his back. She cocked her head as she heard someone moving in the brush. Colin heard it, too. He pulled her up and helped her straighten her gown and remove bits of grass from her hair. Moving a few feet away from her, he cast his line back in the stream. When Brendan bounded into the clearing they looked perfectly at ease.

It lasted only a moment as Mercedes realized Brendan had arrived alone. "Where's your brother?" she asked, stepping forward. "What's happened?"

"Britton's fine. He stayed back to learn as much as he could. I came here to warn you."

It was Colin who spoke. "Warn me? What's the problem?"

Brendan shook his head and gulped the air to catch his breath. His small face was ruddy with the exertion of his run. "Not you. Mercedes. Severn's here with the sheriff and they're looking for Mercedes."

Mercedes was actually relieved. "I'm certain it's nothing," she said. "Probably a few questions left over from yesterday. And Severn's a relation, after all. It is perfectly acceptable for him to visit." She amended this last statement when Colin and Brendan both looked at her with frank skepticism. "I didn't say that I welcomed it, only that it can be tolerated."

Colin's attention turned to Brendan. The boy was not appeased by Mercedes's lack of concern. "What else, Brendan?"

"I don't know, sir. Something's just not right. Severn is . . ."

well, he's Severn. Only more so. And Mr. Patterson is pacing. I think he's worried about something."

"Did they send you to get us?"

"No. Severn sent Mr. Hennepin to look for Mercedes and he doesn't know she's with you. He's gone off to the cottages."

"I don't like this," Colin said. "I want to talk to Mr. Patterson before you come back to the house."

"That's ridiculous." Mercedes brushed the suggestion aside. "This is about the earl's will, that's all. Mr. Patterson's probably here to let us know that you're no longer a suspect."

Colin wasn't convinced. "I'd rather you wait here."

"That doesn't make any sense," she said. "I'm not the one they've been after."

Mercedes hadn't realized how easily that could change. When she met Severn and Patterson in the library and offered them refreshment, she couldn't have imagined what would follow.

Her face paled as she listened to the charges leveled against her. Her mouth was so dry she couldn't answer them.

Standing at the fireplace, Colin's features were impassive. He watched Mr. Patterson closely and accepted that the sheriff actually believed what he was saying. That spoke to Severn's ability to persuade and convince. Severn himself was quiet. He let the law speak for him and he didn't shy from meeting either Mercedes or Colin directly.

Colin waited until Mr. Patterson finished speaking. Brendan had been correct in his assessment of the sheriff. The man was nervous. But then, Colin reflected, it wasn't every day he accused a member of one of England's oldest families of murder.

"There's only one problem with your account of things," Colin told the sheriff. "None of it's true." He saw Mercedes lift her head a notch but it did nothing to contradict the helpless, guilty expression in her eyes. Only he understood that her guilt was related to the lies she had told and that her regret was that she had been overheard. "Yes, Mercedes said all the things that Severn repeated to you, but he didn't stay around long enough to realize she was spinning that tale for my benefit."

"Why would she do that?"

"She was angry with me because I was angry with her. We said things we didn't mean. The earl's murder has all of us talking out of turn and wondering aloud."

Patterson rubbed his chin thoughtfully. "You've never seemed like a man given to speaking before thinking."

Colin shrugged. "I'm not used to dealing with the irrational mind of a female, either." For a moment he thought Mercedes was going to come out of her chair and pounce on him like a wounded lioness. He silently applauded the control she demonstrated by staying put and staying quiet. "You have experience in these matters, don't you?"

The sheriff nodded. "I've been married twenty-one years."

"And I've been at sea that long. I'm still clumsy at not getting a woman so mad at me that she'll say anything to prove me a fool." His glance slid to Severn. "I'm wondering what brought you to Weybourne Park at that time of night and why you thought you could go anywhere you pleased. You're the one with something to gain with these ridiculous charges." He looked at Patterson again. "You took that into account, didn't you? Severn here would inherit the title and tie up the Park if the earl's will is proved to be false."

"I took it into account. I would have been here this morning otherwise. I spent the morning and afternoon in London talking to Ashbrook and Deakins. As far as his lordship's arrival here last night, he explained that he was concerned about the family and returned to offer assistance."

Mercedes spoke up. "He made that offer earlier in the day and I said it was appreciated *and* unnecessary."

"I thought you were merely being polite," Severn said smoothly. "It would be like you not to want to place demands on anyone else. You're aware, of course, that I've always been able to come and go at the Park as I've pleased."

Mercedes felt Colin's questioning glance. She nodded. "He has a key to one of the side doors. Severn often accompanied my uncle home."

"The man was too deep in his cups to use the front stairs," Severn explained. "The side entrance caused the least disturbance." He went on coolly. "I had every intention of announcing myself, but when I arrived in the north wing, you were gone. Captain Thorne's room was also vacant. Since I had already been downstairs I knew you weren't there. I don't know what made me think of the north tower, but there you have it. A chance encounter. You must believe me, Mercedes. I didn't want to hear what I did, but upon hearing, what choice did I have? I locked you in so I would have time to find Mr. Patterson. He was not so amenable to a quick resolution and wanted to make further inquiries, but I could not count myself a friend to the earl if I let his murderer go free."

"You've never been a friend to anyone," she said. Mercedes addressed the sheriff. "You said you spoke to Ashbrook and Deakins. If that's the case then you must know that what Severn overheard was pure fabrication. I've never met these men. And I certainly never went to them with Severn, no matter what he says to the contrary."

"But you were at Tattersall's?" Patterson asked.

"Yes. But I never left the carriage. Severn saw me there and invited himself inside. We went—"

"So you did go with him."

"Yes, but—"

The sheriff raised his hand and shook his head. "No more, my lady. I have indeed met with Mr. Ashbrook and Mr. Deakins. They are willing to testify that you paid them to sign the document in question. They recalled your carriage and in each case they remember you mentioning someone was waiting for you there. Mr. Deakins admits he saw my lord Severn there at the carriage window. His description was accurate enough to satisfy me."

"He's lying," Mercedes said, her voice rising.

Colin came to her side and placed one hand on her shoulder. His touch was light but the message was clear. She needed to calm herself. "Severn's paid them," Colin said.

"There's no evidence of that," Patterson said. "What I do have as evidence is a draft on your account presented to your bank in London for two thousand pounds. It has the signatures of both Mr. Ashbrook and Mr. Deakins and adds credible weight to their story."

"They had another story for Mr. Gordon," Colin reminded him.

"They repeated to Mr. Gordon what Miss Leyden told them to say. They both admitted never having met the Earl of Weybourne. However, they can describe his niece." The sheriff took a deep breath, tugging on his wiry brows. Clearly he was uncomfortable with his business. "I'd like your permission to search your room, my lady."

Mercedes's dark brows came up. "Search my room? Whatever for?"

Colin answered for the sheriff. "He's looking for the weapon. Right now the evidence points most clearly to fraud. As to the murder, Mr. Patterson only has Severn's word that he heard you admit to it."

"I *did* say those things," she said. "But it was a lie."

"Mercedes." Colin said her name sharply. She was adjusting the rope around her own neck. "Do not say another word." He turned to Patterson. "No, you don't have her permission to search."

"There's sufficient cause to conduct one without permission," he said.

"Then that's how you'll have to do it. You may not have the sanction of the accused."

"So be it." He stood.

"I'll go with you," Colin said.

"As you wish. Severn?"

Marcus Severn shook his head. "I'll remain with Mercedes."

"I'll see you in hell first." She came to her feet and went for the door. "I'll be with my cousins in the drawing room." Without a backward glance to see if Mr. Patterson approved, she swept out of the room.

Colin did not shutter the admiration in his eyes. He held the door open for the sheriff. "Shall we?"

The search was conducted with a thoroughness that Colin would have appreciated in other circumstances. The sheriff lifted the mattress, opened drawers, and examined under the bed. He patted down Mercedes's gowns in the armoire and knelt in front of it to search the bottom. Colin knew the moment they were confronted by another problem. The sheriff's brow furrowed and his thin lips tightened. Only his deep-set eyes hinted that his discovery was unwelcome.

"What is it?" Colin asked, stepping closer.

The sheriff sat back on his haunches. His arms were filled with articles of clothing. Boots. Trousers. Neck cloth. A shirt and jacket. All of it men's clothing. Mr. Patterson stood and held up the jacket, partly to display it, partly to judge its size against Colin. It was easily determined the clothes could not have belonged to the captain. "The earl's," Mr. Patterson said heavily. He sifted through the articles, folding each one neatly before he picked up the boots. One was significantly lighter than the other. He dropped that one and reached inside the other. The sorrow in his eyes was quite real as he drew out a pistol.

Colin stared at the weapon. "Is it primed and loaded?"

The sheriff examined it. "Yes."

"Then it hasn't been fired."

"Not since the last time it was primed and loaded. This can't help Miss Leyden."

"You don't really believe she murdered her uncle."

"It doesn't matter what I believe. I only have to gather the evidence. Judges and juries do the rest."

"There's an explanation for this."

Mr. Patterson nodded. "I shouldn't be saying this, Captain Thorne, but I admired Miss Leyden's father and I find myself thinking from time to time that you're a bit like him. My lady's troubles are as high as her neck right now, but yours aren't finished either. You signed the draft that paid for the fraudulent will and you listened to her confession and didn't come to me with it."

Colin didn't repeat again that the confession was a lie. Events had moved far past the point where that was going to be believed.

"Your alibis are suspect because it's plain that one of you is moved to protect the other. I know of only one way that you can't be compelled to testify against her, or she against you." Mr. Patterson picked up the clothes, boots, and weapon and carried them into the hall. "It's something to think about," he said. "Just something to think about."

Mercedes was formally charged and arrested while her family and Colin looked on. Chloe and Sylvia wept softly. The twins threw themselves at Mr. Patterson, battering the hapless man until Colin pulled them off and Mercedes scolded them. She was permitted to take a valise with a few personal belongings and articles of clothing. Colin escorted her to the sheriff's carriage. Severn was riding his own mount.

"Send him away," Colin told the sheriff. "You don't require help taking Mercedes to jail. And if you do, I'll provide you with someone else."

Patterson nodded. He went over to Severn and talked to him briefly.

Marcus shrugged. The smile he cast in Colin's direction was cool and left no doubt that nothing was settled between them.

Colin watched him ride off, then leaned into the carriage to speak to Mercedes. Her face was pale, her lips almost devoid of color. He placed one hand over both of hers. Not surprisingly, they were like ice. "I'm not going to let anything happen to you," he said quietly. There was no response. Mercedes stared straight ahead. He gave her a small shake, his tone urgent. "Tell me you believe me."

Things were already happening to her. Mercedes wondered what there was left to prevent. "I believe you." She said it because she knew it was important to him. Her gray eyes sparkled briefly with tears, then they were gone. Afraid she would shatter, she didn't look at Colin. "I didn't do this thing," she said. "Make certain they know."

Colin glanced back at the group gathered on the front steps of the manor. The twins clung to Mrs. Hennepin but it was difficult to know who was supporting whom. Chloe and Sylvia stood with their arms linked. Mr. Hennepin and Ben Fitch held their hats in hand. The maids wrung their hands in their aprons. Each face was graven with sorrow and anger and fear. Not one among them was accusing.

"They know," Colin told her. He squeezed her hands as Mr. Patterson climbed into the driver's box. "I'll come for you, Mercedes."

She nodded absently. "Yes. You do that."

"I mean it. I'll—" Colin had to step back and close the door as the carriage began to move. "I love you."

He didn't think she heard the last.

The county jail where Mercedes was taken was a small block building at the edge of the village. The other occupants included a man arrested for lifting purses at a recent fair and another being held for drunk and disorderly conduct. The drunk was moved to share quarters with the thief and the cell closest to the sheriff's office was made available to Mercedes.

Mr. Patterson apologized for the conditions but there was little he could do to make the stark block cell more comfortable. The odor of the previous occupant lingered even after the stained cot was turned and the chamber pot was emptied. Fresh air was available from a small, recessed opening in the stone. It was set too high for Mercedes to see out of but it did permit a small beam of sunshine to slip into the room.

It was the turnkey who closed the solid oak door and locked it. Mr. Patterson let his assistant do what he could not bring himself to do. There was a bottle of rum confiscated from the drunk that he had put away in his desk. Once Mercedes was secured, he got it out and began drinking.

The assizes were scheduled for the county in three weeks. The time until these court sessions, where civil and criminal cases were heard, represented Colin's own small window to the outside. While Mercedes sat alone wondering about her future, Colin was planning it.

His first order of business took him to London. He met with his own solicitor and they settled on a barrister to represent Mercedes at the assizes. Mr. Richard Roundstone came highly recommended and Colin liked his thoughtful manner as Mercedes's predicament was presented to him. He agreed to meet with her the following day and begin to prepare for the trial.

Colin had a meal and a pint at the riverfront inn owned by Mr. Ashbrook. He did not introduce himself to the innkeeper, choosing instead to simply observe him managing the Imp 'n Ale. It was Colin's opinion that talk was largely overrated and that much more could be learned by the thoughtful study of a man. This was more difficult to accomplish with Mr. Deakins. The agent for the Garnet Line was a good-natured sort, friendly and verbose, and he wanted to talk at length about Boston when Colin purchased two passages. Still, there was something to be learned from the encounter.

Colin's activities in London kept him away from Weybourne Park for the entire day, but one more task made him pass the Park and head for Glen Eden. It was dark by the time he arrived in the village and he did not make himself known to Chloe's fiance until the following morning. Mr. Fredrick's aunt graciously received him in her small cottage and entertained him until the vicar returned from visiting an ill parishioner. Colin had no idea how Mr. Fredrick would react to the news he brought or the favor he was asking. It was well within the young man's rights to rethink his offer to Chloe. Mercedes's arrest was a scandal that touched her family and therefore the vicar by association.

Colin wondered how much of his relief was visible when Mr. Fredrick merely inquired how he could help.

Upon his return to Weybourne Park Colin met with the family to discuss his intentions. They were remarkably quiet during his short speech and predictably noisy following it, though none of the excited voices offered objections.

Mercedes had enough for all of them.

"How dare you," she said quietly. She was standing at her cell's small, recessed window. Her face was raised toward the opening. A shadow crossed her features as a cloud passed in front of the sun. The tilt of her head gave her a proud, regal air, but her arms crossed protectively in front of her spoke to her vulnerability. "You had no right to do this without my permission."

"I'm asking your permission now," Colin said. He started to approach her, saw her stiffen as she sensed his intent, and sat on the narrow cot instead. "Everyone's agreed it's a good idea."

"I'm so glad everyone has an opinion," she said caustically. "Forgive me if I think mine's the only one that counts."

Colin was silent. He knew from speaking to the turnkey that she already had met with Mr. Roundstone and that the barrister's visit had been a long one. He could see she was discouraged rather than hopeful. His eyes wandered around the cell. There was a small basin and pitcher of water on the floor. A damp cloth lay over the rim of the basin. Fresh straw had been laid in the corner and the chamber pot was pushed out of sight. Except for the flash of sunshine when the clouds rolled on, the cell was without light. Etchings in the stone walls spoke to the boredom and frustration of previous occupants.

He had not given any thought to her distress at being seen in these surroundings. None of it mattered to him, so it hadn't occurred to him that it may matter to her. He knew she had refused to see Mrs. Hennepin earlier in the day when the housekeeper brought a basket of food. He hadn't understood what lay behind her self-imposed isolation. Now he did.

Here, more than at Weybourne Park, Mercedes's mourning clothes suited her.

Mercedes turned away from the window to find Colin studying her. She ducked her head self-consciously. "Marcus came to see me today," she said.

"You're changing the subject," he said.

Her eyes finally met his and challenged. "Yes."

Colin smiled narrowly. "All right. Tell me about Severn. You refused to see him, didn't you?"

"Yes. Mr. Patterson was here then. Severn made a fuss but Mr. Patterson made him respect my wishes." She hesitated. "What do you think he wanted?"

"I don't know." He waited. The subject could not be changed for long. There wasn't much left to talk about.

"Why?" she said finally. "Why would you want to do it?"

"I thought I explained that."

She waved that aside. "I know what you said."

"But you don't believe it." Colin realized then that he had gone about the thing badly. He should have appealed to her practical side. "I understand your reservations," he said at last. "If you can't marry me for love, then you should consider what our marriage could mean to your future. Mr. Patterson was the first to point out that as your husband I couldn't be compelled to testify against you. That offers you some protection. You've had time enough to realize that as word of your arrest gets out, certain people are likely to come forward."

Mercedes *had* thought about it. "You mean Molly, I suppose. And the innkeeper at the Passing Fancy."

He nodded. "It's inevitable that a sketch of you will appear in the *Gazette*. If Molly or the innkeeper recognizes you I imagine they'll have something to say. Your late-night visit to the inn on the eve of my duel with the earl speaks to your character. And what you tried to do that night demonstrates your willingness to—"

Mercedes put her hands over her ears. "Stop it! I don't want to hear any more."

He went on relentlessly. "Your willingness to use violence to solve problems. How will that be heard by a judge and jury? Did you tell Mr. Roundstone about it? If others know you intended to kill me, do you think they would be more or less persuaded that you're capable of murdering your uncle?"

Her hands dropped to her sides, her fists clenched tightly. "Are you threatening me?" she asked. "If I don't marry you, you'll tell that story?"

"It's not a story, is it? And it's not a threat. If questioned, what recourse would I have but to tell the truth?" He paused and allowed her to take that in. "I told you why I wanted to marry you, Mercedes. You're the one who wanted to hear another explanation. Which is more difficult for you to believe: that I could love anyone or that I could love you?"

For the first time she was able to hear his uncertainties. Her heart swelled. Remorse softened her eyes. At her sides her fingers unfolded as she took a step toward him. "I've watched you with my cousins," she said. "Britton and Brendan follow you like puppies and you're never impatient or cruel with them. Chloe and Sylvia seek out your advice and you give them your time and your thoughts. I'm not certain when they stopped seeing you as a guest at Weybourne Park and started thinking of you as family, but I don't doubt that they have. And I don't believe you set out to make that happen. I think you found a home there because you have a great capacity for loving others and for whatever reason, you finally feel free to do it.

"As for loving me?" Mercedes's smile was gentle, even sad. "I think you mistake your feelings."

"I see," he said after a moment. "And you know what's in my heart."

She missed the edge of sarcasm in his tone. "You've shown yourself to be generous and kind and forgiving and it would be easy to confuse your—"

Colin came to his feet, cutting her off. "Those words have never been applied to my nature," he said. His voice was clipped and cold, as if he found her description insulting. "Generous? It's the generosity of a selfish man, one who gives for his own pleasure and because he enjoys the pleasure of others. You, above anyone, should know I'm not kind. A kind man would not provoke you just to see your eyes flash like lightning when you turn on him. And forgiving? What wrong have you or your cousins ever done me that required forgiving?"

"I tried to stab you."

"You *did* stab me," he corrected her. "But it's healed."

"I threw a drawer at your head."

"Also healed."

"I encouraged my cousins to lock you in the tower room."

"So you finally admit it." He smiled as she shifted uneasily, realizing her mistake. "No matter. You let us out."

"I stole two thousand pounds from you."

"I gave you that draft."

"I lied about the flask."

"You thought you were helping me."

"You said I was putting the noose around your neck."

"And you proved me wrong by putting it around your own." He watched her slender frame shudder in reaction to this last statement. When he took a step toward her she didn't back away. By the time his arms came around her, Mercedes was leaning into him, her body unconsciously seeking the shelter and strength her mind would deny her. "Let me do this for you, Mercedes, because I want you in my life."

What could have been a tender moment was cut short by two raucous cries. "MARRY HIM!"

Colin immediately suspected the twins of eavesdropping, but that thought was short-lived as he realized the voices were both baritones, and more pertinent, Britton and Brendan were at Weybourne Park. Mercedes had already jumped back, startled by the intrusion, and Colin made no move to pull her close again.

"What the hell?" he asked, glancing around the cell. "Where did that come from?"

There was the chilling sound of stone grating against stone, then a bit of loose mortar at eye level on the dividing wall crumbled and fell to the ground. Colin walked to the wall and bent his head just enough to peer through the opening.

"Hello."

Colin was not amused by the bright blue eye staring back at

him. The single eye appeared to be gleeful enough for both of them. "Are you the thief or the drunk?" he asked.

There was no lessening of Blue-eye's amusement. His eye actually crinkled at the corner and indicated his smile had deepened. "The thief, I'm afraid. And the drunk's quite sober now but not much in the way of good company. I find myself quite bored."

"Perhaps you should try tunneling through the outside wall," Colin suggested dryly.

"Tried that. Not a loose stone to be had. This seemed a good way to pass the time."

"How long have you been listening?"

The blue eye didn't waver. "All morning actually. Heard most of what the lady told her barrister. Doesn't look good, if you want my thoughts on the matter."

"I don't."

"Still, you'd do well to get her out of here. I understand you're some kind of clipper captain. Seems to me that you should be able to steal her away before she stands trial. Take her around the world."

"I'll consider that," Colin said, not mentioning he already had.

"That's what I would do." Blue-eye pressed his face closer to the small opening. "Would you mind moving to one side," he said. "I'd like a look at the lady."

"I don't think—"

"Is she as lovely as she sounds?"

It was the youth and wistfulness of the disembodied voice that caught Colin's attention. He glanced over his shoulder at Mercedes. A soft, slightly embarrassed smile tugged at her lips. "Lovelier," he said. There was a heartfelt sigh from the other side of the wall.

"I was afraid of that," Blue-eye said.

Colin stepped aside. Mercedes smiled uncertainly in the direction of the small opening in the wall and raised her hand in a tentative greeting. Colin counted to three before he stepped in front of her again.

"Oh my," Blue-eye was moved to say.

"Exactly."

"In your position I'd be selfish, too."

Colin didn't comment on that. "How much can you hear when the hole's closed?"

"Some. Most actually. But a lot's muffled."

"And when it's open?"

"Like I was in there with you."

"That's interesting."

"Might even be useful," Blue-eye offered.

Colin took out his handkerchief. "I'll keep that in mind." He started to plug the hole with the cloth. He paused when Blue-eye cleared his throat.

"One more thing," the pickpocket said.

"What's that?"

"The lady loves you."

"She told you?"

"More or less," Blue-eye said, chuckling. "She's been working it out for herself since she arrived. Mostly out loud."

Colin looked over his shoulder again. This time Mercedes was purposely avoiding his glance. "Talks to herself, does she?"

The thief's eye was dancing now. "Most definitely."

"Thank you." Colin pushed the handkerchief into the crack, muffling the pickpocket's last salute: "Glad to be of service."

Colin leaned against the wall and leveled his dark, usually remote gaze on Mercedes. "That was interesting."

"I believe you said that," she reminded him.

"I said it to the pickpocket. Now I'm saying it to you." His grin was cool and a little superior. "So you talk to yourself. I didn't know that."

"My point all along," she said. "You don't know me."

He straightened. There was no lightness in his tone and his dark eyes were grave. "This is what I know: you're as unpredictable as the weather and as strong and steady as the sea. You embrace your family like sails embrace the wind and stay a course once it's set. And when I hold you in my arms you cradle me like the curve and swell of the ocean. I think I've known you all my life."

She stood there, still and silent, moved by the manner in which he saw her, the way he likened her to all that was familiar to him. "I do love you, you know," she said softly.

"That's the rumor among the inmates." He reached for her, drew her close, and laid his cheek against the crown of her hair. "It's good to have it confirmed." He held her just that way for a long time. When he sensed her peace he lifted his head and raised her face. "My solicitor has arranged for the special license and Mr. Fredrick has agreed to perform the ceremony. We can be married in three days. Mr. Patterson has no objection and your cousins approve of the idea."

"You've thought of everything."

"Not everything. I didn't think you'd say no."

"Well, I'm saying yes now."

Colin's heart slammed hard in his chest but he didn't lose a moment reveling in this victory. He pressed his next concern. "I did some other things in London yesterday besides arrange for the license and meet with your barrister."

"Oh?" There was something in his tone that warned her she would not like what was coming. Mercedes shifted in his embrace and he let her go. "Go on," she said.

"I had dinner at Mr. Ashbrook's inn. He works hard and manages his place with a tight fist. I could see that the earl's man would be impressed by obvious habits. Less noticeable is that Mr. Ashbrook waters his drinks and shortchanges his customers. What's truly remarkable is that he's gotten away with it. I can believe that your uncle had dealings with him and it's even less challenging to imagine Severn being able to buy him off."

"And Mr. Deakins? I assume you saw him."

"I did. I booked two passages to Boston." He saw questions and objections already forming in her expressive eyes. "Don't say anything, Mercedes. They're available if we need them. I'm hoping we won't."

"I suppose I shall have to learn to trust someone besides my-self," she said finally.

"That would be a good beginning."

"Tell me about Mr. Deakins."

"Very talkative. The fact that I wanted passage to Boston interested him. The Garnet Line is based there, same as Remington. He mentioned he had booked passage there just a week earlier for another man. Not the usual thing, he said. Most Londoners are interested in New York, he told me. Especially the toffs."

"Do you think he was talking about my uncle?"

"He could have been." He shrugged. "Or it could have been anyone."

"But you don't think so."

Colin shook his head. "No, I don't think so. We all suspect Weybourne was going to leave the country. But why would he choose Boston? What was there for him?"

"And you think I know the answer?"

"You may. Think of what he's told you, Mercedes. Isn't there something that he's ever said, even off-handedly, that would give you—" He stopped the moment he saw her clouded eyes clear. She seemed struck by her own revelation.

Mercedes's smile was slow to rise, almost disbelieving. "It was you he was after," she said.

"Me? But I was here. He had an opportunity at the Park to face—"

She shook her head furiously. "No. No, that's not it." Her voice rose slightly with excitement. "He once told me . . ." She frowned in concentration. "No, it's no good. I can't remember his precise words, but the gist of it was that what you had done— winning the wager—*couldn't* have been done. I think he intended to prove you cheated him. Where else would he go but Boston to discover the truth?"

"That makes sense."

Mercedes sat down on the cot. "For all the good it does. He's dead. That we might know his intention doesn't help clear me or find his murderer."

Colin was thoughtful. He raked his bright hair back at the temple. "It may," he said slowly. He fixed his eyes on Mercedes. "If you're willing to see Marcus Severn the next time he comes calling."

Her mouth flattened. "I asked Mr. Patterson to tell him not to bother coming again."

"That won't stop him," Colin said. "Not when he learns we're going to be married."

Mercedes was not as confident of Severn's eventual appearance as Colin. She had no idea what she would say to him if he arrived. It was not something that she and Colin talked about and she had no clear sense of what Colin thought Severn's presence would accomplish. When she asked Colin if he thought Severn had murdered her uncle, his answer was an unequivocal no. That was the last he would discuss it.

The remainder of his brief visit was spent sitting side by side on the narrow cot, their backs against the rough stone wall, her head resting on his shoulder, his hand over hers. Mercedes drew up her legs and the black skirt of her gown lay smoothly around her. It didn't seem necessary to talk about anything at all.

Now Mercedes wished she had bent his ear. According to the sheriff, Marcus Severn was due to arrive within the hour and Mercedes's anxiety had reached almost crippling proportions. For all appearance she was numb, nearly expressionless, while on the inside her heart pounded and her stomach churned.

Since Colin's departure, and the removal of his handkerchief, the blue-eyed thief had struck up several conversations with Mercedes. Even her limited responses were more interesting than ones from the sober drunk sharing his cell. For Mercedes it was what she imagined a confessional to be, with both of them taking turns as penitents.

With Severn's visit nearly upon her Mercedes found herself drawn to the small opening in the wall again. "Are you there?"

The blue eye appeared almost immediately. "Always."

"Do you ever think about the hanging?" she asked.

Blue-eye blinked. "You come straight to the point."

"Well, do you?"

"Actually, no."

"Because you're innocent?"

"You know I'm not. But I'm not entirely guilty, either."

She peered closer and could see the single blue eye in her view was brighter with the smile she couldn't see. "You don't think they'll hang you?"

He shook his head. "No. But not because they won't find cause."

"Then why?"

"Because I intend to escape."

It was the last Mercedes heard. Her attention shifted to the door as the key was turned. "He's here," she breathed. For the first time since she had begun speaking to Blue-eye, he failed to reply.

Thirteen

Marcus Severn stepped into the cell. He raised a perfumed handkerchief to his nose to briefly subdue the odors that could not be eliminated. Moving away from the door after he heard it lock, he held out the handkerchief to Mercedes.

"No, thank you," she said softly, politely, but with no feeling.

"Don't tell me you're used to this stench. My God, Sadie, it's time to get you out of here."

"Oh? And you can do that?"

"I'm the one who made certain you were put here, wasn't I?" There was no remorse in his tone. "Have you had your fill?"

"I can't see that it matters to you. As you pointed out, your lies made my confinement possible."

He smiled a little at that. "I don't believe I said it quite that way."

Mercedes managed a careless shrug when what she wanted to do was shiver. She had always been uncomfortable in Severn's presence but the chill was never this pervasive. "Please, sit down," she said, extending her hand to indicate the cot.

"Always gracious," he said, amused. "Even here. Will you join me?"

Her eyes darted to the cot. "No. I've been sitting all morning. But please, do as you wish."

Severn remained standing.

Mercedes tried to increase the space between them without making it look like a retreat. She went to the small window where she could let sunlight glance off her shoulders. "I confess some surprise that you're here," she said. "I made my wishes very clear to Mr. Patterson two days ago."

"And he conveyed them correctly. But you've agreed to see me in spite of what you said, so it was worth the effort."

"Why make an effort at all?"

Severn made a point of looking around the cell before his eyes returned to her. "Can you believe this is where I think you belong?" The question was rhetorical. He did not give her an opportunity to answer. "Any more than I believe you belong with *him?* What can you be thinking, Mercedes? Marrying Thorne is no solution. Oh yes, I've heard about it already. I was skeptical at first—I couldn't credit you with being part of the nonsense— but then I heard the same story from several other sources. It's caused quite a stir in the county." The corners of his mouth lifted in a thin smile but his eyes held no amusement and his tone remained dry. "More of a stir, I would say, than your arrest."

"People are always interested in weddings," she said helpfully. "And for the marriage to take place so soon after the earl's death, well . . ." She let her voice trail off because Severn looked as if he might throttle her. The thought of his hands on any part of her body made it difficult to breathe.

"Tell me about this marriage, Mercedes. What purpose does it serve?"

She frowned. "I don't understand what you mean. It serves its own purpose. I love him."

"I don't believe it."

"I'm not going to try to convince you."

Severn ignored that. "More likely you believe it will help your case. Is that what he told you?" He held up his hand, halting her reply. "No need to say so. I can see that it is. He's been telling you that if you're married he can't testify against you. I hope you have good legal counsel, Mercedes, because Thorne's not giving you full truths."

"It doesn't matter. Nothing Colin says or doesn't say means anything. I'm not guilty of the charges and protection is not why I've agreed to marry him."

"You're so naive," Severn said, shaking his head. "I knew I had to come to protect you from yourself. Haven't you had enough, Mercedes? This is no place for you. Can you even appreciate how you look here?"

"You put me here," she said quietly.

"And I can get you out."

Mercedes said nothing. Her look was skeptical. Severn's price for her freedom was bound to be steep.

"Marry me," he said.

It took her breath away. Mercedes actually recoiled at the notion of being bound to Marcus Severn. "You only wanted me as your mistress before. Perhaps that will do as well."

"I know what I want."

"And if I agree to become your wife you'll—"

"Not merely an agreement. You have to marry me."

"You'll recant your story."

"I'll see that you're released."

Mercedes frowned. "How is that possible? You won't be believed any longer, especially if we're wed. In my eyes you have no credibility whatsoever. I can't imagine that anything you could say in my defense would be helpful."

"Even if I said I always knew your confession to the captain wasn't true?"

It was a struggle to keep her voice steady when her heart was pounding so hard. "Even then."

"I did it to teach you a lesson, Mercedes." Severn approached her. He raised his hand and touched her cheek with the backs of his fingers. His smile was indulgent. "You must have suspected that. Does it surprise you I could be jealous? I am, you know. Weybourne held you out to me like a carrot on a stick. For years. I was incredibly patient where you were concerned. It was only when Weybourne disappeared that I pressed my suit. I thought you would be pleased to accept my protection. Instead you threw my offer back at me and accepted Thorne. Is it any wonder that I was moved to take more serious measures?"

She couldn't keep the horror out of her tone and she recoiled from his touch, pressing her back to the cold stone wall. "But to accuse me of murder?"

"You brought it on yourself, Mercedes." He stepped nearer. There was a certain wildness to her eyes that intrigued him and a cornered quality to her posture that made him want to keep her contained. This time when he touched her his hand grazed her cheek then continued on a downward path. He brushed her throat, her shoulder, her breast, and finally rested his palm against the curve of her waist. "You know you did. I offered my help after the earl's will was read and you turned me down. I came back because I recognized the powerful influence Thorne was exerting on you. You needed to hear from someone else with an interest in Weybourne Park."

"Please go," she said on a thread of sound. The hand on her waist seemed to exert enormous pressure against her diaphragm. She had to remind herself that it was only her imagination that made it seem so. "Your being here serves no purpose. I can't see that you can help me. Nothing you say will make any difference."

Severn gave her a small shake. "Hear me out before you judge. I returned to Weybourne Park to talk some sense into you. Then I found you in the tower room with Thorne, engaged in some absurd argument about the earl's death. He actually *believed* you might have done it. I never thought that, Mercedes. Never for a moment. What does it say when you agree to marry a man who questions your innocence and refuse the man who has never doubted it?"

"Yet you're the one who's made me seem guilty in the eyes of others."

"I had to," he said. "How else could I have you?"

Wrenching away from his light grasp, Mercedes moved to the cot. She stood at the foot of it, trying to place a small barrier between them. "You don't have me," she said. "I haven't heard anything that will make any difference. You went to a great deal of trouble to create the evidence against me."

Severn sighed but remained calm. "You're speaking of Ashbrook and Deakins."

"Two names I wish I had never heard."

"Mr. Patterson would be interested to know that they never heard of you."

"Until you paid them to tell him differently." Anger flushed Mercedes's features. "How could you do that?"

"How could I not? The opportunity presented itself and I took it. Mr. Ashbrook and Mr. Deakins will discredit themselves for the right amount of the ready. No one ever has to know they were paid to lie in the first place. What they were paid to remember they can be paid to forget."

Mercedes closed her eyes and hugged herself. "Oh, Marcus," she said miserably. She implored him to see reason. "My uncle wanted his sons to inherit the title. You set out to undermine his wishes. How can you think I would have you as my husband?"

"Have you no care for your freedom?"

"I care everything for it," she said steadily. "But I have more freedom in these four walls than I would ever have with you."

Mercedes never suspected he could strike so quickly. Severn's blow knocked her against the wall before she realized she was in danger. She tasted blood at the corner of her mouth where she had bitten her lip. Drawing herself up proudly, Mercedes moved away from the wall. "And you wonder why I won't shackle myself to you," she said lowly.

Severn stared at the imprint of his hand on her cheek. Color rushed to fill her complexion, then faded until only a faint outline remained. "You'll hang," he said.

Her gray eyes sparkled with tears she blinked back. "For a murder you committed."

That set Severn back. He actually smiled. "You think I murdered Weybourne?"

"Why not? You wanted the title. You wanted me. His death meant you could contest Captain Thorne's claim to the Park. I believe that when you trapped me in my carriage at Tattersall's you had already met with my uncle. You knew where he was and that he intended to leave the country. I think he told you about the addendum to his will and it infuriated you."

"So I killed him."

"It's a possibility Mr. Roundstone will be looking into."

Severn shrugged. "Let your barrister do what he will but there's no crime to be laid at my door."

"You falsely accused me!"

"I reported things I heard."

"Things you admit you knew weren't true! You paid men to lie about me!"

He actually smiled at her rising passion. Her eyes sparkled and her complexion regained its color. "A small matter, I assure you. One that can be rectified if you would see reason. You really only have yourself to blame. Your own actions have caused you more grief than any of mine. I had nothing to do with the weapon they found in your room or your uncle's clothes being in your possession. There is a record of two thousand pounds paid to Ashbrook and Deakins and it doesn't bear my signature. You've been foolish to place your trust in Thorne. He can't help you, Mercedes. I can."

"Then do it," she said, challenging him. "Tell Mr. Patterson that you lied."

"But I didn't. Don't you see? That's the beauty of it. I told no lies. I paid others to do it for us."

His line of reasoning stole Mercedes voice for a moment. "You did nothing for *us*. It's only been for you." She pressed one hand to her temple. There was a blinding ache behind her eyes. "Nothing you've said changes my mind. Get out, Severn. Leave on your own before I call for the turnkey." When he didn't move immediately, Mercedes started for the door.

Severn caught her by the elbow. "I won't be back, Mercedes. You only have this one chance."

"I never wanted this chance in the first place," she said tightly. She pulled, but he held her fast. "Colin thought I should talk to you. I regret now that I listened to him." Mercedes winced as Severn's grip on her elbow hardened. When she looked at him his gaze was set distantly and she realized he was unaware of what he was doing. "Let me go, Marcus. You're hurting me."

Severn regained his focus. He looked down at his hand on her arm then at her. Now it was his smile that was a trifle sad, even disappointed. "Oh, Sadie, what have you done?"

His response startled her but not as much as the sound of the door being unlocked. "I didn't call for you," she told the turnkey as he pushed open the door. Her eyes widened when she saw the sheriff standing behind his assistant.

"No, but you were going to," the turnkey said.

"Release her, Severn," Patterson said. "My lady, you may step outside. His lordship and I have matters to discuss in here."

Mercedes felt Severn's hand drop away from hers. She glanced at him uncertainly. The look in his eyes could only be described as malevolent. She recoiled and hurried for the safety of the corridor. "I don't understand," she said to the sheriff.

Patterson pointed to the outer office. "Captain Thorne will explain. Please go."

"Colin's here?" Mercedes did not risk a glance back at Severn to see if he heard this news. The men stepped back to let her pass and she hurried down the corridor.

Her initial thought as she walked into the sheriff's office was that she was the target of more trickery. Colin was not immediately visible. Mercedes called to the turnkey, first for assistance, finally in alarm, as she spied Colin's body lying behind Patterson's desk. Dropping to her knees beside him, Mercedes raised Colin's head and cradled it in her lap. She ran her fingers through his hair and over his scalp. There was a lump at the base of his skull and her fingers were tinged with his blood when she pulled them away.

It was the sheriff who responded to her cry. He took in the situation at a glance and called for his assistant. "They've escaped," he told the turnkey. "They can't get far shackled together. I want you to find Douglas and that pickpocket and bring them back."

The turnkey tossed his ring of keys to Mr. Patterson and ran out the door. The sheriff's command that he fetch a physician followed him.

"Here's a sorry sight," Severn said from the doorway.

Patterson sighed heavily. He was going to have words with his assistant. Severn should have been locked in the cell. "I'm not finished with you."

"You are for now." He waited to hear a contradiction. When there was none, he walked out of the jail's open door and into the sunlight.

Shaking his head, the sheriff hunkered beside Mercedes. "How bad is it?"

"Not so bad, I think. He has a hard head. Usually I find it cause for complaint; just now I find myself thankful."

One of Colin's eyes opened. His outlook was blurred but Mercedes's face was still a sweet sight. "I'll remember that." The eyelid closed and Colin groaned as he tried to raise his head.

Mercedes stroked his hair. "Stay where you are. Mr. Patterson has requested a physician be found. There's no need for you to move."

Colin could admit to himself that he had no desire to move. If it were not for the sheriff's watchful and somewhat suspicious regard, Colin would have found himself remarkably content.

"How did this happen?" Patterson wanted to know.

"They rushed me," Colin explained. "I was sitting here at your desk and they were across the room."

"They were still shackled?"

Colin nodded. "One of them clobbered me with those iron wrist cuffs. I admit my attention strayed when I heard you and the turnkey leave the other cell and go to Mercedes's. They saw an opportunity and took it."

Mercedes thought Colin did not sound particularly remorseful. She wondered if Mr. Patterson noticed the same thing.

The sheriff rose and began rifling through his desk. The keys to unlock the shackles were the first thing he couldn't find. That was not surprising. It was when he began digging in a side drawer that he swore softly.

Colin struggled to a sitting position in spite of Mercedes's wish to keep him down. "What is it?" he asked Patterson.

"My evidence drawer." The sheriff slammed the drawer so hard the massive oak desk vibrated. He kicked the corner of it for good measure. "He stole everything."

Mercedes assumed Mr. Patterson was talking about the pickpocket. It did not seem helpful to remind the sheriff that the man *was* a thief by trade. Had he thought that a few weeks in a cell and the threat of a hanging were going to alter Blue-eye's habits? She wisely said nothing.

"Everything?" Colin asked.

Patterson had begun pacing the floor. "Damn him," he said to no one in particular. He clicked off the loss on the points of his fingers. "He got the purses he pocketed at the fair, Miss Callahan's pearl necklace, Mrs. Lynch's beaded coin bag, and that earring no one ever claimed. God, that I have to explain this to his victims. Mrs. Lynch will never let me hear the end of it. And Miss Callahan . . . Miss Callahan never liked the idea that I wanted to keep the articles. I told her it would only be until the assizes."

Colin was unconcerned by the sheriff's litany of loss. "He stole everything?" he asked again.

"Yes." Mr. Patterson stopped pacing. "Didn't I just say so?"

Rising to his feet, Colin then helped Mercedes to hers. He leaned against the desk to steady himself. "The earl's pistol?" he asked. "His clothing?"

"All of it," the sheriff said heavily. He didn't look at Mercedes or Colin but stared morosely at the open door. "Even the flask, though I suspect that may be found again when we get Douglas back. He can't turn away drink."

Mercedes sat down slowly in the sheriff's large wooden chair. She looked uncertainly at Patterson. "What does that mean?"

He turned, stuffing his hands in his pockets, and sighed again. "It merely assures there is no case against you. Your conversation with Severn had significantly tipped the scales in your favor."

"You were listening?" she asked.

"Captain Thorne's idea," the sheriff said. His wiry brows rose and fell in small salute to Colin. "A good one as it turned out.

My assistant and I dropped in on the conversation much the way Severn dropped in on you and the captain."

"Why did no one tell me?"

"I couldn't risk it," Colin said. "If you knew Mr. Patterson was listening, you may have tried too hard to lead the conversation. Severn would have become suspicious." He addressed Patterson. "I take it you heard enough."

"Enough."

"You questioned him?"

"There wasn't time for that. Your inattention to your prisoners cost me the opportunity to keep Severn here."

Colin accepted the rebuke in silence.

Patterson rubbed his chin. He swore under his breath again and when his hand dropped to his side it was curled in a fist. This turn of events was unacceptable to him. "Since there's no reason for me to remain with you, I have a search party to organize and a prisoner to find." He eyed Colin consideringly. "I don't suppose you'll want to join the search?"

Colin winced slightly as he shook his head. He laid his hand over the lump at the base of his skull. "No," he said. "I don't think so. You understand."

The law officer understood far more than Colin admitted. "I didn't suppose you would," he said. He looked at Mercedes and then back to Colin. "In your place, neither would I." He shrugged. "If you'll excuse me." He took his hat off the peg by the door, tipped it politely in Mercedes's direction. "You're free to go, m'lady." Then he was off, heading for the nearest tavern in the hope of gathering men for the search.

Mercedes blinked widely. She stared after the sheriff, stunned.

Colin said nothing. He was patting down his jacket then searching the inside of his vest.

Turning slowly in her chair, Mercedes raised her face to Colin. "Do you suppose they'll catch him?"

Colin had come up emptyhanded.

"Where do you think he'll go?"

Colin had a pretty good idea. "Boston."

"Boston? Why in the world—" She stopped. A grin had transformed Colin's face, lending his features a youthfulness that had rarely been there even when he was young. Then Mercedes understood. "The passages you purchased . . ."

The grin widened. "I've been robbed."

Mercedes found it hard to credit that she was back at Weybourne Park. The bath that had been drawn for her should have been relaxing, instead she kept looking around her room, afraid if she closed her eyes it all would disappear.

In a purposeful attempt to enjoy these moments, Mercedes raised her arm languidly and began soaping it from wrist to shoulder. The desire to scrub herself clean was too strong and she ended up applying the sponge with a vengeance. The smell of the cell was in her hair and under her skin. It lingered in her nostrils even after she was clean from head to toe.

Mercedes climbed out of the tub, wrapped herself in a towel, and rang for assistance. The second bath accomplished what the first one could not. She leaned back in water that was hot enough to flush her skin and curl the ends of her dark hair. Resting her head against the lip of the tub, Mercedes finally closed her eyes. The steamy fragrance of lavender bath salts enabled her to breathe without inhaling the memory of her damp cell.

She slept. She may have denied that she was tired but the evidence was there to the contrary. When she woke she was in her own bed, dressed in a nightshift, covered with a cool sheet and pink and white quilt, and with no recollection of how she got there.

Mercedes sat up slowly. Outside it was dusk. The window was open and a light breeze eddied through the room, raising the curtains until they billowed like sails.

"Do you want dinner?"

Jerking in surprise, Mercedes bumped the back of her head. She made a face as she rubbed it. "I suppose we'll have matching lumps now."

Colin left his chair and moved to the side of the bed. "I didn't mean to startle you. I thought you knew I was here."

Her smile was rueful. "I barely know *I'm* here."

He pushed a strand of damp hair away from her cheek. "I understand. You've had quite a day."

"That hardly describes it." She looked around. They were alone. "Who knows you're here?" she asked suspiciously. It was still early in the evening. If he remained there was little chance that he wouldn't be found out.

"Everyone, I suspect. I told Mrs. Hennepin I intended to sit with you and she didn't raise an eyebrow."

"Are you quite certain?"

"Even Mrs. Hennepin can make small allowances in proper form. We're going to be married tomorrow, remember? I still have the special license."

The last doubt she had about the reasons he was marrying her vanished. "About the wedding . . ."

Panic paralyzed Colin. Only his eyes moved as he searched her face.

"I wonder if we might have it in the garden."

He leaned forward and laid his mouth over hers. She had to have known she had almost stopped his heart. He even thought she was reveling in it; certainly she was reveling in the kiss. Her arms were raised and circling his shoulders. Her fingers threaded in his hair. The taste of her was sweet as she opened her mouth under his.

The kiss lingered after Colin sat back. Her fingertips rested lightly on his shoulders as though she was reluctant to let him go. Her face was still turned up to him, her gray eyes clear and guileless and . . . trusting. He felt this last as a gift and a burden. He had asked for it but he also knew it was misplaced. Mercedes had given it without knowing things that could make a difference. It was this very uncertainty that kept him silent.

He kissed her lightly again then came to his feet. "You never said if you wanted me to ring for dinner."

Not knowing the turn Colin's thoughts had taken, Mercedes

thought that he was determined to play the gentleman. She was not so confident that she could say she wished he might do otherwise. "Yes, please," she said instead. "I find I'm hungry. Is it so late?"

"After seven. You obviously needed to rest. You were exhausted." He gave the brocade pull a yank. "Have you slept at all these last few days?"

Mercedes shook her head. Unconsciously she drew into herself, pulling her knees up and raising the quilt around her. "A nap now and again and only because I couldn't help myself. I didn't want to sleep. It was as though I was losing my life there."

It was with some effort that Colin kept himself from approaching the bed. A touch now would undermine Mercedes's own strength. She needed to know she had survived the experience, not that she had been a victim of it.

"It helped when I could finally talk to Blue-eye," she said.

"Blue-eye? You mean Ponty."

"Ponty? Was that the pickpocket's name?"

Colin nodded. "Ponty Pine."

"That's rather odd, isn't it?"

"That's the name he gave me."

Mercedes made a small dismissive motion with her hand. "No, I mean it's odd that I never asked him. He never asked me, either. I suppose I appreciated the anonymity."

"I think it's safe to assume he knew who you were."

She shrugged. "I didn't think about that. I couldn't have told him the things I did if I had."

Colin was intrigued. "What sort of things?"

Mercedes shook her head. A vaguely rueful smile changed the shape of her mouth. "I'm not telling you."

"It's not as though your secrets are safe," he said. "If you recall, Ponty the pickpocket is the one who told me you were in love."

"I never said I told him secrets. That was your word. In any event, I don't believe we'll be hearing from Mr. Pine again."

Colin touched his vest pocket again, reconfirming the bills of fare to Boston were really gone. "You're right," he said. "And I wish him God's speed. If he provided some measure of comfort to you, then he deserves this turn in his fortune."

Mercedes felt precisely the same, but Colin's generosity suddenly made her suspicious. "You wouldn't have had anything to do with his turn of fortune, would you?"

"What do you mean?"

"I mean did you allow him to escape?"

Colin's hand went to the back of his head. The lump was still sizable and the throbbing had only diminished marginally since the physician examined it. "Of course," he agreed dryly. "I invited him to clobber me. Turned my back on him and pointed out where to strike for maximum effect and minimal damage."

Regarding him consideringly, Mercedes said, "You might have done just that."

Colin was saved responding by the arrival of Sylvia with Mercedes's dinner tray. He helped her uncover the dishes and set them out on the small bedside table. Mrs. Hennepin had prepared light fare for Mercedes. The steamy aroma of the roast chicken breast and small red potatoes filled the air quickly. He noticed Mercedes was leaning toward the table, eyeing the dishes as the lids were removed. It was a good sign that she was hungry. Sleep was not the only thing she denied herself during her incarceration. Mrs. Hennepin had despaired that Mercedes ate next to nothing of the food she prepared and sent to her.

Sylvia set the tray over Mercedes's lap and plumped pillows behind her back. Unaccustomed to the pampering, Mercedes protested that she was not an invalid. No one paid her any heed, talking around her as if being bed bound had also made her deaf. It wasn't until she was comfortably settled with fork in hand that Sylvia began to take Colin to task.

"Mrs. Hennepin says you've been in here alone quite long enough and if you won't leave I'm supposed to chaperone." Sylvia waggled her finger at Colin to emphasize her point—the one the housekeeper insisted she make. "And Mrs. Hennepin also says that the next time you throw her out of a room, she won't go so easily."

Colin sighed softly and avoided Mercedes's interested glance. "Traitor," he said to Sylvia. He held up his hands in surrender. "I'm leaving." Swooping down, he kissed Mercedes before she could duck her head. His action flustered Mercedes and delighted Sylvia. He backed out of the room, closing the door just as Mercedes was calling him an ill-mannered rogue. He did not think he was imagining a certain amount of affection in her tone.

A downpour forced the ceremony from the garden into Weybourne Park's chapel. Mr. Fredrick was visibly more nervous than either the bride or groom, although everyone agreed later he managed the rites with both gravity and grace. Chloe was particularly complimentary of her intended's performance.

Mrs. Hennepin wept copiously while Sylvia, wondering if she might ever plight her troth, shed a more discreet tear or two. The twins were amused by all the fuss although they thought Captain Thorne was rather splendid looking in his black morning coat, trousers, and intricately tied neckcloth. He did not appear predisposed to make either one of them walk a plank for their antics.

The gathering had to strain to hear Mercedes recite her vows, but Colin's voice was clear and fearless. The pronouncement that they were joined as husband and wife rocked them both with equal force. For the first time they looked at each other uncertainly, less confident of their future than they had been only moments before. Mercedes twisted the gold band on her finger and wondered what she had done. Looking at her now, Colin wondered that she had done it.

The silent expectation of those gathered moved Colin to bend his head and urged Mercedes to raise her face. Their eyes met. Held. Her clear gray gaze did not waver from his darker one. His had a question, hers an answer.

His mouth laid softly over hers. It was a chaste kiss. Reserved and reverent. Undemanding yet filled with promise.

When Colin and Mercedes turned to face their guests they were met with a silence more profound than the one that had prompted their kiss. Even the twins were subdued.

Colin gave Mercedes an arch look. He said nothing. The look was enough to convey that, had he known a kiss could have such a powerful quieting effect on her family and staff, he would have made a point of kissing her often and publicly.

That silence didn't last, of course, as they were rushed by well-wishers. Brendan launched himself at Colin, hugging him hard enough to make him stagger back. Britton also attached like a barnacle. It was not the twins' display of affection that made tears glisten in Mercedes's eyes, but seeing how deeply Colin was moved by it.

A splendid wedding breakfast was laid out for the family in the dining room. The staff also enjoyed a celebratory meal in the kitchen, complete with champagne, thanks to Colin's thoughtfulness.

Mercedes let her heart fill with the chatter and excitement around the table. She had no regrets that the ceremony had been indoors rather than out, that the bride was wearing black rather than white, that proper form had been abandoned rather than observed. It was all insignificant in light of the way Colin was watching her. She wondered that she had ever thought his dark eyes unreadable. The look in them now was very clear. Had she ever been prone to blushing, her face would have been a beacon of color.

In many ways the day was like any other. Mercedes was intent on putting her arrest behind her and she poured over accounts and inventories as if she had neglected these duties for months rather than days. Accompanied by Chloe and Sylvia, Colin escorted Mr. Fredrick back to Glen Eden and didn't return until dusk. The twins demanded his attention then and he complied, beating them soundly at whist even though they happily admitted to cheating. It was not until Mrs. Hennepin took them firmly in hand that Colin found himself alone with Mercedes.

He glanced around the library to make certain neither Chloe

nor Sylvia was lurking in the shadows. Satisfied, he rose from
the table where he had been playing cards and crossed the room
to Mercedes's chair. A book lay open in her lap but she had made
no real pretense of reading it. Her gaze had wandered too many
times in his direction for her to put up that front now.

The morning's downpour had shifted to a steady shower. The
occupied rooms of the manor had fires laid in the hearths to ward
off the damp chill. Colin took Mercedes's book and put it aside.
She didn't murmur a protest. When he held out his hand, she
placed hers in it and came to her feet.

He had changed out of formal attire for his trip to Glen Eden.
This morning, in his handsomely cut coat and tails, he had almost
been a stranger to her. Now he was an achingly familiar figure
in buff trousers and riding boots. He had removed his jacket to
play with the boys, but he still wore a vest a few shades darker
than his trousers. His shirt, for all that he had traveled today, was
largely unwrinkled. He was careless of fashion yet the casual
ease with which he wore his clothes spoke to his comfort and
confidence.

Colin drew Mercedes toward the fireplace. He added a log,
poked at the fire, then invited her to sit on the hearth rug. She
looked at him questioningly, but complied. Colin poured wine
in two glasses before he joined her. Mercedes took her glass and
moved closer so that Colin's chest offered partial support for her
back. The leaping, licking fire was hypnotic. Orange and yellow
flames shimmered as they consumed the logs. The light that was
cast lifted the rich hidden colors in Mercedes's hair to the surface.
Dark chocolate strands were threaded with shades of auburn and
copper and the play of light across her face was more interesting
to Colin than the fire she was looking at.

He touched his glass to hers, pulling her attention away from
the hearth. "Mrs. Thorne."

The husky tenor of his voice quickened Mercedes's pulse.
"Yes?"

His narrow smile touched his eyes. "Nothing. I wanted to try
it out. Mercedes Leyden Thorne. I like it."

She liked it, too. Smiling agreeably, she sipped her wine.

Watching her, Colin was moved to taste the wine on her lips. He took the glass from her hand and set it on the marble fireplace apron. He placed his own glass beside it.

Colin had no grand seduction plan. The fire, the wine, the informality of sitting on the rug, it was accomplished more by accident than design. He lifted her chin. Her skin was soft under his fingertips. He could feel her warmth and knew better than to credit the fire. Her mouth was damp and for a moment her breathing was trapped in her throat.

He kissed her long and deeply, fulfilling the promise of the kiss that had sealed their vows. She turned into him and his hands framed her face, holding her still and steady while his mouth ravaged hers. Mercedes felt the kiss in her breasts which swelled tautly, the nipples hardening and pressing against her camisole. She felt the kiss along the length of her spine as she arched to match the curve of her body to his. Between her legs she could feel the rise of moist heat.

It did not seem she could get close enough. Her arms came around his shoulders. She rose to her knees and then she was straddling him without ever knowing quite how it was accomplished. Her gown and petticoats fell around her modestly, but beneath them she was cradled intimately to Colin's thighs. Mercedes gave herself up to his hands and his mouth. Her head fell back, exposing her throat, and Colin's lips laid a trail from her chin to the base of her neck. He unfastened the buttons at the back of her gown and slipped the material over her shoulders. In contrast to the dark fabric, her skin had the luminescence of a pearl.

The corset and camisole and shift were all removed and she knelt in front of him, naked to the waist. His eyes, so dark now they seemed black, were all that covered her. Her heart raced as she raised his hands and laid them across her breasts. She moved, her nipples caressed by the center of his palms, and raised herself higher, offering herself up to the hot suck of his mouth.

Mercedes moaned softly as his lips caught her nipple. Colin's tongue flicked the tip. His hands moved under her gown, caught her hips, and settled her hard against his groin. Her body rocked against him. She tore at his vest, his shirt, and laid kisses across his jaw and shoulder. Her hands slipped under his shirt and the hard muscles of his chest and belly retracted as he sucked in his breath. He found the anticipation of her touch almost as intensely pleasurable as the touch itself.

Colin tugged at Mercedes's drawers. He opened the front of his trousers. He lifted her again and this time brought her down on his hard tumescence. There was only a faint darkening of her eyes as she was filled by him. Her slender, elegant fingers closed around his shirt more tightly as though to gain purchase. Her head tilted to one side and she leaned into him, slanting her mouth across his in a kiss that robbed him of breath and thought, everything in fact, except sensation.

She rose slowly, contracting around him, drawing out the exquisite pleasure of their joining, then lowered herself again. The rhythm was hers this time and she made it a sweet torment.

Mercedes closed her eyes but he couldn't stop looking at her. Nothing in his life had prepared him for the enormity of the gift she was giving him. She touched him in ways that had nothing to do with her hands in his hair, her mouth on his skin, or the joining of their bodies. What she offered was the raw honesty of emotion and the fierce passion of a soul that had never been opened.

In healing him she found herself healed.

Mercedes was captured by the pleasure that flooded her. At her back heat from the fire licked her skin. At her breast it was the damp edge of Colin's tongue that caused the same sensation. His fingers unbound her hair. It fell like a cascade of water around her naked shoulders and the fragrance was reminiscent of the flowers she had carried that morning. He breathed deeply as she rocked forward.

One of Colin's hands slid across her hip and caressed her inner thigh. Mercedes's body tensed in response to his touch. He teased her, straying closer to the center of their joining until she trapped his hand between them. His fingers grazed her most intimately and the intensity of it caused her to arch and cry out incoherently. His mouth covered hers, cutting off the sound and tasting her pleasure.

Colin's chest swelled. His skin was stretched taut over the muscles of his back and shoulders. In response to his need her rhythm changed. He arched under her, thrusting upward and twisting so that she was finally under him. He drove into her hard and she gave up another cry at the back of her throat.

A shudder shook his body first, then hers. The tension that had strung them so tightly vibrated now. For a few seconds pleasure was crystalized, tangible. Then it was gone. In its wake was a satisfying lethargy. Neither of them moved. Neither of them spoke.

They might have remained that way for the best part of the evening if Mercedes hadn't minded the occasional spark that leapt from the fireplace and singed her hair. She let one pass. The second time she sat up and repinned her hair.

Colin watched her slender arms rise elegantly. Her breasts lifted. Her skin glowed in the aftermath of their loving. He sighed when she finally raised her shift straps to her shoulders. One of them immediately fell back when she leaned over him. He appreciated the swift response to his prayers.

"Why are you smiling?" she whispered.

"That must be what you call a rhetorical question."

She kissed him lightly. "Clever man," Mercedes's eyes strayed to the library doors. "Did you lock those?"

"It's a bit late to be asking, don't you think? Are you quite certain you want to know the answer?"

Mercedes jumped to her feet and went to the doors, straightening her clothes as she crossed the floor. She shook the handles. They were secure. Turning on Colin, she placed her hands on her hips. "You might have just told me," she said. "Instead of letting me think the worst."

He sat up and righted his own clothing. "But you rise to the bait so beautifully."

"I've seen the trout you've landed," she told him with some asperity. "There's no compliment in being likened to a great gaping fish."

He stood. "I shall strive to make more flattering comparisons in the future. Will that satisfy you?"

What he had just done to her *satisfied* Mercedes. Flattery would merely have to do. She couldn't quite contain her smile. "I suppose," she said primly.

His glance lowered to her mouth. She was looking very pleased with herself. He hoped in some small measure that it had something to do with him. Colin picked up both glasses of wine and balanced them carefully in one hand. With the other he took the bottle. "I believe Mrs. Hennepin will have prepared our room by now," he said. "Would you care to join me?"

Mercedes looked past him to the place where they had made love on the floor. She couldn't quite check her smile. "It seems that nothing about this day has gone quite the way I'd imagined."

Before Colin could ask what she meant by that, Mercedes had opened the doors and was leading the way to the staircase.

In Colin's room fresh flowers filled vases on the mantelpiece and bedside table. Rose petals were scattered across the lace pillowshams. Mercedes recognized some of her toiletries on Colin's dresser. She imagined the armoire in the adjoining dressing room now contained part of her wardrobe. Colin was nudging the door closed with the heel of his boot when she turned on him.

"Was this your idea?" she asked.

"The flowers?" He set the glasses and wine on the small table between the two wing chairs. "That's Sylvia's touch, I imagine. Or Chloe's."

"No." Mercedes was shaking her head, her distress visible. "I mean was it your idea that we would share one room?"

Now Colin was puzzled. "We're married," he said. "Of course we'll share a room."

"You should have asked me. It's not done here. Not in a house like Weybourne Manor, not when there are dozens of bedrooms at our disposal. We can have rooms that connect here in the south wing if you prefer the privacy, or in the north wing if you don't mind being close to my cousins."

Colin sat on the edge of the bed and removed his boots. He stretched his legs, crossing them at the ankles. "Mercedes," he said patiently. "We've shared this room before. I don't see what difference it—"

"It was *different* before. When I came here I could leave. I had a room of my own. I can't stay here with you . . . not all the time."

"You're my wife, Mercedes."

She twisted the ring on her finger. "I had more freedom when I was your mistress."

He sat up straighter and he leveled her with a cold glance. "It's a little late for cold feet, but then you've already mentioned nothing about this day has gone as you imagined it. Add this to your list of complaints."

"I've had no complaints," she said, her voice rising. "Until now. It didn't occur to me that you would want a single bedroom."

"And it didn't occur to me that you'd want to sleep apart."

Mercedes blinked. Anger subsided as the wind was taken out of her sails. She shook her head, her smile shaded by regret. "I didn't say that I wanted to sleep apart," she said. "Only that I wanted a room of my own. They're very different things." She approached the bed. Colin uncrossed his legs and she walked into the opening he provided. Mercedes laid her hands on his shoulders. "And as far as today not being as I imagined, you don't know that I've always thought I'd be sold to one of my uncle's friends. He threatened me with them often enough. Had I been any less helpful in keeping Weybourne Park afloat, or caring for his children, the earl would have had me auctioned off a long time ago."

Colin knew she was telling the truth. He felt his insides clenching. "Then you weren't disappointed?"

"In what?" she asked.

"You wanted the wedding in the garden."

"It could have been in jail," she reminded him. "And you filled the chapel with flowers. It was lovely."

"We didn't spend the day together."

"It made me appreciate being with you later."

"We consummated our marriage in the library."

"Think of it another way: we put off this argument." Mercedes expected him to laugh. At the very least, to smile. He did neither. Instead he searched her face and the naked need in his eyes captured her breath. "Colin?" she said softly.

He drew her close. His face was pressed against her breast. He felt her fingers gently stroking his hair. Her hands cradled him.

"What is it?" she asked. "There's something. I know it."

A long moment passed before he put her from him and stood. He added wine to his glass and offered her some. She declined. He felt her eyes follow him as he put distance between them. "There's something," he said at last. "The problem is you don't know it."

Mercedes's arms automatically crossed in front of her. The protective posture usually helped settle the roiling in her stomach. This time there was no relief.

He had no idea he was going to say it until it was said. "I've never told you about my parents."

She had no clear expectation of what he might tell her, but she would have never guessed this. Bewildered rather than anxious now, Mercedes drew a slow breath. "Go on," she said.

There was no gentle way to put it. "They were murdered," he said. "Like yours."

Mercedes's first reaction was to offer her condolences. She held back because there was so obviously more.

"Exactly like yours."

Now she frowned. "I don't understand."

"Six months before your parents were killed there was another robbery on the same stretch of road. Remember? You told me about it the first evening I was here."

"I remember" she said. "The driver was shot. The parents of three boys were murdered."

He waited for her to make the connection. She had known the story for so long that she recited it without feeling now. It was part and parcel of her own tragedy, the larger background to the events that had claimed her parents.

Her chin came up and her delicate brows came together. "Three boys," she whispered. "You and Decker and Grey."

"That's right."

She still didn't offer her sympathies. "Why didn't you tell me this before?"

"Because I didn't think you'd marry me if you knew I believed your uncle murdered them."

Fourteen

Murdered them . . . murdered them . . . mur—

Mercedes shook her head slowly, partly in disbelief and denial, partly to clear it. "You're mistaken," she said quietly. There was no real force behind her words. She was too shaken to make a defense. "Is that why you sought out the earl in the first place?"

"He sought me out," Colin said. He watched her closely. She looked as if a chill had swept her body. The fire's glow could not hide the pale, icy mask that held her features rigid. "I had no suspicions, no expectations, until I arrived here."

"And you spoke to me."

"And *you* spoke to *me,*" he reminded her. Colin took a sip of his wine. He had only told the story a few times in his life. The Cunningtons hadn't believed him when he was eight. That kept him silent until he was twelve, when he shared the story with Jack Quincy. Later he told Mrs. Remington. More recently he had disclosed it to Aubrey Jones.

It wasn't that the telling was particularly difficult that made him reluctant to repeat it. It was so long ago that when Colin thought about it now he could almost believe it had happened to someone else. The opposite was true, however. The events of that night were intensely personal. What kept him quiet was that with each telling it seemed less real. He was afraid of losing the connection to his past. The older he got, the more he understood why the Cunningtons hadn't believed him in the first place.

"I witnessed my parents' murders," he said without inflection. "I saw the driver fall from the box almost immediately after he stopped our carriage. There was no warning shout. No demand that he stand down. He was unarmed so I know he drew no weapon. He was murdered because it was the intent all along."

She was simply staring at him, her features without expression. Colin wasn't sure she was even listening. He went on anyway.

"My father was yanked out of the carriage. He offered the little money he was carrying. He told them they could have my mother's jewelry. His bargaining gave Mother enough time to hand me her earrings and push me back on the bench. She gestured that I should pretend I was sleeping and I curled up beside Decker." If he let himself, Colin could still feel his younger brother's trembling body. He had absorbed Decker's shudders then, cowering in the corner with all the same fears but trying to let none of them show. Sometimes at night sleep would fail him and he'd wake with the metallic taste of terror in his mouth. He never remembered the dream but the taste was enough to raise the memory of that night.

"My father was still alive when my mother was pulled out of the carriage. The man took Greydon from her arms and thrust him into mine then he shut the door." Colin finished his wine though he took no pleasure in it. "I gave Grey to Decker. Grey was awake now and crying. I made Decker cover his mouth to keep him quiet. I thought they might kill him because he was making so much noise." Colin shrugged. "They had already murdered for reasons less obvious and provoking."

Mercedes's complexion had taken on a waxen cast. She remained unmoving.

"I went to the window. The shades had been pulled but I could see out a crack. The carriage lanterns had been extinguished. It was dark but not impossible to see. The sky was clear and there was a fingernail of moon to lend pale light. There were three men. Two of them had climbed off their horses. The third was still mounted. Clearly he was the one they looked to for direction, although he rarely said anything.

They were all wearing hats that shaded their eyes and scarves that hid the lower portion of their faces.

"They took my father's purse. They stripped my mother of her rings and her necklace." He paused, looking away from Mercedes for a moment. "We weren't wealthy," he told her. "The earrings that I held were my mother's most valuable pieces. Our carriage bore no markings. I think we may have rented it. The driver was not in our employ. We were on our way to visit my father's father—a man I'd never met before. My father had only made the decision to go a few days before.

"We had stopped at an inn earlier. I remember that he began to reconsider the wisdom of the journey we were making. Not that he was thinking of any danger we might face. It was his own reluctance to reconcile with his father that made him question continuing. It was at my mother's urging that he decided we would go on." Colin's brief smile was at odds with the bleak expression in his eyes. "He couldn't refuse her anything. She told him it was time that his sons knew their grandfather."

Colin turned and walked to the fireplace. Mercedes was shivering but she wouldn't move from her place by the bed. He poked at the logs, making them give up more heat and light. "There were a number of other patrons at the inn that evening and I took little notice of them."

It was why he noticed everything now, Mercedes thought. Why he was watchful, vigilant. Why he studied people around him. That was the lesson a young boy learned and took to heart: never lower your guard. Nothing is insignificant.

"The thieves were there at the inn," she said.

Her voice startled him. It was hollow, remote. "Yes," he said. "That's what I think. They made us a target there."

"And followed you."

He nodded. "The location was remote. They made certain no one would come upon us quickly." Colin put the poker aside. No amount of rearranging the logs would add enough warmth for what was chilling Mercedes. "It didn't matter that my father gave them what he had. They had planned at the outset to kill him.

They shot him in the back as if he were fleeing. What he had done was throw himself at my mother to protect her. It took both men to pry him loose. My mother came at them, clawing and kicking and screaming. I think she knew she was going to die and she wanted death on her terms. Provoking them prevented her from being raped. The one who hadn't spent a shot on my father used it on her."

Colin remembered watching her fall, her arms outstretched to his father. She lay very near him, almost touching. Colin blinked, erasing the picture from his mind. "The men on foot offered a share of what they had taken to the man still on horseback. He didn't accept it. In fact, it seemed he was . . ." The description had always eluded him in the past. Now he found a word that suited. "He recoiled a bit. As though he was insulted by their offer. 'You have proven you can do it,' is what he told them. 'Keep your souvenirs.' He reached inside his jacket and brought out a bag of coins. They jingled as he tossed them to the highwaymen.

"The one who caught the money wanted to know what to do with the children. The man on horseback glanced at our carriage. For a moment I imagined he saw me at the window and knew what I had witnessed. I couldn't move. Couldn't breathe. I waited to discover what he would do. The rider merely shook his head and dismissed us as unimportant. He turned his horse, waited for the others to mount, and then they disappeared."

Once they were gone Colin found his courage. He ran after them until tears and rage blinded him and he could go no further. Winded, defeated, he returned to the carriage. Decker still clutched his baby brother. He took Grey away and helped Decker down. They kept vigil by the bodies of their parents until they were discovered by the next travelers to use the road.

Mercedes went to the window. She wanted to look past the room to the expanse of Weybourne Park. The darkness outside and the firelight within conspired to make only her own reflection visible. When she looked beyond her own ghostly apparition she could make out Colin standing behind her, watching her, his dark eyes gravely intent.

"There are similarities," she said after a moment. "I've always known there were other robberies. I don't know why you think they have anything to do with my uncle."

"I've talked to Mr. and Mrs. Hennepin and other people in the area who remember," Colin said. "Yes, there were other robberies, but only one other that ended in murder. Accounts of robberies before my parents' deaths reported only two thieves."

"And only two were held responsible for the murders of my parents," Mercedes said.

"I was a witness to three men," he told her. "And so were you."

Mercedes spun on him. Her gown whipped around her legs, falling back into place slowly. "I wasn't there."

He ignored her. "Two highwaymen on the post road," he said. "Rather successful at what they do. They come to the attention of a certain younger son, a jealous man who has been thinking his brother the earl has everything he himself has always wanted. The brother has an estate, a title, a place in government. He has a beautiful wife, a woman the younger man had actually believed would marry him. He has a daughter, but no son. Therefore the man still has hope that he can claim his brother's property, if not his brother's wife. Time is not in his favor. There may be more children and the brother can make no claim if the next one is a boy."

Mercedes closed her eyes briefly, shutting him out. At her sides her fingers curled. "You don't know this," she said tightly. "There's no proof."

Again he ignored her. "This young man seeks out the services of the highwaymen. Not for robbery alone this time, but for murder. He has to be certain they have the mettle for it, so he arranges a test. They meet in a small inn where travelers frequently stop and where they will not be noticed among so many others. He selects a family." Colin shrugged. "Or perhaps they do. The presence of the children is important because the younger man knows

his brother rarely travels without his wife and daughter. Now the
highwaymen must convince this man that they are up to the task."

Colin took a step toward Mercedes. She remained where she
was. "They showed him they were. He let them keep what they
had taken and he gave them more besides. Robbery was not what
he cared about."

Now Colin took Mercedes's hands in his. Her skin was cool.
When her fingers unfolded her palms were clammy. "Six months
later," he told her quietly, "it happened again. People who had
been lulled into thinking the first incident would be the last, knew
better now. The highwaymen may have had no clear idea who
they were preying upon this time. It probably wouldn't have mattered except they would have been more cautious about celebrating their success within five miles of the scene of their crime.
They must have thought themselves very safe."

Mercedes shook her head. "They would have said something
before they hanged. They would have pointed to the third man."

"Not if they didn't know who he was. They didn't necessarily
understand his motives. And perhaps they did say something and
no one believed them or could find evidence of an accomplice.
The robberies they committed prior to the murders worked
against them. The only people who could have supported a fan-
tastic story like that were children. Grey was an infant. Decker
had already left the workhouse, and I was in Boston when they
were arrested. You were a mute four-year-old. No one was going
to question us."

Mercedes shook her head and tried to break away from his
grasp. "I wasn't there," she said tautly.

"You were. Ask Mrs. Hennepin. I did. She can recount everything about that time. To her way of thinking it's God's blessing
that you can't remember what happened that night."

She snapped at him. "Only you would be arrogant enough to
interfere with God's blessing."

He let that pass. "For almost a year you were silent. Your Aunt
Georgia didn't know what to do with you. She brought in phy-
sicians who could find nothing wrong or suggested you were

dangerous and needed to be kept from Chloe and Sylvia. Mrs. Hennepin says you spent most of your time alone in the north tower so there was nothing to be done. Your uncle apparently had a different view of the matter. One day he followed you. No one knows what went on there, but when you came back down it was as if the last year had never happened."

Colin gave her hands a small shake, keeping her with him when she began to withdraw. "That frightened your Aunt Georgia, but Mrs. Hennepin wanted to believe it was all behind you. Except for your fear of horses—which she says you never had before—and the odd times you slip away and become so introspective that you're lost to everyone else, she likes to think that it is."

This time when Mercedes tried to pull away he let her go. "Then you should have let it rest. What purpose does it serve to tell me now? My uncle's dead. He can't defend himself."

"What does that matter?" Colin asked. "When he has you."

Mercedes slapped him. "Oh my God!" She covered her face with her hands, not because she expected him to retaliate, but because she knew he wouldn't. Ashamed, she couldn't look at him.

Colin's voice was soft, his eyes intent on her bent head. "I didn't tell you before the wedding because I didn't think you would marry me. All your life you've accepted responsibility for what others have done. You protected your cousins, the staff, the Park itself from your uncle. You protected him and found some way to blame yourself. I had no reason to believe this would be any different. Indeed, it's not."

"I'm not protecting him," she said, letting her hands fall. Anguish clouded her gray eyes. She stared at a point past his shoulder. "I just don't believe you."

"I don't care that you don't believe me," he said. "I wanted you to know it's what *I* believe."

"You're not going to tell my cousins, are you?" she asked. She looked at him briefly. "You can't be that cruel."

Colin felt his heart being squeezed. "No, of course I'm not

going to say anything to them. And cruelty has nothing to do with telling you."

Her short laugh held no joy. "You'll forgive me if I think differently. You've just named my uncle a murderer. More than that, you've said he murdered my own parents and that I've known it all along. If that's a kindness, then I hope to God I am never the subject of your cruelty."

Mercedes looked to the door. There was no escape there. She had all of the manor at her disposal and no room she could properly call her own. She went into the adjoining dressing room and stood at the basin, wondering if she was going to be sick.

Colin went to the doorway but didn't enter. "You would have asked about my parents," he told her quietly. "Someday you would have asked about the circumstances of their deaths. I would have a choice then: to lie or tell the truth. Lying would be disrespectful to you. The truth would have led to other questions and eventually we would have traveled this road. The journey might have been longer if I had only told you a little at a time, but I believe we would have arrived exactly at this point. Only then you also would have been hurt that I hadn't told you sooner."

Mercedes said nothing. He was right.

Colin stepped back and pulled the door closed, giving Mercedes her privacy.

It was thirty minutes before Mercedes reappeared. She had changed into her nightshift and brushed out her hair. She padded quietly to the edge of the bed. Colin was lying on his side under the covers. The rose petals had all been brushed aside but their fragrance still clung to the pillows. He raised the blankets and she slipped under them.

Mercedes lay on her back, not touching Colin, but close enough to feel his warmth. He didn't speak but she knew he was watching her. It didn't even bother her anymore. "What did you mean when you said it would be disrespectful to lie to me?"

Colin was silent a moment longer. "Lying would have meant

that I didn't believe in you, that I thought you were weak or incapable of thinking for yourself. I don't think any of those things, so lying was never a choice."

She considered that. "That was a compliment, wasn't it?"

He smiled in the darkness. "Yes," he said. "That was a compliment."

Mercedes turned on her side. "I need time to think about what you told me," she said. "It may have been different if I had worked it out on my own, but to be confronted with it . . ."

"I understand."

"And you have no proof."

"None."

"But you believe it."

"Yes."

Mercedes drew her knees up. Firelight slipped over her shoulder and touched his face. She reached up and touched his cheek with her fingertips. There was no evidence that she had slapped him. The color had long since faded. "I'm sorry," she said. "If I could change anything about today, I would take that back."

He laid his hand over hers and held it against his cheek. "Why are you here now?" he asked.

If she had still borne him malice she could have said it was because she had no place to go. Instead she told him the truth. "This is where I want to be."

Colin moved her hand to his mouth. He pressed his lips against the heart of her palm. Relief washed over him. Somehow they had survived the worst truths he knew. She had heard him out, railed against him, and in the end only asked for time to think it through herself.

Mercedes withdrew her hand and turned over so that her back was to Colin. He didn't move closer until she reached behind her and placed his arm across her waist. She snuggled into him. The fire was almost out in the grate when she said, "Whatever he did or didn't do, it's not about me, is it? I'm not to blame."

"No, Mercedes." His breath ruffled her hair. "You're not to blame."

* * *

Mercedes lay on a blanket near the trout stream. Sunshine peeked through the canopy of leaves above her and dappled her face with light. She closed her eyes then rested her forearm over them for good measure. Beyond her she could hear the twins splashing in the water as they bedeviled Colin. He wasn't likely to catch any fish this afternoon and he didn't seem to particularly care. If his silence was any indication—and she knew it was—the captain was getting ready to pounce.

Poor Britton and Brendan. They were so unsuspecting.

Mercedes bolted upright as water splashed her face and the bodice of her gown. She squinted against the light, expecting to see the twins standing over her. Their giggles were still far off, however, and it was Colin flicking water at her. He dropped beside her, tossing the rod aside, as she made a face at him.

"You're not allowed to use the twins as a diversion," she said.

"Is that a rule?"

"It should be."

He stretched, leaning back on his elbows, and watched Britton and Brendan teeter across the stream on slippery, moss-covered rocks. In a few weeks they would be going off to school. It was hard to believe the summer days were growing shorter but the evidence was everywhere.

The crops required less tending and the farmers were preparing for harvest. Although the days were clear, mornings and evenings were cool. Smoke was more often visible from the manor's chimneys as fires were laid in the occupied rooms. Blooms that faded in the garden were not so quick to replenish themselves.

It had been five weeks since the earl's funeral, a month since the wedding. Three days ago Aubrey Jones had returned. Colin's glance shifted to Mercedes. She was still watching the boys, the corners of her mouth pulled faintly upward in a contented smile. That smile had been a rare pleasure these last few days. Its disappearance had coincided with Aubrey's arrival. Whenever Colin brought up the purpose of his visit, Mercedes skillfully changed the subject.

Her hair was plaited. The curling tip reached more than halfway down her back. Colin pulled on it lightly. She glanced over her shoulder and for an unguarded moment he was graced with the sweet purity of her smile. He watched it fade. He let her hair go.

"We have to talk about it sometime," he said.

Mercedes shrugged. "There's nothing for me to say. Whether you stay or go has to be your decision. I know Mr. Jones expects you to take the *Mystic* on a run to China."

"How do you know that?"

"Sylvia told me. You can imagine how she learned of it."

"I can make it to Hong Kong and back in under two hundred days."

She nodded and turned around to watch the boys. "And I won't ask you not to try."

Colin let it go for now. This time together was too important to him to be spent arguing.

"I thought I would pay a visit to Mr. Patterson," she said casually.

"Why?" His posture was less relaxed now. "Have you heard something about Marcus?"

She shook her head. "I don't look for him to return any time soon." At least, she thought, not while Colin remained at Weybourne Park. She was not so certain of Severn's absence once he learned she was alone. It was not a fear she intended to share with her husband. It wasn't that she would have felt foolish for expressing it, but that it would have been tantamount to asking him to stay.

Days after her marriage to Colin, Marcus Severn had abruptly decided to tour the Continent. Mercedes couldn't remember that he had ever expressed a penchant for traveling. His quick exit seemed to have more to do with the sheriff wanting to ask him questions.

"His departure made him look guilty," Colin said, thinking

aloud. "He should have stayed and explained himself. Mr. Patterson doesn't seriously believe Marcus killed the earl." He tugged on Mercedes's braid again. "If it's not because of Severn, then why—"

"Ponty Pine," she told him.

"The pickpocket?"

"The same. Really, Colin, you can't expect that there would be two Ponty Pines in all the world."

He pulled the braid harder and brought her tumbling backward. He could taste laughter on her lips when he kissed her. Later he tasted hunger. For the first time since coming to Weybourne Park, Colin regretted the twins' presence. It was hard to forget they were around with them crashing through the water to come to Mercedes's aid. Did they think he was wrestling her?

Colin found himself laughing. Yes, they probably thought just that.

Ponty Pine was forgotten in the melee that followed. Colin took Britton by the elbows as the boy dived and flipped him over his head. Mercedes scrambled out of the way but managed to get a foot out to trip up Brendan. He sprawled across Colin and was tickled mercilessly.

Mercedes looked on, her gray eyes clear, her smile gentle. Unconsciously her right hand rested on her abdomen as she thought of Colin with his own children. They had never talked about it, but sometimes after he made love to her he would lay his hand over her flat belly and stroke her lightly. She didn't think he was even aware of the motion or that she was calmed by it.

If she wasn't carrying his child already it wasn't because they hadn't been doing the right things. At Colin's insistence they moved to another suite of rooms in the south wing. Now Mercedes had a bedchamber to herself but she had never slept there. She had never even tried.

She counted lying beside Colin at night as one of her greatest pleasures. He slept soundly in her arms and his light, steady breathing was as soothing as water slipping over rocks. She slept deeply, too. Cradled. Comforted. Mercedes no longer lay alert in response to every creak and crack she heard in the hallway, tense with fear that the earl was approaching.

Sometimes in the early morning hours, when the first faint suggestions of light slipped into their room, Mercedes would wake and find herself engaged in making love to her husband. She never knew who initiated the caresses and kisses that led to their joining, but she liked the idea that their need transcended conscious yearnings and that in the aftermath there was the sense of profound peace.

That same sense of peace came to her now as she watched Colin wrestle the twins into laughing, squealing surrender. The power of the moment brought a familiar ache to her throat. This time she didn't force herself to swallow it or blink back the tears that accompanied it. Her heart swelled, pushing all the evidence of her emotion to the crystalline purity of her gray eyes.

Mercedes was unaware that the clearing had quieted or that she was now the one being watched.

Brendan was the first one to reach her. "I say, Mercedes, are you feeling quite the thing?"

Britton dropped to his knees beside his brother. He put his small hand on Mercedes's forearm. "We were playing," he told her. "See, we're not hurt. It wasn't like that."

The boys looked at each other, then at Colin, alarmed as Mercedes's tears flowed with more force. They backed away when Colin put his hand on their shoulders.

Colin reached for Mercedes. Her hand went into his, gripping it hard, and he drew her to her feet. She buried her face against his shoulder and hung on, her fingers clutching his shirt like a lifeline. Over her shoulder Colin addressed the twins. "She's fine, boys. In fact, she's very happy."

Britton and Brendan exchanged confused, uncertain looks.

"Trust me," Colin said.

And they did. Without waiting to be told, they trotted away like frisky, obedient puppies toward the manor.

Colin's mouth lay close to Mercedes's ear. "You are happy, aren't you?" he whispered.

She nodded. Her watery smile was pressed against his shirt. A handkerchief was thrust into her hand as Mercedes sniffed inelegantly. "I wasn't going to use your shirt," she said.

He ignored that. "Blow."

Dutifully she did. Her eyelashes were spiked with tears. When she blinked they dropped over her cheeks.

Colin took the handkerchief, folded it, and wiped her face gently. He kissed her eyelids, her damp mouth. "Mercedes," he said. There was reverence in his voice, adoration.

Her heart swelled again. Tears threatened. For a moment she couldn't speak. "Love me," she whispered.

He did. The rushing water covered her soft cries and the urgency in his husky voice. They stripped away some of their clothes and all of their hearts. She matched his need and answered his hunger. He held her close and gave himself.

Their hands clasped. Mouths met. Held. His palm hovered just above her breast. The air warmed between them. The pleasure of anticipation separated them.

Her tongue flicked across his shoulder. Saltysour. Bittersweet. The texture of all the tastes was there. She moved lower and felt the retraction of his skin, heard the catch in his breathing. She took him in her mouth and his fingers threaded in her hair. He closed his eyes. Surrounded by the moist heat of her lips and tongue, by the suck of her mouth, he surrendered and gave them each what they wanted.

Their bodies twisted. Half on the blanket, half off, she found herself beneath him, her thighs cradling him. She guided him into her. After the first thrust he was still.

Her eyes were luminous. He watched the centers darken and widen. Her mouth parted and the edge of her tongue was just visible. She contracted around him and the pressure was a sweet agony. He kissed her hard but it was no punishment. She laughed joyously as he began to move inside her.

Finally there was only the rushing water and the rustle of leaves overhead. Their breathing was silent, their hearts steady.

Sunlight glanced off her bare shoulder and highlighted the sculpted lines of his face.

"I'm not afraid anymore," she said. For all that this announcement was made quietly, there was a hint of a revelation in it. Mercedes tilted her head to see Colin better. "I've been afraid so long I was numb to it. It dulled every other feeling I've ever had." She searched his features for some sign that he understood. "There's never been room for anything else."

There was the merest suggestion of a smile shaping Colin's mouth. He had always known she was holding back, always sensed the reserve that kept her from him even when she thought she was giving him everything. "And now?" he asked.

"I love you," she said. She said it with abandon and joy. She said it again as though saying it for the first time and she listened to the words and understood their meaning. Her heart was in her eyes.

They argued after dinner.

"You are making no sense," she said. The book that lay unopened in her lap was put aside. "I thought you'd be pleased. Didn't you just tell me this afternoon that you could do a China run in two hundred days?"

"Yes."

"Well?"

Colin splashed a crystal snifter with a small measure of brandy. He raised it, swirling the glass, but didn't drink. "I've already informed Aubrey that I intend to quit as master of the *Mystic*. He's taking my resignation back to Miss Remington. Jonna will place him in command and he'll make the same run in a few days more or less. I don't have to be at the helm. In fact, I plan to invest in the run."

"Why are you doing this?" she asked. "I was so certain you wanted to go."

"You never really asked, did you?" Colin said. "You wouldn't even discuss it. All I ever wanted to do was discuss it."

Mercedes ducked her head guiltily. "I told you I was afraid before. I was afraid of everything. Of losing you. Of keeping you. Of chasing you away or making you feel bound to me." She glanced at him sideways. "I don't want you to resent me in a month or two when you regret your decision to stay at Weybourne Park."

Colin sat opposite her. He leaned forward in his chair and rested his forearms on his knees. The snifter rolled on its slender stem between his palms. "Why do you think I'll regret it? This is where I want to be, Mercedes. I thought you knew that."

"I wanted to believe it," she said softly. "It's not precisely the same thing as knowing."

Colin was quiet. He considered his words carefully. He imagined it would be difficult to say his thoughts aloud. In truth, it wasn't. Mercedes was not the only one who had stopped being afraid. "I don't know if I'll ever see my brothers again. I don't know what they look like, what their names are, or the kind of men they've become. The search for them, the fear of *failing* them, has kept me alive at times and kept me from living at others. The act of looking for them became running from everything else.

"I *am* bound to you, Mercedes. I want to be. It's my choice and there's no chance that I'll regret it." His eyes lightened with the smile that raised the corners of his mouth. "Being here, with you, is more liberating than the open seas ever were. I don't know that you can understand that, but from my perspective it's true."

Mercedes's eyes were troubled. "Oh, Colin," she whispered. "You can't mean it."

"I do." He paused, studying her face, the confusion in her eyes. "Does it frighten you that I love you that much?"

She shook her head emphatically. "No," she said quickly. "Not now. Before . . ."

Colin put his snifter down. He hadn't tasted the brandy. He reached across the space that separated them and pulled Mercedes into his lap. She came without hesitation. "Before?" he prompted.

"Before I would have thought I didn't deserve you. I would have thought you'd see through to my heart and know what a frightened little rabbit I was, always jumping at shadows, flinching from an extended hand. You'd see that I wasn't nearly as brave or confident as I pretended. I wouldn't have wanted you close enough to learn the truth."

Colin pressed his smile against her hair. "Have you forgotten how we met?" he asked. "That was no frightened rabbit at the Passing Fancy."

"Liar. You know I was terrified."

"You were magnificent."

She gave him an arch look. "You didn't think so at the time."

"I've revised my opinion."

That warmed her. She cupped the side of his face. "I hope you're not abandoning your search for your brothers because of me," she said.

"I'm not giving it up," he said. "I'm simply going to stay in one place."

"You're certain?"

"I'm staying here," he told her. "Aubrey's known it longer than I have. He'd tell you that himself if you'd talk to him."

Mercedes knew she had been neglecting her guest. She'd been polite but cool and it was not only on Colin's account. "What are his intentions regarding Sylvia?" she asked. "Has he told you? She's in love with him, you know. I don't like to think that she's going to be hurt."

Colin didn't like to think it either. "We have to trust them to sort it out."

"Like we did?"

"I don't know that I'd wish *that* on them."

Mercedes wasn't certain she appreciated his dry response. She poked him lightly in the ribs but managed to elude his grasp when he would have kept her on his lap. There was a saucy swing in her step and laughter in her eyes. She sashayed out the library's doors and didn't have to glance behind her to know that he was following.

* * *

"Take me with you," Sylvia said. She blushed at her forwardness but her eyes were lifted, challenging Aubrey's.

Aubrey's fair complexion took on a ruddy cast. He felt the heat in his cheeks in contrast to the light breeze coming out of the woods. "I can't do that."

"You mean you won't."

Aubrey thrust his large hands in his pockets to keep them from straying toward Sylvia's neck. It was a slender throat, very vulnerable. He was perfectly capable of snapping it in half. Not that throttling her was the only thing on his mind. "All right," he said. "I won't."

"Now you're agreeing with me to avoid an argument."

"Yes."

"It's no good if you won't fight. Don't you feel any passion?"

The evening was cool, but to Aubrey's way of thinking it wasn't nearly cool enough. Sylvia's blond hair took on a silver cast in the moonlight. She was perched on the stone balustrade at the rear of the manor, her small hands folded neatly in her lap, her face raised expectantly. The shawl around her shoulders fluttered, but she made no move to hold it more tightly.

Aubrey glanced behind him. On the second floor of the manor the lights were all extinguished. Lamps burned in the servants quarters and in a few rooms on the main floor. He knew that Sylvia's sister and brothers had gone to bed. He had been heading in that direction himself when Sylvia surprised him on the main landing. At her insistence and against his better judgment he had followed her outside.

Aubrey Jones was at his ease with saucy serving girls and the women who frequented the harbors. He never minded when they remarked on the breadth of his shoulders or the size of his neck or wondered aloud about proportions that were hidden from their gaze. Now, next to Sylvia Leyden, Aubrey felt ham-handed, tongue-tied, and clumsy. His feet were too big, his chest too wide, his thighs too much like tree trunks.

"I think it would be better if you'd go back inside," he said, ignoring her comment about passion. If she had been even a tenth as experienced as a tavern wench, she'd have known where to look to see the proof of his passion. "Please, Sylvia. Colin trusts me. Mercedes trusts you."

She wasn't certain what he meant by that. "Of course they trust us. And why shouldn't they? You haven't so much as kissed me. I think you want to. I know I want you to."

"You can't possibly know what you want," he said gruffly. She was so dainty, like a china figurine, cool and exquisite and irreplaceable if broken. Aubrey glanced down at himself as he rocked back on his heels. He would break her. Surely she would break if he touched her.

"That's a horrible thing to say." Sylvia's pale blond hair shimmered as she shook her head angrily.

Aubrey strove for patience. He ran a hand through his thick red hair. "You have plans for a London Season," he said carefully, as though explaining it to a child. "You'll meet lots of fellows there with money and titles and family trees that are so big you can swing on the branches. I'm not the one you should cut your teeth on. Better you should stick to your own kind."

From her bedroom window, shielded by the darkness of the chamber, Mercedes watched the combatants square off. Even at this distance, without benefit of hearing any of the exchange, she knew that she was witnessing at least a disagreement, perhaps an argument.

"Come to bed," Colin said sleepily. He patted the space beside him, which was already cooling since her departure, and moved the covers back as an invitation.

"In a moment." Mercedes rolled the glass of water she held between her palms. Thirst was the reason she had left her bed. Since her first glance out the window, she hadn't given it another thought.

She wasn't star-gazing. Colin saw Mercedes's eyes were focused in the wrong direction. "What has your interest out there?"

"Sylvia and Aubrey."

Colin pushed himself upright. It was not so long ago that he and Mercedes had been on the portico at night, unchaperoned. He hadn't cared about proper form then. Neither had she. That thought didn't comfort him when he applied it to Sylvia and his first mate. Colin sighed. He grinned lopsidedly as he realized how responsibility had reformed him on this count. "Am I going to have to demand satisfaction from my best friend?" he asked, padding toward the window.

"They're arguing," Mercedes said quietly, as if speaking too loudly would alert them. "Look at Sylvia. She has her chin up and whatever she's saying is pushing Aubrey back on his heels."

Colin suddenly felt a wave of sympathy for Aubrey. He had been in that position. "She's more than able to hold her own."

"Of course. She grew up at Weybourne Park, didn't she?"

Colin took the glass from Mercedes's hands and put it on the bedside table. "Do you want me to go down there?"

Mercedes took comfort from the arm he slipped around her waist. "No, I don't think so. Aubrey's actions speak well of him. I'll have to talk with Sylvia though. She's the one behaving recklessly."

Even as Mercedes said it Sylvia launched herself from the balustrade and into Aubrey's arms. Unprepared as the large man was, Sylvia's slight weight made him waver. He clasped her by the waist to put her aside, but her arms were locked around his neck and her mouth was fused to his.

Beside him, Colin felt Mercedes stiffen. "I'll go," he said.

"No. Look. He's detaching her." It was exactly the right word for what Aubrey was doing. Sylvia had secured herself like a barnacle to the hull of a ship.

"The *Mystic* is scheduled to leave in four days," Colin said. "Do you want me to tell Aubrey to move it up a day?"

"He can do that?"

Colin nodded. "One day forward won't cause a hardship for the crew."

Mercedes considered it while Aubrey turned and began walking away from Sylvia toward the house. Sylvia stood where she was, her pale hair almost silver in the moonlight. She was looking after Aubrey, and Mercedes noted there was nothing bereft about her features or posture. Sylvia's shoulders were hunched against the cool night breeze, not because she was dejected. "A day more or less," Mercedes said. "I don't think it will matter. Will Aubrey understand if you ask him to take up lodgings in London?"

"He'll understand. He may even thank you for the suggestion. I don't think he knows quite what to make of Sylvia. Aubrey's more comfortable with—"

Mercedes held up one hand. "You don't have to tell me. And you really are in no position to cast stones. I remember Molly well enough."

Without warning Colin swung Mercedes into his arms. "I don't know who you mean." Ignoring her surprised squeal and laughing protests, Colin carried her to the bed and tossed her in. She bounced and rolled, expecting Colin to pounce on her. Instead, he innocently handed her the glass of water.

"Thank you," she said. She sat up, leaned against the headboard, and drank. "And thank you for understanding about Aubrey. I know he's your friend. I don't like asking him to leave. It's just that—"

Colin sat on the edge of the bed. "You don't have to explain or apologize. As you said, I understand. I'm afraid I've become that terrifying arbiter of proper manners: a reformed rake."

Mercedes looked at him suspiciously. "Have you really?"

"What are you questioning? That I'm reformed? Or that I was ever a rake?"

She gave him her empty glass. Her right brow was still arched, her look patently skeptical. "Both, I suppose."

"I'm prepared to exile my best friend from Weybourne Park to save Sylvia from herself," he said. "So you judge whether I've been reformed. As for having been a rake . . ." His kiss was deliberate and slow and deeply passionate. He didn't raise his head until Mercedes was fully engaged and just a little dazed by his ardor. "I never was." He touched her forehead with his and whispered. "What I learned about loving, I learned from you."

The skeptical look had long since faded. Mercedes was a believer. She put everything else from her mind and devoted herself to this moment. Reaching for Colin, she drew him down beside her to teach him what else she knew.

Aubrey Jones took his leave the following morning. He bore no animosity toward either Colin or Mercedes. He had been packing his belongings, already resolved to leave, when Colin came upon him. There had been very little to say.

"She should have her London Season," Aubrey said, stuffing shirts into his valise. "If she hasn't met anyone that strikes her fancy then . . ." He shrugged and stuffed harder.

Colin noted that Aubrey's belongings were now so compact that he could have had room for twice the wardrobe. He wisely made no comment. "I prepared a letter for you to carry to Jonna."

"Aye," Aubrey said heavily. "Miss Remington's expecting as much. When I told her about your lady . . . well, I think she began preparing herself. Quincy wanted me to haul you out of here but she wouldn't have it."

"So you'll make the China run yourself."

"And beat your record."

Colin didn't doubt that he would. Aubrey Jones had something to come back to. Sylvia Leyden would be waiting for him. A London Season wasn't likely to make her stray from her course. "I'll be counting the days," Colin said. "Money's riding on it."

For Aubrey Jones the stakes were higher. "I'll be counting them, as well." He took Colin's extended hand in his own larger one and clasped it hard. "Good luck to you, Captain. It's a fine thing you've found for yourself here."

He was gone before Colin could return the sentiment.

Sylvia learned that Aubrey was gone at breakfast. She retired to her room and neither the entreaties of her sister or Mercedes could dislodge her. Colin was only glad he was not asked to intervene. He would have rather faced a winter storm on the

Atlantic than the young lady's anger. He knew what to do with a cold and icy wind.

"Ride it out," he told Mercedes later that day. "Take in your sails and get out of her wind. This will blow over."

Mercedes patted his hand gently, amused. "You don't mind if I ignore your advice, do you?"

Rather than being offended, Colin was quite comfortable with it. "I hope you do." He picked up a small sandwich from the tray a maid had just delivered to the drawing room. "If I'm right I can gloat—within limits, of course. And if I'm wrong, I can be fairly certain I'll never be consulted again." His response had the desired effect. Mercedes was smiling. Colin believed he was willing to do most anything to bask in that radiance.

He changed the subject. There was no point to dwelling on Sylvia's distress when there was nothing to be done about it. "I recall you saying something about Mr. Patterson yesterday. You were going to call on him?"

"What?" Mercedes was slower to shift topics. "Oh, yes. Mr. Patterson. Yes, I thought I would." She took a small bite of the sandwich she held. "There was no time yesterday. I suppose I could go today since Sylvia won't see me."

"What's your interest in the pickpocket?"

Mercedes shrugged. "I'm not certain I understand it myself. I think in part I need to assure myself that he got away. I know I'll feel better if the sheriff tells me there haven't been any more complaints of the type Mr. Pine caused."

Colin laughed at that. "Mercedes, there have probably been dozens of complaints. Mr. Pine is not the region's only light-finger. No doubt there are scores more like him in this county alone."

"Yes, but Ponty specialized in ladies' jewelry. He took some purses, to be sure, but I think he must have had a particular fondness for women's pieces. Remember? The necklace. The combs. Earrings."

"One earring," Colin reminded her. "Ponty must have lost his touch there, to come away with only one."

"Was he handsome?" she asked. "I always thought he was likely to be handsome. I mean handsome enough to charm the women he robbed."

"Don't you know?"

"I saw a blue eye. I had to imagine the rest."

One of Colin's brows kicked up. "Stop imagining. Except for that eye he was hideously deformed."

She sat back, surprised. "You're making that up," she accused.

"I am," he said, unrepentant.

"You're not jealous of Ponty Pine, are you?" She clapped her hands together and smiled brilliantly "You are! How lovely!" Mercedes was also without remorse. "Then he *was* rather handsome, wasn't he?"

Colin sighed. "Any better looking and women would have offered the rogue their baubles. If he returned their things and apologized they'd most likely be moved to forgive him."

"I thought it might be something like that," she said, satisfied. "That will help us know if he's safely out of the country."

And, Colin realized, that was that. Her interest was no more than she had related in the first place. As her smile faded and her expression became more distant, he knew Ponty Pine was forgotten and Sylvia had come to the forefront of her thoughts. "Give her time," he told her. "In a few days Aubrey will be gone and Sylvia will make her own way."

Colin did not suspect then how true his words would be.

In four days the *Mystic* was set to sail and Sylvia Leyden had made her way to London.

Fifteen

"You'll find her."

Colin finished shrugging into his jacket before he took Mercedes's hands. They were cold. He squeezed them lightly and gave her the reassurance she sought. "Of course, I'll find her."

"And bring her back?"

"Yes, and bring her back." He looked over his shoulder at the doorway where Chloe stood. At his command, the twins had already run off to the stable to make certain a mount was readied for him. "Do you know how many bags your sister took with her?" he asked.

Chloe's eyes were damp, her complexion even paler than her cousin's. "One valise is missing. Sylvia packed very little." She bit her lip to quell the hiccup. Her entire body jerked as it overtook her anyway. "What can she have been thinking?"

Colin wasn't sure if Chloe was lamenting her sister's elopement or the fact that Sylvia had gone with so little regard for what she might wear. He gave Chloe the benefit of the doubt. "Do you have any way of knowing what she was wearing when she left?"

Chloe shook her head and dabbed at her eyes. She straightened a little as a thought occurred to her. "But perhaps I could look through her wardrobe and determine what's missing," she offered helpfully. "That would narrow it down."

"Good girl."

Chloe's smile was fulsome and eager. She dashed off to the

north wing, glad at last to be of some assistance rather than solely the bearer of bad tidings.

Colin turned back to Mercedes. He gathered her close, hugging her and rubbing her back. He kissed the crown of her dark head. "It's going to be all right," he said. "You don't have to worry yourself sick."

Mercedes closed her eyes. "That she could be so irresponsible," she whispered.

"And you don't have to blame yourself."

She pulled away. Her small smile was uneven and a shade guilty. "You know me so well. I thought I might blame Mr. Jones to relieve my own culpability, but I find I cannot. He'll send her back, won't he? I mean, he's a sensible man, he must know how worried we would be. He wouldn't take her on the ship, would he?"

Colin was confident of Aubrey's response. "He'll deliver Sylvia to Weybourne Park himself," he said. *"If* he knows she's there."

Mercedes frowned. "What do you mean? How could he not know? Surely Sylvia will announce herself to him."

"Not if she suspects that Aubrey will march her back here. She may wait until the *Mystic* has sailed."

"You mean she'll stow away?" Mercedes stared at Colin wide-eyed. Clearly the thought had not occurred to her before.

He nodded. "It's not as difficult as you might think." Especially if Sylvia, as he suspected, was wearing men's clothing.

"But—"

"I'll bring her back," he said simply. "Even if the ship's sailed, Mercedes. I'll bring her back."

She believed him but she didn't know if she could bear waiting for his return. "I want to go with you." It was not so much a plea as a command.

"No."

Mercedes's head jerked back. She wasn't prepared for Colin to refuse her. "But I can help. Two pairs of eyes will be more vigilant."

"No," he repeated firmly. "I'm not taking a carriage and you cannot ride horseback." He saw her shoulders sag a little at this realization. "I can travel more swiftly alone and that's how I intend to go."

Mercedes recognized he was set on the matter. Arguing would simply delay his departure. "I do not like feeling so useless," she admitted softly.

"Staying here, where I know you are quite safe, is not useless to me. I couldn't devote myself to looking for Sylvia if I knew you were set on following or up to some scheme to bring her back yourself."

She shook her head swiftly. "No, I wouldn't do that to you." Standing on tiptoe, Mercedes kissed him full on the mouth. "Bring her back safely, Colin. And do not set her down too harshly. She's in love and that makes us all foolish sometimes."

Sylvia had little experience in London. The people were as unfamiliar to her as the streets. She was not prepared for the crowds or the odors or the noise. It was, quite simply, the most exciting adventure of her young life.

A less prepared young lady would have been hopelessly lost already. Sylvia was able to arrive along the river harbor because she had paid particular attention to Aubrey's description of the city. She had asked questions that had sounded innocent enough at the time but were serving her well now. She negotiated the narrow thoroughfares with relative ease, asking directions only when she could not find a landmark to guide her.

The citizens of London, when they noticed her at all, were pleasant. Traveling through the crowded market, she was implored to buy baked goods and sausages, tomatoes and corn, fish and fresh flowers. Her response to all the entreaties was the same. Sylvia touched the brim of her hat in a vague salute and kept moving, never fully making eye contact or studying her surroundings too long.

The journey from Weybourne Park to London had mostly been

accomplished at night. She had not had the opportunity to test the efficacy of her disguise until she reached the outskirts of town. Sylvia knew she could not hope to fool anyone who had reason to study her, therefore she was careful not to call attention to herself. The alterations she had made in her father's clothes were not clever or complete enough to pass scrutiny. On close inspection, Sylvia believed quite correctly, she would be found out as a woman. The hat helped, shading the upper part of her face, and because the morning was cool, she had a good excuse for keeping the scarf around her neck and chin. Even with these precautions, Sylvia's size worked against her. Gloves helped hide her delicate hands, but on the back of the mare she had chosen she looked especially slender if not precisely short of stature.

Sylvia arrived unaccosted at the wharf two hours after daybreak. Although she was feeling quite full of herself for her accomplishment, the first moments of alarm and uncertainty were beginning to tap at her psyche.

Panic made her clutch the reins tighter when she became aware of just how many ships filled the harbor. She had imagined being able to find the *Mystic* without difficulty. Now she realized it would not be the case. The hundreds of masts and crossbeams gave the waterfront's skyline the peculiar appearance of a winter wood. Moreover, she had timed her arrival to coincide closely with the clipper's departure. She was very much afraid she may have left it to too late.

Giving her mount a nudge, Sylvia began her first pass along the riverfront.

Sailors and dock hands moved with purpose and precision. Barrels and bales were wheeled from warehouses, across the wharf, then up the gangboards. On dollies and wagons and carts the cargo weaved in and out. The timing, the rhythm, the musical squeaks and clatter, gave the work a choreographed beauty. Although the raised voices were often guttural and prone to cursing, and the clothes were drab, there was rarely so much grace on the floor of a Brighton ballroom.

With her attention focused on the sea of ships, it was not surprising that eventually Sylvia ran afoul of the cargo loaders.

"See here," one of them shouted. "Watch where yer goin', pretty boy."

Sylvia tugged on the reins, swinging her mare around to avoid colliding with a wagon.

Another man brought his cart up short. "If you can't keep yer mount steady, get off and lead 'er."

"What's yer business here, lad?" someone else called.

A big man chuckled. "Doxies are mostly indoors now if that's yer pleasure."

Panic caused Sylvia to look around for a savior or an exit. She found neither. What she saw, however, made her careless of the consequences as she pushed through the crowd. Carts and wagons were pulled out of her way and the men jumped back, no match for her skittish mare. They cursed her as she rode off but Sylvia paid no heed. She sought out the *Mystic* with a new sense of urgency.

Sylvia's heart lightened when she found the ship. It was exactly as Aubrey had described it and she wondered that she hadn't seen it immediately among all the others. It was not difficult to imagine how proud she would look with her sails unfurled over the open water. Even loaded as she was now, her masts stood a little taller than those around her.

Ignoring the passengers who stood milling around on the wharf, waiting for their turn to board, Sylvia dismounted and secured her horse, then charged up the gangboard.

She was stopped from jumping to the ship's deck by a sailor with a manifest.

"Not so quickly," he said, throwing up his hand to prevent her entry. "Passengers wait until we've loaded all the cargo."

Sylvia's glare was icy. "I am looking for your master," she said. "Mr. Jones."

"Sir?" the man said. As his stare narrowed he became more uncertain. "Ma'am?"

"It's Lady Sylvia Leyden," she said in cool accents, lifting her chin. "And Mr. Jones would not wish you to detain me." The man hesitated. His arm bobbled a little giving Sylvia an opening and she jumped to the deck. "You may tell me where I can find him."

The sailor dropped his manifest to his side. "Beggin' your pardon, but Mr. Jones isn't on board right now."

"Then you'll tell me *how* I can find him."

"I'm afraid I can't. He didn't tell me where he was going, only that he'd be back directly."

Sylvia stepped out of the way as several trunks were pushed on board. "Then I'll wait," she said in a voice that brooked no argument. She walked to the taffrail and braced herself against it. Her posture alone announced she would not be moved. Out of the corner of her eye Sylvia saw the sailor start to come forward then think better of it. He shrugged and held up his manifest, checking off items as they were brought aboard.

The wait was interminable. Sylvia had no interest in any of the activity laid out in front of her. The chill that had coursed through her minutes before finding the *Mystic* eventually numbed her. Her eyes wandered the length of the wharf as far as she could see, looking for Aubrey's bright red head towering above other men.

The last of the cargo was loaded and the passengers were brought on board. Sylvia felt glances in her direction but she gave them scant attention. Had events come about differently, Sylvia would have gotten to know the *Mystic* passengers. Now she knew she would not be sailing with them.

She spied Aubrey first. He could be forgiven for not recognizing the dervish that raced down the gangboard and overtook him on the wharf. Much as she had done a few evenings earlier, Sylvia flung herself into his arms and hung on. Aubrey knew the subtle difference in the way he was held. On the previous occasion it had been passion that launched her. This time it was fear.

Ignoring the cat calls from the ship as his men gathered at the rail, Aubrey held her close. Her hat fell as she tipped her face back. Her loosely bound hair cascaded over her shoulders and back. There was stunned silence on board the *Mystic*. "You have a lot of explaining to do, Sylvia."

She hardly knew she was trembling. Aubrey set her back on her heels and urged her up the gangboard. When they were on deck again he ordered his crew back to work, then led Sylvia to his cabin.

Aubrey closed the door, but before he could say anything of the things that had come to his mind since seeing her, Sylvia held up her hand.

"There's no time to scold me," she said quickly. "You must take me back to Weybourne Park."

"My intentions exactly."

She went on as if he hadn't spoken. "I've seen him, Aubrey. He's here, in London. It can only mean that he's going back to the Park. I can't know when, but I know that he will. Captain Thorne may be in danger if we don't warn him."

Aubrey raked his hair with one large hand as he frowned. "Who have you seen?"

"My father, of course."

Aubrey simply stared at her. His dear, dear Sylvia was quite mad.

"I'm not a lunatic," she said sharply. "And it's very bad of you to think that of me. I tell you, I saw him. He was walking along the wharf with Severn and another man I don't know. Severn and my father were talking. It was he. I swear it."

Aubrey's cabin aboard the *Mystic* was a small affair. Besides the bed and trunk, there was a desk and chair and a wall cupboard that held books and liquor. Aubrey poured a glass of whisky in a tumbler and held it out for Sylvia.

"I don't require spirits," she said. "I'm frightened, not addled. You must see that I have to go back."

Aubrey sighed and downed the liquor himself. "Sylvia," he said gently. "I know you believe what you're saying, but you also must realize how it sounds." She was angry with him. He could see that now. Her delicate features were flushed and her pale blue eyes had turned frosty. Aubrey pressed on, as willing to be hanged for a sheep as a lamb. "Naturally I'm prepared to take you back to Weybourne Park. You don't have to elaborate on some fantastical story to make me do it. Anyone can see that you've thought better of your decision to come here—though not soon enough to stop you—and need some method of extricating yourself from your folly."

Sylvia actually sucked in her breath. "Anyone can see that, can they? Then you take no special credit for your prescience." She lifted her hair and secured it with more pins and a comb from her pocket. "I am very sorry for this inconvenience," she said tightly. "If it were not for seeing my father and Severn, I would regret making this trip. Clearly I mistook your feelings for me."

"Now, Sylvia."

Her eyes widened at his condescending tone. She held up one finger. "Do not say another word to me, Mr. Jones." Sylvia looked around for her hat, realized she lost it on the wharf, and rewound her scarf instead. Her voice was muffled. "My mare will not support us both. I suppose you will have to hire a mount." Turning her back on him, Sylvia left the cabin for the upper deck.

Several times during their journey Aubrey attempted to initiate conversation. Sylvia had no use for it. She kept her face averted so that he could not see her tears. She knew that he was concerned. He would have apologized if she had let him, but she didn't want to hear it, not when he thought she was creating a story to save her pride.

Aubrey reined in his horse when the road opened up in front of them as they crested a hill. The deep green of the countryside lay like a carpet at their feet. A patchwork of fields bordered the road on either side.

Sylvia slowed and glanced over her shoulder. "Why have you stopped?" she asked. "We're not halfway to Weybourne Park."

Aubrey pointed across the hillside to the ribbon of road far in the distance. "That's Colin," he said without astonishment. "Come to fetch you."

Raising one gloved hand to shield her eyes, Sylvia followed

Aubrey's direction. She could make out a single rider in the distance, but it was impossible for her to say it was Captain Thorne. "Wishful thinking does not make it so," she said tartly. She urged her mount forward again.

When Colin came upon them Aubrey had the good sense not to say with either a look or words that he told her so.

"Did you see them?" Sylvia asked by way of a greeting. "If they came this way you must have passed them."

Colin's eyes grazed Sylvia's male attire. "I thought as much," he said to himself, shaking his head. He came out of his reverie and looked at Aubrey. "I take it Sylvia's escapade has set you back a day."

"A few hours anyway," he said. "Now that you're here you can complete my escort. Sylvia takes no pleasure in my company."

"Must you *both* speak as if I were absent?" she demanded. "I know you are put out with me but I can't see that it's any excuse for bad manners." Sylvia drew her horse close to Colin's and ignored Aubrey. "Have you seen Severn?" she asked.

Colin's brows lifted. "Severn? He's on the Continent."

"Not according to Sylvia," Aubrey said. "She thinks she saw him in London." He paused a beat. "With the earl."

"Severn was with his father?" Colin asked.

"No, blast it!" Sylvia said feelingly. "He was with *my* father!"

Aubrey was not certain what he expected Colin to do. Slide him a knowing glance, perhaps. Attempt to reason with Sylvia. Clear his throat to cover a chuckle. None of these things occurred, however. Instead, Colin gave Sylvia his full attention.

"Where?" he asked.

"You believe me?" she asked, stunned. Sylvia had been prepared to go on at length about the clarity of her mind and her vision. Once she realized that Aubrey did not believe her it was conceivable that no one else would either. Her silence had not been completely in aid of ignoring Aubrey, but in planning her own defense. She suddenly realized how her surprise might sound. "It's true," she said quickly. "I swear it, Captain Thorne.

Aubrey thinks I'm making it up because I changed my mind about going with him to Boston, but that's not true. Not that I haven't changed my mind, but that I'm not making it up. I wouldn't have noticed him at all if it weren't for the traffic on the wharf. A man with a cart charged in front of me and my mare turned skittish. Other men raised their voices at me and I became confused. I looked around for someone to come to my aid and that's when I saw him."

"Severn?" Colin asked. In the face of Sylvia's breathless recitation he found himself oddly calm. His eyes slid to his friend. He saw Aubrey was listening to Sylvia without rushing to judgment this time.

"No," Sylvia said. "My father. I saw him first. I admit I thought I mistook my own eyes, but then I saw Severn and knew that I hadn't."

"Do you remember where along the riverfront you saw them?"

Sylvia closed her eyes and tried to recall her father and Severn in a broader scene. "There was a tavern," she said at last. "The sign hung crookedly from an uneven chain. It was faded. I couldn't make it out." Her brow furrowed with the effort to remember. "There was a warehouse beside it. That's where the carts were coming from." She opened her eyes. "Gaylord's Mercantile." Sylvia regarded Colin hopefully. "It's all I can recall. Is it enough to make you believe me?"

"I believe you," Colin said. He looked at Aubrey. "Do you remember me telling you about Mr. Ashbrook?"

Aubrey nodded. "The tavern owner that Severn paid off."

Colin prompted his memory. "The Imp 'n Ale . . ."

". . . is directly beside the mercantile," Aubrey finished. It lent credence to Sylvia's story. Aubrey was moved to apologize, but when he looked in her direction she was holding up her hand, palm out.

"You may as well speak to my hand, Mr. Jones, for all the good it's going to do for you to apologize." She turned her head away from Aubrey and gave Colin her full attention. "I'm glad to find you here and all of one piece," she said. "I believed you were the one most likely in danger. I had such a strong sense of it when I saw them together. Though why that should be, I don't know. They were in deep conversation as they walked along, but that can hardly be called sinister. My first thought was to find Aubrey and return to the Park to warn you."

Sylvia continued softly, more to herself than her companions. "Do you know I didn't feel a moment's joy knowing he was alive? There was no comfort in it. Only fear." It distressed her now to think on it and she addressed Colin. "I want to go back to the Park," she said. "I want to be with Mercedes and Chloe and the twins. They'll have to be told. I suspect they will feel much as I do."

Colin nodded. "Go on, Sylvia," he said. "Aubrey and I will catch up."

"I take it you mean to talk about things you don't want me to hear."

"That's right."

"Very well," she said. "I appreciate your honesty." Giving her mare a light kick, she moved out of eavesdropping distance.

Aubrey nudged his horse forward. "You think she's telling the truth." It was less a question than a statement.

"I do."

"But the earl's dead. They found a body. There was a funeral. Hell, Colin, Mercedes was arrested for his murder."

"And Severn's supposedly touring the Continent. It doesn't make sense."

"She told me there was a third man with them. But she didn't seem to recognize him."

"Mr. Ashbrook, perhaps." Colin shook his head as if to clear it. Sylvia was already farther ahead than he liked. "Let's move on," he said. The sky was nearly cloudless. Sunlight brightened the fields from deep green to emerald. In Colin's current state of mind he saw it all in shades of gray.

"You're not surprised," Aubrey said.

"No," Colin admitted. "I'm not. I wanted to believe I was

wrong. It was something of a comfort to think Wallace Leyden was actually dead, but I could never quite accept it."

Aubrey swore softly. "You should have told me."

"I had no proof," he said.

"Just your gut," Aubrey said. "Which I'd trust sooner than a charred, unrecognizable corpse."

Colin grinned. "I wish I could have been so certain."

"What do you think they have planned? It's a sure bet Severn and the earl are working together."

"I don't know. I imagine Sylvia's not far off the mark to suppose that Leyden will return to Weybourne Park."

"To what purpose?"

"Mercedes said once that he wanted to prove that what I did couldn't have been done."

"What does that mean?"

"He was speaking of the wager. I think he believes I cheated to win it."

Aubrey gave a bark of laughter. Ahead, Sylvia turned around, gave him a cursory look, then faced forward. It was going to take powerful groveling to make him fit in her eyes again. He sobered just thinking about it. "Weybourne doesn't know you then."

"No, he doesn't. But perhaps he's found some way to discredit me. That would explain his sudden appearance."

"And Severn?"

Colin's eyes were fixed on the horizon. Sunlight glinted off the gentle slopes in the distance. Treetops formed a dark outline that seemed familiar to him because he wanted to believe it was the rooftop and chimneys of Weybourne Manor. Unsettled, he could only repeat himself. "I don't know," he said quietly. "I just don't know."

Mercedes had no choice but to sit beside Severn. He was driving a small open carriage and there was nowhere else for her to go. It was less objectionable than being trapped in a closed conveyance with him as she had been at Tattersall's. There was some safety in being able to be seen. Anyone might come upon them on the road between Weybourne Park and Severn's estate at Rosefield. It eased her mind that the twins and Chloe and Mrs. Hennepin all knew where she was going with him. A passerby could confirm the same thing.

She slid a glance sideways at Severn. He was guiding the horses expertly, his touch on the reins both light and sure. They were covering the ground at a rapid clip, faster than the rutted roads warranted. Mercedes wisely said nothing. It was the price to be paid for electing to be in Severn's company, she thought. She could not ask him to slow down *and* be rid of him straightaway.

He had said very little since helping her onto the carriage bench. It occurred to her that perhaps he found her company as unwelcome as she found his. In his defense, it could not have been easy for him to rush from the Continent to his dying father's bedside and have the earl request her presence. It confirmed her impression gleaned over the years that Severn was something of a disappointment to his father. It did not explain why the earl would take it in his head to see her.

"Your father knows I'm married, doesn't he?" Mercedes asked. It was the logical extension of her last thought. She wasn't aware she had said it aloud until Severn answered.

"He knows," he said. "Or rather, he knew. His mind is not so sharp as it once was. He may have forgotten. Why do you ask?"

Mercedes refastened the ribbon on her bonnet. "I thought it might explain his desire to see me. I believe he would have favored a match between us."

"Indeed," Severn said dryly.

She wished she had not broached the subject. The memories of Severn's offer were unpleasant. To her surprise, Severn did not pursue it. His mind was clearly elsewhere and Mercedes felt rather small for thinking he could not be so moved by the impending death of his father.

Deep in consideration of this matter, Mercedes did not immediately notice Severn had taken a less traveled fork in the road.

* * *

"Why on earth would she go with Severn?" Colin demanded.

The twins looked to each other, then to Chloe. All three of them knew the answer but not one of them wanted to respond. The captain's cold, tightly leashed anger was terrible to behold. They had no desire to be at the center of its focus.

Pleasure at Sylvia's return was shortlived. Now she sat on the edge of the divan casting nervous glances between Colin and Aubrey. They could sense she had something to say but she remained uncharacteristically quiet.

In the end Chloe believed she was responsible for the reply. "Mercedes felt she could not refuse the request of the earl," she said. When this was met by blank stares from the returning trio, she went on in a rush. "Severn's father is dying. That's the news he received on the Continent and why he returned. He came to get Mercedes because his father had asked for her. He liked her, you know. His lordship always remarked on enjoying her company though he did not often have cause to do so. I think the earl admired my uncle, Mercedes's father. They both shared a passion for astronomy." She came to an abrupt halt, then finished lamely. "At least that's what I've heard Mercedes say."

During Chloe's discourse Colin had moved to the window. He stared out at the grounds of Weybourne Park with no appreciation for the sun-dappled landscape.

Aubrey's mouth had flattened in a grim line. "Do you think it's true, Colin? Severn came at his father's request?"

Colin turned slowly. His dark eyes were still distantly focused. The remoteness of his gaze separated him, made him seem less touched by the humanity that bound the others. "I think Severn hit on the single most effective way of gaining Mercedes's cooperation," he said without inflection. "He used her compassion against her."

No one responded. It was easy to believe of Severn. Sylvia left the sofa and sat on the arm of Chloe's chair as her sister began to weep softly. The twins moved closer together.

"He won't hurt her," Aubrey said. "He wouldn't dare."

Colin was already crossing the room. "I intend to make sure of it."

Aubrey opened the doors for him. "I'm coming with you. I'll see about fresh horses now."

"No." The reply was swift and intractable. "Stay with the family." His voice dropped so the others could not hear. "He has to know I'll come for her. It's better that I meet him alone."

Colin was gone before Aubrey could ask if *he* referred to Marcus Severn or the Earl of Weybourne.

Mercedes recognized the hunting lodge only because her uncle had described it to her. It was a favorite place for him at Rosefield, although it was little used. During hunts he preferred the lodge to staying at the main house and Severn obliged this preference by making it available to him even without special invitation.

The lodge was constructed of fieldstone. It had the rustic look of a tenant's cottage but the size of a country squire's residence. Situated in the deep wood of Rosefield, the lodge was almost entirely shaded from the sun by the trees on all sides. Even before midday shadows fell across the lodge's sloping roof and lent the structure a certain gloom. Neither the lamps lighted in the windows nor the smoke rising from the chimney could entirely erase it.

As soon as Mercedes realized that Severn was not taking her to the manor, she began making plans to escape. That she had not come upon any workable scheme did not daunt her. She promised herself that patience would be rewarded. Severn would expect her to do something and when she did not, he would lower his guard.

Severn alighted from the carriage, reins in hand. He secured the horses before he offered assistance to Mercedes.

She ignored his extended hand and eased herself down onto the narrow footplate, then the ground. There was a short flagstone walk leading to the lodge. Severn indicated she should follow it.

She did so with scant eagerness. "I do not pretend to understand the bent of your mind, Severn, but you must know nothing but misery can come of it. I can find reason for rejoicing, however, knowing that your father is not dying."

Severn pointed to the door of the lodge again. The gesture was impatient. "I could not imagine another pretext that would have had the same result."

"You were right," she said. She started up the walk. "Did you know that my husband was gone from the Park?"

Severn's mouth flattened. Knowing that Mercedes was deliberately needling him with her pointed reference to Colin did not lessen the impact. It was with difficulty that he kept his hands at his sides—but pleasures of that nature would have to wait. He wished he could savor the anticipation. "I knew," he said. "I inquired of your gardener."

"And had he been in residence?" she asked.

"I would have waited another day."

The way he said it made Mercedes suspect he had been biding his time. Sylvia's disappearance had served his needs.

Severn opened the door and ushered Mercedes inside. The two men in chairs in front of the fireplace immediately came to their feet. They turned simultaneously toward the open doorway.

"You know your uncle, of course," Severn said by way of introduction. "The other gentleman is Mr. Epine and he has a story to tell you."

Mercedes understood what it was to be struck dumb. It was no longer an expression but an experience. Her gaze alternated from one man to the other while her legs began to give way beneath her. As though from a great distance she watched them move forward and she realized they were coming for her. The darkness at the edge of her vision made it difficult to think. I was the hand that Severn placed under her elbow that gave Mercedes the focus she needed.

Recoiling from his touch, Mercedes bumped into the banister and her. On her right the door was still open. Without signaling her intention with a glance, she lifted her skirts and sprinted for it and the flagstone walk beyond.

"She does not seem happy to see me," Wallace Leyden said dryly. "One might think she would be grateful to give up mourning clothes. She is not well suited to black, is she?" He looked to his silent companion for help, not an answer to his question. "Mr. Epine, perhaps you would be so good as to bring her back?"

"I'll do it," Severn interjected quickly.

"I'll help you," said Mr. Epine. His offer wasn't accepted or refused. Severn was already in pursuit of his quarry. Mr. Epine hurried after him. Behind him he thought he heard the earl chuckle. Not for the first time Mr. Epine wondered what he had stepped into.

Thistles and underbrush impeded Mercedes's progress. She was quick and light on her feet, but no match for Severn's strength and endurance. Without looking behind her Mercedes knew he was gaining ground. The fact that he tripped over the fallen log that she gracefully cleared only bought her time. It did not change the outcome.

Mercedes sprawled on the forest floor, brought down by Severn's tackle. Bits of detritus clung to the bodice and skirt of her black gown. The ribbons on her bonnet were undone and the hat rested askew on the back of her head. She struggled to rise but Severn's weight and her own winded condition conspired to keep her precisely where she was. Mercedes closed her eyes.

"Let her up," Mr. Epine said. He touched Severn on the shoulder. "You've winded the lady."

Severn lifted his weight off Mercedes but only so he could straddle her. "Stay out of it, Epine. You're Leyden's friend, not mine." Severn tore the bonnet away from Mercedes's hair and turned her onto her back. Although she had ceased struggling, he leaned forward and trapped her wrists with his hands. "There was no reason for you to run, Mercedes," he said quietly. "You have to stop running from me. Where would you go?"

Mercedes wasn't listening. Severn's words washed over her. She wasn't looking at him, either. Her startled glance had found

another target in Mr. Epine. Her uncle's handsome friend was
bent over Severn but his blue eyes were focused on her. He placed
one finger to his lips and winked.

Blue-eye. Ponty Pine.

The pickpocket straightened. He took aim at Severn's bent
head with the only weapon he had: his fist. A roundhouse punch
would lay Severn out. He drew back.

"You found her," Weybourne said. His tone was unruffled,
even congratulatory. "She was able to go rather farther than I
would have thought possible."

Ponty Pine shook out his arm as if he had been straightening
his jacket sleeve. Only time would tell if the gesture was believ-
able. He noticed Weybourne was giving nothing away. The earl's
sharply defined features were impassive.

"Do get off her, Severn," the earl said in bored accents. "I
know you must be beside yourself at having her under you at
long last, but it's most unbecoming as a public display."

Severn's eyes narrowed on Mercedes's upturned face. His fingers tightened on her wrists until he saw her wince. For now it
was enough. Still straddling her, he rose and brushed off his
jacket. Dried fragments of leaves and bits of stone rained on
Mercedes's gown. At his leisure he stepped aside and offered his
hand.

Mercedes ignored it and pushed herself upright. She accepted
Ponty Pine's hand instead.

Weybourne's smile did not touch his eyes. "It seems you have
another rival for your affections, Severn. Come. We should all
return to the lodge. I, for one, am in need of libation."

The housekeeper at Rosefield had been at her post for a quarter
of a century. So when Colin asked her if she was quite certain
the earl and his son were not in residence, she was visibly af-
fronted. She actually recoiled from the notion that she may have
somehow mistaken the matter and pursed her thin lips disapprov-
ingly.

"Quite certain," she said. "The earl has been in London for a little better than a month now."

"And his health?" Colin asked tersely.

"He fairs as well as he did one month ago," she said. "No information has reached Rosefield to the contrary."

"What about Viscount Fielding?"

The housekeeper was thinking better of her decision to allow Colin into Rosefield's spacious entrance hall. His eyes had darted several times toward the main staircase and he looked as if he was of a mind to search the rooms abovestairs himself. "His lordship only recently returned from abroad," she said. "But yesterday he went to London and has yet to return."

"You expect him today?"

The housekeeper's hands were clasped firmly in front of her. The knuckles whitened a bit at this question. "I am not apprised of his lordship's plans," she said. Clearly it was a sore point with her.

"What business took him to London?"

"I'm sure I don't know," the housekeeper said. "A messenger arrived and his lordship left posthaste."

Colin saw she was uncomfortable with his questions but felt some compunction to answer them. "The message had nothing to do with the earl's health?"

"I'm certain of that. News of that nature would have come to me in order to prepare for his arrival. The earl would move heaven and earth to return to Rosefield if he were ill. He has always been quite adamant in that regard."

Colin supposed that meant the earl intended to die at Rosefield.

"More to the point," the housekeeper went on, "I don't believe the earl knew his son was in residence." Her hands fell to her sides as she realized she had said more than she meant to. "If that's all . . ." She glanced hopefully toward the door.

"Only one small matter more," Colin said. "I require the London addresses for the earl and his son."

The housekeeper hesitated only briefly. Colin's silence moved her to action more quickly than further entreaties would have done. She excused herself long enough to write down the addresses, then handed the note over quite willingly.

Colin gave it a cursory glance then thrust it into his jacket pocket. "If Severn returns, you'll be sure to tell him I was here. You will also tell him I'll meet him anywhere."

The housekeeper nodded before she clearly understood what was being asked of her. It was only after Colin was riding away that she realized she had agreed to carry a message that could cost someone his life.

Mercedes watched her uncle pour himself a drink. She recognized his mood as one which had been fermenting a good part of the morning and perhaps the previous night. His movements were the careful gestures of one who did not want to appear foxed but nevertheless was deep in his cups.

Upon returning to the lodge Mercedes was directed to sit in one of the chairs by the fireplace. She knew it was no accident that Marcus had set her back to the window. If she could have looked out there would have been hope. He had been careful to take that away from her.

The pickpocket's presence was a mystery to her. He was at his ease with her uncle and only slightly less so with Severn, though both men were faintly contemptuous of him. Mercedes was certain he had intended to help her in the wood, but now it seemed he had cast in his lot with the others. She tried to catch his eye but he very purposefully avoided looking too often in her direction.

"Don't imagine that you will have the opportunity to run again," Severn told her. He was gone from the room for a few minutes and returned with a silk scarf. He dampened the length of silk with water from the sideboard, stretched it once, then went to Mercedes.

She heard her uncle chuckle deeply as her hands went protectively to her throat.

"It's not your neck he wants, niece," Weybourne said, raising his glass to his lips. "Not now. Give him your hands."

Mercedes turned her head and slowly offered up her wrists. The wet silk was cold against her skin. Severn wove the material in a figure eight and pulled tight. He secured the binding with a double knot and Mercedes knew the pressure would increase as the silk dried. Her comfort was not Severn's concern. It seemed he, like her uncle, took pleasure in her pain. Mercedes made every effort to keep her expression neutral.

Satisfied with his work, Severn moved to sit, only to find the wing chair opposite Mercedes was now taken. He smiled coolly and chose to sit on the long sofa when Weybourne's rough friend did not move.

Seeing Severn thwarted, Weybourne was amused. "You must excuse Mr. Epine, Marcus. He's not accustomed to showing deference to his betters. I suppose it could become tiresome, but right now I find it enormously entertaining." He did not seek a seat for himself, choosing instead to hover at the sideboard and sip his liquor. "Well, Mercedes? Have you nothing to say? I find your silence rather remarkable. Has marriage so thoroughly tamed your tongue?" Out of the corner of his eye he saw Severn grimace. Marcus did not like any reminders that Mercedes was married. "Or is it that you find us tedious conversationalists?"

Mercedes stared at her bound hands and said nothing.

Severn grew impatient. His hand sliced the air. "Enough. Weybourne, tell her what you told me when you summoned me to London."

The earl's brows rose. "Summoned?" he asked. "Isn't that putting too strong an emphasis on it? I believe I merely mentioned I was alive and well and returned to these fair environs. I may have mentioned where I had taken my lodgings but I don't think I actually summoned you there." He topped off his glass. His slight smile communicated his enjoyment of Severn's simmering anger. "You mustn't be so anxious, Marcus. Or at least you mustn't appear to be so. I imagine you have hours yet before the captain finds us here. After all, it was your intent to make it difficult for him. Otherwise, he'd know it was a trap, wouldn't he?"

Mercedes closed her eyes briefly. The tightening around the silk bonds was nothing to the tightening around her heart. Colin couldn't possibly know that her uncle was alive. Even if he was able to find her, he'd never suspect that he would not be facing Severn alone.

Severn's eyes were cold. "Tell her," he said again.

"Oh, very well." Amber liquid swirled in Weybourne's glass. "The last time we spoke, Mercedes, you knew it was my intention to go abroad. I did exactly that. I can tell you that Boston has nothing to recommend itself. For all that the people give themselves airs, it's really quite provincial."

Concerned that Weybourne intended to go on at length about the city, Severn interrupted. "Resist lecturing, Wallace. Tell her what she needs to know."

Weybourne sighed. "You must forgive Severn," he said to Mercedes. "He's taken it in his head that once you hear my tale you'll be moved to see him in a more favorable light. I've told him that a thousand Roman candles going off above his head wouldn't illuminate him in your eyes, but the poor boy still has his hopes." He shrugged and smiled carelessly. "Love. There is no accounting for it."

Mercedes started as Severn came to his feet. He had straightened to his full height and fairly vibrated with his agitation. That he contained it made it somehow seem more fierce. Had it been directed at her she knew she would have recoiled. What she did not expect was that her uncle would. She watched a droplet of liquor splash on the back of Weybourne's hand and for the first time recognized that her uncle was not necessarily in command of Severn's friendship. It occurred to her to wonder if he ever had been.

Severn sat down slowly. He had no need to punctuate his point with words.

Weybourne set his glass on the sideboard and removed a handkerchief. He dabbed at his wrist. In spite of Severn's silent threat, he took his time before speaking. "My purpose for going to Boston, of course, was to find someone who would speak the truth about Captain Thorne's last voyage on the *Mystic*. I learned very quickly that the captain is something of a local hero. It was not so easy as I supposed to locate a man willing to say something against him."

"Lie, you mean," Mercedes said.

Weybourne shrugged. "As it turned out, it wasn't necessary. Mr. Epine came forward and is quite willing to discredit your husband's victory. He sailed on the *Mystic* on that occasion."

Mercedes's eyes darted to Ponty Pine. She knew it was quite impossible for that to be true. If Ponty's jailhouse confessions could be believed, then he had been lifting jewelry from bedchambers in Bath at about that time. It was on the tip of her tongue to say as much, but a single glance from Ponty kept her silent.

"It seems suspicious that you could only find one man to speak against my husband," she said instead. "Perhaps Mr. Epine has reasons for lying of which you're unaware. Is that right, Mr. Epine? As I understand it, the *Mystic*'s crew was handsomely rewarded for their record voyage. Were you slighted in some way?"

Ponty Pine was less relaxed than his posture indicated. He sat back in the large chair, his arms resting casually across the deep maroon leather. His legs were crossed at the ankles and his head was tilted slightly to one side. There was once again a certain distance in his blue eyes, a look that could have been thoughtful or bored. "Slighted?" he said at last. "No. I wouldn't say I was slighted. Cheated, more like it. Came aboard the *Mystic* in London. Thought I'd sign on, make the trek to Boston, and abandon ship there. Never told a soul what I was about. I'm not trusting that way."

Mercedes schooled her features and listened. She could feel Severn's impatience with Ponty's account and could almost believe that the pickpocket was drawing it out on purpose.

The thing of it is," Ponty went on. "The *Mystic* never went as far as Boston. I can't say where we were—I don't know much about the longitude and latitude of these things—but men told me we were only a few days shy of making port when the captain hailed another ship. She was coming straightaway from Boston and she pulled alongside us. There wasn't much discussion as I remember. I thought to myself that this had been done before. With the two crews working side by side we exchanged cargoes in a few hours. The *Mystic* circled and the next thing I knew the sun was behind me and we were coming back to London."

Mercedes *knew* he was lying, yet he told his story with convincing simplicity.

"I got my portion of the reward for the record but I knew just like every other man that it was undeserved." He smiled narrowly. "Not that I complained. That would have been foolish."

"I thought you met my uncle in Boston," Mercedes said.

"That's true," said Ponty. His calm demeanor was unruffled. His thick hair was a dark contrast to the startling blue clarity of his eyes. "I jumped ship in London, waited for the *Mystic* to leave again, then signed aboard another clipper. I finally got to Boston, left the ship, and kept mostly to myself the next few weeks. Then I heard this rumor about an Englishman looking for someone who had been on the *Mystic*'s last record voyage. It tickled my curiosity. The truth is, I found the Earl of Weybourne before he found me."

Sixteen

Colin refused the seat that Aubrey offered him. The area in front of the fireplace was an inadequate substitute for the pacing dimensions of a clipper, but confinement in a chair would have been worse. The restlessness that was upon him, the need to *do* something, was so powerful that he was having difficulty keeping his head clear for thinking. Only one other time in his life had he not known what to do.

On that occasion his parents had died.

"Think," he told the gathering, asking them to do what he could not. The twins were sharing a single wing chair. Sylvia and Chloe were huddled on the love seat. Aubrey's large bulk occupied another chair. Mrs. Hennepin and her husband had been asked to join the family and Aubrey in the library. They stood like sentries just inside the doorway. "There must be some place besides London that he would take her. Somewhere closer."

Mrs. Hennepin twisted the corner of her apron. "Pardon me, sir, but how can you be so certain he *didn't* take her to his London house?"

Colin ran one hand through his hair. The truth was, he didn't know. He still had the addresses given to him by the housekeeper at Rosefield. He could dispatch Aubrey in that direction but he was strangely reluctant to go there himself. Lines creased the corners of his eyes and there was a tightness along his jaw. "I have to trust Mercedes," he said finally. "I don't believe she would have agreed to go that far with him. Not alone. Not even to see his father. And she would have wanted to be here for Sylvia.

If I leave for London, and she's not there, I won't be back before nightfall." His voice dropped. He looked away from them all. "There's no time to do the wrong thing."

Chloe edged closer to her sister and slipped her hand under Sylvia's. Her lips moved in a silent prayer.

Mrs. Hennepin continued to wring the corner of her starched white apron. Her husband turned his hat in his hand as he considered the problem. He cleared his throat and shifted his weight from one foot to the other.

"What is it, Mr. Hennepin?" Brendan asked.

Britton chimed in. "Do you know something?"

Mr. Hennepin's shoulders drew in defensively as everyone looked at him. The hope in their eyes was a terrible burden on account of a little throat clearing. "Well," he said slowly. "There's the hunting lodge at Rosefield."

The twins squeezed out of their chair and leapt to their feet. "The hunting lodge!" They were fairly dancing. "Of course! That's *just* where he would go!"

Sylvia didn't try to restrain them. She caught their excitement instead and hope soared. "Tell us why."

Britton stopped wiggling first. "He takes his lovebirds there," he said in very adult tones.

"Britton!" Chloe admonished.

"It's true." Brendan defended his brother even though it meant admitting to eavesdropping. "But it doesn't mean we think Mercedes is his doxie." He made a face to show what he thought of that. "And our father used to stay there sometimes." He went on helpfully. "Though I don't know if he had a mistress with him."

Chloe started to scold him but thought better of it. Reaching for him instead, she kissed him on the head.

Brendan blushed and pulled away. He rubbed his hair to slough off the kiss. "I say, Chloe. You had no call to do that."

Colin felt the first faint stirrings of a smile. "If she hadn't, I would have," he said. His eyes turned grave. They lifted above the twins' bright heads and rested on Mr. Hennepin. "Tell me how to find this lodge."

* * *

Mercedes stared at Ponty Pine blankly. "You sought out my uncle?" she asked after a moment. Could that much be true? she wondered. The pickpocket's expression hadn't changed in the least yet Mercedes felt he was willing her to believe him.

"That's right," he said. "When I heard what he was looking for I realized I could help. No one else was coming forward. I thought we Englishmen should stick together."

"So, after going to so much trouble to get to Boston, you simply decided to come back."

Ponty shrugged. "As his lordship noted, the city did not have much to recommend it. I find I prefer London."

Mercedes's head swiveled toward Severn. "This is what you wanted me to hear? Do you think I'd believe this man over my husband? Mr. Epine's tale may be enough to discredit Colin with those who don't know him, but I assure you, it means nothing to me."

Weybourne lifted his glass again in mock salute to his niece. "I told you she could be stubborn, Marcus. No matter. You can always beat it out of her."

"Shut up," Severn said lowly. He did not take his eyes from Mercedes. "Mr. Epine's story changes everything. You must be able to see that. Weybourne Park hasn't been lost in the wager. It's been won. Captain Thorne owes your uncle a great deal of money and therefore his debts will be cleared. It's the captain who will be shamed and penniless."

Mercedes would have covered her ears if not for the silken bindings. It was an effort not to flinch from Severn's words. "You're wrong."

"I'm right. That's why you're frightened. And you *are* frightened, Mercedes. I can see it. The captain is facing ruin." His smile was meant to calm her fears even as his words evoked the opposite. "You can separate yourself from it," he told her. "You can denounce him. Leave him. You can come to me."

It was what she expected to hear but she wasn't prepared for her own response. She heard the laughter before she realized it was coming from her.

Severn's features became rigid. He flushed and his fingers tightened on the arms of the chair. It would have taken little effort on his part to pull himself out of his seat and push Mercedes more firmly into hers.

Ponty Pine uncrossed his legs. The movement was casual. His posture remained relaxed, his demeanor unconcerned. His eyes didn't dart between Mercedes and Severn and he didn't break the tense silence with his own voice, yet he was ready to stop Severn if he had to. It only concerned him that he would have to play his hand too soon. He might be able to hold his own against Severn alone, but not if Weybourne joined the fray. The earl's untimely arrival in the wood had stopped him once. He did not want to be stopped again. There would be no help for Mercedes then.

Severn demonstrated remarkable restraint by remaining as he was. His voice took on a gravel roughness. "Perhaps you need time to think it over, Mercedes. Weybourne, show your niece to her room. She may remain there until the captain arrives."

Mercedes stood without assistance from the earl and she coolly shrugged off the hand he placed near her elbow. "Colin doesn't know this place," she said. "Why would he come here?"

"Why is it I'm more confident of his ability to find you than you are? You really need to have more faith in the man. The one thing I've never done is underestimate him."

Mercedes was careful to step around Severn as she made her way to the staircase. She half expected him to grab a handful of her dress and hold her back. She doubted she could have borne his hands on her just then.

The room her uncle showed her faced the rear of the lodge. Looking out the sole window, she could see only the wood. The road, and therefore the approach that Colin would take, was not in her view. There was no balcony, no roof that would give her an escape route from the window. The trees had been cleared for twenty feet beyond the lodge so there were no branches she might use to lower herself to the ground.

She turned to face her uncle. Her smile was grim. "It appears Severn has thought of everything."

"He is thorough."

Mercedes was silent as she studied her uncle. In her eyes he was remarkably unchanged by the passage of time. He looked the same to her now as he had when she was sixteen or twelve or nine . . . or four.

She actually stepped backward as a powerful sense of déjà vu assailed her. This meeting had taken place before, not at Rosefield but at Weybourne Park. The north turret suddenly came to her mind and Mercedes was rocked again by the warring sensations of distance and familiarity.

The Earl of Weybourne became her point of reference as Mercedes's surroundings began to shift. There was no longer a single window at her back. Instead she was surrounded by them. Even the carpet beneath her feet faded and was replaced by the intricately patterned Oriental one she remembered from childhood. Her dolls were arranged in a protective phalanx against intruders to the north turret, but on this occasion they were useless. Her uncle was unaware or uncaring of them. He stood over her in the middle of the tower room, his shadow swallowing her tiny form.

Mercedes blinked. She did not have to see any more. She remembered everything.

Weybourne watched as a measure of color returned to Mercedes's complexion. He had thought she was going to faint, much as she had almost done downstairs, but then, as on that occasion, she seemed to find some focus and bring herself back. He had no patience for these fits. To his way of thinking they were merely a variation on her long practiced withdrawal. He had never had any patience for that, either.

He flinched a little at the way she was looking at him. There was too much clarity in her gray eyes, too much knowing. He had only seen that expression one other time. It unnerved him now as it had a score of years ago.

Weybourne lifted his drinking hand only to realize he had left his glass belowstairs.

Mercedes observed the motion of her uncle's arm and knew what he had been hoping to find at the end of his hand. Her smile was pitying. "It's not so easy without a drink, is it?"

"What isn't easy?" he asked impatiently. "Speak plainly."

"Looking at me," she said. "I remind you of her." She did not have to elaborate. She saw by her uncle's reaction that he knew she was speaking of her mother. "And perhaps a little of him. My father. Your brother."

"You're speaking nonsense."

She ignored that. "This is the moment you've been preparing for, isn't it? The moment when I would finally remember. And here you are without a glass in your hand. One would think twenty years of drinking would have numbed you, but I wonder if that's entirely true." Mercedes thought he might leave but he seemed incapable of taking any action save to let his arm fall to his side. It had only been a few days ago that she had told Colin she was no longer afraid. If further proof was required she showed it now. "If you loved my mother so much, how could you plan her murder?"

Weybourne's eyes narrowed but he said nothing.

"It's all right," Mercedes said. "You don't have to admit to it. I was there. I saw you. You stayed back from the others when they took my father's money and my mother's jewels, but I recognized you. I called to you, didn't I? I suppose in my mind I thought you were there to help us. I called you uncle. Only that. Only once. The pistols fired immediately afterward, but I like to think you heard me. Did you, Uncle? Did you hear me?"

Weybourne took a step forward. In the past it might have made Mercedes think better of her next words, but now she went on relentlessly. There was nothing he could do to her that hadn't already been done.

"I got out of the carriage and I ran. You must remember that. The others, those thieves you hired, they started to come after me, but you stopped them. You let me go, then, with all the compassion of a hunter for the fox, you ran me to ground on your horse. It almost trampled me before you got it under control and I'll never believe it wasn't on purpose. I think you might have killed me if I hadn't been mute with terror. The fact that I was suddenly insensible to what was happening, or what had already happened, saved my life. You plucked me off the ground and set me on your mount." Mercedes felt her skin prickle as the long-buried memory came to her conscious mind. "And you led me back to the carriage and put me inside. I was still there when the next travelers passed.

"You must have wondered if you'd done the right thing by letting me live. Was it relief you felt when you realized I was incapable of speaking a word against you? Or guilt? Or a mixture of both?"

"You credit me with too many finer feelings, Mercedes," said Weybourne. "I felt nothing."

Mercedes shook her head. "I don't believe it. Don't misunderstand, Uncle. I *choose* not to believe. I want to know that you have suffered every day since then. I want to know that it was fear and self-loathing that took you to the north tower room almost a year after the murders. I hadn't spoken in all that time and yet you felt my very presence as an accusation. Do you remember what you did that night?" It was so clear to Mercedes now that she wondered how she had ever forgotten.

"I believe I demonstrated how easily dolls can be broken," he said without remorse. "Is that how you recall it?"

It was as if the earl's cool, measured words had created a shift in the room's very air. Mercedes wanted to cross her arms to counter the chill and could not. "You broke one of my dolls," she said. Her voice surprised her. It sounded breathless and childish and hurt.

"You were like a doll," he said. "Pale porcelain features. Expressionless. Vacant eyes. There was no life in you. That's what I gave you back that night, Mercedes. I showed you what you could expect if you said the wrong things, but I freed you to say *something*. You came out of that tower room more like the little girl everyone remembered." He paused a beat. "I could have broken more than your doll. I could have broken you."

It was the threat that he had held over her head all these years. It was the reason she had never fully challenged him, the reason she gave in when she wanted to resist. He had given her back her voice that night, but taken away the things she might say. He had not broken her body as he had her doll's, but he had broken her spirit.

Mercedes asked quietly, "Are you going to challenge Colin? Is there to be a duel afterall?"

Weybourne was thoughtful a moment. Finally he nodded. "You don't disappoint, Mercedes. I knew you would come upon the purpose of this confrontation."

It was true that she was no longer afraid of him. It was also true that she no longer had any defenses. The return of the memories made her feel less liberated and more vulnerable. "I'm surprised you've agreed to it," she said. "Colin will kill you, you know."

The earl's smile was unconcerned. "You can't be right about everything." Without any further explanation he backed out of the room, closed the door, and locked it. He stood in the hallway a moment, quite surprised to hear the sound of weeping.

It was two hours later that Ponty Pine entered the room. He balanced a tray in one hand while he pocketed the key. He kicked the door shut with his heel. "Severn said I could bring you something to eat," he told her. He placed the tray on the bed and raised one finger when she would have spoken. Pointing to the door, he gestured that they could be overheard and began to speak of inconsequential matters. "You probably don't want to eat, but you must know you need to keep up your strength. Things always look better when you have a full stomach. That's the one thing life's taught me. Full is better than empty."

The bedchamber was furnished with a small writing desk in addition to the rocker, commode, and armoire. While he spoke, Ponty Pine rifled through the desk for paper, pen, and ink. His hastily scrawled message was badly misspelled and barely legible: *"Do nott dispare."* He gave her a moment to read it before he shredded the paper and stuffed the pieces in his pocket. He prompted Mercedes to keep up her end of the conversation.

"I don't want anything, Mr. Pine," she said.

"Epine," he corrected. "Épine, really." He gave it the proper accent, pausing between first and last name, and said it again. "Pont . . . Épine."

"It's French." At his silent suggestion, Mercedes raised her bound wrists.

"Yes." He produced a knife and began to pick at the knot, loosening it, but not undoing it.

"Then you're French?" she asked.

"No. My mother was."

Mercedes could not help herself. It was impossible to make meaningless conversation. "They mean to kill Colin," she whispered. "You must *do* something."

He quickly placed a hand over her mouth. "Won't you eat a little?" he pretended to plead with her.

"Let me have the knife." Her words were muffled by his palm but understandable. *"I'll* do something."

Ponty's blue eyes rolled at the thought. He dropped the knife into his boot and released her mouth. "Very well," he said. "Severn said you would have none of it. I'll leave the tray here in the event you change your mind."

When he opened the door to leave Mercedes saw his precautions were not without merit. Severn was standing in the hallway, completely unembarrassed at having been caught out. Ponty gave him the key and left. Severn smiled coolly in Mercedes's direction before he pulled the door shut and locked it.

There were a few hours of daylight left when Colin reached the hunting lodge. Had he wanted to hide his approach, he would have waited until nightfall. He decided against it because he believed there was more danger to Mercedes that way. He had made the decision not to have Aubrey accompany him the entire way for the same reason. As long as Severn and Weybourne thought they were in control, Colin felt he could expect them to act in certain relatively predictable ways. Cornered or threatened, neither would have any compunction about hurting Mercedes to gain his own release.

Colin saw the curtain drop in the large front window as he dismounted. They knew he was there and no one had fired a shot. It was a good sign.

He tied his mare's reins to the post beside the carriage then removed the box of matched dueling pistols from her back. Placing the lacquered case under his arm, Colin started up the flagstone walk.

The door was opened for him. Colin felt a very real shock when he recognized Ponty Pine as the one ushering him inside. He knew immediately that Severn had seen his unguarded reaction.

"I see you *do* remember me," Ponty said immediately. He turned to Severn. "There, you can be satisfied now that my story is true. Captain Thorne knows I was on his *Mystic* crew. I don't think he'll deny it." He glanced at Colin. "Will you, Captain?"

Colin did not answer the question that was posed. "What are you doing here?"

It was Severn who spoke. "I would think it's obvious, Thorne. Mr. Epine is the one who can discredit your *Mystic* victory."

"Mr. Epine?" Colin wondered how badly he had miscalculated the risks. He saw neither Mercedes nor Weybourne and he was being confronted by a pickpocket who should have been in Boston. What was even more disconcerting was that the thief's presence made some sort of sense to Severn. "What are you talking about? Where is Mercedes?"

The answer came from the top of the stairs. Weybourne appeared on the landing with Mercedes at his side. "She's here, Captain Thorne. Shall I bring her to you?"

Afraid that Weybourne intended to push her down the steps, Colin dropped the case from under his arm and swung around the banister to break her fall.

"Very nicely done," Weybourne said. He indicated Mercedes should precede him. "But quite unwarranted. I have no intention of harming my niece. That would be like playing my trump card out of turn."

Colin caught Mercedes in his arms. He held her close and kissed the dark crown of her hair. "Are you all right?" he whispered.

She closed her eyes, buried her head in his shoulder, and nodded.

He wanted her arms around him. Colin's hands slid down her arms and grasped her wrists. He had only started to pull at the silk scarf when Severn stopped him.

"Let her be, Thorne. It's very touching that you want to see her comfortable, but I tied her wrists because I wanted them that way." Severn felt no reluctance in making his confession. The pistol he was now leveling at Mercedes was Colin's own.

Colin's eyes dropped from the weapon to the opened case. Both pistols had been removed. Severn had tucked the other in the waistband of his trousers. Colin looked pointedly at that one. "It's primed, Severn. I'd be very careful if I were you."

Severn ignored that. He smoothed the front of his jacket. "Come here, Mercedes. You will stand at my side until I say differently." At her infinitesimal hesitation he moved the pistol fractionally. He now had Colin squarely in his sights. "That's better," he said, as she came toward him. "Stand here." He pointed to his right side. "Wallace, you will relieve the captain of any concealed weapons."

The Earl of Weybourne had no liking for the task or being ordered to do it. "Really, Severn, Mr. Epine's your man here."

Ponty moved to begin the search but Severn stopped him.

"Not you, Mr. Epine. I said the earl and I mean him to do it."

For a moment Colin thought Severn's pistol might actually move in the direction of his old friend. Weybourne stepped down the last few stairs before such an action was necessary.

The earl examined Colin's jacket and patted down his vest and boots. "Only this," he said, straightening. He held Colin's knife between his thumb and forefinger.

Severn nodded. "Place it on the sideboard. Captain, you may come here. Have a seat in the chair closest to the fireplace. Weybourne. Mr. Epine." He invited them into the sitting area. As they took their places he and Mercedes remained standing. "I confess, Captain, you seemed more surprised to see Mr. Epine than you did to see the earl. Can it be you suspected he was alive?"

"I don't see that it makes any difference."

"Humor me," Severn said.

"Very well. Yes, I suspected."

Severn nodded, satisfied. "So did I." He lowered his gun but the look he gave Weybourne seemed potentially as deadly. "You never did tell me who it was you murdered," he said.

The earl shrugged. "There were no introductions. Under the circumstances, they hardly seemed important."

"I wonder that you thought the deception was necessary," Severn said.

Weybourne did not bother to hide his impatience. "I wanted time undisturbed in Boston. Arranging my own death seemed the best way to accomplish that."

"I wonder," Severn said softly. "What if you hadn't found Mr. Epine? What if no one had ever come forward to clear your name or discredit the captain's?"

Ponty Pine's blue eyes slid casually to Colin. The exchange was brief but in that moment the pickpocket believed he at last had made his presence understood.

Weybourne got up from his chair and went to the sideboard. He poured himself a drink. "You know the answer, Severn. Why ask at all?"

Mercedes was close enough to Severn to feel anger hold him rigid. She suddenly understood Severn's fury. "It's because of the will, isn't it?" she asked Severn. "When we thought the earl was dead you had a chance again at Weybourne Park. The addition to his will changed that." Her eyes widened as another thought struck her. "You think he did it purposely to stop you! He didn't want you to have Weybourne Park."

Weybourne lifted his glass. It was an uneven salute but perfectly recognizable. "I always said you were a bright one, Mercedes. You see, Severn, she's up to the mark in every regard. Do you know what she told me abovestairs?" He sipped his liquor. Above the rim of his glass his smile was wry. "She told me she knows I was responsible for her parents' deaths."

Mercedes felt Colin's eyes on her. She turned toward him. It was impossible to tell him that she had come to terms with his suspicions long before she was confronted with the memory of that night. She was so desperate for Colin to understand that she hardly heard her uncle speaking.

"Can you believe it, Marcus?" he was saying. "For so many years I've paid you to keep the secret and somehow she's come upon it all by herself."

Mercedes spun on Severn. "You *knew?*" The thought revolted her and it showed clearly on her face. "You knew and you did nothing?"

"Hardly nothing," Weybourne said. "Oh, you mean did he go to the authorities. No, he didn't do that. How long has it been, Severn? Eight years? Nine? How long have you been living in my pockets and picking them clean?"

Severn didn't blink. "Georgia was carrying the twins," he said.

"Aaah, yes. My heirs. Of course we couldn't be certain they would be boys. We didn't even know there would be two. I believe I was celebrating my good fortune with champagne that evening when you felt compelled to tell me I was a cuckold. I deserved to know, I think you said."

"You did deserve to know," Severn said.

Mercedes felt the impact of these words as a blow. It had been Severn who poisoned the earl's mind against his wife. There was only one reason she could imagine he had done it. "You wanted Weybourne Park so long ago?" she asked.

"He's always wanted it," Weybourne said.

Severn's laugh was dry. "In that we're very much alike, aren't

we, Wallace? You wanted it enough to kill for it. I merely lied."
He looked at Mercedes. "I suppose I planted a seed of doubt that
night," he told her. "But your uncle found it easy to believe that
his lady had found a lover. He was rarely at the Park even in
those days. It wasn't hard to convince him that Georgia had
sought pleasures elsewhere. The celebration turned sour after
that. I don't know that I've ever seen him as self-pitying or maud-
lin as he was then. He hardly knew what he was about. The next
morning he had no memory of telling me about the robberies on
the road to London or his part in them."

Scotch settled warmly in the pit of Weybourne's empty stomach. "You wasted little time reminding me." He poured another
finger in his glass and explained to Mercedes, "His father is not
so generous as Marcus might have wished. He came to me when
his debts outpaced his allowance. I've been paying ever since."

Mercedes shied from the whine in her uncle's tone. Was he
really asking her to believe he had been wronged? She felt un-
clean being in the same room with him.

"I think they've heard enough," Severn said, watching Mercedes's reaction. "Captain Thorne wronged you, Weybourne. Mr.
Epine has offered himself as proof that your wager should not
have been lost. Do you still want satisfaction?"

The earl set his glass aside. His hands were steady and hatred
burned in his eyes. Everyone was witness to the fact the hatred
was not directed at Colin Thorne but at Marcus Severn. "Yes, I
want satisfaction," Weybourne said. His smile was cold. "If I
can't reclaim the Park then I have no means to pay you."

Severn nodded. "Just so," he said smoothly. "Shall we step
outside then? I believe there is enough of a clearing to serve our
purpose." He moved aside and gestured with his pistol for the
others to go first. "Mercedes, if you will take that box from the
mantelpiece and bring it with you."

She recognized the case as one belonging to her uncle. She
knew it held dueling pistols that were of a lesser quality than
Colin's, but no less deadly. Because of the silk restraints Mercedes picked it up awkwardly but managed to hold on. Severn

stood back so she could follow the others. She heard him whisper as she passed.

"You can save his life, Mercedes. Say the right words."

She stopped. "I don't believe you," she said. Then she kept on walking.

Outside the lodge Mercedes was directed to give the case to Mr. Epine. She placed it in his hands. Her eyes beseeched him. If he was going to do anything to help them, then it had to be now.

"Gentlemen," he said, opening the case. "Your weapons."

The earl did not examine the weapons. He had prepared them. He chose the one on the right.

Colin smiled thinly as he tested the weight and balance of the pistol that was left for him. "I take it we're going to play out this farce."

Severn's eyes were like ice chips. "I know I want to see it to its end."

Mercedes did not think she could bear to watch, yet somehow she could not take her eyes away. Colin and Weybourne moved to the far perimeter of the clearing with no direction from anyone. Her uncle's easy confidence worried her. The alcohol had made no visible mark on his gait or the steadiness of his arm.

"Please, Severn," she begged quietly. "Stop them."

"I can't stop them," he said. "I can only change the outcome."

Mercedes's fingers clutched the sleeve of his jacket. A breeze rustled the leaves overhead and an eerie moan whistled through the branches. It gave sound to Mercedes's own despair.

"Let go of me," Severn said. "I can shoot the captain from here."

Mercedes gave up her hold reluctantly as Ponty unfolded her fingers. Severn had to grip his pistol more tightly when he was jostled by Ponty Pine.

"Carefully, Mr. Epine," he said. "You could have this pistol ball as easily as Captain Thorne."

"My apologies," he said. He slipped the pistol case under his arm and used both hands to wrest Mercedes's fingers away from

Severn. When he had her free he held her back. "You're distract-
ing him," he whispered.

At first she thought he was talking about Severn. Then she
followed his sharp blue glance and saw he meant Colin. Mercedes stilled immediately and she felt the pickpocket's hands
slide away from hers. It was only as she lowered her arms that
she realized her wrists were no longer tightly bound. The scarf
remained but the knots had disappeared.

By not so much as a twitch did Mercedes reveal her newfound
freedom.

"Count it off, Mr. Epine," Severn said. "Ten paces."

Colin and the earl stood back to back, pistols held at attention.
Severn's own weapons guaranteed their cooperation.

"One!" Ponty Pine called. "Two!"

A shadow crossed the clearing as the sun ducked behind the
clouds. The wooded site was mired in the blue-gray hues of twi-
light. Mercedes felt the hair at the back of her neck rise.

"Three! Four! Five!"

"Severn," she pleaded. "What would you have me do?"

"Six! Seven!"

Tears blurred Mercedes vision. In a fair match she believed
Colin would kill her uncle, but she had no faith that this challenge
was fairly met. "If I agree to marry you," she said. "Is it
enough?"

"Eight! Nine!"

"Severn! I'll do whatever you want!"

"Ten!"

She had no voice as Colin and the earl turned to face each
other. Simultaneously they straightened their arms. Their fingers
tightened.

It was then, without signaling his intention, that Weybourne
suddenly shifted his aim.

Mercedes was rocked back on her heels as the pistols fired.
The earl's lead ball was wide of the mark, splintering a tree a
yard from where Marcus Severn stood. The other ball found its
target.

The acrid smell of gunpowder made Mercedes grimace. The faint blue cloud of smoke burned her eyes. This assault on her senses made her realize it was Severn's pistol that had been fired.

The Earl of Weybourne collapsed to his knees, his expression a mixture of both pain and fear. His fingers unfolded around the pistol and it dropped to the ground. Looking down at himself, he saw the first small blossom of blood appear on his chest. His last glance was for Severn, and this time his eyes were accusing.

Mercedes's small cry of alarm propelled her forward. Her uncle lay face down on the ground, unmoving. She held out no hope for him but she could not do nothing.

Ponty made a grab for Mercedes as she crossed in front of Severn. With a handful of her skirt locked in his fist, he managed to bring her up short. Her struggle was brief and ineffectual. He hauled her back against him. "He's beyond your help," he said quietly. Then, in a more urgent whisper he added, "Stay out of the way."

Severn could not hear the exchange. He was more amused by Mercedes's attempt to help than angered, and his low laughter covered Ponty's words. "Do you see, Captain?" he addressed Colin. "She's made another conquest in Mr. Epine. It would seem she's hardly worth fighting for. She barters her affections too easily. Something she learned from her uncle, I think. You observed he was not to be trusted, either. He meant to kill me."

Colin did not lower his pistol and his eyes never wavered from Severn. "I'm not convinced it's Mercedes you really want."

Severn remained calm in the face of Colin's level aim. His shrug punctuated his lack of concern. He let his discharged pistol fall to the ground. "It wouldn't be very gallant to admit it," he said pleasantly. "Please don't force me to say so now."

Colin had never thought of Severn as particularly courageous. His casual posing now could only mean he still believed he held the upper hand. Colin wondered if the person he had misread was the pickpocket. Was Severn right to be expecting help from that quarter? "You set this up to kill Weybourne," he said flatly.

The accusation raised Severn's small smile. "And you," he said. "You would do well to remember that I intend to kill you."

"No!" It was Mercedes who cried out. "You promised!"

"And you believed me after all?" Severn asked dryly. "That *is* unfortunate."

Mercedes tried to pull away but she was held fast. Her throat constricted with unshed tears. Her vision blurred and it seemed that Colin's arm wavered from its target.

Colin hadn't forgotten the pistol Severn had tucked into his trousers earlier. Did he really think he could draw it and fire before Colin discharged his own weapon? "I think you found some satisfaction in killing the earl," Colin said. "You couldn't bring yourself to let me do it."

"He was annoying," Severn said without inflection. "He left London to get away from me. Oh, I know he said he wanted to prove that he won the wager, but that was another way of getting back at me." He believed he had Colin's complete attention. Beside him he heard Mercedes stifle a sob. "You must have supposed by now that the wager was my idea," he told them. "Weybourne could be surprisingly easy to influence. He had already lost so much it was merely a matter of dangling the hope of recovery in front of him that made him leap and wriggle like a fish."

Colin nodded. "And if he won he would be on his way to being clear of his debt to you."

Severn actually laughed aloud at that. "That wasn't possible. Weybourne could never have relieved the debt he owed me. He could only have bought himself time with other creditors. He set up his murder to gain his freedom but he couldn't resist coming back when he found Mr. Epine. I have no illusions that he would have remained here long. He wouldn't have come to Rosefield if I hadn't insisted. His plan was to blackmail you, Captain. He thought you'd be willing to pay to keep your reputation and that you would keep on paying. I imagine he thought to set himself up in India or Bermuda and live on the overflow from your pockets."

"Which wouldn't have left much for you," Colin said.

Severn nodded. "I'm afraid not."

"So you killed him."

"Well, actually not," Severn said. *"You* killed him. Your pistol, remember?"

"What about this pistol?" Colin asked, his finger tightening on the trigger.

"Not loaded, I'm afraid," he said, feigning regret. "Weybourne knew it, too. He chose the only weapon that was primed. Unfortunately, there was no accounting for his aim. I really had no other choice but to act first." He held up his hands slowly, palms out as if surrendering. "Go on, Captain. Fire."

Colin pulled the trigger. His shot, had there been one, would have caught Severn on the shoulder, not the heart. Not waiting for Severn to draw, he threw down the useless pistol and charged across the clearing.

Severn reached for his weapon and came away with nothing. Startled, he looked around. For the first time his features registered something close to panic. He had a glimpse of his pistol in Pont Epine's hand before Colin's tackle dropped him to the ground. They skidded and bumped in the sparse grass and dirt. The horses grew skittish and pulled on their tethers. Mercedes found herself released just long enough to jump out of the way of the rolling bodies. Ponty's arm blocked her from throwing herself into the fray.

"Let them finish it," he said, lowering the pistol.

She looked at the weapon, stunned. "How did you—"

Her question was cut off as Severn's fist connected for the first real blow. Colin's head snapped back and he rolled over. Severn clambered to his feet but when he kicked out Colin brought him down again and landed a punch to his midsection. He was already winded, and Colin's hard delivery pushed the last breath of air from Severn's lungs. His gasp was silenced and color left his face.

Mercedes unwound the silk scarf from her wrists. It fluttered softly on the back of another gentle breeze and the movement caught Severn's eye. His moment's inattention as he staggered sideways let Colin land a glancing blow on his jaw. Severn was thrown in the direction he was already going. He crashed into Mercedes and they both fell backward. His weight pinned her to the ground and she found herself captured again.

Captured, but not helpless. When Severn attempted to pin her wrists she threw the scarf up and lassoed his neck. She gripped the ends of the scarf so that as he held her down, she also held him. She almost smiled as she secured his head for the chopping block.

Intent on pulling Severn off Mercedes, Colin started forward just as he began to wrest free.

Ponty Pine raised his hand and stopped Colin's approach. "I've been here before," he said in almost bored accents. Bending over the struggling viscount, he caught Mercedes's eye and winked.

Then he brought down the butt of his pistol on Severn's head.

Epilogue

Mercedes nudged open the doors to the library. The tray of tea and cakes bobbled in her hands as she stepped into the room. Colin set his book aside and got to his feet to help her. He took the tray and carried it to the desk while Mercedes secured their privacy.

"You know," he said in confidential tones while he poured. "We employ enough staff at Weybourne Park now to have each piece of this service carried in separately. There's no need for you to do it at all."

"I only relieved Mrs. Hennepin in the hallway." Mercedes touched his arm as she accepted her cup. He had taken off his jacket and the sleeve of his crisp shirt was cool beneath her fingers. She liked to touch him at odd times. It was a reassurance and a pleasure. "I'd say that was hardly a burden."

Colin's dark eyes dropped to her delicate hand. He had a vision of it suddenly lying on the pillow next to his head. He glanced at the clock. Perhaps he could persuade her to retire early this evening. "The twins are abed?" he asked casually.

"I just came from their rooms," she said. She sipped her tea. "Chloe?"

"Doing needlework." She smiled, searching his eyes and reading his mind. "Sylvia is writing a long letter to Mr. Jones and Ponty is packing in anticipation of finally being able to leave Weybourne Park. Mr. Hennepin is—"

Placing a finger to her lips, Colin stopped her. "We're alone."

"We're never alone." Standing on tiptoe, she kissed him. Her

lips were warm from the tea. "But perhaps we have a little time
to ourselves . . ." Her voice trailed off.

"With no interruptions."

It was a heady thought they shared. Time alone had been a
rare luxury these past four weeks. First, there had been the inevitable involvement of the authorities. Mr. Patterson was a frequent visitor to Weybourne Park as he tried to settle the earl's
death. He came to accept that Wallace Leyden was responsible
for the body in the burned-out cottage, but he was not so eager
to judge him guilty for murders that had happened twenty years
ago. There was no evidence and he found it difficult to accept
Mercedes's newly found memory as fact. He was equally reluctant to give credence to Severn's account of the earl's drunken
confession.

It concerned neither Mercedes nor Colin that the matter was
unresolved by Mr. Patterson. It was enough that they knew the
truth. Mercedes had no desire to lay open the murder of her
parents for public dissection. She was satisfied when the sheriff
chose not to pursue it.

It was a different matter with Marcus Severn. Now lodged in
the same cell Mercedes once occupied, he continued to claim the
earl's murder was by Colin's hand. Although refuted by Mercedes
and Colin, it initially raised the suspicion in Patterson's mind
that Severn was the one being falsely accused.

Days of questioning followed. Risking her own reputation,
Sylvia related seeing her father and Severn on the London waterfront. The twins confessed to overhearing that the hunting
lodge was a favorite haunt for the earl and Severn. Chloe explained she was a witness to Severn announcing himself at Weybourne Park with the news that his father was gravely ill.

Severn flatly claimed all of it lies but Patterson was finally
moved to believe the majority. Absent among the accounts was
one from Ponty Pine. Severn did not mention his presence in the
clearing because he knew the man wouldn't support his story.
Mercedes and Colin were silent because they knew the sheriff
would arrest him.

When Aubrey brought Mr. Patterson to the hunting lodge at Rosefield, Ponty Pine was already gone. At Mercedes's urging he had hidden in the woods until Colin could safely get him to Weybourne Park. Since then he had been a boarder in the north wing. The twins took great delight in secreting him away whenever Mr. Patterson approached. It had been planned for Ponty to leave with Aubrey when the *Mystic* sailed, but he refused. The investigation was too unsettled at that point and he wanted to be available in the event the stories came unraveled.

The pickpocket's presence was not intrusive. He kept mostly to himself unless someone made a point to include him. He was invariably cheerful, almost purposely so, but sometimes Mercedes caught him in an unguarded moment watching Colin with the boys. She saw a look of such longing that it made her heart ache for him.

Mrs. Hennepin was the one who found his stay at the Park most trying. Anticipating that he would take anything that was not hammered to the floor, she watched him closely. At the housekeeper's orders, the maids were occupied with a daily linen inventory and Mrs. Hennepin herself counted the silver. Embarrassed and apologetic, there was little Mercedes could do to stop the endless counting. Their houseguest, she noticed, pretended he wasn't aware of the housekeeper's suspicions, but he bedeviled poor Mrs. Hennepin by moving jade figurines from one location to another and rearranging the silverware drawers.

The start of Britton and Brendan's school year was delayed by the affairs of Weybourne Park. They were restless now and up to every trick. Waiting had never been their strong suit and what one of them didn't think to do, the other one did. It was Colin's patience that kept Mercedes from locking them in the north turret until they were twenty.

When the twins weren't requiring her attention it was Sylvia or Chloe who came to her. On the occasion they came together, announcing their plans to have a double wedding, Mercedes actually retired to her room to recover her wits. Sylvia's engagement to Aubrey Jones in the midst of so much confusion was one thing, but planning a wedding for sisters with ever changing minds, was quite another.

In the midst of all the activity, Colin Thorne was the eye of the storm. Mercedes did not need a reason to seek him out. He made a place for her in whatever he was doing. She appreciated his silence and came to understand that it made her more thoughtful.

In the beginning there were nightmares. She dreamed of things long suppressed and woke up cold and frightened. He listened to her then. Sometimes he would slip his hand into hers. Sometimes he was only a presence. He seemed to know what she wanted without her giving voice to it.

One evening he carried her out to the portico and she sat huddled in his embrace on the stone balustrade. They counted six shooting stars before she fell asleep in his arms. For Colin it was the answer to every wish he had made.

The odd turns of fate and coincidence that had ultimately brought them together did not seem so remarkable to Mercedes now. Rather they seemed inevitable, as if cast in the very stars they took pleasure in watching. It was a fanciful notion and one Mercedes didn't share with Colin. He had a more pragmatic nature, and until now, she thought the same was true of her.

Colin balanced his cup of tea in one hand and took Mercedes by the other. When he sat down in the large leather wing chair she needed no urging to join him. She was tucked comfortably across his lap. Her sigh was telling.

Leaning forward, Colin kissed the crown of her dark hair. He didn't press her to go to bed. For now this was all that she wanted and all that he needed. "Are you worried about Severn's appearance at the assizes tomorrow?" he asked.

"No," she said. "Not any longer. I only want it settled. Even Mr. Patterson is in agreement that the Park is legitimately yours. Severn can't really say you cheated to win the wager, can he? Not when he doesn't want anyone to know there was another witness to what happened at the lodge."

Colin nodded. "He must wonder why we've never mentioned Ponty."

"I hope he's eaten up with curiosity," she said.

One of Colin's brows kicked up. "A most uncharitable thought."

"I don't care." And she meant it. Mercedes sipped her tea. "Have you considered how it could have turned out without Ponty's help?"

Sobering, Colin said, "Every day."

"He doesn't want to hear it."

"That's because in part he blames himself."

Mercedes sat up a little straighter. "What? Why would he do that?"

"Because he believes if he'd never heard the rumors in the Boston taverns, if he'd never looked up the earl to learn his game, and if he'd never lied about sailing with me on the *Mystic*'s record run, your uncle would have stayed in Boston. Ponty's first thought was that his involvement would protect us. Everything that followed has made him wonder if he didn't place us in more danger."

Mercedes set her cup on the table at her side. "Then he doesn't really appreciate my uncle's nature. Or Severn's, either."

"I'm not the one you have to convince."

"You're right." She sighed again. "I should have known he was thinking along those lines when he refused to leave with Aubrey. Mrs. Hennepin's convinced he stayed because he plans to steal the few valuables we have left in the manor."

Colin chuckled. His cup joined Mercedes's. "Like he stole the pistol from under Severn's jacket."

"He proved what a clever pickpocket he really is." Her fingers tripped lightly down the front of Colin's shirt then brushed back and forth along the edge of his trousers. She stared straight in his eyes. "How do you suppose he did that without Severn noticing?"

"I don't know, but I can feel your hand."

"You can? Hmmm. I must not be so light-fingered as Ponty."

Her smile teased him as much as her hands. "Do you think he might teach—"

Colin grasped her wrists as she fondled him. "No," he said. "I like it this way."

Mercedes leaned forward and kissed him deeply. His grip loosened on her wrists and her hands were free to move again.

Neither of them immediately heard the scratching at the doors. It was when the sound changed to a hesitant knock that they broke apart. Mercedes jumped to her feet, repairing her hair and smoothing her gown. Colin tucked his shirt and straightened his jacket. He raked his hair with one hand and cast Mercedes an accusing glance. Except for the dark, widening centers of her eyes she looked remarkably innocent. If she ached it was not so noticeable as the one she had caused between his thighs.

"I thought they were all abed," he fairly growled. Feeling much like an untried schoolboy caught out with the headmaster's wife, Colin picked up the book he was reading and pretended to give it his attention.

Mercedes opened the doors. It was the housekeeper on the other side of the threshold. "Yes?" Mercedes may have appeared all untouched sweetness, but her voice held a husky timbre she could not disguise. She cleared her throat and tried again. "What is it, Mrs. Hennepin?"

"Begging your pardon, but you and the captain have a visitor. The earl's come to call."

For a moment Mercedes couldn't think what that meant. It flashed through her mind that Mrs. Hennepin was talking about her uncle, no matter how impossible that was. Behind her, she heard Colin coming to his feet and crossing the room.

"What's this?" he asked.

"Lord Fielding's here," she said. "I couldn't turn him away."

Mercedes frowned. "Severn's father is here? Now? At this hour?" She didn't expect an answer from Mrs. Hennepin. She looked to Colin. "What can he possibly want?"

Colin touched Mercedes's shoulder lightly. "Show him in, Mrs. Hennepin. We'll be honored to receive him here."

The Earl of Rosefield entered the library unassisted except by his ebony-knobbed cane. His gait was slow but deliberate. His complexion had a gray cast and where the veins were close to the surface it took on a cold, marble appearance. The lines of his face were nearly immobile, as if permanently and deeply etched in stone. He looked every one of his seventy-eight years.

"Thank you for receiving me," he said stiffly.

Mercedes was gracious. "It's an unexpected pleasure. Please, won't you sit down and allow me to ring for a fresh pot of tea?"

"Something stronger," Colin said. The earl's expression wasn't merely haggard. The man looked as if he was in the throes of some shock. "Scotch?"

"Tea," the earl said. "My doctors tell me that—" He interrupted himself with a dismissive wave of his hand and cane. "Bah! What do they know? Scotch will be fine. Three fingers."

Colin poured a generous amount for the earl and a little for himself. He presented Lord Fielding with the tumbler then joined Mercedes on the sofa. There was no exchange of pleasantries. The earl came to the point of his visit immediately.

"I've only just come from the jail," he said. "There has been an accident. Lord Severn . . . Marcus . . ." He looked down at the tumbler. His hand shook and the liquid rippled. "My son is dead." His eyes found Mercedes as she gasped softly. "It's rather more shocking than it is sorrowful. I'm afraid that is as much pain as I have been able to feel at his passing. These past weeks . . . learning of his passion for cruelty . . . the extent of his deceit . . . it has been . . ." His voice, or words, failed him. He drank deeply.

"How could this happen?" Mercedes said softly.

"You may well ask, but the particulars will not surprise. With court tomorrow Marcus took it upon himself to attempt an escape. He struggled with the turnkey and his head was hit against the stones. The physician that was summoned said it was not the blow but the angle at which his head hit. The injury was to his neck. It was broken by the fall."

Neither Colin nor Mercedes spoke and the Earl of Rosefield

was glad for it. "It is difficult to know what to say, is it not? Do not trouble yourselves to make a reply. I well know the hardships my son has visited upon you. You may both think that I have come only as a bearer of this night's grim news, but in truth, I had planned this visit all along. It was only Marcus's death which kept it to so late." Mercedes's surprise was near the surface. Captain Thorne, he noticed, was a deeper well of emotion.

"Captain, if you will see my man in the drawing room, he has some papers which will be of particular interest to you. Fetch them, please. I will explain them in full."

With only the slightest hesitation, Colin rose and complied with the earl's request. He returned in a few minutes. Mercedes and the earl were talking in low tones and they stopped when he entered the room. He handed the earl the documents. They were bound by a black ribbon and the color of the paper attested to their age.

The earl let his cane rest against the arm of his chair and set the documents in his lap. "I found these in Marcus's London house. He had no right to them, of course. They were mine. I came in possession of them when my solicitor passed away some twelve years ago. I cannot say at what point Marcus found them, read them, or understood their import. He never told me he had them and I did not miss them. As far as I knew they were safely stored in the same place where I keep all things I can't part with but don't wish to remember daily."

His hand trembled as his fingers smoothed the ribboned documents. "Forgive me," he said. "You are kind to be patient."

"Please," Mercedes said, genuinely concerned. "If it troubles you so much, then let it rest. Perhaps those papers, whatever their content, are best put back in that safe place."

The earl would have none of it. A measure of color returned to his face as the Scotch settled warmly in his belly. "No, I will have my say. I told Marcus as much and he knew what it meant for him." His voice dropped to a gravel pitch. The admission was a difficult one to make. "It may be that it prompted him to act as he did tonight."

"You take too much on yourself," Mercedes said quietly.

Lord Fielding held up his hand and stopped her. "No more than I deserve," he said. "Probably less." He clasped his fingers together and formed a single fist. He rested it heavily on the documents in his lap. "I will allow you to read these after I'm gone, but permit me to explain their context. They represent the tireless work of Mr. Elliot Willoughby who was in my employ for more than thirty years. The last eight years of his life he devoted entirely to finding the whereabouts of my grandsons."

Mercedes frowned. "Not Severn's children."

"Hardly. He was a very young man himself then. These were the children of my firstborn son and Marcus's half-brother. I had three children, Mercedes. John and James and Marcus. James was an infant when he died. Scarlet fever took him and my wife, but John was untouched by it and grew up to be a fine man, headstrong and opinionated and proud, like his father, but unlike me, blessed with tolerance and a charitable heart." The earl cleared his throat and for a moment he looked uncomfortable. "If I may speak plainly?"

Mercedes nodded. Colin, she saw, reserved judgment.

"Marcus is my bastard son, the by-blow of an unfortunate and ill-advised liaison. He lived with his mother the first fourteen years of his life and may have continued to do so if it weren't for the death of my other son. It was after confirming that event that I finally did what John had asked me to do years earlier: recognize his half-brother."

"I never knew," Mercedes said, shaking her head.

"It was a long time ago," the earl said. "You were a child yourself and Marcus never remarked on his origins, not when he was so anxious that they be forgotten." He reached for his drink and sipped it when his voice became hoarse. Recovering, he continued. "In a way Marcus was at the source of the rift between John and myself. John was a bright one, full of promise and possessed of an exceptional character. I had high hopes for his accomplishments in the political arena. Yet he also had a mind of his own in matters of the heart and he made a bad marriage.

At least what I believed was a bad marriage. The woman he fell in love with had no title or dowry or family to speak of. She was an actress, of all things. The idea of them marrying was ludicrous to me and I was vocal in my displeasure. I had also had an affair with an actress, I told him. But I had had the good sense not to marry her."

The earl's laughter was self-mocking and bitter. "You can't imagine how he looked at me then. Even in those days I carried a cane. More of an affectation than a necessity. I hit him with it. Not once, but half a dozen times. He stood there, stoic, unyielding, and he took it and he would have kept on taking it if I hadn't broken it across his shoulder. You may think he would have walked out of my life that day, but he didn't. He believed I would come to my senses. Can you imagine? My son insisting I was the one who needed to see reason. He asked me to consider seeing Marcus and recognizing him as my son. I wouldn't hear of it. I had met my obligations, providing for Marcus and his mother for years without objection. It was enough, I said. More than enough."

"So he left," Colin said. He felt Mercedes slip her hand into his. "Because he would not be moved from his course. He loved her, you know. Emily. That was her name. She supported him in the early years of their marriage with her acting. I don't remember those days. She had given it up when he found a position as a clerk in a law office."

The earl showed no surprise that Colin had come upon the truth. "You have the look of her. You don't take after John at all."

Colin said nothing.

"Except, perhaps, your bloody silence. My John could do that. And the way you're looking at me now. I haven't the strength to take a cane to you."

"I wouldn't let you."

Lord Fielding's narrow smile was rueful. "No, I don't suppose you would. You're harder than he was. I can see that. But then you've had to be, haven't you?" He lifted the documents a fraction and let them fall again. "When my son left me he made a thorough job of disappearing. He changed his name and moved away from London. I was too proud to hunt him down then and in the end I left it to too late." His uneven sigh was more of a sob caught in his throat. "It was your mother who wrote to inform me of the birth of each of my grandchildren. There were no names, no descriptions, and little narrative, and yet I committed every one of those missives to memory. I prayed for another grandson only that I might hear from her again.

"Her last letter arrived unexpectedly. I knew she could not have given birth. It was too soon since the last and I trembled at the opening of it, afraid it was news about John this time."

Colin guessed the content of his mother's letter. "She told you we were coming to see you."

The earl nodded. "Yes. Just like that. Without invitation or any thought that I might not want you there, she made her announcement."

"It still rankles a bit," Colin said.

Lord Fielding snorted. "Yes. Yes, it does. Damnable thing, pride. I can tell you, I swallowed it hard that day. I had everything made in readiness for my prodigal son." His voice lowered as his shoulders slumped. "He never arrived. None of you did."

Silence stretched between them. The pressure of Mercedes's hand in Colin's increased. She knew he was remembering that day. She was recalling her uncle's part in it.

The earl spoke again. "It's all here," he said, referring to the documents. "Willoughby kept a record of all the contacts he made. I set him on the task of finding my son when no one came to Rosefield. I had no thought then that he was already dead. I only supposed that he had changed his mind about reconciling . . . or that Emily had changed hers. It was months before Willoughby made the connection to the ill-fated family on the road from London. It was the name that finally got his attention. Thorne."

When the earl smiled this time it held a certain fondness. "That would have been so like my John. Rosefield's thorn. A thorn in my side. I used to say that to him. I suppose he took it to heart."

Fielding leaned forward and handed the ribbon-bound papers to Colin. "Take them," he said. "You'll read for yourself the lengths that Willoughby went to to find you. He arrived at Cunnington's only weeks after you had left. They were not so helpful there."

There was only one thing Colin wanted to know. "My brothers?"

The earl shook his head. "There was so little to go on. Willoughby made it the end of his life's work, but this is what he had to show for it. Forgive me, but I stopped trying after that. I had no stomach for it any longer . . . no heart."

Colin said nothing but he understood. His fingers tightened on the documents.

Mercedes watched Colin's hands. She knew he had been hopeful. She had felt it herself. "You say Marcus had these papers in his possession?"

"That's right," the earl said.

"Then he knew who Colin was," she said.

"I believe so. He denied it when I confronted him, but that has always been his way. I believe he encouraged Weybourne to make a wager with Captain Thorne to set forces moving on a collision course. It would have amused him. Marcus never believed there was anything outside his manipulative talents. It certainly seems he encouraged Weybourne to challenge your husband. It was more than the Park that was at stake, but my estate, as well."

The Earl of Rosefield's solemn eyes moved from Mercedes to Colin. "It has yet to be said plainly, Captain Thorne, but you are now Viscount Fielding and heir to all that I own."

"You're awake," Mercedes said softly. She was glad she had not drawn the drapes. Moonlight edged Colin's handsome profile. He was lying on his back, staring at the ceiling. When she lightly touched his chest he uncradled his head and slipped one arm under her shoulders. Mercedes turned more fully on her side and leaned into him. She did not think he had slept at all since they had come to bed. The earl had departed long ago but much of the intervening hours had been used to pour through the documents he left behind. It wouldn't be long before moonlight gave way to dawn. "Are you sorry you know, m'lord?"

"Only if you persist in calling me that."

She tapped his jaw with her finger. "You'll never get used to it, will you? That you earned Weybourne Park through your efforts suits you just fine, but the knowledge that it's yours by rights of entailment and inheritance doesn't sit so well."

"I'll never be as English as my birthright suggests," he said.

"I'm coming to appreciate that and I find I can accept it."

His low growl was menacing but his kiss was not. She unfolded in his embrace and kissed him back, long and deep and slow. It was with some reluctance that she pulled back. "What is it?" he asked.

Mercedes searched his face. "You won't ignore him," she said. "Lord Fielding, I mean. Your grandfather. You won't dismiss him from your life, will you? There's already been so much pain because of heated words and a surfeit of pride. He didn't have to come here this evening. I think he is a much changed man from the one your father knew."

"You don't have to convince me, Mercedes. I don't blame him."

"But you were so distant tonight."

"It's quite a lot to get used to. He may be my grandfather but I don't know him."

Mercedes accepted that. All things in their own time, she thought. And this was her time. Her capacity to enjoy life had only been tapped. Mercedes opened her heart.

"Make love to me," she whispered. "Give me your child."

He touched her hair. His fingers were gentle. They slipped to her neck, then the curve of her shoulder. He slid lower in the bed so his face was close to hers. Their knees bumped. Then their noses. He smiled.

"I'll see what I can do." His huskily spoken words tickled her lips. He closed the small space of air that separated their mouths and kissed her.

Passion unfolded. Their bodies met and held. She cradled him. He stroked her. His bright hair mingled with the bittersweet chocolate of hers. His mouth opened over her breast and the heat and dampness and pressure of his lips made her arch under him. She raised her knee and caressed his thigh and hip. Her fingertips ran the length of his spine.

His touch treasured her. She was loved with abandon, with joy, and finally with a certain selfish fierceness that made her cry out her pleasure. The sound of it tripped along his skin. Her arms came around him as tremors eased the tension in his own tautly arched body.

She lay curved against him then. In that familiar, dreamy gesture of his, Colin's hand rested lightly on her flat belly. Mercedes's fingers threaded through his and she smiled.

They slept soundly in the aftermath. Whether it was on account of their late night or their lovemaking, neither noticed the surge of sunlight that would have wakened them on other mornings. It was the commotion in the hallway that roused them. Britton and Brendan were demanding entrance.

"So it begins," Colin said.

Mercedes groaned softly and pressed her face back into the pillow. She thought he seemed indecently cheerful about it.

Colin glanced at the clock on the mantelpiece as he shrugged into his dressing gown. He tossed Mercedes her robe. "We're late," he said. "That's why they're here. Come to get us to accompany Ponty to London." He gave her a few moments to digest that then opened the door as she was scrambling to put on her robe.

Britton nearly tumbled into the room. Colin picked him up and pitched him on the bed. He skidded to a halt beside Mercedes. Brendan looked at him hopefully. "Me, too, sir?" he asked. Colin lifted the boy to his shoulder and tossed him head over bucket on the bed.

"Are there more of you in the hallway?" Mercedes asked.

"You make as much noise as any five children. One would think we're going to London."

Undaunted by her rebuke, they spoke in near unison, finishing each other's sentences. "Hurry! Ponty is afraid he'll miss his ship. He's packed and ready for us to join him. And he's making Mrs. Hennepin very nervous with the way he's eyeing her pocket watch. I think she means to inspect his bags before he leaves."

Mercedes's eyes began to lift heavenward but they stopped when they met Colin's. He was clearly enjoying himself and she loved him for it. "No doubt Ponty is trembling at the very idea of staying here a moment longer than he has to."

The journey to London was a high-spirited excursion. Ponty and Colin took turns regaling the boys with stories from their own youth, only a quarter of which Mercedes hoped had any foundation in truth.

It was when they made their farewells at the gangboard of the *Remington Siren* that they sobered.

"You'll ask for Miss Jonna Remington when you reach Boston this time," Colin said. It was more a question than a statement.

Ponty's blue eyes danced as he held up his right hand. "I swear," he said. "Miss Jonna Remington. And I'll tell her you recommend me."

"That will only get you in the door."

"I intend to make my own way." He sounded solemn enough. It was his grin that was incorrigible.

Mercedes hugged him. "Don't change too much, Ponty." She had to stand on tiptoe to kiss his cheek.

He held her face in his hands and looked at her for a long moment. "He's very lucky, you know," he said quietly. Smiling, he withdrew. He dangled her earrings from his fingertips. "In remembrance," he said and pocketed both.

Laughing, she stepped back into Colin's loose embrace and let the twins take their leave. They hugged Ponty in turn and wished him well. They surprised Mercedes and Colin by thanking him. It was only then that Ponty looked genuinely uncomfortable. He gave the twins a look that closed their mouths and hurried up the gangboard.

Colin and Mercedes and the twins stood on the wharf until the *Siren* was out of sight. Even then they were strangely reluctant to return to the carriage.

"Why did you thank Mr. Epine?" asked Mercedes.

Britton shrugged. Brendan found something to interest him across the pier.

Mercedes knew when she was being held at bay. She touched Brendan's chin with her forefinger and lifted his eyes to hers. "Well?"

Brendan caved immediately. "He taught us some tricks," he mumbled.

"What?"

"Some tricks," Britton said more clearly than his brother. He reached in his pocket and drew out a small gold earring. "I got one of yours back. Mr. Epine didn't even suspect."

Colin tamped down his smile and tried to look as appalled as Mercedes. He knew he failed when she nudged him in the ribs. "Perhaps we should have inspected his bags after all," he whispered in her ear.

Mercedes gave him a quelling look and spoke to the twins. "Tricks? Is that what you're calling theft now?"

Brendan dropped his head sheepishly as Mercedes removed her finger. He reached in his jacket pocket and withdrew something. He opened his palm for Mercedes to see. "I have your other earring."

But he didn't. Colin and Mercedes saw that right away. This one was a pearl stud with a raindrop of pure gold hanging from it. The letters ER were engraved on the drop and the pearl was set in a gold crown. It wasn't any earring. It was the earring.

"He must have stolen it," Colin said slowly. "Ponty Pine couldn't be my brother." But there was hope in his voice and Mercedes heard it.

"One can see how he became Ponty," she said. "But it's Pont Epine. Odd, don't you think? So odd, I never thought beyond it."

"What do you mean?" Colin asked. He had plucked the earring from Brendan and was turning it over in his hand. "It's French, isn't it?"

"Yes. My point exactly. L'épine is a prickle. A thorn. And le pont means bridge . . . or platform . . ."

Colin was looking at Mercedes again. "Or deck," he said. His voice carried no further than her ears. "Decker Thorne."

Mercedes touched his arm lightly. This time it was she who offered reassurance. She turned so she could see the river Thames. "Do you think he knew?" she asked.

The *Remington Siren* was invisible to them. Colin's fist closed over the earring and he pulled Mercedes to him. "I think he may have," he said. "But you heard him. He intends to make his own way."

Mercedes slipped her arm around Colin and rested her head on his shoulder. It wouldn't be the last they saw of Colin's brother. Heat pinkened her cheeks as she remembered how Colin had loved her only hours earlier. "Give me a child," she had said. In her heart she believed he had.

Mercedes thought she would have reason to write Decker soon and in nine months he would return. He would want to see her and Colin and the twins and all of Weybourne Park, but he would come for the baby first.

ABOUT THE AUTHOR

Jo Goodman lives with her family in Colliers, West Virginia. She is the author of sixteen historical romances (all published by Zebra Books) including her beloved Dennehy sisters series: WILD SWEET ECSTASY (Mary Michael's story), ROGUE'S MISTRESS (Rennie's story), FOREVER IN MY HEART (Maggie's story), ALWAYS IN MY DREAMS (Skye's story) and ONLY IN MY ARMS (Mary's story). Jo is currently beginning work on Decker's story, the second installment of her new trilogy, which will be published in February 1998. Jo loves hearing from her readers and you can write to her c/o Zebra Books. Please include a self-addressed stamped envelope if you wish a response.

ROMANCE FROM JO BEVERLY

DANGEROUS JOY   (0-8217-5129-8, $5.99)

FORBIDDEN   (0-8217-4488-7, $4.99)

THE SHATTERED ROSE   (0-8217-5310-X, $5.99)

TEMPTING FORTUNE   (0-8217-4858-0, $4.99)